Fran 2/20
BK .0120 -3/22
Nah 8/22
Shatt 10/22

# LUCKY PENNY

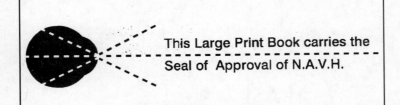

This Large Print Book carries the
Seal of Approval of N.A.V.H.

# LUCKY PENNY

# CATHERINE ANDERSON

**THORNDIKE PRESS**
*A part of Gale, Cengage Learning*

 GALE
CENGAGE Learning®

Detroit • New York • San Francisco • New Haven, Conn • Waterville, Maine • London

Copyright © Adeline Catherin Anderson, 2012.
A Coulter Family Historical Novel.
Thorndike Press, a part of Gale, Cengage Learning.

**LIBRARY OF CONGRESS CATALOGING-IN-PUBLICATION DATA**

Anderson, Catherine (Adeline Catherine)
    Lucky penny / by Catherine Anderson. — Large print ed.
        p. cm. — (A Coulter family historical novel) (Thorndike Press large print romance)
        ISBN 978-1-4104-5159-0 (hardcover) — ISBN 1-4104-5159-3 (hardcover) 1. Domestic fiction. 2. Large type books. I. Title.
PS3551.N34557L83 2012
813'.54—dc23                                                2012024588

Published in 2012 by arrangement with NAL Signet, a member of Penguin Group (USA) Inc.

*To my husband and hero, Sid.*

*I didn't have a lucky penny in my pocket when I met you, but it was still the luckiest moment of my entire life. Thank you for all the years of happiness, support, and love.*

# ACKNOWLEDGMENTS

I would like to thank my editor, Ellen Edwards, who has been behind the scenes throughout most of my career. You've always been open to new ideas and have a wonderful talent for making a book the best that it can be without changing my writer's voice. Together, we've become a great team. I would also like to thank everyone at New American Library for the unflagging enthusiasm and support, and I absolutely must express my gratitude to my agent, Steven Axelrod, for his professional advice over the years and his great sense of humor when I need a good laugh.

# PROLOGUE

*No Name, Colorado*
*Monday, April 6, 1891*

David Paxton couldn't quite credit that his little town had grown so quiet that he could rock back on his chair outside the jailhouse with nary a care to sour his mood. Over the past four months, since he'd changed his peacekeeping tactics, the barroom brawls and gunfights, common occurrences in the past, had become a rarity. At first he hadn't felt confident that the change would last, but now he was finally starting to believe it would. No more tension, no need to keep an eye out for potential trouble. It had taken him a while to adjust to the change, but now that he had, his job as marshal seemed so easy it was almost boring.

In the early-morning breeze, his shoulder-length hair drifted across his face, making everything look limned in gold before he lazily pushed the strands back. How long had it been since he'd felt this relaxed? At least a year, damn it, or his eyes weren't blue. Being tense and on guard all the time wasn't good for a man's constitution. Feeling certain he wouldn't be awakened by the sound of gunfire last night, he had slumbered deeply. Hell, he felt so good he could swear he wasn't a day more than twenty instead of the venerable thirty that he actually was. It was hard to believe he'd turn thirty-one in only a couple of months.

Old Mose Hepburn, the local drunk and David's only prisoner, was sleeping it off in the cell block, as happy as a grub worm in a rotten log to be snoozing on a lumpy cot. Most times, he had to compete with rats for space in the hayloft of Chris Coffle's livery stable. If the cantankerous old fart kept to his usual pattern, he wouldn't come around until along about noon, and by then Billy Joe Roberts, one of David's deputies, would be on duty to walk across the way to get Mose some breakfast. David sighed with contentment and flexed his shoulders, glad to be slothful for a change and let his mind wander. No appointments, no meetings, and no rowdy cowpokes. His languorous mood was magnified by Sam, his fluffy gold and white dog, who lay beside him, snoring louder than a two-man crosscut saw.

It was a long-missed pleasure for David to watch the town of No Name awaken. And, oh, what a fine morning it was, putting him in mind of his early years, when he'd sometimes had nothing better to do than sit on the back stoop and watch the grass grow. The planks of the boardwalk creaked as he shifted his weight. A fly, the first David had seen since last autumn, buzzed in to cut circles in front of his nose. Sunlight spilled over the roof peaks at the opposite side of Main Street and slanted under the overhang. Butter yellow warmth bathed the lower half of his face where his hat brim didn't cast a shadow and seeped through his leather duster and shirt to make him feel toasty despite the chill temperatures of early spring. Yep, and boy howdy, it was shaping up to be a great day.

Slumped on the tottery contraption of ancient wood he still called a chair, David extended his long legs and crossed his booted feet to study his spurs. He hated the damned things, would never use them on a horse, and felt silly wearing them, but his sister-in-law Caitlin insisted they were "necessary accoutrements" to his new marshal's outfit. Trust her to come up with a big word for every little thing. Turning his ankles, he noted with grim satisfaction that

11

the once-silver rowels were now pewter gray and specked with dry mud. Not so long ago, he would have rushed over to Gilpatrick's general store for some polish to restore their sparkle. Not anymore. He'd learned the hard way that a town marshal who paraded about in a starched shirt, pressed blue jeans, and spit-shined boots was asking for trouble. Now, under the direction of his elder brother Ace, a renowned ex-gunslinger, David dressed more like a roughrider than a peacekeeper, and he sure did appreciate the results. No upstart fast guns had called him out into the street in well over three months.

A loud thump brought Sam's snoring to a halt and caught David's attention. Squinting against the light, he directed his gaze across the way to the source of the noise. Roxie Balloux, the buxom and ever-cheerful proprietress of No Name's best restaurant, had just emerged from the establishment from a side service doorway with a five-gallon slop bucket in each hand. Reddish brown hair caught at her crown in a coiled braid, she looked fetching in a tidy, blue-checked gingham housedress with lacy shoulder caps and a fashionable new bustle that was supposedly more streamlined than its predecessors. To the delight of most men, the effect was lost on Roxie. She was plump in all the right places and needed no posterior enhancement. Hell, Roxie wearing a bustle was sort of like ladling whipped cream over apple pie à la mode, a bit too much of a good thing. Not that any man with blood still moving in his veins could think about food when he admired her backside. Sadly, she would turn thirty-five in August, making her a mite too long in the tooth for David, who still hoped to marry and raise a family.

As Roxie descended the porch steps, Old Jeb, a black dog belonging to Jesse Chandler, the chimney sweep, appeared out of nowhere, barking excitedly and circling at her feet as she upended the buckets over the trash barrel. She let loose with a sigh, audible even at a distance, and gingerly routed through the slop to find the shaggy beggar a treat. She tossed the canine a ham hock generously peppered with what looked like coffee grounds. Jeb wasn't fussy and dropped onto his belly in a patch of grass, still yellow from winter, to gnaw happily on the bone.

Sam, who either heard Jeb chewing or caught the smell, jerked awake and whined. David lowered a hand to his pet's head. "No way, you rascal. Every time you eat Roxie's slop, you get the squirts."

13

The shepherd grunted and went back to snoring. David rocked, shifted, and went back to lollygagging, his gaze idly scanning the businesses across the street. Next door to the eating establishment, Tobias Thompson, so thin he didn't cast a shadow standing sideways, emerged from his dry-goods store with broom in hand. Same as always, he wore a blue bib apron over black trousers and a white shirt with a turned-down collar that sported a red necktie. Even in the shade of the boardwalk overhang, his bald pate gleamed like polished agate as he bent to the task of sweeping his doorstep.

Watching the man work, David reached under his hat to scratch, hoping to high heaven he'd never lose his hair. He guessed he'd just wear a hat all the time when he got old. He wore one most of the time, anyhow.

The batwing doors of the Golden Slipper saloon creaked open just then. David glanced to his left, expecting to see Mac, the owner of the establishment, stepping out for a breath of fresh morning air. Instead, Marcy May Jones, the newly hired upstairs girl, posed in the doorway. David damned near swallowed his tongue. She wore a pink wrapper — in a manner of speaking — with the sash looped carelessly at her waist, one slender shoulder and most of one breast artfully displayed. David was so taken aback that he couldn't think what to do or say. He was the marshal, after all, responsible for law, order, and upholding the decency codes of the town, but how in the Sam Hill did a man tell a lady to get her pretty little ass back inside where it belonged?

David wasn't the only male on the street who reacted with a start. Tobias froze with his broom in midswing, and his grown son, Brad, the town's newly appointed garbage collector, almost took out an overhang post with the right rear wheel of his fully loaded wagon as he cut the corner from the alley onto Main. One of the mules brayed in protest as Brad jerked hard on the reins to stop.

"Good morning, Mr. Thompson," Marcy crooned to Brad as she caressed one hip, smiled, and tipped her head so that the henna tint of her brown hair flashed in the morning light. "I keep hopin' you might pay me a call one of these nights, and my little heart's just broken that you never come."

Trying to back up his team, Brad turned three shades of crimson and gripped the lines in one hand to tug at his shirt collar, which apparently had shrunk a size between one breath and the next. "I . . . um . . . Well, lands, Miss Marcy, I'm a happily married man."

"I'm partial to happily married men, Mr. Thompson. They know how to treat a lady."

Brad coughed and ran a hand over his face. "Well, um, my Bess — she wouldn't like it if I visited you. No, ma'am, she wouldn't cotton to that at all."

Marcy sighed theatrically. "Too bad. Her bein' in the family way and all, I bet you're not gettin' any at home. If you should start to feel cross and out of sorts, you come see me. I'll cure what ails you. You have my personal guarantee."

Tobias glared at Miss Jones and then at his son's broad back. He was clearing his throat and about to speak when Brad's wife, Bess, a petite and very pregnant blonde, emerged from the dry-goods store. Prior to having children, Bess had been the schoolteacher, and despite her diminutive stature, she still carried herself with an air of authority even though she now had the swaybacked posture common to so many women heavy with child. She stepped off the edge of the boardwalk into full sunlight, circled the wagon, and stood between her husband and the saloon as she met Marcy's gaze. The sparks that shot from her green eyes could have set fire to stone. David realized her anger stemmed from jealousy, which baffled him. Miss Marcy was easy enough on the eyes, he guessed, but she didn't hold a candle to Bess.

"Where is Mac?" she demanded of the prostitute. "I'm guessing he doesn't know his upstairs *girl* is indecently exposing herself on the town boardwalk in broad daylight!" Bess had perfected the schoolmarm haughtiness that always snapped kids to attention. Chin up, eyebrows arched, she almost made David want to dive for cover. "You'll kindly remove yourself from public view, Miss Jones, or I shall report you to the city council. We do have laws in this town to protect the innocent!" With a fling of her left arm, Bess gestured up the street at the schoolhouse. "*Children* are out and about, my good woman. I don't believe that Charley and Eva Banks would be pleased to learn that their boy Ralph witnessed this indecent display on his way to school." Bess fluttered her fingers in front of her chest and added with shrill accusation, "Your feminine *protrusions* are showing."

"They're called tits, honey," Marcy replied drily. "You got so much starch in your petticoats, it's a wonder you don't crackle when you walk."

17

David was greatly enjoying himself until Bess turned that fiery green gaze on him. He leaped to his feet as if he'd just been prodded with a pitchfork tine. "We do have a city ordinance about appropriate public attire, Miss Marcy," he said loudly, so Bess would hear, hoping as he spoke that *ordinance* was the proper term. The city council had so many names for laws — *appendages, bylaws,* and all manner of other shit — that he could never keep them straight. Bottom line, he had been appointed marshal because he was halfway smart and fast with a gun, not because he had a gift with words. "Standing about on the boardwalk in nothing but a —" David glanced at Miss Marcy and, like Brad, had a sudden urge to loosen his collar. Even worse, he plumb forgot what that pink thingamajig she wore was called. It had slipped farther off her right shoulder, and the brown of her nipple was playing peekaboo with him every time the breeze shifted. "Well, ma'am, no offense, but parading about in one's birthday suit, even if it's sort of covered, is against the law. You need to go back inside."

Wearing a jade dress that matched her eyes and sporting a belly as big as a Texas watermelon, Bess pointed a rigid finger at the prostitute. "Immediately!"

18

"I'm goin', I'm goin'," Marcy replied with a seductive thrust of her hip as she turned away. "Don't get your lacy little knickers in a twist. I ain't never stole anybody's husband yet and don't plan to start. They come of their own free will."

Bess's face turned as red as her husband's. She reached up to rest a fine-boned hand on Brad's knee, and the man jerked as if he'd just been touched with a hot brand. David, who'd been courting Hazel Wright, the new schoolteacher, and was thinking about asking her to marry him, got an itchy feeling at the nape of his neck. If this was any indication, maybe wedded bliss wasn't so blissful. Hell's bells, all Brad had done was accidentally look, and as a result, he'd probably get burned biscuits for supper.

Bess abandoned her husband to march across the rutted street, which was still muddy in spots from a recent rain. As she approached David, he wondered how a perfectly wonderful morning had so quickly gone to hell.

"Marshal Paxton," she said, using a tone that took David back in time to the classroom, when nuns had cracked rulers over the backs of his knuckles when he misbehaved. "We, the citizens of No Name, pay you well to keep this town respectable, yet you sat there on that dilapidated chair doing absolutely nothing while a harlot hawked her wares on Main Street at eight o'clock in the morning!"

David rubbed his whiskery jaw and repositioned his hat. "You heard me tell her to go back inside, Bess. What else can you expect me to do, get her in a headlock and drag her back in?"

"That is *not* the point!" Bess's lips drew back over her teeth in a snarl so fierce that David cringed. Sam whined and crossed his snow-white paws over his eyes. "The *point* is that you *gawked* at her for a full three minutes before you said a single word."

"Gawked? I didn't gawk." Well, he guessed he had, but not on purpose. "I was just taken aback, Bess, and as the marshal, I can't go off half-cocked. I needed to think of an appropriate way to handle the situation."

Judging by the flare of pink on her cheeks, Bess was less than mollified by his explanation. "Mark my word, I will attend the next city council meeting and lodge a complaint. You never hesitate to arrest a *man* who disturbs the peace, yet you fail to act when the perpetrator is a half-dressed female of ill repute!"

David scratched beside his nose. "That

isn't fair. It's different with a woman."

"How so?"

David scuffed his heel on a plank. "Well, when a man breaks the law, I can go to fisticuffs with him if it becomes necessary — or shoot him if all else fails. It's a whole different story with a lady."

"Marcy May Jones is *not* a lady!" Bess ran a molten gaze from the top of David's head to the toes of his dusty boots. "Not that I'm certain you'd recognize the difference anymore. You used to be a fine, upstanding marshal. Now just *look* at you! A saddle tramp has better personal hygiene." She jabbed a dainty finger at his duster. "That *thing* is absolutely filthy! And just look at your face. I'll bet you haven't shaved for the better part of a week."

David put a blade to his jaw every three days now, usually right before bedtime so he could sprout a new crop of whiskers before sunrise. "My duster isn't dirty. I just greased it up to make it look that way."

Bess held up a staying hand. "I've heard all about your reasons for changing your appearance, and it's a bunch of stuff and nonsense, if you ask me. Looking mean and disreputable to keep the peace? Ha. There's more to the job than just dispensing with the riffraff. A marshal should represent our community in fine fashion and set a good example for our children! He should be clean shaven and keep his hair cropped short. He should change clothes every single day! He should —"

"Hold on just one minute," David protested. "I change clothes every blessed morning. And just because I look dirty doesn't mean I am. I bathe regular, and I brush my teeth morning and night." He gestured at his duster, which Ace's wife, Caitlin, had designed and made from soft leather purchased at the cobbler's shop. "You have to admit that there's been no trouble around here for almost four months now. Say what you want about how I look, but it scares off the rowdies."

Bess rolled her eyes. "You have become a disgrace! Your poor mother must be embarrassed half to death."

In truth, David's mother slept better at night now that no upstarts were calling him out. That said, she tolerated no slovenliness in anyone, so she did try to sneak up behind David with her scissors now and again to trim his hair. But he wasn't about to mention that to Bess. "How my mother feels about my changed appearance is none of your business, Mrs. Thompson."

"My husband and I help pay your wages,

Marshal Paxton! I guess I have some say."

Bess waddled back across the street. *Damn.* He'd heard tell that pregnancy made women emotional, but this particular female had become downright ornery. Normally Bess was mild tempered. Didn't she realize that Miss Marcy was no threat? Brad wouldn't look at another woman if he was paid to do it, not willingly, anyhow. He'd been taken by surprise this morning, but that didn't mean he'd liked what he saw. Not enough to be unfaithful to Bess, anyhow.

Sam whined again. David glanced down and saw that the dog had finally uncovered his eyes. "Coward. You kill rattlers without blinking, yet you quake and hide from a pregnant female? Explain that to me."

Sam groaned and rolled over on his back, legs sprawled for a belly rub. David gave him a scratch with the toe of his boot. "You worthless mutt. Bess wouldn't hurt a fly. She's just out of sorts right now. While carrying Dory Sue, Caitlin took offense at every imagined slight and cried all during her last month. Remember that? Everybody had to carry an extra handkerchief to help mop her up."

David had lost his yen for whiling away the morning, but as he started into the office to catch up on paperwork, someone shouted his name. He turned to see a man riding up Main on a sorrel gelding.

"Yes?" David called.

The man guided his horse over to the boardwalk. "You the marshal?"

"That's right." David tucked the left side of his duster behind the butt of his Colt .45 to expose his badge and softly shushed Sam, who growled in warning because the fellow was a stranger. "What can I do for you?"

"If your name's David Paxton, I brung you a heap of mail."

"That's my moniker, but I get all my mail here at the No Name post office."

"Not all of it, I reckon." The fellow had a canvas tote on the saddle in front of him. He tossed it at David's feet. "The Denver postmaster's been holdin' these here letters for goin' on six years. He returned a few of 'em, but mostly he just tucked 'em away, hopin' David Paxton would show up someday to get his mail."

David's brows snapped together in bewilderment. Who would send him letters in Denver? He visited the larger town every now and then, mostly by train to get his cattle to market, but he had never lived there.

"Anyhow," the man continued, inclining

24

his head at the bag, "as you can see, the amount of unclaimed mail is substantial and was takin' up a lot of needed space. Postmaster was about to dispose of it when the sheriff told him the marshal down here goes by the name of David Paxton."

"There must be a mistake," David replied. "You sure there's not another man with the same name up that way?"

"Not so far as I know. And if there is, he ain't never gone to the post office to collect his mail." He nodded at the bag again. "The sender must think you live there. All the letters is addressed to you, general delivery."

David had to admit, if only to himself, that he'd never met anyone outside his family with the surname Paxton, let alone another Paxton with the same first name. "Strange."

"Yeah, well." The other man shrugged. "If you figure the letters ain't meant for you, throw 'em out."

David watched the fellow turn his horse and ride away. Then, after tossing the dregs of his coffee into the street, he bent to pick up the bag, which was weighty with mail. Whistling for Sam to follow him, he carried it inside and emptied the contents on his desk. The letters had been grouped in small bundles and bound together with twine. The return address on one of them sported the name of a gal named Brianna Paxton who lived in Glory Ridge, Colorado, a place David believed was southeast of No Name.

As Sam settled in his favorite spot behind the wood box, David lifted the blue speckled pot simmering on the rusty stove to refill his mug. Then he sat at his battered old desk, drew his knife from his trouser pocket, and sliced the twine on a bundle of envelopes. After cutting the first seal, he settled in to read a missive picked at random, which was dated only a few weeks ago and written in an elegant feminine hand. He was barely aware of the rumbling snores that vibrated through the wall that separated the cell block from the front office.

Darling David:
  I hope this finds you well and that you have finally struck it rich in the Denver gold fields.

David frowned. Nobody had done any gold mining to speak of in the immediate area of Denver for many years.

I write again, as I have many times before, to plead with you to come for me and our little girl, only this time I do so with more urgency. My employer, Charles Ricker, wishes to marry, and when he takes a wife, he will no longer have need of a housekeeper, cook, or tutor for his sons. In Glory Ridge, there is very little by way of respectable employment for a lady. Our daughter and I will shortly be in dire straits. I miss you dreadfully, especially at night when I recall our brief but delightful times together. If you come for us, I promise that I will be a loving wife and more supportive of your dreams.

Forever yours,
Brianna

David's frown deepened. Who the hell *was* this lady? He knew no one named Brianna, sure as heck hadn't married her, and had *not* sired her child. Or had he? Sweat beaded on his brow.

Just then a light tap came at the door and David glanced up to see Hazel Wright stepping into the office. As pretty as a spring morning in a yellow day dress and green shawl, with her honey-colored hair swept up in a fluff of curls atop her head, she smiled brightly as she closed the door, her blue eyes sparkling.

"I just wanted to stop by and say good

morning before going to the schoolhouse," she said, fingering the gold pendant that David had given her the previous evening. "We had such a lovely time last night. At least, I thought so." A blush stole into her cheeks, telling David she was recalling their farewell kiss, which had been pleasant and stirring. "How is your day starting out?"

It had started off great, but now David was getting a bitch of a headache, and Hazel, the woman he might marry, was the last person he wanted to see. "Fine." *I just found out I may have sired a daughter out of wedlock, but everything else is just dandy.* Remembering his manners, he pushed erect, swept off his Stetson, and tossed it on the mail, hoping the hat would prevent Hazel from noticing that the sender of all the letters bore his surname. "Would you care for a cup of coffee? It's fresh, not coffin varnish like Billy Joe always has on hand."

She shook her head, curls bouncing. "I'd love to, but I need to go. The children will run wild if I'm late."

"Well." That was all David could think to say. "I'm pleased you stopped by to say hello."

She pinned shimmery blue eyes on his, giving David the uncomfortable feeling that she wanted him to kiss her again. It bothered him that he felt no urge to hotfoot it around the desk. Hazel was lovely, a well-educated lady, and perfect for him. Her acceptance of the pendant last night also told him that she would be receptive to a proposal of marriage. It was inappropriate for a woman to welcome such an expensive gift from a gentleman otherwise.

David should have felt jubilant. He wasn't the only man in No Name who'd tried to win Hazel's affection. But something — David couldn't pinpoint precisely what — was missing in his feelings for Hazel. He liked her and enjoyed her company. Practically speaking, he should have been as happy as a cow in a cabbage patch that she'd chosen him when others had tried so hard to gain her favor.

So why was he waffling? Maybe it was because he still harbored fanciful notions about finding his one true love. His older brothers, Ace and Joseph, had found the women of their dreams. Sadly, it hadn't occurred for David yet. If he waited around much longer for something magical to happen, he might grow too old to raise a family. He wanted a brood of children. A practical man would tie the knot with Hazel before some other fellow beat him to it.

David circled the desk, grasped Hazel's shoulders, and pressed a chaste kiss to her forehead. "Have a wonderful day. Maybe, if things are quiet around here this evening, I can take you to supper at Roxie's. She serves roast beef on Mondays. As I recall, that's one of your favorites."

Hazel nodded, still searching his gaze as she fingered the pendant. "Last night when you gave me this, I —" She broke off, looked away, and moistened her lips. "Please tell me if I read something more into it than you intended."

"No, of course you didn't." David chucked her gently under the chin. "My intentions are —" David hauled in a deep breath, feeling like he had as a kid when he'd been about to jump into a swimming hole. *Crazy.* He'd been thinking about proposing for weeks. Giving Hazel the pendant had been his way of testing the water. So why did he feel like a bear with its paw caught in a trap? "My intentions are honorable," he settled for saying. "I, um — just need some time to think things through and do some planning before taking the next step."

Her timorous expression suddenly grew radiant, her smile as sweet and warm as sorghum on hot flapjacks. Going up on her tiptoes, she kissed David on the mouth.

Before he could respond, she drew back to leave.

"Supper at Roxie's!" she said cheerfully. "I'll look forward to it all day."

David stared solemnly at the door after it closed. Was this how it felt when a man was in love? Maybe it didn't get any better than this. Hazel stirred David physically. He felt confident that he'd enjoy the intimacies of marriage with her. They got along well, shared a few interests, and hadn't thus far disagreed on any important moral issues. Maybe that combination of things was what constituted love, and he just had his head in the clouds, wishing for earthshaking emotions that would never come to him and possibly didn't even exist.

David turned back to the letters piled on his desk, most of which were still unopened. *Brianna.* The name didn't ring a bell, but there was no denying that he was the addressee on every envelope. He resumed his seat to continue reading. Because Brianna's more recent letters made little sense — he might forget if he'd bedded a woman, but he sure as hell wouldn't forget if he'd married one — he searched for letters written four or five years ago. Sadly, the content of those made little sense, either, more or less mirroring the more recent missives except that she failed to mention how much she missed him at night. David was frowning over this when he came across a newer envelope that included a note written by a child, the printing awkward and comprised of a few brief sentences. There were no misspellings or errors in punctuation, which made David suspect that the little girl's mother had supervised the composition.

Dearest Papa:
Mama says you are far too busy mining to come visit me, so I write to tell you we are fine and doing well. Mr. Ricker has lots of spring calves, and we've got many chicks that will soon be old enough to lay eggs. This morning I am helping Mama make dumpling stew. I hope you will come see me soon.
Your loving daughter,
Daphne

David stared thoughtfully at the name. *Daphne?* There it was, definite proof that he wasn't the child's father. He'd never in a million years curse a little girl with that name. Rose, Iris, or Violet, maybe, but *Daphne?* Her classmates probably teased her unmercifully.
Sifting through the mountain of mail, Da-

32

vid located an envelope that had been addressed to him in that same childish hand. At least the kid had written something halfway interesting in her last note, unlike the mother, who seemed fixated on repeating herself, the recurring theme, "Please come for us."

David's heart squeezed as he began reading Daphne's second offering.

Dear Papa:

The man at the genrul store gives me pennys to post letters to you now becuz mama has vary little munny. Mr. Charles her boss got mareed and his new wife sed there wasn't enuff room in one howse for too laydeez.

Clearly Daphne's mother had not been present to help the child write this note. The misspellings and lack of punctuation made it difficult to read.

Mama had to find other work in gloree rij. She kleens howzes washiz uther peeples cloze duz dishez and sohs dressuz at nite.

David paused and had to back up where commas had been omitted.

33

We have a room in the atik at the bording howse but mostly I sleep on a pallut by mamas chare while she sohs until the we ours.

After finishing that letter, which was grimmer in content than the last, David fished until he found another envelope addressed to him in Daphne's handwriting. He paused less frequently now, mentally inserting commas where they were absent and deciphering the child's misspelled words by sounding them out.

We dont alwaze have enuff food but mama sez she iznt hungry and gives every bit she finds to me. I am smart and know she goze without only becuz there isnt enuff for too. Sometimes the food is from peeples garbuj drums but I eat it anyhow becuz there is nuthing else.

The most recent letter from Daphne tugged at David's heart even more.

I gess you wont ever come to see me papa. Mama says you are way to buzy trying to find gold and make us rich. But if you could send me munny so mama can make me a dress, I would be very hapy. I am in school now, and the other girls make fun of me becuz my dress is to short and has pachez all over it. Mama trys real hard to make the pachez purty, cutting budderflize and starz out of scraps but evrybudy can still tell they are pachez. I'm not vary big, so the cloth for a dress won't cost vary much.

David made a good income from his cattle ranch, had plenty in the bank, and also earned wages as a marshal. Even though he felt reasonably certain this little girl wasn't his, he could afford to send her money for clothes. If there were a child in No Name in such dire straits, he wouldn't hesitate to reach in his pocket.

Troubled, David addressed an envelope to Daphne Paxton and slipped in enough money to provide her with a half dozen school dresses, a pair of decent shoes, any other necessities, and food for several months as well. He refrained from writing a note to accompany it. He wasn't the child's father, and he didn't want to kindle hope within her that her papa was undergoing a change of heart.

It was the best that he could do. And, hey, it was quite a lot in the general scheme of things. Many men would send nothing to a child not their own.

■ ■ ■ ■

A few minutes later, while en route to the post office, which lay at the south end of town between the Chandler couple's combination chimney sweep/candle shop and the livery, David was haunted by Daphne's last letter. He'd lost his pa at a tender age and knew firsthand about hardships. But eating food from garbage drums? He shuddered at the thought. And it tore him up to imagine a little girl wearing patched, undersize dresses and worn-out shoes that pinched her toes. From the sound of it, Brianna Paxton turned her hand to every kind of work available and still wasn't able to keep the wolves from her door. What kind of man abandoned his family and left them to fend for themselves? Not any kind of man, and it made David ashamed to think anyone of that ilk bore his name.

Incensed, David shoved open the post office door with a little more force than necessary, startling Baxter Piff, the postmaster, a stocky fellow of about fifty with a shock of unruly red hair, a bushy gray beard, and sharp blue eyes that missed nothing. Sam preceded his master to the window. When David slapped the envelope down on the counter, the other man glanced at it and said, "Didn't know you had any other kin here in Colorado, only a sister out in California."

"Oregon," David corrected, dimly aware of Sam settling at his feet. "And this person isn't kin," he added gruffly. "Only a friend with the same last name."

"Hmm." Baxter weighed the envelope and quoted David an amount for postage. "Strange, that. Never met no other Paxtons so far as I recall."

The headache that had been bedeviling David throbbed with increased intensity, pounding like a fist in his temples. "I've never met anybody else named Piff, either. That doesn't mean I won't someday."

Baxter nodded. "Maybe, but I doubt it. My grandpappy changed our name. Originally it was something French, and nobody could say it right. Ain't likely that anybody else came up with the same idea unless they're related to us."

"Well, Paxton isn't French, it's easy enough to pronounce, and it's the last name of lots of folks."

"How do you know it's not French? Ain't like you've traveled the world and seen faraway places, meeting folks with different names along the way."

"I've traveled enough — all the way from Virginia to California and then back here." David's neck went hot. Paxton wasn't that common, but at the moment, he would guzzle kerosene rather than admit it. "You'd argue with a fence post, Baxter. This job doesn't keep you busy enough, and your boredom's showing." He fished in his pocket for coins and plopped them on the other man's outstretched palm. "How long before that letter reaches its destination?"

The postmaster licked his finger and leafed through a thick tome. "Glory Ridge," he muttered. "Hmph. Three days, best guess. It'll go by train partway. Then it'll be switched to a stagecoach for delivery. No main railway anywhere close, and the town's probably too small for a connecting branch like we got."

Until this morning, David had been only vaguely aware that Glory Ridge existed. Now he had reason to hope he never heard tell of it again. He just wanted Daphne to get the money as soon as possible, and then he'd return to his office, discard those letters, and wash his hands of this whole damned mess.

As he left the building and turned north, he saw his brother Ace braking his wagon near the hitching post in front of the marshal's office. Sam gave a happy bark and raced ahead to greet David's family. Caitlin's red hair gleamed like copper as her husband took fifteen-month-old Dory Sue from her arms and assisted her from the wagon. Little Ace, almost three and a half, barely gave his father a chance to release Caitlin's elbow and hand her the baby before leaping from the driver's seat. While catching his son, Ace lost his hat. His jet-black hair shone like polished onyx as he bent to retrieve his Stetson.

David swore under his breath. *Not today.* He loved his oldest brother and always enjoyed when Ace dropped by to chat while Caitlin took the kids shopping. But this wasn't a good time. There was all that mail piled on David's desk, and Ace, who seldom missed anything, wasn't likely to overlook those return addresses. That would prompt him to ask questions — lots of questions — and right now, David had no answers. Sweat sluiced down the cleavage of David's spine as he strode toward his office.

Balancing Dory Sue on her hip, Caitlin waved, then lifted her blue skirts to gain the boardwalk. "Loafing as always, I see," she accused teasingly, her cheek dimpling with pleasure as she went up on her tiptoes to kiss David's. "And prickly, too," she added with a smile when her lips met with whiskers. "How are you?" She leaned back to study him, her blue eyes filling with concern. "What a scowl! Where's that famous grin I'm so accustomed to seeing?"

David did his best to smile as he bent to peck his niece on the forehead. Except for the jet-black hair Dory Sue had inherited from her father, she was the picture of her mama, delicate of feature, with big blue eyes and porcelain skin. She thrust out her chubby arms, saying, "Unca Day-Day! Unca Day-Day!"

David chuckled and soon found his arms filled with lace-trimmed pink gingham and baby-girl softness. He pressed his nose to the child's ebon curls to breathe in the clean, sweet scent of her. Over the top of her head, he met Caitlin's questioning gaze.

"It's just been a troublesome morning," he confessed. "Nothing serious, and even if it were, seeing all of you is just the thing to take my mind off it."

A flush of pleasure flagged Caitlin's cheeks. She caught Little Ace by the arm as he tried to scale David's leg like a miniature pole climber. "Wait your turn. Uncle David is saying hello to your sister right now." To David, she said, "We're hoping you can join us for lunch at Roxie's. My errands won't take long. I need a few things from dry goods, and then I'm taking the children to the cobbler shop to be measured for shoes." She rolled her eyes. "Ace refuses to order any from Montgomery Ward. He says ill-fitting, mail-order shoes are bad for their feet."

David nodded. "I agree. Even if you specify the size they're in right now, it'll be a few weeks before the shoes arrive." He handed Dory Sue back to her mother and swept Little Ace up to sit on his shoulder. "The way this little pistol is growing, his feet may be an inch longer by then."

"Or two," Ace put in with a smile directed at his wife. "Stop fussing. I know cobbler-made shoes are more expensive, but Shelby can use the business."

"But, Ace, the kids will outgrow them in nothing flat!"

"And when they do, we'll have more made. I'm not a poor man who has to pinch pennies on his children's footwear."

Little Ace chose that moment to grab David's camel-brown leather hat. When the child put it on, his tiny dark head disappeared inside the bowl. When he pushed at the brim to peek out, everyone laughed.

"I think you need to grow some before you steal Uncle David's hat, boy." Ace

41

fetched his son, returned David's headgear, and set the child on his feet beside his mother. "No bargaining with Shelby," he told his wife as he bent to kiss her cheek. "He's a fair man, and the prices he quotes will be fair as well."

Caitlin sighed, caught hold of Little Ace's hand, and smiled in farewell. "You can drink some coffee, but don't you dare eat any of those cookies from Roxie's that David keeps in a tin," she said over her shoulder as she started across the street. "You promised me lunch at her place, and I mean to hold you to it."

Ace grinned and shook his head. To David, he murmured, "Is it my imagination, or is my wife getting headstrong and bossy?"

David laughed. "Now, there's a question I wouldn't touch with the tip of a long-barrel rifle."

"No, truly. If a problem's developing, maybe I should get a handle on it."

David stifled a chuckle. Ace worshiped Caitlin and catered to her every whim. Only her sweet nature saved her from being spoiled and impossible to please.

"What's so funny?" Ace asked.

David held up his hands. "Nothing! She's one of the dearest people I know. If she's getting a little headstrong and bossy, it's nobody's fault but your own."

Ace bent to scratch Sam behind the ears. "So you *do* think she's bossy."

"I don't think any such thing. Didn't you just hear me say how dear I think she is? Damn it, Ace. Don't put words in my mouth."

Ace straightened from petting the dog. Though David wasn't considered by most people to be a man of diminutive stature, he'd always felt short because Ace, who was actually only his half brother, was so blooming tall. In some parts of the country, there were full-grown trees that hit him below the chin. Big, muscular, and as solid as a chunk of rock — that was Ace. It was mind-boggling to realize that a tiny woman like Caitlin had not only brought the infamous Ace Keegan to his knees but now ruled his every thought, word, and gesture. A tear in her eye filled Ace with panic.

Slapping his brother on the shoulder, David led the way into his office. Sam danced to enter first and find his favored spot behind the stove. As David removed his hat and made to toss it at the hook on the wall, he stopped dead, remembering the mail on his desk. A knot formed in the pit of his stomach.

Ace glanced at the mound of envelopes

and took his usual place in the chair across from David's. Rocking back, he crossed his ankles and arms, the very picture of nonchalance except for the tic of his jaw muscle.

"So," Ace said, still aiming for a cavalier manner, "that's a heap of mail from someone named Paxton. Do we have a chatty relative I'm not yet aware of?"

After taking a seat, David slumped his shoulders and looked Ace in the eye. Since Joseph Paxton Sr.'s death, when David had been knee-high to a grasshopper, Ace had been the only father he'd ever known, stern and demanding in many ways, but also David's best friend. He could have more easily cut off his right arm than lie to him. Family honor was a bitch sometimes.

"All these letters arrived this morning," David replied. "The Denver postmaster has been saving them for about six years. They're written by a gal named Brianna Paxton to her husband, David Paxton, who apparently married her, got her with child, and then abandoned her to find his fortune in Denver."

"Well, little brother, that counts you out. You've never been a gold chaser, and I didn't raise you to be a spineless pollywog that leaves a pregnant woman to fend for herself."

Oh, how David yearned to leave it there, to just laugh and say, "You are so damned right." Instead his scalp prickled, and his lungs ached as if he'd run three miles. "In my younger years, I wasn't exactly an angel, Ace. When I went to Denver alone, I did plenty of honey dipping, and I was usually too far gone into a bottle to think about consequences."

*There,* David thought. *I've said it.* And with the utterance, he felt sort of nauseated.

Ace rubbed beside his nose. "You ever get so drunk you had loss of memory? I've been there, waking up with no recollection of the previous night, sometimes with a woman in my bed whose face and name I couldn't recall."

David sank deeper into the embrace of his chair, elbows pressing hard on the arms. "I drank heavy. Gambled heavy, too. It was exciting to me back then. Denver seemed like a big city compared to No Name. Still does, only it's gotten fancier. Now that I'm older, it just doesn't hold the same appeal for me."

"That isn't what I asked." Ace sat forward. "Were you ever so drunk that you could have been intimate with this woman and not remembered it the next day?"

David puffed air into his cheeks. "Only if

she was a sporting woman, and they always take care of things like that with a sponge soaked in vinegar."

"They *try* to take care of things like that with a sponge, but it's about as effective as pulling out before the gun goes off. Sporting women do get pregnant. You know that. Sometimes they get rid of it. Sometimes they don't. Many a child has grown up sleeping under the staircase of a whorehouse. Now, I asked you the question, square and honest. Were you ever *that* drunk?"

David could now pinpoint the source of his headache and nausea, and it had a terrible name: *Truth.* He closed his eyes, willing it away because suddenly Hazel Wright seemed mighty appealing. David didn't want his nice little life messed up by a child he'd sired with a woman he couldn't remember. "Yes," he pushed out. "There were times when I got that drunk."

Ace made a sound that reminded David of a bellows releasing a blast of air. A creak of wood signaled that he had gone limp and slumped back in his seat.

Finally David opened his eyes. "I don't know what to do next," he confessed. "If this woman used to be a working girl, and I got her pregnant, why didn't she look me

46

up? And why would she pretend to be married to me?"

"It's possible that she didn't realize she was pregnant for two or three months," Ace replied, "and maybe she looked for you in Denver and couldn't find you. As for taking your name and claiming to be your wife, I'll remind you that Christian folks don't look kindly upon an unmarried woman with a bun in her oven. It's possible that she finally left the area and pretended she had a husband so *decent* folks wouldn't shun her and the child."

Ace didn't take kindly to holier-than-thou churchgoers. He worshiped weekly with Caitlin, sometimes even taking her to Denver to attend Mass, but he drew the line at acting as if he were sinless. He felt that many people lost their way as Christians, and David agreed with him. That was undoubtedly why he'd been hesitant earlier to embarrass Miss Marcy. Her being an upstairs girl didn't make her less of a human being.

"So you think this woman" — David gestured at the mail — "might actually have had my child?"

"It's possible. That doesn't mean I'm saying it's probable."

"Ever since I read some of the letters, I've

47

been trying to convince myself of that," David said. "That it's improbable, I mean. It's the *possibility* that has my guts tied in knots." In a rush, he told Ace about sending Daphne money. "My gut tells me I've never clapped eyes on this woman, Ace." He broke off and swallowed a lump of guilt. "But my conscience won't let it go. What if I did bed her? She could have been a fancy girl in one of the Denver saloons and mistook me for a gold miner. Back then, before you got the railway connection built, I drove my cattle to market, and I was as dirty as any nugget digger you ever saw when I reached town. How do you tell the difference between a miner and a cowpoke? By the boots they wear? It isn't like I talk a whole lot about myself when I toss a skirt. Fact is, I don't talk much at all, except to say nice stuff, leaving off before I tell a woman I love her." David felt like a ten-year-old again. "Even working girls like to hear nice stuff. Right?"

Ace nodded. "I raised you right. What you do with what I taught you is your business. If you choose to burn those letters, I won't hold it against you. I'm hard put to say I'd do differently. A woman and child, out of the blue? You have your life here in No Name. They aren't a part of it. I guess what I'm saying is, do what your heart tells you to do, David. If you can live with it, I sure as hell can."

David's headache suddenly eased. He pushed at the heap of letters, his fingertips sensitive to the rasp against grained paper. "I can't live with fathering a child and leaving her to eat scraps from garbage drums. If I was once with that woman — if I got her pregnant —" David broke off and released a breath he hadn't realized he'd been holding. "Well, if I did that, I have an obligation to the woman and the kid. Drunk or not when he makes a mistake, any man worth his salt takes responsibility for his actions. I can't burn the letters and just let it go."

"I'd feel the same. But let's not jump the gun. It's possible there's another man around Denver, or was a few years back, named David Paxton. I suggest you head up there and scour the area, not only Denver, but all the outlying mining communities, for any trace of a man of that name. If he exists, there should be some record, a signature when he checked into a hotel, a transaction in his name at the assayer's office if he was a miner, a bill at a dry-goods store, *something*. And if you find evidence that another David Paxton exists, it's my feeling that you have no obligation to hang your hat on this gal's hook."

"And if there is no evidence of another David Paxton?" David didn't know why he asked the question, because he already knew the answer, but for some reason, he needed to hear Ace say it. "Do I go find the woman? Will I know when I see the child if she's mine? Look at little Dory, damn it. Except for your black hair, she looks nothing like you. What does a man do in a situation like this?"

Ace shoved at the mail again, his dark face taut. "He does what his heart and conscience tell him to do. If you decide it's possible this child is your daughter, can you live with ignoring that fact?"

David shook his head. "I wouldn't have much respect for myself as a man."

"Then you need to hop the train to Denver. Do some checking. Hit the saloons, talk to people, see if anyone remembers this fellow."

"That'll take a spell, especially if I visit outlying towns," David mused. He glanced toward the cell block. "It's been pretty quiet around here lately, though. My deputies can handle everything if I'm gone for a few days, I reckon."

"It may take more than a few days if you find no evidence that another David Paxton ever stepped foot in Denver. In that event,

50

you'll have to put your foreman in charge of your ranch and let your deputies do the marshaling while you make another trip."

David nodded grimly. If he could find no trace of another man with his name, he'd be taking quite a long trip to a tiny little town named Glory Ridge.

# CHAPTER ONE

*Glory Ridge, Colorado*
*April 10, 1891*

The hum and clack of the Singer sewing machine sang as softly in Brianna's ears as a lullaby, the sounds so familiar and soothing to her that she could lose herself to the rhythm for hours, barely aware of the ache in her ankles from constantly working the pedal. A window to her right offered the only brightness in her work cubicle, and that was precious little on an overcast day. Even so, Brianna squinted to see rather than fire up the lantern before sundown. Kerosene cost dearly, a fact the shop owner, Abigail Martin, pointed out when anyone but herself needed extra illumination. Providing sufficient light so her employee didn't struggle to see came under the heading of wasteful. Brianna's lips compressed. She was in no mood for another scold today.

A lock of Brianna's curly auburn hair

escaped its coronet to tickle her cheek, but she ignored the irritation and kept pushing the two pieces of rose taffeta forward, ever gauging the evenness and tightness of the stitches. Abigail cawed like a disgruntled crow when she found a flaw. At present, the tempting fragrance of toasted bread and hot tea drifted from the old hag's living quarters, irrefutable testimony that the woman loafed behind the closed door, indulging in afternoon treats instead of working.

Brianna knew it was wrong to have hateful thoughts, but since leaving Charles Ricker's employ two months ago, she'd come to detest Abigail. The lady was mean-spirited and miserly, never offering to share the bounty from her kitchen, not even with a child. She also had a propensity for hogging the glory. The shrew presented all finished gowns to her customers and took credit for their innovative design. Oh, how Brianna yearned to speak up and claim the creations as her own, but the fangs of hunger, always threatening to slash at her daughter's belly, kept her silent. She needed this job. The paltry sum she received each week, along with what she made at the restaurant and doing odd jobs, paid their rent and usually, though not always, provided sufficient food for Daphne. For now, that had to be Brianna's only focus.

Nevertheless, she dreamed as she worked of owning her own dress shop. The display windows would sport the very latest in fashion and the finest quality available. Wealthy women would pay dearly to purchase Brianna Paxton originals. They would, oh, yes, they would, and Brianna's coffers would overflow with the profits, putting an end to this hand-to-mouth existence.

To Brianna, sewing was similar to a waltz, her partner a machine. She followed its lead, aware of every hitch in its gait. Even when pain stabbed like knives beneath her shoulder blades from sitting hunched over, she was grateful for her talent with a needle, for that alone would one day free her and Daphne from the clutches of poverty.

Brianna often sent up prayers for the nuns at the Boston orphanage where she'd lived as a child. They had been wise to teach her a trade. Without this job to supplement her other income, she and her child would be out on the street, begging for handouts from the citizens of Glory Ridge, who were hard put to take care of themselves. As it was, Brianna occasionally had to snatch hunks of bread and cheese from the restaurant kitchen she cleaned every night and was sometimes left with no choice but to forage in trash barrels for food.

It shamed her, that. Her Irish pride burned hot every time she thought of it. Fortunately, she'd been blessed with a goodly amount of stubbornness, which stood her in good stead when circumstances drove her to do things that went against her grain and humiliated her. She'd heard people say that the end justified the means. In Brianna's case, the end, keeping Daphne nourished, justified the depths to which she sometimes sank. Until their circumstances improved, there was no room in her life for a fierce sense of dignity. That was a facet of her nature she had to bury deep within herself. Daphne had to eat, and the child had no one in the world but Brianna.

Brianna sometimes wondered from which of her parents she had inherited her strong personality. They'd both been Irish, according to the nuns, and apparently impoverished, because they'd left their infant daughters on the orphanage doorstep with only a note to provide the good sisters with their first and last names. Other than that, Brianna knew nothing about her sire or dam. Her identical twin, Moira, had been humble and malleable of nature, giving Brianna reason to believe that one of their parents had been iron willed and the other possibly complaisant.

Or perhaps life itself had molded Brianna into the willful person she'd become. Growing up in an orphanage had made her feel unimportant. She'd been one of a flock, like the offspring of a brood hen that had laid all her eggs in a communal nest. The nuns had been affectionate, but their attention was spread thin. Only determination and an abundance of individuality made Brianna stand out. To this day, she could remember how she'd yearned for her favorite nun, Sister Theresa, to notice her. Maybe that craving had pushed Brianna into becoming bolder. A harsh reprimand from the sweet little nun had been better than no special consideration from her at all.

Brianna frowned thoughtfully as she fixed a gathered sleeve to the armhole of the garment. It had been from Sister Theresa that she'd first heard the proverb "Pride goeth before destruction." Those had been only words to Brianna as a child. It had taken the harsh lessons of experience years later to teach her their meaning.

Well, she had learned, all right, and the events triggered by her reckless behavior at age eighteen would haunt her for the rest of her life. Tears of regret stung Brianna's eyes whenever she thought of those times, for it had been her sister, Moira, who had paid the price for Brianna's indiscretions, her sister who ultimately was destroyed.

*Spilled milk, and no sense in crying over it.* Moira had been dead for more than six years, and the time for weeping had passed. Now all Brianna could do was keep her promise to raise Moira's daughter as her own. She'd been unable to do it in fine fashion, but at least she'd managed. Not even Daphne knew Brianna wasn't her real mother, and unless Brianna allowed herself to dwell on the past, she seldom remembered it, either. Daphne was her child in every way that counted.

Running footsteps thumped outside on the boardwalk. Then, as if Brianna's musings conjured her up, Daphne burst into the shop. Brianna didn't have to see the child to know it was her. No adult would create such a clatter and bang with door and bell. Biting back a smile, Brianna turned, swept aside the curtain that separated her cubicle from the display room, and settled a censorial gaze on her daughter, who now added to the din, slamming the portal closed without a thought for the additional noise.

"Quiet! You know how angry Miss Martin gets when you make a racket!"

Flushed from running in the chill breeze, the six-year-old bounced across the plank floor, golden curls tumbling over her shoulders. Sometimes Brianna wondered where the girl had gotten her church-angel fairness. From the man who'd raped her mother, she supposed, for neither Brianna nor Moira had ever been blond, even in early childhood. Daphne had blue eyes instead of green. Only her finely arched brows, so like Brianna's own, marked her as an O'Keefe. Right now she shifted from one foot to the other with excitement as she waved a fat envelope beneath Brianna's nose.

"It's from Papa!" she cried. "Look, Mama! He sent heaps and heaps of money! I just asked for one new dress, but this is enough for a hundred!"

*Papa?*

Bewildered, Brianna plucked the envelope from her daughter's hand. A cold sense of unreality washed over her as she perused the return address, written in a bold, masculine hand: *Marshal David Paxton, No Name, Colorado.*

It couldn't be. David Paxton didn't exist. Brianna had invented him one long-ago night in Boston, and forever after she had claimed he was her husband and the father

59

of her child. He wasn't an actual person, only a man she'd dreamed up to lend her an air of respectability in a world that ostracized women who bore children out of wedlock.

"Look, Mama!" Daphne cried. "He sent lots and lots! Maybe even enough for" — the child gulped before voicing her dearest and most oft-repeated wish — "shoes, too?"

Trembling with shock, Brianna shushed the child again and parted the envelope to peer at the currency. *Dear God in heaven.* In all her twenty-six years, she'd seen this much money only once, after she'd left Charles Ricker's employ and emptied her five-year savings account to rent the attic room of the boardinghouse, purchase blankets for the cot, and buy Daphne eats. Pulling out the bills, Brianna stared in stunned amazement. A quick glance told her there was at least a hundred dollars, if not more.

Incredulous, she fixed her gaze on Daphne's glowing countenance. For an instant, she wanted to shout with delight and bounce across the floor with her daughter. Then reason banished the urge, trickling into her mind like ice water and filling her with foreboding. Her husband, David Paxton, did not exist, yet figments of one's imagination could not address an envelope or fill it with cash. David Paxton, her counterfeit husband, had suddenly taken on substance. This was *not* manna from heaven but a catastrophe. What if this man showed up in Glory Ridge?

"Mama?" Daphne studied Brianna with worried blue eyes. "What is it? Aren't you pleased that he sent us money?"

Brianna fished in the envelope, hoping to find an accompanying note, something — anything — to explain this strange turn of events. Over the last six years, during which she'd written to David Paxton in Denver repeatedly under duress by her employer and never received a reply, she'd grown confident that no man of that name dwelled in the city or surrounding area. *No worries.* Her invented marriage was safe from exposure. No one would ever respond to her missives, in which she'd been forced by her boss to plead countless times for assistance. She and Daphne were secure, their social status protected by a fragile guise of legitimacy. On her left hand, Brianna wore a simple gold band, which she'd purchased from a Boston pawnbroker, enabling her to pose as a married woman who could apply for employment out West. There had been no jobs in Boston — well, next to nothing, anyway, the alternatives now best forgotten

— and her infant niece had required constant care. Brianna had desperately needed a position where she could keep the baby with her while she worked.

Charles Ricker's advertisement in the *Boston Herald* had saved the day. Reeling from the death of his wife, the rancher had needed a cook, housekeeper, and tutor for his sons, preferably a widow, with or without a child of her own. Brianna had learned the hard way that a woman without male protection was often victimized by men, so she decided it would be safer to portray herself as a lady with an errant husband who might resurface. So it was that David Paxton had been born. Brianna had written to Ricker, fabricating the story that she still told now. Ricker had found her trumped-up qualifications satisfactory and wired traveling funds for Brianna and her daughter.

Brianna tried never to recall those disastrous first months when her lack of knowledge about cooking and ranch animals had been a torment that had almost cost her the job. Fortunately, her tutoring skills were genuine and well above average. Ricker had eventually come to accept that his housekeeper would never warm his bed, and he'd been marginally satisfied with Brianna's work. The years had passed pleasantly enough until Ricker met a lady he wanted to marry. With his boys almost grown, Brianna's services had become superfluous.

Now here she sat, staring stupidly at an envelope that threatened to destroy the life she'd built in Glory Ridge for herself and Daphne. David Paxton was *real.* Panic welled within her. "My, my, it *is* a fair sum of money, dear heart. You'll have several new dresses and new shoes as well. Apparently your papa found a huge gold nugget!"

Daphne beamed with pleasure. "And he remembered me, Mama! You always say how much he loves us. But sometimes I wondered. I did, and that's a fact. But this proves I was wrong."

Brianna's heart caught. It concerned her to know that Daphne felt unloved by her sire, for if any child on earth deserved to feel cherished, Daphne did. That was the problem with pretend papas. They could show no affection because they didn't exist.

The thought drew Brianna's attention back to the thick stack of silver certificates on her palm. With a brush of her thumb, she uncovered three tens, several fives, a number of ones, and four twenties. If the money had been from Daphne's real papa, Brianna would have felt it was little enough and long overdue, but the child's biological father, Stanley Romanik, was in Boston, the spoiled son of a prosperous farmer. Seven years ago, he had raped her sister, Moira, in the convent conservatory, accepted no responsibility for the pregnancy, and gotten away scot-free.

"Mama, is there enough money for you to have a new dress, too? The ones you wear don't fit right, and one of them keeps splitting on the side."

Brianna gathered the child into her arms for a fierce hug. How many six-year-old girls, deprived as Daphne had been, would think to share money that had been sent in an envelope addressed solely to them? Brianna had no intention of wasting a cent of this blessing on herself. Daphne would have new dresses and a pair of good shoes, but the remainder would be saved to ensure that the child had a roof over her head and food in her stomach for a few more months. As for David Paxton — well, that was a worry for later. She mustn't betray by expression or action that she was shocked or disbelieving.

"Do you think he may come for us soon?" Daphne asked.

"I doubt it, dearest. One gold nugget doesn't make a man rich. It was kind of him to share some of his find with you, though."

"And with you!"

Brianna stopped short of shaking her head. She mustn't unwittingly reveal to this intelligent child that the story she'd grown up believing was a pack of lies. "And with me. Of course, with *me!* I am his wife, after all."

"And he loves us both dearly. You've been right all along, Mama. He's just been working so hard to find gold that he hasn't had time to write letters or come for us!"

"Yes," Brianna agreed, without much alternative. She'd tried to make Daphne believe her father was a good person, and it looked as if she'd succeeded. Brianna tucked the certificates back into the envelope. "May I have this for safekeeping?"

Daphne nodded and then twirled in her patched and faded dress. "Mama, I'll soon look like the other girls! Maybe Hester and Hope won't tease me anymore. Maybe they'll even let me play with them. Do you think so?"

If Brianna had her way, Daphne's new clothing would outshine anything her classmates wore. "You'll look even better than they do, and I'm sure they will let you play!" She slipped the envelope into the pocket of her skirt and guided her daughter through the shop to look at cloth. Daphne was

65

embracing a lovely pink, patterned with delicate roses, when Abigail's harsh tones interrupted them.

"*What* in tarnation is going on out here?" With a scathing glare at Brianna, she fingered an imaginary film of dust on a glass case filled with ribbons and gewgaws. "I pay you a good wage to *work,* and time wasted will be taken into account when I tally your pay! When you're not sewing, you should be cleaning."

"I beg your pardon, ma'am." Brianna injected humility into her voice. "Daphne's papa sent her some money to buy dresses, and we were trying to choose some cloth. Of course I thought of purchasing it here, rather than going elsewhere."

Though Daphne had suddenly become a paying customer, Abigail pinched her nostrils in disapproval. At forty-plus, she was a bitter woman, plainer than flat bread, with white-blond hair slicked back into a chignon and a pallid complexion offset only by glittering, raisin-colored eyes. The latter were beady and ever watchful, reminding Brianna of a raptor hunting for a hapless creature to injure with a snap of its beak. In an attempt to brighten her appearance, Abigail wore colorful gowns that accentuated her paleness. When men entered her shop, she fawned over them, hopeful that a masculine eye might wander her way. If the woman had been kinder, Brianna might have given her advice on how to showcase her face, but as it was, she felt no such inclination. The lonely result of Abigail's harsh nature was no less than she deserved.

"You'll work overtime to make up for your idleness." Abigail added sibilance to the last word. "If you fail to do so, I shan't forget come Monday when I calculate your wages."

Exhaustion threatened to slump Brianna's shoulders, but she stood erect even though she knew her infraction of five minutes would cost her an hour of toil without pay. "As you wish, of course, but please bear in mind that I only just left my seat."

"Poppycock." Abigail wagged a thin forefinger. "You'll put nothing over on me, Mrs. Paxton! I know how long you've been dillydallying."

"Yes, ma'am." Brianna nearly choked on the words. "I only beg you to remember I seldom leave my station, and today the infraction has been five minutes, no more."

Regal in posture, Abigail sniffed her disdain, turned, and vanished into her apartment, where she supposedly toiled. Brianna knew better. The walls were thin, and she seldom heard her employer's machine in use. She didn't know what the woman did all afternoon and during the night while Brianna stitched gowns that sold for a handsome profit. Maybe, like Brianna, Abigail had a passion for dime novels. God knew she could afford to buy as many as she wished. Brianna's reading was limited to rare moments when she wasn't working. A few ladies in town lent her books when they'd finished with them. Raised to appreciate fine literature, Brianna had at first scorned the grand portrayals in dime novels of the Wild West. After a time, however, she'd been starved for fine print and had come to anticipate with great eagerness any work of fiction or nonfiction. Her favorites were the stories featuring Ace Keegan, the infamous gunslinger who'd once killed three men with one bullet.

"I'm sorry," Daphne whispered after Abigail's angry departure. "Now she'll make you work longer with no money. I know she's never fair when she tallies your wages."

Brianna bent to hug her daughter. "No, she's never fair, so we may as well enjoy the infraction! You have some yardage to select, young lady."

Daphne grinned, displaying the gap where she'd lost two front teeth. "I like this one!" she cried, returning to the pink floral print.

"It is a particularly fine choice." Brianna turned the child's attention to a polka dot pattern, white on dark blue. It would make up nicely with appropriate trim, piping possibly, with a bit of lace. "And we mustn't forget that you're in desperate need of a winter cloak and muff!"

Daphne beamed with delight. "I need to write Papa a thank-you note!"

"You do, indeed. Run over to the boardinghouse to fetch my writing materials."

After the child raced from the shop, Brianna briefly considered returning the cash to the sender, but envisioning the resultant look of disappointment on Daphne's face, she quickly banished the thought. The money was a godsend, and the child now had her heart set on new dresses her mother couldn't afford. That man never would have parted with such a large sum if he were in dire straits. So in a separate note, written secretly, Brianna would thank Mr. Paxton for the kindness and apologize for the mistake. She would explain that Daphne's father was a gold miner in Denver, not a town marshal. Then she'd add that no further gifts of money would be accepted and express her intent to keep Mr. Paxton's address and pay him back with interest when her finances improved. Surely that would be enough to clarify the situation in his mind.

Hours later, Brianna was still hunched over the Singer sewing machine, its shiny black surface, trimmed in gold, a blur as she focused burning eyes on a blue silk creation. The light cast by the hissing lantern was not the best to see by, and her temples throbbed. Tomorrow afternoon and evening, she would spend hours doing handwork on both the rose and blue gowns, and by night's end, when she scurried to the restaurant to do the cleanup, her fingertips would burn from pushing on the blunt head of a needle because Abigail was so miserly with her thimbles.

*Oh, precious Lord, the restaurant cleanup.* Brianna nearly groaned, for she had that yet to do before she could drop like a rock onto the narrow cot in the boardinghouse attic room that she and Daphne called home. For now, the little girl slept on a pallet near Brianna's chair, and there she would stay while Brianna tidied the kitchen of Glory Ridge's only restaurant. When that task was completed, Brianna would return to collect her child and then stumble under her inert weight as she carried her to their humble abode, which was barely large enough to accommodate the narrow bed and wash-stand.

If only she truly did have a husband, Brianna thought hazily. Perhaps then she could see an end to this life of toil. Unfortunately, even if Brianna conveniently killed off her fictitious spouse, there seemed little demand in Glory Ridge for a widow with a child. Besides, Brianna had gotten her fill of men, not only in Boston when she'd struggled to support an infant daughter, but also here in Glory Ridge. Charles Ricker had tried to force himself on her more than once, and now she was bedeviled nearly every weeknight by the aging owner of the restaurant, who was supposedly happily married but had a hankering for something new.

She was better off single even if her grand dreams of opening her own dress shop never came to fruition, which was a distinct possibility. Since leaving Ricker's household, she had been able to save nothing for that ambitious endeavor. Like syrup simmered overlong, life had boiled down to a thick, sticky substance that clung to her weary feet. She saw no way out. No matter how hard she worked, she never made enough money to set a penny aside. And as Daphne grew older and her needs increased, it would get worse. She couldn't expect envelopes full of cash to arrive on a regular basis, after all.

*Maybe this is all there is. You might spend the rest of your life working for Abigail, lining her purse instead of your own.* Everything within Brianna rebelled, but her practical nature made it impossible to keep her head in the clouds. If only she could afford a subscription to a large city newspaper, she might be able to acquire another live-in position. Unfortunately, even though she could now spare a few coins for a single issue, there were none available in Glory Ridge. And the local paper, a weekly edition, had no section set aside for paid advertisements.

Daphne moaned and stirred in her sleep, whispering, "Papa." The word electrified Brianna's nerves. She still shivered when she recalled that envelope filled with money. After so many years of writing letters and receiving no responses, she could scarcely believe that a David Paxton actually existed. The very thought made panic nip at her spine. She couldn't allow herself to fly into a flutter and pace the floor. In her mind, she heard Sister Theresa's gentle intonations from her childhood, always the voice of reason. *All will be well. Pray about it, have faith, and all will be well.*

Brianna paused in her sewing to take a deep, fortifying breath. As calm settled over her, she was able to think more clearly. Yes, David Paxton had sent a great deal of money, but he'd included no note. He had most likely been given the letters by mistake and, after reading Daphne's letters, had felt sorry for the child, thus the generous gift. That did *not* mean the man believed Daphne was his daughter and might journey to Glory Ridge. Brianna had never stepped foot in Denver, had never even visited a town in that vicinity, and had never clapped eyes on a flesh-and-blood man named David Paxton. It followed that this gentleman knew he was not Daphne's sire.

Leaving her chair for a brief stretch of her spine, Brianna circled the shadowy shop. She paused over the three bolts of cloth that the child had chosen for her new dresses. Fingering the material, Brianna smiled softly and ordered herself to stop fretting over possibilities that would never happen. Unless David Paxton was daft, he'd never in a million years take it upon himself to visit Glory Ridge. For what reason? To lay claim to someone else's wife and child? No man in his right mind would ever do that.

# CHAPTER TWO

*May 1, 1891*

An icy prairie wind, as sharp as a frozen straight razor, sliced across David's jaw, diminished only slightly by several days' growth of whiskers. Shifting in the saddle, he ran a hand along Blue's neck and gave the gelding a pat. Not for the first time, he was grateful for the blue roan's unflagging energy and smooth gait. Poor old Lucy, long ears flopping as she trailed behind them, got no stroking, but he'd make up for it when they reached Glory Ridge that evening. The gray pack mule had the toughest job, eating Blue's dust and lugging their gear.

It had been a tiring journey. David had traveled by train as far as he could, making Blue and the nervous Lucy as comfortable as possible in a stock car. Unfortunately, here in the far eastern reaches of Colorado's high plains, railway service was sparse. At the last stop, he'd been told there was a train that went toward Glory Ridge, but it wouldn't show up for days, and the tracks would end sixty miles short of that destination. David couldn't wait around; he had marshaling duties in No Name, and he'd already been absent longer than he liked. He could either hit the trail or take a stage. It wasn't a difficult choice. Rattling across country in a crowded coach was his idea of purgatory, and tethering Blue and Lucy to the rear of a carriage would be cruel. The teams of horses that pulled the coaches were swapped out at nearly every station, but a domestic equine or mule traveling behind could rest only during the stops. Otherwise they had to run all day and sometimes well into the night. David refused to put Blue or Lucy through that. He preferred traveling alone, keeping a slow pace for the sake of his animals.

"We should get there in a few hours," David informed the roan, whose ears flicked in response. "At the livery stable, you can have all the hay and oats you can eat. You, too, Lucy," he tossed over his shoulder.

Lucy emitted a noise peculiar only to her, a cross between a bray and a whicker that always made David smile. He'd left Sam at his ranch to spare him getting foot worn,

75

but now he wished he'd brought the silly mutt along. He missed the shepherd, especially at night by the fire. Sam sang along when David played his fiddle, barking, howling, and growling, and when David shook out his bedroll, the canine snuggled close, helping him stay warm.

David hunched his shoulders against the chill, grateful for the protection of his leather duster and the applications of grease that had rendered it windproof. Sadly, it reached only to his knees when he was standing and fell open astride a horse to leave his legs exposed. He could stop to don his chaps, but it was too much bother. Better to keep moving and put this trip behind him. With any luck, his stay in Glory Ridge would be short. He'd meet this Brianna Paxton, she would explain everything to his satisfaction, and he'd head home tomorrow.

If it didn't play out that way — well, David's imagination had been working overtime. He just wanted to get this whole mess settled and put it behind him. How could he have fathered a child with a woman he couldn't remember? It seemed impossible, yet he couldn't escape the fact that it might have happened. Thinking about it gave him a sour stomach. His thoughts alternately stampeded like maddened cattle or swirled in his head like dust devils, tangling his emotions like a popcorn garland after a year in storage. What if Daphne was his little girl? If so, was he obligated to make an honest woman of the mother? Where did that put his future with Hazel Wright? If he knew Hazel, she wouldn't take kindly to the news that he'd fathered a child with another woman.

David looked across the landscape. Folks who hadn't been here thought the plains were flat, with little of interest to see. They were dead wrong. The high prairie undulated with swells and dips that could have concealed a drove of bison just over the next rise if there'd been any large herds left. Nowadays the buffalo grass grew tall and mostly unmolested by the huge mammals from which it had gotten its name, forming a thick moving carpet of wind-driven green that struck a stunning contrast to the broad expanses of blue sky. Off to his right and sheltered by a stone outcropping, his mother's favorite little meadow anemones made a splash of bright color. Near them, beard-tongue made a splendiferous showing. On a sandy hill ahead of him, two male prairie chickens were strutting, dancing, flapping their rust-colored wings, and filling the bulbous orange sacs on each side of their necks to make a booming sound that could travel for miles. It was late for mating season, but the cocks had apparently misplaced their calendars. Not that David blamed them. Being limited to romancing the ladies for only a short while each spring would drive any male to drag it out as long as possible.

Nope. The prairie wasn't boring to him. And his ma, an amateur botanist, shared his interest; weather allowing, she loved to take her daily constitutional on the grasslands around Ace's ranch.

Blue whickered, and Lucy emitted a soft sound, distracting David from his musings. Narrowing his eyes, he searched the horizon. *Buildings.* He hadn't expected to reach Glory Ridge until evening, but there it was. He would be facing Brianna Paxton soon.

The thought made his stomach twist. Her thank-you note had been polite. She was grateful, but she would accept no more financial gifts, and she would someday pay him back, with interest. She'd also made it clear that Daphne wasn't his child. All very fine, David thought, but then why had Daphne herself referred to him as her father?

David didn't expect his first meeting with Brianna to go well. For reasons unspecified, she'd done a turnaround, pleading with him for years to come fetch her, and now, suddenly, hell-bent on keeping him away. Maybe she'd met some fellow and didn't want David to interfere with her plans to marry. Or perhaps he was just the wrong David Paxton. He hoped it was the latter, but he wouldn't sleep well until he knew for certain. The men in his family didn't sire children and then shirk responsibility, damn it.

Well, the grim possibilities would have to wait. He wasn't going to meet with Brianna when he looked like a drover hitting town after a cattle drive. He had a powerful craving for a glass of ale to wash down the trail dust, followed by a bath, a fresh change of clothes, and a shave before he enjoyed a sit-down meal. Most towns had a restaurant of some sort. Meatloaf sounded really good, a juicy steak even better. And, boy howdy, he wouldn't curl his lip at hot biscuits and sausage gravy, either.

Keeping his gaze fixed on the clutch of buildings ahead, David felt his heart sink as he drew closer. Why in Sam Hill was a place like this named Glory Ridge? There was no ridge in sight, and there was nothing glorious about it. As he rode in at the west side, he decided the community could serve as a model for the term *one-horse town.* He could have chucked a stone the full length of the main street. At the opposite end, the sagging roofs of a community church and tiny schoolhouse bore testimony that the ranching profits in these parts were meager. The short expanses of boardwalks and shop awnings were in no better repair. Clumps of bastard toadflax had sprouted up to line the walkways with spots of brightness, and field bindweed, sporting delicate pink flowers, formed knotted mats in between. The whole town looked shabby. David couldn't help but draw comparisons to No Name, which was at least kept tidy and in good repair, with a layer of fresh paint slapped on all the buildings every summer.

The hotel looked none too inviting. The letter E was missing from the sign that hung at an angle out front, and the windows looked too grimy to admit much light. David sighed. The beds probably weren't much better. He hated lumpy mattresses. He could only hope that the sheets and linens were clean. Time to worry about that later, though. Clucking his tongue to Blue, he guided the gelding toward the livery, a dilapidated structure with weathered plank siding and a battered billboard above the stable doors that hung catawampus and flapped in the breeze.

David dismounted out front, eyeing a rickety buckboard that sported a For Rent banner fluttering on the sidewalls. Gathering Blue's reins, he started into the building only to find his path blocked by an elderly fellow in blue denim dungarees held up by purple suspenders that clashed with his bright red shirt.

"Howdy, stranger," he said. "How can I hep ya?"

The man's drawl told David he harkened from somewhere south of the Mason-Dixon Line. He rested a hand on Blue's neck. "I need to put my stock up for the night."

The man nodded and spat a stream of tobacco juice before rocking back on his bootheels and hooking his thumbs under his suspender straps. A growth of grizzled whiskers lined his jaw. "I got three empty stalls, so ye've come to the right place."

David inclined his head. "Sounds good. I'll see to their needs myself, if you don't mind. My horse has been ridden a long stretch, and the mule has been carrying a load. I'd like to walk them and rub them down before they're fed or watered."

"Happy to accommodate ya." He smoothed a hand over his ruffled gray hair. "Got me a hitch in my get-along. Hip injury

81

years back. Walkin' a horse is a trial for me."

As the man turned to lead the way, David noted how he swung his right leg out to the side with every step. "Upkeep around here must be taxing for you."

"Don't do much of it," the proprietor called over his shoulder. "Hired me a young fellar for the heavy work. I run the place during the day, and he takes over at night. In exchange for muckin' out stalls and handlin' the rare customer after hours, he gets three squares, the use of a cot in the tack room, and a fair to middlin' wage."

The stalls were better than David had dared to hope. Both were clean, with layers of fresh straw, and the feed troughs held no remnants of hay from prior feedings. No sign of mouse or rat droppings, either. He was equally glad to note that the water buckets had been upended instead of left to sit half filled with stagnant, slimy water.

Despite the tumbledown condition of the building, David felt compelled to say, "You run a first-rate operation here."

"Love horses — mules, too, as far as that goes," the older man replied. "Yer welcome to check the hay. Ya won't find no mold or cheat grass. I only buy quality."

One devoted horseman recognized another. David knew he would find good fodder. "How much for a measure of oats for my friends? They deserve a treat."

"Oats are covered by the fee. Same goes for hay and fresh water." The man gimped into the adjacent stall to take the load from Lucy's back while David relieved Blue of the riding gear. The moment her pack was removed, Lucy buckled her front legs and rolled in the clean straw, grunting with pleasure. Glancing over the dividing wall, the livery owner said, "That is one *fine*-lookin' blue roan, son. Never seen his like."

David chuckled. "His sire is a magnificent black, and I was aiming for a duplicate when I let him cover my blue roan mare. Didn't happen the way I planned, but I can't complain about the results." Stroking Blue's arched neck, David added, "He is fine."

"Breedin' for color is like tossin' dice. When you cross a black with a blue roan, the foal's color can go either way, with the off chance of some other colors poppin' up."

"You know your horses."

"I do, and that's a fact." Lucy, who had regained her feet, seemed to realize she was being slighted and let loose with a full donkey bray, startling both David and the other man. They both laughed, and the proprietor patted Lucy's shoulder. "Yer right fine, too, darlin'. Never seen a purdier girl, and ya got grit, to boot. Been a long ride, ain't it? Yer due for some coddlin'."

David liked the way this fellow talked to animals — as if they understood and had feelings. Sad to say, he didn't see it very often. The tension flowed from his body. Allowing his mount and mule to be at the mercy of a stranger always made him nervous. No need for that tonight. Blue and Lucy would be in good hands.

As if the livery owner sensed David's approval, he smiled as he left Lucy's stall. "Got a round pen out back. Ya can walk 'em both out there. When yer ready for the hay, oats, and water, give me a holler."

Amazing what a difference two hours could make. David had dispensed with the trail grime in a luxurious hot bath, scraped off his whiskers without nicking himself, and put on clean clothes before heading for Glory Ridge's only restaurant. Lucky for him, it was a good one. The two-inch-thick steak with all the trimmings that he'd just wolfed down had been every bit as tasty as the fare at Roxie Balloux's. The hotel had proved to be a pleasant surprise, too. His room was spacious, if a little threadbare in spots, and immaculately clean. The window glass had grown cloudy with age, not layers of dirt as he'd first thought. The freshly turned, soft down mattress beckoned to him after days of sleeping on the ground with a saddle for a pillow. All in all, David couldn't complain.

After leaving a generous tip, he exited the restaurant, crossed the rickety boardwalk, and stepped out onto the packed-dirt street. A glass of chilled, foaming ale sounded just fine, but first things first. He'd better get this Brianna Paxton business over with. He'd locate the dress shop where she worked as a seamstress in the afternoons and evenings and hope he'd catch her there.

Well, okay, *hope* was a little strong. Now that the meeting was upon him, David felt as jumpy as an unbranded calf at roundup time. How should he approach this unknown woman, who might or might not be the mother of his daughter? If the child was his, and he couldn't recall Brianna, she would have every right to be madder than a bear with a bee up its nose. He just hoped her claws weren't quite as sharp.

He'd dressed carefully for the meeting. He didn't want to look too formal, like some stuck-up city swell. He'd finally settled on a clean pair of tan trousers and the long-sleeved blue shirt Hazel Wright had complimented him on. Thinking of Hazel made him recall how difficult it had been to leave No Name without letting the nature of his journey slip. She'd tried everything to wrangle an explanation out of him, and she'd gotten downright ornery when he refused to give her one. It was a side of her he hadn't seen before.

The restaurant was at the end of Main. If he turned left he'd be headed out to commune with prairie dogs and coyotes. Turning right, David set a slow pace and scanned the businesses that lined both sides of the street, looking for anything that resembled a dress shop. When he glimpsed a shine of copper brightness from the corner of his eye, he stopped, focused on the coin that lay in the dirt a few feet ahead of him, and was about to pick it up when a little girl, a whirlwind of pink ribbons and lace, darted in to grab it. David saved them both from a painful collision of heads by jerking back in the nick of time. Her noggin barely missed his nose. He grinned down at her.

"Well, now," he said. "I've always heard tell that finders are keepers, but nobody ever said what to do when there are *two* finders."

Without picking up the coin, the child straightened and blushed. "I'm sorry, mister. I didn't know you'd seen it, too."

"Well, ma'am," he said, tipping his hat, "I wouldn't dream of depriving a lady of anything she wanted that much, so please —"

David forgot what else he meant to say. *Sweet Jesus.* The child standing before him was the spitting image of his mother, with the same golden curls, big blue eyes, delicate turned-up nose, and pointy little chin. Her mouth was even shaped like Dory's, and she had the same deep dimple in her left cheek. David had the queer impression for an instant that everything stopped. His innards felt like they had a few years back when a dun-colored steer had kicked him in the gut during the annual town rodeo. Cold prickles scuttled all over him.

"Daphne?" His lips formed the name soundlessly. A puzzled look came over the child's face, and David forced his tongue into action. "Daphne?" he said again, wondering why he made the word sound like a question. There *was* no question. This child had the Paxton stamp all over her. "Daphne," he said again on the crest of a sigh, feeling as if all the air in his body rushed out through his mouth.

Her eyes went wide. Her perfect little mouth popped into an O of astonishment as she peered up at his face. "Papa?" she said incredulously.

Oh, Lord. *Papa.* David wasn't a man to get weepy over every little thing, but his eyes stung as he looked down at the little girl. *His.* No question about it. His knees went shaky. He felt a mite dizzy. Myriad emotions pummeled him. His throat ached, his chest hurt, and the urge to snatch her up into his arms and never let go was so strong that his fingertips throbbed.

But, no. If he touched her, he might frighten her. He looked down into those clear blue eyes, now fixed on his face. Waves of sickening shame swelled inside him, crowding his heart until it felt as if it might burst through his rib cage. *Dear Lord, what have I done?* This was without question his daughter, and he'd failed miserably to do right by her. David half expected lightning to flash from the sky and strike him dead, for surely siring a child and abandoning her was high on God's list of reprehensible acts. He had no memory whatsoever of having been intimate with this child's mother, but the family resemblance was too marked to refute.

Snippets of Daphne's letters to him swirled in his mind — her plea for money to have just one new dress, her reference to sometimes eating food from trash barrels, and her repeated pleas for him to come visit her. She'd been without a father all her life, she'd suffered for it, and it was no one's fault but his. In that moment, he made a solemn vow to himself that she would never want for anything again.

David tried to speak, but his voice failed him. Just as well. He hadn't a clue what he was going to say. He just stared at her, taking in every detail. She was all-over beautiful in her pretty pink dress, patterned with rosebuds of a darker hue and trimmed with ribbon and lace. Her tiny feet were encased in brand-new patent leather slippers. A silk bow, tied pertly at the top of her blond head, fluttered in the breeze.

Just then, her corn-silk curls shifted to expose the side of her neck. Below her ear was a tiny strawberry splotch, the Paxton birthmark, passed down from his mother's side of the family for generations. If he'd had any lingering doubts, seeing that mark erased them. Practically every child in his family was born with that mark. David's skin had darkened over time from exposure to the sun, but his mark was still visible. There was no mistake. His blood flowed in this child's veins.

David sank down onto one knee, which brought him close to eye level with the girl.

"Well, well," he finally managed to push out. "What an auspicious moment this is." He fetched the penny and held it up before her cute, freckled little nose. "And, by gum, we found us a lucky penny, to boot. That's a good omen. Don't you think?"

Her eyes went sparkly, and her mouth trembled as she said, "Does auspish — um — that big word you just said — does that mean you're my papa?"

David figured his abandonment of this child was already a count against him in heaven. He wouldn't add to the wrongs he'd committed by lying to her. "I am," he whispered, his voice gone gravelly with emotion. "I am, or my name isn't David Paxton."

Daphne blinked and nodded. "Oh." Seeming suddenly shy, she jerked her gaze from David's and eyed the upheld coin. "I didn't know a penny was lucky."

David collected his composure, swallowed hard to steady his voice, and replied, "You've never heard about lucky pennies? Darlin', this is the luckiest penny either of us will ever run across in our lifetimes. It brought us smack-dab together, didn't it?"

The dimple flashed in her cheek, putting David so much in mind of his ma that he blinked away tears again. Dory would be wild with joy to know that she had another granddaughter. And, oh, that gap where the child had lost two front teeth was so darned cute he wanted to grin. Before he could, a sense of loss swamped him. His ma had saved all her children's baby teeth. His own were pasted to a tattered page in a scrapbook entitled *David.* What had happened to Daphne's? Losing those first few teeth was a huge occasion in a kid's life. Had she worked the first one loose with her tongue? Or had she bitten into an apple? David could well remember standing with a string tied around his first loose tooth, the other end of the twine attached to a doorknob. He'd quivered in his knickers because Ace and Joseph kept saying, "Slam the door, David. Don't be a pansy ass."

"It did, for certain," Daphne replied.

David was jerked back to the moment but couldn't remember what they'd been talking about.

"We almost bumped heads over that penny!" she exclaimed. "You should be very glad we didn't." With a giggle, she added, "Mama says my head is harder than a rock."

David laughed. "Well, you came by that from me, I reckon. I've been told many a time that I've got solid rock between my ears."

He rested his weight on his bootheel, dimly aware that there was no traffic on the street and grateful for it. He had to clear his throat before he went on. "Most times, the saying about pennies goes like this. 'Find a penny, pick it up, and all the day, you'll have good luck.' And I can tell you from personal experience that it's true. Any old penny can be lucky if you find it and pick it up, but in a case like that, it's only lucky for a day." He touched the shimmery coin to the tip of her nose. "This is no ordinary lucky penny, though."

"It isn't?"

"Nope," David assured her. "This one is the luckiest of all pennies because you and I found it together." He turned the coin so it would catch the fading sunlight. "See that? It's even winking at us. We've got ourselves a treasure, for sure."

"What'll we do with it?" she asked, her voice touched with awe.

"We'll keep it safe for future use. You hold on to it for now." He tucked it into her hand. "Whenever we get in a pickle or have a powerful hankering for something important, we'll make a wish on this penny, and sure as shootin', it will come true."

Daphne pushed the coin back at him. "You'd better keep it, then. I've got a sweet tooth, and when I find pennies, I spend them on candy at the general store. I might spend our magic one by accident."

David accepted the coin and tucked it into his shirt pocket, where he never carried change. "You're right. We can't risk spending it accidentally. I'll drill a hole in it so we can thread a length of chain or leather through it. That way, we can wear it as a necklace, and we'll both always know it's our special penny. Deal?"

Daphne nodded and thrust out her small hand to shake on it. As David enfolded her tiny fingers in his, his heart panged. Somehow the handclasp turned into a hug, tentative at first, but then becoming fierce on both their parts. David had to gentle his hold for fear of hurting her. She locked her thin arms around his neck, flattened her small self against him, and whispered, "I thought you'd never come, Papa. I prayed and prayed, but it never happened. I thought maybe —" Her body jerked. "I thought maybe you didn't love me enough to come so far."

David felt as if he'd just guzzled a pint of lye water, his esophagus paining him as if it were on fire. He couldn't answer the child right away. When he finally regained his voice, it sounded like a blade scraping over sandpaper. "Oh, honey, no. How could any papa fail to love a sweet little girl like you? I didn't come sooner because I never got your letters. They got sidetracked at the Denver post office, and I didn't get them until a month or so ago."

"Was that when you sent me the money for new dresses?"

David turned his face against her golden curls and inhaled her sweet scent. When he thought of all the years he'd missed, of all the hugs he'd never experienced, he felt half sick. He deserved to be kicked from here to San Francisco. "Yes, little miss, that was when."

She drew back to turn a full circle in front of him. "You sent so much that Mama made me *three,* plus a plain frock for after school. I also got two pairs of shoes, underclothes, and a winter cape and muff! Used to, the other girls wouldn't play with me and poked fun at my clothes. Now Mama says I outshine them all."

"I'll just bet you do." Looking at her, David could honestly say he'd never clapped eyes on a prettier child. "That is a mighty fine dress."

"Do you like it? I picked the yardage, and Mama chose the trim. Then she stayed up one whole night making it for me. I found a picture in a fashion periodical, and she made my dress look just like it."

David wondered if all six-year-olds said things like *periodical*. His daughter was either uncommonly smart or she'd been reared up hearing big words. He made a great show of admiring the frock. "It's gorgeous. Your mama is a fine seamstress."

"She's the very best." Daphne hugged her waist and beamed a smile. "Most times, I have to change into my new play dress after school, but today is special."

"It is?"

She beamed a smile at him. "It's May Day."

Out on the trail, David had lost track of time. "By Jove, I guess you're right. It is May Day, isn't it?"

"Yes! And my school is doing a recital tonight at the community church to celebrate. Only two girls in my class were selected to do a solo recitation, and I'm one of them. That's how come I'm still wearing my special school dress. I need to look very nice."

She did one more turn, so proud of her finery that it nearly broke David's heart. This was his daughter, for Christ's sake. She should have a wardrobe stuffed with pretty dresses.

She stopped twirling to say, "Mama is going to be so surprised to see you!"

David figured that was probably an understatement. He had come unannounced, after all. Brianna had obviously intended her thank-you note to end their acquaintance, if you could even call it that. Imagining her possible reaction — so far as he knew, she might be a shrew — David decided their meeting should take place outside of Daphne's earshot. He pushed to his feet, fished in his trouser pocket, and placed some coins in the child's hand. Her eyes went as round as the quarter she held on her upturned palm.

"For *me?*"

David chuckled. "Some candy money. Just don't spend it all today. If you get a bellyache, your mama may snatch me bald headed."

Daphne fisted her fingers around the money. "I can spend it another time, Papa. Can I show you where Mama works? She'll be so excited to see you."

*I'll just bet,* David thought. He glanced along the street, then met the child's gaze. "It's not that big a town, pumpkin. I can find the shop fine without your help. Run along. It's not every day your papa comes to visit and gives you candy money."

Daphne looked undecided. Her blue gaze clung to his. "What if you're gone when I get back?"

"I won't be gone." David ached to tell the child that he would never leave her now that he'd found her, but until he discussed this mess with her mother, he couldn't make far-flung promises. "You'll see me again, darlin'. You've got my word on it."

Visibly reluctant to leave him, Daphne seemed to have put down taproots. Her bottom lip started to tremble. Looking down at her, David thought, *Oh, to hell with it,* and swept her up into his arms. Like a little organ monkey he'd once seen in San Francisco, she wrapped her thin legs around his waist and clung desperately to his neck. David pressed a kiss to her temple, nearly losing his hat in the process.

"You're right," he whispered. "The candy can wait."

"I love you, Papa," she whispered back, her shoulders jerking with a sob. "I'm so glad you got my letters and finally came to see me."

Her clinging arms, her smothered words, and the way she trembled against him almost took David to his knees. She'd waited so long for him to come, and the entire while, he hadn't even realized she existed. Tears slipped from his tightly closed eyes, trickling down his cheeks and turning cold from the breeze. He felt moisture on his neck as well and knew Daphne was crying with him. She felt so *right* in his arms. The weight of her was a burden he'd never missed, but now he felt as if he might die if he turned loose of her. He lost track of time as he stood there, embracing his child — a beautiful little girl he'd never known he had.

So this was how it felt to be a father. David had watched both Ace and Joseph act like blithering idiots the first time they held their babies in their arms. Now he finally understood. This child was a part of him, flesh of his flesh and blood of his blood. The love was instantaneous and ran so deep it was almost frightening. David loved his family, he truly did, but this feeling was different. On the way here, he'd hoped countless times that he would learn Daphne wasn't his — that he'd be free to head home in the morning and resume his nice little life with no kid or unwanted wife to mess up his plans. Now he couldn't imagine leaving Daphne behind in this shabby town. *No way.* From this moment forward, it was his job to protect her — with his very life, if it came down to it — and he couldn't do that if they were separated again.

A wagon turned onto Main, jerking David back to awareness. Loath to release his hold on Daphne, he stepped back on the board-walk.

"Don't leave me! Not ever again, Papa. Please? I'm a good girl. Truly I am."

"I won't, sweetheart." The moment David said the words, he knew it was a promise he'd needed to make, and damn it to hell, it was also a promise he would keep. This was his child. She would never wear undersize dresses again or shoes that pinched her toes. And, God as his witness, she'd never consume another scrap of food from a trash barrel, either. Her mother would either accept that, or David would wage war in court for custody. "No more letters," he said, his voice gone thick. "No more wishing and waiting. From now on, I'm going to be stuck to you like a tick to a hound's neck."

She lifted her tearstained face from his shoulder. Her wet lashes formed dark spikes, framing the intense blue of her eyes. "Does that mean stuck really tight?"

David laughed through his tears. He realized his whole body was shaking. His baby girl, dear God, his baby girl. He'd never burped her or changed her diapers. He'd never walked the floor with her when she had colic. He'd probably missed fevers, chicken pox, and heaven only knew what else. Well, he'd be damned if he missed anything more. From now on, when she was sick, he'd be there. When she was afraid, he'd be there. When she needed anything, he'd by God be there.

"Daphne, you ever seen a hound's neck?"

Her brow wrinkled in thought. He'd seen his ma look that way when she was trying to decide what herbs to use to cure an illness. "Most folks here have sheepdogs."

"Well, the skin on a hound's neck hangs in folds, kind of like ruffled curtains. When a tick takes up residence on a hound's neck, the only way to make it turn loose is to set fire to its arse with a lighted lucifer. That's stuck pretty tight."

Daphne burst forth with a wet, tremulous laugh. "Stay away from lighted lucifers, Papa. If you leave me again, it'll fair break my heart."

David grinned and gave her a jostle. "Sweetheart, Lucifer himself could set fire to my arse right now, and all I'd do is dance circles around you. I'm not leaving you, no matter what."

# CHAPTER THREE

Brianna heard a rattling sound and glanced warily at the closed door that led to her employer's living quarters. Abigail liked to burst in without warning, hoping to catch Brianna "loafing." The sudden appearances startled Brianna when she was deep in concentration, and she hated the feeling of her heart catching in her chest. Today she particularly dreaded having the old witch sneak up on her because she was groggy from lack of sleep. She didn't need Abigail hovering to pick apart everything she did.

Brianna flexed her aching shoulders. She hadn't finished at the restaurant until two in the morning, washing stack after stack of dishes and then tidying up the dining area for the breakfast trade. Five thirty had come early, and she would have given almost anything to sleep in. As it was, she'd barely had time to walk to Mrs. Dawson's, get the woman's ironing done, and return to the boardinghouse by seven to wake Daphne for school. After the little girl left, carrying bread and cheese in a knapsack for lunch, Brianna had scurried the length of Glory Ridge to spend the morning ironing at the Wilson place. Their seven children, six of them boys, regularly produced a mountain of laundry, and the mother, Charlotte, still ailing after the birth of her daughter, could no longer keep up with all the work, a boon for Brianna, but a terrible hardship for Mac Wilson, who could ill afford to pay for household help.

Brianna had hoped to snatch a couple of hours' sleep before starting her shift at the dress shop, but there had been no time. School had adjourned shortly after lunch because it was May Day and there was to be a recital at the church tonight. Daphne had been chosen, along with one other girl, to do a solo recitation. Abigail had denied Brianna permission to take time off from work in order to attend, so Daphne had insisted on doing an attic-room performance this afternoon for her mama. She'd looked so adorable, standing on her washstand stool, all decked out in her new dress and fancy patent leather shoes. As desperate as Brianna had been for a nap, she hadn't had the heart to disappoint her daughter by saying so. Then, to make matters worse, Daphne bungled her lines, so a practice session had ensued, the child strung taut with last-minute nervousness, Brianna struggling to keep her eyes from drifting closed.

Blinking to clear the film of exhaustion from her gaze, Brianna resumed pumping the foot pedal of the sewing machine, wondering how one could toil as much as she did and still fail to make ends meet. The rent was due on Monday morning. The attic room ran three dollars a week, and she had only two, a fourth of which she'd found on the restaurant floor on Wednesday night while sweeping the dining room.

Mrs. Brighton collected the rent bright and early, and she expected to be paid in full. Brianna felt the rate for a closet-size room was astronomical, but the silver-haired widow refused to budge on the amount. So far, Brianna had always managed to come up with the money because those who didn't were immediately evicted. No period of grace was offered. Without ceremony or apology, any tenants in arrears were given a half hour to collect their belongings and get out. Brianna had seen it occur, and so had a very frightened Daphne. Brianna had promised the child that it would never happen to them. Brave words, indeed, and now she might live to regret them.

*There is Daphne's dress money,* she thought blearily. But, oh, how Brianna detested the thought of dipping into the funds David Paxton had sent her daughter. Nearly half of his generous gift remained unspent. Brianna kept it tucked safely away in a deep pocket of her skirt, but it wouldn't remain there for long if she borrowed from it.

She needed to think about next winter, when business at the dress shop would slow down again. Brianna had started working for Abigail three months ago, in early February, when customers had been so few that she'd been needed for only a short while each day. Now, with spring on its way, women were ordering new summer gowns or having old dresses made over, which gave Brianna more hours. But spring would soon slip into summer, summer into fall, and then winter would come again to tighten everyone's purse strings. If her money ran out in the middle of January, she and Daphne would be out on the street in subzero blizzard conditions. The thought made her frantic.

Daphne's money had to be saved for truly dire situations — to pay the rent during the slow months, to take the child to the doctor if she got sick, and to buy her food when the coffers ran empty. *Please, God, help me. I'm not asking for a huge miracle, only a tiny one. I'll be ever so thankful. I'll never entertain another evil thought, not even about Abigail. Just, please, hear my prayer and send me an itty bitty miracle.*

Tears threatened. Brianna blinked them away, angry with herself for giving way to weakness. Tears never solved anything. She'd learned that long ago as she wept over her twin sister's lifeless body.

The wonderful smell of hot vegetable soup drifted from Abigail's apartment. Brianna's stomach churned. Oh, how she yearned for a taste. She'd been going without meals as much as she could to trim expenses. No breakfast, followed by a hunk of bread and a cup of lukewarm tea for lunch. Ah, well, she'd sneak some cheese when she cleaned the restaurant kitchen tonight. That would sustain her. Losing more weight posed no great concern. Her gowns, fashioned for her by the nuns when she was eighteen and now out of style even in this isolated community, had grown too snug. Maybe, by eating less, she would grow thin enough to take a deep breath without splitting her underarm seams.

Today Brianna was altering a dress for

Mrs. Pauder, a sheep rancher's wife who'd gained weight over the winter and couldn't afford a new wardrobe. Normally Brianna detested doing alterations, which in this case involved ripping out stitches and reconstructing the garment to utilize the inseams. The unexposed cloth didn't fade as quickly as that on the outside, which gave the refashioned gown a striped look. It was tedious work, requiring no imagination, but for once she was grateful. She was too exhausted to take on a truly creative project.

From behind her curtained cubicle, Brianna heard the bell jingle as someone entered the shop. Her ever-thrifty employer had assigned Brianna the duty of dealing with customers to eliminate the cost of hiring a clerk. Sighing, she stopped peddling, pushed Mrs. Pauder's dress onto the machine's work surface so it wouldn't slip to the floor, and rose from her chair. When she heard the thud of a man's boots on the plank flooring, she grimaced. Occasionally a gentleman stopped in to buy his wife a bonnet, trinket, or length of ribbon. Males invariably took twice as long to decide as most women did. Brianna's eyebrows arched when she heard the chink of spurs. The farmers and ranchers around Glory Ridge didn't normally wear them.

She tried to tidy her hair and then swatted at the wrinkles in her skirt. Why she bothered, she had no idea. The sound of a man's footsteps inside the shop would bring Abigail running, and then Brianna's presence would be unnecessary. Whether the poor fellow was married or not, her employer would bat her scanty lashes, chatter inanely, and titter like a schoolgirl. If ever a woman had hungered for masculine attention, it was Abigail Martin. *Hmph.* If Brianna lived out the rest of her days without ever again drawing a man's interest, she'd be inexpressibly grateful. She had enough trouble avoiding the groping hands of Adam Parks, the restaurateur.

As Brianna swept aside the curtain to greet the customer, she froze in motion. The fellow who stood at the center of the display area held Daphne in his arms. What was a stranger doing with her child? At a glance, Brianna knew he wasn't a local. She'd lived in or near Glory Ridge for years and recognized practically everyone. Her first thought was that her little girl had met with an accident. Daphne loved horses and sometimes ran out into the street when ranchers rode into town. Once, she had been knocked down. Brianna held out her arms for the child, but before she could utter a word, she noticed the way Daphne clung to the man's neck. The glow of happiness on the little girl's face spoke volumes.

*Oh, dear God.* The front panels of the man's oily leather duster were tucked behind the butts of his six-shooters, and a flash of silver jerked Brianna's gaze to the left breast pocket of his blue shirt. *A badge.* The floor felt as if it turned to water beneath her feet, and she caught hold of the counter to steady herself. An icy chill crawled up her spine. Her heart squeezed and missed a beat. *David Paxton.* As surely as she lived and breathed, she knew it was he. Questions bounced inside her mind. Why had he come? What did he want? How dare he show up here after she'd told him in her last note that he wasn't Daphne's father?

Though lean and not overly tall, he projected a "big man" aura, his stance not precisely threatening but signaling that he had lived with danger as an almost constant companion and was always on guard. His gold hair, visible beneath the brim of his tan leather hat and only a few shades darker than Daphne's, hung as straight as a ruler to his broad shoulders. He wore his two-gun belt low on his hips in the manner of a fast draw. Except for the badge, his overall appearance was more suited to her idea of a desperado than a lawman. Tawny trousers, scuffed riding boots, and tarnished spurs completed his outfit. The faint scent of bay rum and the silken gleam of his lower jaw indicated that he'd recently shaved, and his clothing looked clean enough, but he was one of those men who would project a slightly disreputable air even in a fancy suit.

When he loosened one arm from around Daphne to remove his hat, Brianna got a clear look at his sharp blue eyes, which seemed to miss nothing. They were underscored by chiseled features, a square jaw, and a full mouth that might have softened the hard angles of his face if not for its grim set.

Keeping one thin arm locked around his neck, Daphne twisted on his hip to flash Brianna a jubilant smile. "Look, Mama! Papa has finally come to see us!"

The room seemed to tilt. Little black spots danced before Brianna's eyes. Her limbs remained frozen, and her mouth felt as dry as sunbaked rawhide. She was imagining things. She had to be. Stuff this horrible didn't happen, not even to her. She squeezed her eyes shut and opened them again. He was still there. For the life of her, she couldn't think what to do.

"Hello, Brianna," he said, his deep voice

pitched low. "It's good to see you again."

*Again?* She'd never clapped eyes on this man in her life.

"Isn't it wonderful, Mama?" Daphne chortled with unbridled delight. "Aren't you excited? Why don't you say something?"

Brianna didn't know what to say, and excitement was way down the list of her emotions, well behind horrified, appalled, and stunned. She felt like a defenseless rabbit caught out in the open by a long-toothed predator, and all she wanted was to bolt for the nearest hidey-hole. Only two things forestalled her: the presence of her child and the forbidding glint in David Paxton's eyes. It took every shred of self-control she possessed to collect her wits.

*Don't panic,* she cautioned herself. *Calm down.* Because of her letters to a man of the same name in Denver, this fellow was somehow under the impression that Daphne might be his. Just how he thought he'd managed to sire a child with a woman he'd never met could be worked out at another time. Right now, she had to get Daphne out of earshot, and fast, so she could make it clear to *this* David Paxton that he was the wrong man.

Brianna Paxton wasn't what David had

expected. Braced to recognize her, even if only vaguely, he realized that nothing about the woman seemed remotely familiar. As best he could see in this poor light, she had a memorable head of hair, a striking color somewhere between dark brown and fiery red, large, shamrock green eyes, flawless ivory skin, and delicate features. Altogether not a package he'd be likely to forget under normal circumstances. Problem was, he had a hunch the circumstances surrounding their meeting had been a long way from normal.

He'd been taught better manners than to take stock of a woman's figure unless he did it on the sly, but in this situation, he found himself staring at her generous breasts, the indentation of her slender waist, and the swell of her hips, hoping against hope that *something* about her might jar his memory. Had he actually gotten so drunk that he'd had intercourse with this woman and could recall nothing about her? Stupid question. He held the proof of his indiscretion in his arms, a beautiful little girl who was undeniably a Paxton. Whether he remembered it or not, he had trifled with this lady.

And she hadn't missed his less-than-subtle appraisal. The lift of her chin and the light of battle in her eyes told him that. It was a look of insulted dignity, calculated to reduce the victim to shreds. He'd seen his ma do the same.

That mental comparison was another thing about Brianna that bothered David. Looks could be deceiving; as a marshal, he knew that better than most folks. But unless this gal had experienced a come-to-Jesus moment and completely transformed herself from the skin out, she'd never been a sporting woman in Denver or anyplace else. If the collar of her gray dress had reached any higher, it would have covered her chin. She wore her gorgeous, glossy hair done up in a severe chignon. Curls had escaped to frame her face and lie upon her nape, but he had a feeling she would quickly dispense with them if she saw herself in a mirror. She was comely, exceedingly so, the kind of woman who could make her fortune by plying that most ancient of female trades in a rowdy saloon or bawdy house. But there was a haughty stiffness in her posture that told him she'd never lower herself to cavort with foulmouthed, uncouth men, no matter how much money lined their pockets. She had that indefinable quality his ma called breeding.

So where the hell had he met her? At a Denver community social, possibly, or at a cattlemen's potluck? At shindigs like that, there were always a couple of punch bowls heavily spiked with booze. David could scarcely believe he'd offered a proper young lady alcohol at some forgotten public function. Paxton men didn't prey on innocents. Ace had started drilling that into David's head as he entered adolescence. Sadly, back in his early twenties while visiting Denver, David had been drunk so much of the time that the line between right and wrong had gotten very blurry.

Brianna stood with one slender hand pressed to her waist, as if she had a stomach ache or something. He'd had a lot of different reactions from women in his time, but he'd never before suspected that his mere presence was enough to make a lady sick. Ignoring him, she fixed her gaze on their daughter. "Daphne, darling, can you run along and play for a while? Or better yet, perhaps this is a good time to practice your recitation. We adults need a moment to talk privately, please."

David gave Daphne a reassuring pat and whispered in her ear, "Remember the candy money? Now would be a good time to buy yourself a peppermint stick."

David set her on the floor. He straightened the rose-colored ribbon in her hair. The expression in her eyes told him without her saying a word that she was still worried about him leaving. "Do you, by any chance, like sarsaparilla?"

"I *love* it!" the child cried.

"Well, I'm fond of it, too. Later, we'll go to the restaurant, and I'll buy us both one."

Assured by the promise, the little girl bounced across the plank floor. The door crashed shut behind her as she ran outside. David settled a thoughtful gaze on the child's mother. Damn, but she was pretty. David couldn't deny that. But the possibility of a fractious disposition still couldn't be ruled out. Even her speech, refined and laced with an accent he couldn't quite pinpoint, screamed "proper."

"My dear sir," she said shakily, her hand still splayed at her waist. "It appears you have traveled a very long way for absolutely no reason. We've obviously never met, and you have no obligations here."

When she said *sir,* it sounded like *suh.* Southern, maybe? Nope. David had been born in Virginia, and he didn't detect a drawl. An Easterner, he decided. How he had hooked up with her, he didn't know, but it didn't matter. After seeing Daphne, he was convinced beyond any shadow of a doubt that he was her father.

Just then a door at the rear of the shop swung open and a skinny woman in a scarlet dress emerged, accompanied by a faint smell of vegetable soup. David had seen some fair-skinned people in his day, but this gal looked as if she'd been dipped repeatedly in a bleaching agent, her skin, hair, lashes, and lips so white that the bright color of her gown was startling by contrast. Only her eyes — a dark, beady brown — saved her from being mistaken for an albino. Her mouth curved into an overeager smile as she greeted David.

"My, my, it's not every day we have a handsome stranger drop in." She stepped forward, offering him a clawlike hand. "I'm the proprietress, *Miss* Abigail. It will be my great pleasure to assist you in any way I can."

David shook hands with the woman and resisted the urge to wipe his palm clean on his tan jeans after the contact ended. She was sweating like a horse that had been run too hard for several miles. Thwarted lust, or was she coming down sick? Either way, he wanted no part of it. Deliberately neglecting to introduce himself, David said, "Thank you for your kindness, Miss Abigail, but I'm here to speak with Mrs. Paxton."

Abigail's eager smile thinned into a moue of distaste. She directed a glittering, resentful glance at Brianna. "I see." Her bony shoulders lifted in a shrug. Then she jabbed a rigid finger at her employee. "You'll not entertain men inside my shop, Mrs. Paxton. You may take your leave until your business with this gentleman is concluded, and I shall dock your wages accordingly for the time missed."

Brianna shot David an accusing look, then nodded in meek acquiescence to her boss. "I'll be gone a half hour, no more."

"*I'll* keep track of the time you miss, thank you very much," Abigail flung back. Then, with a sniff, she disappeared and slammed the door behind her.

David shot Brianna a commiserating look. "Well, now, she's all-over unpleasant. Working for a termagant like her must be a constant trial."

"Positions of respectable employment for ladies are few and far between in Glory Ridge, Mr. Paxton."

"I know. You mentioned that in your letters."

She shot him a wary look over her shoulder before stepping through the parted curtain to collect her wrap. As she stooped over, the way she moved struck him as odd.

116

There was no curve of her back, no dip of her head, and she bent slightly at the knees to prevent her posterior from protruding. That was a shame. The limp folds of her wash-worn skirt did little to hide her figure, and in his estimation, she had a very fetching backside.

As she returned to the main room, she drew a tattered black shawl around her shoulders. Judging by her complexion, green eyes, and given name, David guessed her to be of Irish descent, and he found himself wondering if she had a temper as fiery as the shimmer of red in her hair.

"Shall we?" she asked.

David noticed faint blue shadows of exhaustion under her lovely eyes, which were the deepest green he'd ever seen. He knew from Daphne's letters that Brianna turned her hand to any honest toil she could find in order to support their daughter, but judging by her appearance, she spent precious little of her earnings on herself. In addition to being rail thin, she wore a gown that was faded, badly worn, and too snug across the breasts. Her kid boots were old and battered. He had an awful suspicion that she slept little, ate infrequently, and did without other basic necessities. The very thought made him feel like a lowdown skunk. If not for him, she wouldn't be in such a pickle.

When they exited the dress shop, the breeze had picked up, and it had a sharp bite. Brianna clutched her shawl close and walked ahead of him along the uneven, sagging boardwalk until she reached a break between the buildings, whereupon she vanished into the narrow alley. David followed her into the shadowy chasm, where the weather-beaten structures on either side provided a windbreak. And a sound barrier. No passersby would overhear them, and he suspected that was why she'd chosen this secluded spot, despite her obvious wariness of him.

She turned to face him, her countenance pale, her eyes gleaming with purpose. "You've made a huge mistake by coming here, Mr. Paxton. I told you in my last note that Daphne isn't your daughter."

David tried to take a mental step back and keep his temper. He had seen the child in question, and if she wasn't a Paxton, he'd eat his boots and have his hat for dessert. Still, he needed to hear the woman out. Having him show up unexpectedly had to be unnerving for her. One tryst, a resultant pregnancy, and so many years of separation didn't make them lovers, close friends, or even acquaintances. He was, to all intents and purposes, a total stranger.

"Look," he said, trying to inject a gentle note into his voice, "I'm not here to cause you any trouble. I only want to do right by you and the little girl."

She blinked and, as if her lashes were attached to a drain-plug chain, all the remaining color slipped from her face. "Did you not hear me, Mr. Paxton? This isn't about your doing the right thing. It's a case of mistaken identity. You bear my husband's name, but you are not my husband, and you are *not* Daphne's father. Can't you *see* that? You can't honestly say you've ever met me before."

David bent his head and dug at the dirt with the heel of his boot, a habit of his when he grew angry or tense. It gave him a chance to think before he stuck his foot in his mouth. She looked scared half to death, and he sure as sand didn't want to end this conversation prematurely by pushing her into a full-blown panic. From her standpoint, this might be a frightening situation. In custody suits, fathers, who had greater earning power, normally prevailed in court. Maybe she feared that he meant to take Daphne away from her. David hadn't come here to separate the mother from her little girl. The way he saw it, he was as obligated to Brianna as he was to Daphne. Hazel Wright's appeal seemed dim by comparison to the very real need he saw here. He'd do whatever was necessary to make this right, and if that meant being saddled with a wife he didn't love, so be it. At least she was easy on the eyes, and under better circumstances, she might even be congenial.

"Like I said, I'm not here to do any harm."

She squeezed her eyes closed. When she lifted her lashes, David saw the shadows of anxiety and fear that darkened her irises. He regretted that, but what the hell was his alternative? After seeing Daphne, he couldn't just ride away to spare this woman grief.

"As I told you in my thank-you note, Mr. Paxton, my husband is a miner in Denver, not a marshal in an outlying town."

David dug a deeper hole in the dirt, wishing he were better with words. "No offense intended, ma'am, but I've searched high and low for another man named David Paxton in or around Denver. I've visited the saloons, the post offices, the assayers, and all the stores, searching the books for a transaction under his name. I've also interviewed countless people, hoping to find just one person who might remember him. Plain and simple, another David Paxton in that area simply doesn't exist."

She looked as if she might faint. Her mouth compressed into a thin line. She weaved on her feet. David gripped her shoulder to steady her. She jerked and cringed from his touch.

"That isn't possible," she told him. "I'm married to the man. I had a child with him. No more than a month ago, I received a letter from him, postmarked in Denver! He's there, mining for gold, I'm telling you. Just because you didn't locate him doesn't mean he doesn't exist. Why would I lie about such a thing?"

David had no idea why she might lie; he knew for a fact only that she had. About a month ago, he'd spoken to the Denver postmaster at length. The man had a mind like a steel trap, took a personal interest in all his customers, and never forgot a name. If another David Paxton had posted a letter at his window at any time over the last few years, the postmaster would remember him.

As if Brianna sensed that he didn't believe her, she rocked forward onto her toes and extended her neck. "He mines in Denver, I tell you. In the gold fields! All of his letters have been postmarked there!"

David didn't want this discussion to get

ugly, but Daphne's sweet face kept swimming in his mind. Her resemblance to his mother was uncanny, and that birthmark on her neck was undeniable proof that his blood flowed in her veins.

Trying to choose his words carefully, he replied, "The placer mining in the Denver gold fields petered out years ago. Only a fool would sift through that dirt now, trying to find enough color to amount to anything."

"Are you calling my husband a fool, sir?"

Well, no, he wasn't, at least not exactly. David was saying, as politely as he could, that her alleged husband didn't exist. He looked deep into the alleyway, searching the shadows, wishing he could find answers there. "I'm saying no other David Paxton resides in the Denver area."

"Then maybe he mines somewhere else! Maybe he moved on!" she cried. "Maybe he only goes into Denver for the amenities, a hot bath, a good meal, and a night at a hotel. He enjoys a game of cards now and again, and also an occasional drink. A man can't live his entire life working without taking a break now and then."

It appeared to David that she was doing pretty much that, toiling long hours with precious little rest. "The mining towns in the mountains west of Denver are well established with their own hotels, saloons, bathhouses, and postal services," he informed her. "Why would a man travel clear to Denver when all the things you just mentioned are readily available in the town where he works? I'll also add that I checked out those distant mining communities. Leadville, Central City. I even went as far as Summitville. There's no record of another David Paxton ever having been in any of those places. Quite simply, the man doesn't exist. Do you think I'd be here otherwise? That I've got a strange hankering to take on a ready-made family? I have a nice life in No Name — a job as the town marshal and a prosperous cattle ranch."

"Then go back to them!" she cried. "I didn't invite you here."

"Yes," he corrected, "you did. In dozens of letters written over the last six years, you not only invited me here, but you begged me to come."

She sank against the clapboard wall behind her. "Please, just go. Don't do this."

"I don't have any choice," he replied.

*"Why?"* she demanded, her voice rising to a shrill pitch. "Are you out of your mind? I guess I know who the father of my child is, sir, and you are not he!"

"Then why did you send me those letters?"

"I didn't!" She practically screamed the words, then pulled in a gasping breath in an obvious fight for self-control.

David was fast moving beyond diplomacy. "I've seen Daphne. That child is the spitting image of my mother. She even has the Paxton birthmark on her neck. Don't stand there and deny she's mine. I know better."

She laughed — a brittle, frantic little bleep of sound followed by a gulp that bobbed her pebble-size larynx. "You're delusional. That spot on my daughter's neck is *not* a birthmark." She paused and her gaze shifted nervously. "Hot grease splattered from a skillet while I was cooking when she was just a baby. The burn left a scar."

David had interrogated too many people to be easily deceived. The hand she used to grasp her shawl had gone white at the knuckles. Instead of looking him directly in the eye, she kept her gaze fixed on the building behind him. He didn't believe a word she was saying. Maybe he'd guessed right about there being a new man in her life and marital plans in the making. The unexpected appearance of her child's father would sure as hell be a fly in her ointment.

"Bullshit," he shot back.

She jerked at the word, which told him she was unaccustomed to rough language. Well, he was no longer in any frame of mind to mince words.

"I know a Paxton when I see one," he added. "She's my kid, God damn it! And now you expect me to just walk away? Think again. You look like you haven't had a decent meal in weeks. Your clothing is threadbare. My daughter would be wearing rags if I hadn't sent money. Yet you stand there denying me the right to care for her — and for you?"

"I've done the best I can by her! You have no right to criticize me or how I've provided for my child. You're stepping beyond your bounds."

"I meant no criticism. Under the circumstances, I think you've done a swell job. But with my help you can do better."

"I don't *want* your help."

"Not even if it makes things better for Daphne?" he thrust at her, and saw her flinch. He pressed his advantage. He had a feeling he wouldn't get many of them. "Whether you want my help or not, Paxton men don't sire children and then walk away. We're honor bound to do right by the child *and* the mother. Get that straight in your head. Now that I'm here, I'll by God not leave without my daughter."

She looked at him as if he were a five-headed coiled rattler. "Are you *threatening* me?"

"Read into it what you like. I didn't stutter my words."

Even in the dim light, tears sparkled like diamonds in her eyes. "You have to listen to me," she said jaggedly. "You're wrong, I'm telling you. My husband, David, was once a rancher here in Colorado."

"Where at in Colorado?" he broke in.

She fixed him with a blank look. "It's — um — a tiny place. I'm sure you've never heard of it."

"Try me."

She flicked the tip of her tongue over her full lower lip. "Taffeta Falls," she blurted.

David almost chuckled. *Taffeta Falls?* She was a dressmaker, so he supposed it followed that she'd draw from her ready store of knowledge when she lied. "You're right. I've never heard of it." Undoubtedly because such a place didn't exist. He gestured with his hand. "Please, do go on."

She drew up her shoulders, breathed deeply through her nose, and visibly collected her composure. "Where was I?"

"Your husband was once a rancher here

126

in Colorado near a tiny town called Taffeta Falls."

"Oh, yes, of course." She drew in another breath before continuing. "I met David in Boston when he journeyed there to visit his relatives. After we married, I returned to Colorado with him. Shortly thereafter, he heard of the gold being found in Denver, and he set out to find his fortune. Not long after he left, I realized I was with child, and I was soon unable to do the work required to keep the ranch. The bank foreclosed. David didn't respond to my letters or return to collect me. At that point, I was homeless, so I went back to Boston, prevailing upon David's family to help me."

"You don't have any relatives of your own?" David interjected.

"No, I was left on the doorstep of an orphanage when I was an infant."

David filed away that bit of information for later.

"After Daphne was born, I found that I missed the wide-open spaces of Colorado and responded to an advertisement in the Boston paper, applying for a job as a housekeeper and tutor in a widower's home outside of Glory Ridge. I worked for him until three months ago, when he took a second wife."

David almost rolled his eyes. She had her story down pat; he'd give her that. It was like listening to a kid's recitation of the Gettysburg Address, a fine bit of memory work, but delivered too perfectly and without a hitch of emotion.

"Why, after you realized you had a bun in your oven, didn't you stay in Denver until you were able to locate me?" he shot back.

"Locate *you?* Did you hear *nothing* I just said?"

"I heard you, but I have to go with the evidence of my own eyes. That little girl is a Paxton."

"She is not a Paxton!" she flung at him. "I mean, she is — but she's not yours! Look at me," she cried. "Really, *really* look at me. Have you *any* recollection of ever having met me before?"

David had already considered how insulted she might be if he confessed the truth, so he decided to say something flattering rather than answer her question. "How could any man with blood in his veins forget a beautiful woman like you?"

She gaped at him. He felt like a cockroach that had just appeared on her supper plate. "You, sir, are completely out of your mind. We've never met. You are *not* my child's father. Perhaps, in your countless conquests, you have lost the ability to remember each and every woman with whom you've consorted, but I have perfect recall of the *one* man I've been with, Daphne's father. I'll add that it is patently obvious, at least to me, that I would never keep company with a man of your stratum."

His *stratum?* David's folks had it in them to spew some fancy words, but he'd never heard that one. All the same, he knew an insult when he heard one. Okay, this was going to get ugly whether he wanted it to or not. He hauled in a bracing breath and searched his memory for any highfalutin words he knew. His brain went as blank as a freshly scrubbed chalkboard. "What the hell's wrong with my stratum?" As he asked, David wished he knew the exact meaning of the word because he'd shove it right back down her throat. "I come from good people, *upstanding* people, damn it. And you obviously don't know who you're dealing with. You will *not* keep me away from my daughter or deprive me of my right to fulfill my obligations to her. Are we clear on that? My offer still stands to take care of *both* of you, but you'd best recognize, here and now, that you're not dealing with some pampered Boston dandy who runs at the first sign of trouble. I'm going to be there for my little girl, and nobody will stop me. If you think different, come with an army to back you up, and while you're at it, tell the bastards to pack a lunch."

"This is, without question, the most *ludicrous* exchange I've ever had the misfortune to participate in. She is not your child! What possible reason would I have to lie to you about it?"

"I don't know," David admitted. "But you've sure got a reason. And yeah, I may be ludicrous, but you're fixin' to discover the cut of my cloth, lady. I've decided this disagreement isn't going to be settled in any damned alley. We need to take the issue before someone of authority." David had to bite down hard on his back teeth to keep from following that with a string of curses to turn the air blue. She was fast becoming one of the most infuriating women he'd ever met. That snooty Eastern accent of hers could get under his skin quicker than an Oklahoma chigger. "So far as I can see, talking any further is pointless."

She visibly groped for calm and relaxed her shoulders. "Perhaps we should both take a step back, Mr. Paxton. We *are* both adults, correct? Surely we can discuss this matter and reach a conclusion satisfactory to both of us without involving anyone else."

David sure as hell considered himself to be an adult, but at the moment his *stratum* seemed to be something of a problem. Nevertheless, he forced himself to shove away the anger — and, okay, his offended feelings. She clearly didn't feel comfortable about a hearing before the authorities, and if the two of them could settle this without anyone else making the calls, he was all for it.

"Okay," he agreed. "Start discussing."

She turned up her palms in a gesture of helpless bewilderment. "I defer to you, sir. Discuss away."

"All right, I'll start with how I think it happened."

"How you think *what* happened?"

"What happened between us, in what I guess you'd call the *biblical* sense."

Two bright spots of color appeared on her cheeks. "We have *never* been together in any sense, Mr. Paxton, biblical or otherwise."

"There you go again, not letting me talk. Maybe my first instinct was right, and we need some referees."

"Arbitrators, you mean."

David clenched his teeth. She apparently noticed because she flapped her wrist, muttered something under her breath, and said, "I'm sorry. Please, do continue."

"Thank you." He laced that with an edge of sarcasm. "Here's how I think it came about." David jerked off his hat, raked his fingers through his hair, and slapped the damned thing back on his head. "I think you and me met —"

"I," she interrupted. "That is the proper form of the first-person pronoun in that sentence."

David arched an eyebrow. She had more brass than a rich man's door knocker. "Excuse me?"

"I'm sorry." She flapped her hand again. He'd never seen anyone so loose at the wrist, making him wonder if she had gelatin for bones. "Your improper use of pronouns isn't really important. It's just that 'me' is only used as an object in a sentence. For instance, you'd never say, 'Tell *I* what you mean by that.' It makes no sense at all."

"I think I made perfect sense the way I said it. If you want a mediator, fine, but if not, please refrain from finding fault with my goddamned English." David silently congratulated himself on coming up with a big word of his own. *Mediator.* Not bad for a man with a questionable stratum.

"I beg your pardon," she said. "Truly, I do. Not another correction, I swear. I'm just very upset right now. Things simply pop out."

Like telling him her husband's ranch was near Taffeta Falls, maybe? David jerked on the front panels of his duster, flexed his shoulders, and tried to remember what the hell he'd been about to say. Oh, yeah. His stratum might be lacking, but his memory was good — *except* when it came to a roll in the hay with this woman.

"I think you and *I* ran into each other in Denver a few years ago, a one-night —" David broke off because every description that sprang to his mind was too coarse to say to a lady. "A one-night *romance,* I guess you could call it. I think we met, were having fun, and, oh, well, never mind. Back then, I drank pretty heavy when I went to Denver, not only at saloons, but even at cattlemen's meetings and potlucks, which is likely where I met you."

"We never met anywhere, let alone at a cattlemen's potluck."

David held up a hand for silence. "Let me say my piece. I think we met that way — or in a situation close to it. You don't have the look of a sporting woman."

She jerked up her chin. "Thank you for that much, at least."

David nodded. "That accent definitely

pegs you as a lady from back East. I'm not saying you went looking for trouble, or that I did. But, hello, honey, shit happens." Glimpsing her appalled expression, he wished he could call back those words. "*Bad* things happen. Things we never plan to happen. If you lost your parents at a young age, maybe you came out West to live with relatives who didn't look after you properly at social functions. I've always had an eye for fetching females. I probably approached you and struck up a conversation, and while we talked, we drank too much spiked punch.

"When we were both well into our cups, maybe we went for a walk in the moonlight, and the situation got out of hand. Knowing me, I was probably pie-eyed and not thinking straight before I even got to the function. Back in those days I tended to follow my nose straight into trouble, and I obviously found it that night. After I left the potluck, I undoubtedly went to a saloon and got even drunker to finish off the evening. It wasn't uncommon back then for me to wake up of a morning with no recollection of what went on the night before, so I would have had no memory of my encounter with you. So I took off for my ranch outside of No Name. A few months later, you realized I'd left my calling card, and you didn't know how to find me. You ended up in desperate straits, borrowed my name, possibly the only thing you could clearly remember about me except that you thought I lived in Denver, and set out to raise a child born out of wedlock with some semblance of respectability."

He broke off and swallowed to steady his voice. "No proper young lady should be placed in that position. If we drank spiked punch, it was my responsibility to look after you, not take advantage of you. All the hard times and misfortunes that have befallen you since are entirely *my* fault. The situation you and my daughter are in right now is *my* fault. Why can't you understand that I can't walk away from that or that I didn't come here to cause you grief? And, damn it to hell, why do you refuse to admit what's as obvious to me as the nose on my face, that Daphne is my daughter?"

"Because she *isn't!*"

David could scarcely credit her response. He'd given her every out, accepting the blame for everything, and she still wouldn't acknowledge the corn. "I am here to right a wrong. You can't stand there and tell me you don't need help. It's obvious that you do, and I'm offering it. If you choose not to marry me, fine. But at least let me get you and my child out of this hellhole, set you up in a decent home, cover your living costs, and allow me to be a part of my daughter's life."

"Never. I can't accept help of that magnitude from a complete stranger. You're not her father. Your story is plausible, I suppose, but it is nothing but that, a story you made up. It has no relation to the actual truth. There's no earthly reason why I should even allow you to see Daphne again."

David had done his best to remove the fuse from this keg of dynamite. Now she was waving a lighted match again. He hadn't set out to ride roughshod over this lady, but he'd be damned if she would deprive him of the right to be a proper father to his child. "Don't bite off more than you can chew," he said softly. "I *will* see my daughter again — trust me on that — and you'll play hell trying to stop me."

She pushed away from the building and took a step toward him. The Irish temper David had suspected might lurk beneath her proper, ladylike exterior finally revealed itself. She spat words at him like they were bullets, and the expression in her eyes told him plainly enough that she wished they were. "After listening to this piece of fiction, Mr. Paxton, I've come to agree with you. This is clearly a matter to be taken before the town marshal. You, sir, are a lunatic of the first order. I would not consort with a man of your caliber even if I were inebriated. We never met at a Denver potluck. We never sipped spiked punch together. We *never* created a child together. In point of fact, we have never even *met*."

David wasn't intimidated by her flare of anger. Even with some meat on her bones, she'd still be a woman of diminutive stature. Then, to his utter amazement, she dared to poke him in the chest with her finger — sharp little thumps that might have unbalanced him if he'd been standing on uneven ground. Grown men who were fast with guns avoided confrontations with him, but this pint-size female thought she could stand toe to toe with him? He almost laughed. Luckily for her, he'd been raised to respect the opposite sex and would never lift his hand to a woman, no matter what she did to provoke him.

That didn't mean he had to stand there and let her thump him. He caught her wrist. The network of bones that pressed against his fingers felt as fragile as a bird's. "You'll get no argument from me. This is definitely a matter to be taken before the authorities, but I'll not be satisfied with pleading my case to only a marshal. Is there a bona fide judge in this poor excuse for a town?"

She jerked free of his grasp. "There most certainly is! So make free. You've no proof whatsoever that Daphne is your child. You can't just waltz into our lives and claim paternity, based on the flimsy fact that we bear the same last name. You'll leave with my daughter over my dead body!"

"We'll see about that. I'll be off to arrange a hearing with both the judge and the marshal."

She tried to push past him to gain the street. David was so angry that he braced a shoulder against her and set her back a step. She staggered, caught her balance, and treated him to a glare that made his face burn. What he'd just done was unpardonable, and he knew he should apologize, but when he tried to push out the words, he almost choked on them.

"I've lived in this town for six years," she told him. "Daphne was only an infant when I arrived. The judge knows me. The marshal does as well. Do you *really* think either of them will take the word of a stranger over mine?" She jerked her head up to make a regal exit as she swept around him, skirts held high. "Poppycock! You may be wearing a badge, but you could have gotten it

138

anywhere. You look more like a roughrider than a lawman. They will laugh and send you packing."

David couldn't help but admire her pluck. He leaned a shoulder against the corner of the building and called after her. "Mrs. Paxton?"

At his form of address, she stopped like she'd run into a wall and turned to face him.

David had a lot of practice with show-downs, and in that moment, he knew he had her outclassed nine ways to hell. It didn't take fancy talk and a highfalutin accent to get his point across. "We've got a performance at the schoolhouse to attend tonight. I think Daphne deserves to have both her mother *and* father there. I'll come back with you and tell that simpering old maid that you're coming with me. And I'll arrange a meeting with the judge for tonight, if possible. I've got a job and a ranch to tend to back home, so the quicker this is settled, the better."

She glared at him, her cheeks flagged with crimson. "I have a position of employment, sir. I've already taken one leave of absence today, and I can't afford to take another. I can't possibly attend the schoolhouse enter-tainment tonight — or a meeting. Make ar-rangements for tomorrow."

139

"From now on, I'll be assuming responsibility for the support of our child. That being the case, you can afford to miss a little more work. You'll be leaving soon, anyhow."

For a moment, David half expected her to launch a physical attack on him. Instead, she drew herself up to her full height, which wasn't all that impressive, and turned her back on him. As infuriated as he was, he couldn't suppress a smile. She was one hell of a lady. He had to give her that. And even in a temper, she was, hands down, the most beautiful woman he'd ever seen.

# CHAPTER FOUR

Somehow, Brianna stumbled back to the shop, groped for the door handle, and nearly fell inside. Her hands were trembling with such violence that her shawl slipped from her shoulders to form a black pool on the floor. She sank numbly onto her sewing chair, too rattled to care whether Abigail had heard her return and marked the time. Right now, getting paid for the hours she worked was the least of Brianna's worries.

*Oh, God, oh, God.* David Paxton was dangerous. Out in the alley, she'd bungled the exchange, trying to stick to her original story even after he started rebutting her claims. Over the last six years, no one else had picked apart her tale, let alone asked where her nonexistent husband's fictitious ranch had been located. What earthly difference did it make? To a normal person, it was a small detail and of no great importance, but for reasons beyond her, David

Paxton seemed bent on discrediting everything she said. Was he daft? How else could he possibly believe that he had fathered a child with a woman he'd never met?

In truth, Brianna had never been intimate with anyone. *Sweet Mother Mary.* What if *that* came out — that she wasn't Daphne's real mother, but only her aunt? She might have no legal claim to the little girl at all then.

Her stomach rolled, and she swallowed down the salty taste of nausea. Paxton had even gone so far as to say he wouldn't leave Glory Ridge without Daphne. Was she over-reacting to perceive that as a threat? He *couldn't* take Daphne! She was the child's mother in every way except biologically, and the only people who knew the truth were clear back in Boson. There were *laws.* He was a stranger who'd shown up out of the blue. Surely neither the marshal nor the judge would credit his outrageous claims of paternity. That stupid birthmark story, for instance. That splotch on Daphne's neck had indeed been there since birth, but it wasn't dark enough to be an actual birthmark. It was only a strawberry patch. Lots of people were born with one, and over time it faded away.

Brianna pressed her shaking fingers

against her eyes with such force that she saw spots. After several deep breaths, her heartbeat slowed, and she felt the sweat born of panic dry on her skin. She had to keep calm if she planned to find a way out of this mess.

She rose to drape her shawl over the trunk where she kept Daphne's blankets, yardage scraps, and sewing notions. Her hands, still cold from being outdoors, felt numb. She began to pace the small cubicle, chafing her arms with brisk passes of her palms over the puffed sleeves of her shirtwaist. The smell of hot bacon grease and sautéing onions drifted from Abigail's quarters. The odor turned Brianna's stomach. How did that disagreeable woman manage to remain pencil thin when she ate so often? The question no sooner entered Brianna's mind than she tossed it out. She needed to concentrate on far more important matters. If Paxton arranged a meeting with the judge and marshal, she would have to be rock solid with her story, not allowing his questions or allegations to unnerve her. To all intents and purposes, she *was* Daphne's mama. No one could disprove that. Could they?

An alarming thought occurred to her. Paxton didn't look like any lawman she'd ever seen, but he did wear a badge. What if he actually was a marshal? Might he not have the resources to check out her story? She never should have told him she'd been abandoned as an infant. There weren't that many orphanages in Boston. If he started digging and had the necessary funds to hire investigators back East, he would eventually contact the correct institution, and the truth about Daphne's mother would come out. Such a discovery would nullify Paxton's claim that he was the child's father, but it might also invalidate Brianna's entitlements. Would a court grant Brianna the right to raise her niece when she was all but penniless? And, oh, God, if the authorities took Daphne, what would happen to her? So far as Brianna knew, there were no decent orphanages closer than the one in Denver, and she could not attest to its quality.

She spun to a dizzying halt to stare at Mrs. Pauder's crumpled dress. *Stop this,* she ordered herself. *You're working yourself into a fine dither. That won't help the situation. You must keep a clear head. Stay calm. David Paxton doesn't have the look of a wealthy man. He will never part company with enough money to hire professional investigators, and even if he does, a process like that takes time. You can run with Daphne, if you must. You have the remainder of her dress money. That should be enough to hire a horse and travel to the nearest railway. You can book passage from there to a large town, change your name, and no one will ever find you.*

She felt better with that half-formulated plan taking shape in her mind. She heard Abigail bumping around in her quarters. The warning sent her diving for the sewing chair. By the time the proprietress flung back the cubicle curtain, Brianna was, to all appearances, hard at work.

"You'll be docked an hour," the woman said. "You were gone longer than that, but I've decided to be generous."

Brianna had been absent from the shop for no more than twenty minutes, but she'd learned the hard way that contradicting her boss only made matters worse. "Thank you," she pushed out. "I need all the time I can get."

"Who was that man?"

Brianna wanted to lie, but in a tiny town like Glory Ridge, the word was probably already out. "His name is David Paxton."

Abigail sucked in a sharp breath. "Your husband?"

A dagger of pain stabbed behind Brianna's eyes. Her thoughts were in such a tangle, she couldn't think how to reply. *He isn't my husband. He only bears the same name.* That

145

would incite a dozen questions she wasn't prepared to answer. *He believes he is Daphne's father, but he isn't.* Again, such a reply would stir curiosity. In short, Brianna couldn't think how to respond, but she had no choice but to say something. She settled on, "No, he's not my husband."

"But that's your husband's name."

"Yes, that is my husband's name. You are correct. But he is not the same David Paxton."

Abigail smelled a juicy tidbit of gossip and entered the cubicle. "That's peculiar. What is he doing here? What did he want?"

Desperation made Brianna bold. She met Abigail's birdlike gaze. "Miss Martin, you are my employer, and I hold you in high regard, but my position here in no way privileges you to pry into my personal affairs."

Abigail's bony cheeks went pink with anger. "Well, I never! Don't forget your place, madam, or you shall find yourself without a job. You aren't the only woman in Glory Ridge who is skilled with needle and thread."

Brianna was well aware that times were hard in the community and others had applied for her position. That said, those applicants lacked Brianna's ability to design gowns of high fashion and quality, and Abigail was no fool. "That's true," she dared to reply. "Have you someone else in mind that you might prefer?"

Abigail thinned her lips and turned to leave the cubicle. Brianna knew she'd just bested her employer, but she was too unnerved to feel smug. Others were bound to ask the same questions Abigail just had. How on earth would she answer them? *Oh, God, oh, God, why is that man here? I asked you for a miracle, and instead you sent me a catastrophe.* Brianna had worked hard to build a life for herself and Daphne in this tiny town, inhabited by narrow-minded, judgmental provincials who stood ready to shun anyone touched by even a hint of scandal.

David Paxton had brought with him far more than a hint.

David sat on the edge of the boardwalk outside the restaurant, his daughter perched beside him. She'd fetched a pretty new cloak of deep blue wool from the boarding-house to protect herself from the chill, but she'd drawn her small hands from the matching muff to drink her sarsaparilla. As the wind whipped up dust devils in the street, David questioned the wisdom of al-

147

lowing the child to consume a cold drink. With every sip, she shivered.

Oh, well, he was new to this father business. He had wanted Daphne to have her refreshment inside the restaurant, but she'd felt uneasy in the more formal surroundings and asked to come outdoors. Had she never eaten at the restaurant? Probably not. Sighing, David lifted the side of his duster to drape it around her shoulders before taking another sip of his drink, wishing it were beer instead of soda pop. She grinned up at him, her mouth ringed with dark liquid, Dory Paxton's dimple flashing in her cheek.

"Thank you, Papa. It *is* a bit chilly, isn't it?"

"Just a mite." He tucked her close to his side, enjoying the feeling of her slightness against him. New at the job though he was, he liked being a father. "Is the sarsaparilla tasty?"

"Very tasty." She took another swallow and then lowered the half-empty bottle to her knees and leaned closer to David's warmth. A yawn tugged at her lips, finally won the war, and stretched her mouth wide. "Hmm," she said, resting her head against his rib cage. "I *like* having you here, Papa."

"Why, because I make a good pillow?" he teased.

She giggled and loosened one hand from around the bottle to rub her eyes.

"Are you sleepy, pumpkin?" David asked.

"Only a little."

"Do you normally take a nap after school?"

She bobbed her head. "On the pallet beside Mama's chair. Afterward, she gives me supper, and I do homework or play quiet games until bedtime."

"Then you go to the boardinghouse?"

"No, I sleep on the pallet until Mama finishes cleaning the restaurant. Then she comes back and takes me to the boarding-house."

"Ah." David wondered when Brianna ever rested. He drew out his pocket watch. It was half past three. He guessed it was well past Daphne's usual nap time. "When does she finish at the restaurant?"

The child yawned again. "I dunno," she said drowsily. "I'm always asleep when she carries me home."

David had already determined that Brianna worked almost ceaselessly. A pretty woman like her deserved better. She had the most tempting mouth he'd ever seen. *Inappropriate thought.* Allowing himself to feel attracted to Brianna Paxton might undermine his resolve to sort out this situation, and for Daphne's sake, he had to remain focused, not on the mother but on the future well-being of the child.

He settled his gaze on the marshal's office across the street, more determined than ever to set up a hearing with the lawman and judge. Brianna might balk and dig in her heels, but in the end, she would be much better off with him paying all her expenses.

Bending his head, he whispered to Daphne, "I think the rest of your drink will keep. It's time for you to go inside with your mother and take a short nap."

Daphne leaned back to fix him with a worried look. "You might be gone when I wake up. Won't you please come to my May Day presentation tonight, Papa? Hope Blinstrub has hers memorized perfectly, and she always laughs when I make a mistake. I won't be as scared if you're there. Mama can't come because she has to work."

David hated to hear that Brianna's boss — or the dictates of her budget — would prevent her from attending the child's performance. He had a good mind to do something about that. Taking on *Miss* Martin, the termagant, would be a challenge, but he had a feeling the silly woman was so hungry for masculine attention that maneuvering her might be fairly easy.

"I wouldn't miss your recitation for anything," he assured the child. "As for me taking off while you're asleep, no way, little lady. From now on, you're stuck with me. Tight as a tick to a hound's neck, remember?"

She didn't seem convinced. Thinking quickly, David fished the coin from his shirt pocket. "I'll tell you what. While you're napping, you stand guard over our lucky penny. That way, you can be extra sure I won't go haring off while you're asleep."

Daphne accepted the collateral and stuck it in the pocket of her cloak. "You'd *never* run off without our penny, 'cause it's magic."

"You've got that right. Our lucky penny is almost as good as having a genie in a bottle."

"A what?"

David made up a quick tale about a man who had a genie trapped in a jug. As he spun the story, Daphne went limp against him. When he heard her emit a soft little snort, he was once again reminded strongly of his ma, who swore up and down she never snored. It had become a family joke, with him and all his brothers often asking her if she stayed awake all night to make certain sure of that.

After depositing his own sarsaparilla at

the edge of the boardwalk, he recapped Daphne's and put the half-finished drink into the deep pocket of his duster, leaning the bottle just so to prevent a spill. Scooping his daughter into his arms, he walked to the dress shop, only a few yards away. By juggling his burden, he was able to open the door, enter the establishment, and nudge the portal closed behind him. Brianna immediately appeared, her eyes wide, her expression filled with censure. David had a bad feeling she was afraid of him as he sidled past her into the cubicle. *Why?* He knew it could be a hard world for a woman alone. Had she been ill-treated by some of the men in town? As shabby as Glory Ridge was, the residents seemed to be God-fearing enough. Even so, David knew a respectable, kindly air often concealed a black heart.

"Where's her napping pallet?" he asked.

Brianna opened a trunk to withdraw a folded quilt, which she spread on the floor beside her chair. Once again, David noted how stiffly she held herself as she bent over. It went beyond strange. He'd seen someone move like that, but for the life of him, he couldn't remember who. He knelt on one knee to gently lay Daphne down. She murmured in her sleep. It didn't escape David's notice that she had one small hand in her cloak pocket, no doubt to protect their lucky penny. He couldn't resist smoothing her tousled golden curls.

As he pushed erect, he withdrew the bottle of sarsaparilla from his pocket and set it on the windowsill. Brianna jerked at the movement of his hand. David gave her a long, searching look. He had never struck a woman in his life, and it bothered him that this particular female thought him capable of that.

As he left the cubicle, he glanced into the open trunk, noting an array of sewing notions and yardage, but what caught his eye was a stack of dime novels, uppermost a far-fetched tale about Ace Keegan, the infamous gunslinger. He almost chuckled. What would Brianna say if he told her Ace was his half brother? Not a wise move, he quickly decided. Somehow he didn't think that would ease Brianna's mind much about his *stratum,* and it sure as hell wouldn't assure her that he was harmless.

Meeting her gaze, he tried to ignore the lovely curve of her cheek and the shadows of fear in her green eyes. He regretted that he unsettled her so, but he didn't see that he had a choice but to continue on his present course. "I'll be off to the marshal's office to arrange that hearing," he said.

"For in the morning," she inserted.

"As I said, I'm hoping to get it over with tonight. The sooner this is settled, the better."

She knotted her hands at her sides. "There is *nothing* to settle, sir."

David forced a smile. "Save your breath for the marshal and judge, darlin'. It's wasted on me."

David thought for just an instant that he saw steam coming out of her ears. He turned and walked out.

After Paxton left, Brianna paced the cubicle. He was the most insolent man she'd ever had the misfortune to meet. That arrogant stance, with one lean hip cocked and his knee slightly bent, smacked of self-importance, and when those incredibly blue eyes met hers, she got the unsettling feeling that he saw far more than she wanted to reveal. He had a way of smiling slightly — a condescending twist of his lips — that made her want to slap his handsome face.

*Handsome?* Brianna could scarcely believe that she had allowed her mind to wander in that direction, but there it was, an inescapable fact. That chiseled countenance, so burnished by exposure to the sun, was undeniably attractive, possessing a masculine appeal that undoubtedly made female hearts skip beats. *Not mine,* she assured herself. Well, only when she was enclosed in a small area with him. Then her heart definitely went out of rhythm, not because she found him attractive, but because he was intimidating. He towered over her, and his breadth of shoulder made her feel dwarfed. Though she'd yet to see him without the duster, she knew his upper body had to be as powerfully muscled as his long, lean legs. If he turned that strength against her, she would be helpless to defend herself.

The thought made her lungs hitch. She would never be truly alone with the man, so worrying about it was silly. Here in town, he'd never dare touch her. Help was only a shout away.

Grabbing for calm, Brianna went over to close her trunk, a habit drilled into her by her boss, who insisted that the cubicle always look tidy. As she started to lower the lid, her gaze caught on the books that had been lent to her by women in town. She kept them stored in the camelback so she might return them when the ladies came into the shop. A cold, clawing sensation ripped at her belly. She dropped to her knees, rifled through the cheap publications, and closed her hand over the one that was now striking terror into her heart. It was entitled *Slave Trade in Mexico,* which was underscored with a subtitle, *Little Girls and Young Women, Kidnapped for Profit.*

Brianna had read the book more than once. Oftentimes at night, she was so keyed up from working feverishly at the restaurant that she couldn't fall asleep. Losing herself in a story helped her grow drowsy. Normally, she read dime novels, which were, by their very nature, quite short, the aim of them being to entertain and titillate. But this particular issue was different. Instead of embellishing on the derring-do of Western heroes, it was a factual account that incited terror into the heart of any female who resided in the West. It was about horrible men who would go to any length to abscond with a young girl or woman who would bring a high price across the border. Little girls had been stolen. Older girls, on the cusp of adulthood, had also disappeared. They were taken across the Rio Grande and sold to the highest bidder, after which they became the toys of wealthy men. What truly struck trepidation into Brianna was the author's repeated warnings that blondes commanded the most money, and little girls Daphne's age were especially prized.

Brianna's hands shook as she opened the

publication. Her vision hazed over so she couldn't make out the print. No need. She had most of the text memorized. *Dear Lord.* From the first instant that she'd clapped eyes on David Paxton, she'd pegged him as a ruffian. He didn't look, or *act,* like any lawman she'd ever seen. What if he was a criminal? In many dime novels, mention was made of the men without conscience who resided in Deadwood, South Dakota, that most evil of all towns. That lawless cesspool of humanity was a gathering spot for scoundrels, many of them hiding from the law to avoid punishment for their foul, incomprehensible deeds. Murders were rumored to be committed in Deadwood on a daily basis, and the inhabitants often rode out to rain terror upon the law-abiding folks in Montana and Colorado.

Brianna snapped the book closed, determined not to let her imagination run away with her. Only now that the suspicion had crept into her mind, she couldn't shove it back out again. Who was David Paxton? Was that even his real name? What if he had gotten his hands on all her and Daphne's letters by foul means? From the start, Brianna had prayed she was writing to a nonexistent person. She had envisioned the Denver postmaster holding the missives for a time and then tossing them out onto a burn pile or into a trash barrel to be carried away to the local dump. What she hadn't considered was that the correspondence might fall into the wrong hands.

Now, suddenly, Paxton's crazy behavior didn't seem so crazy, after all. A blond little girl like Daphne, so fair and blue of eye, might bring as much as a thousand dollars in Mexico, making it well worth the while of a criminal to get his hands on her. Brianna's employer, Ricker, had always dictated what she should write in the letters. Had he encouraged her to tell David that his little girl was a flaxen-haired beauty? Brianna had written so many missives she couldn't remember. Ricker had been anxious to be rid of Brianna from the beginning. He'd hoped to hire a more accommodating woman who would not only keep house and tutor his sons, but also warm his bed. On that count, and others, Brianna had been a huge disappointment to him. Within a month of her arrival in Glory Ridge, he'd started insisting that she write weekly letters to her errant husband in Denver to bring him back to heel. It made sense that he might have told her to include specifics about Daphne: her age, her coloring, her progress with academics.

If so, Daphne's physical description would have been enough to make any slave trader drool over the profit he stood to make if he could get his hands on her.

Tossing the book back in the trunk, Brianna faced the unthinkable. The events today had not been twists of fate. That ruffian who called himself David Paxton wasn't here with honest intent. He'd somehow gained possession of those letters, and now he was bent on taking Daphne to sell her across the border so he could lounge about in a cantina somewhere, swilling tequila and availing himself of prostitutes.

"Drat and tarnation!"

Brianna muttered the exclamations under her breath so as not to wake Daphne. Hands shaking, she held up Mrs. Pauder's gown, staring with dismay at the left underarm seam, which she'd just sewn to the waist with the wrong sides together, leaving the raw edges showing. What in heaven's name had she been thinking? Blast that man to perdition for rattling her so. Now she'd have to carefully rip out each stitch, no easy task with dusk soon to descend and the light of only one lantern to see by.

Just then Brianna heard a tap at the front door of the shop, which she'd locked a few seconds ago when the clock struck five. She groaned and tossed the dress aside. As she circled the curtain, she saw her new nemesis through the glass and stopped dead in her tracks. *David Paxton,* or whatever his *real* name was, bent to peer past the Closed sign and poised his knuckles to knock again. Brianna considered ignoring the summons, but she'd seen the glint of determination in his eyes earlier and knew he wouldn't hesitate to make a racket if she dared. She wanted no more unpleasant exchanges with her employer today. She absolutely could *not* lose this position.

Her stomach felt as if she'd just swallowed an entire handful of jumping beans, but she forced her feet to move. He wasn't going to conveniently disappear, and like it or not, she had to deal with him. As she neared the glass, she took measure of his person. To her frightened gaze, his chest looked at least a yard wide, an illusion she felt sure was enhanced by the saddlebags that he carried over one shoulder. She felt diminished by him. Disengaging the deadbolt with trembling fingers, she cracked the door to peer out at him. He straightened, forcing her gaze upward in order to maintain eye contact. His chiseled features were cast into shadow by the brim of his leather hat. The faint scent of bay rum drifted to her on the chill air.

"The judge and marshal have agreed to see us in ten minutes at the marshal's office. I would have given you more warning, but I had to fetch my saddlebags."

Brianna clenched her hand on the doorknob. "I *told* you, I cannot afford to miss any more time today. Do you have cotton in your ears?"

His even white teeth flashed in a slow grin. He leaned his right arm against the doorframe, forcing the portal to open wider despite her attempts to brace against his weight. "No cotton in my ears, but I do have money in my pocket. I'll reimburse you for the lost wages."

"I don't *want* your money, Mr. Paxton, if that's even your real name! I want nothing to do with you, period!"

He didn't budge, making it impossible for her to close the door. "You should have made that call seven years ago, darlin'."

Rage surged through Brianna so hotly she felt the burn at the back of her throat. She yearned to stomp on his foot to make him back away from the opening. "I can't leave right now. Daphne is doing a recitation at the church hall this evening. When she awakens from her nap, I must get her ready

161

and make sure she arrives there on time."

"This meeting won't take long — thirty minutes, maybe, an hour at the most — and I can help get Daphne ready for the recital."

Brianna glared up at him. "The program starts at seven, sir! It is now shortly after five."

"I said I would help get her ready."

"No!" she cried. "I refuse to allow you to interfere with my work schedule twice, and you will not so much as *touch* my daughter again, you low-account reprobate."

He actually chuckled. "A low-account reprobate? My, my, I'm flat moving up in the world."

Ever since Moira's death, Brianna had struggled, day in and day out, to be a mirror image of her sister — sweet, well-mannered, and difficult to rile, a lady of the first cut who was fit to be Daphne's mother. But right then, seeing David Paxton's smirk, she wanted to toss all that aside and give way to her *true* nature, which was volatile and Irish to the bone. This man would have the surprise of his life if she socked him in the eye with all her might and then slammed the door on his foot.

But, no. She couldn't allow him to attend that meeting alone. Then the judge and marshal would hear only his side of the story.

Brianna stepped back from the doorway. "Very well. Have it your way. I shall inform Miss Martin of my forthcoming absence and get my shawl."

Paxton pushed into the shop and closed the door behind him so softly that the bell failed to tinkle. "While you do that, I'll collect our daughter."

"*My* daughter."

Grinning again, he hooked a thumb under the saddlebag strap on his shoulder and nudged up the brim of his hat with his other hand. She wasn't surprised that he had failed to remove the grimy, sweat-rimmed thing. Men of his ilk knew nothing of how to comport themselves in society or how to show deference to a lady. The nuns had warned her about his kind. This miscreant could smile all he liked. She wasn't fooled.

"There's no need to interrupt her nap," she told him. "The shop is closed. I can lock up as we leave. We should let her sleep."

Paxton swept by Brianna as if she hadn't spoken. "I'll not be leaving my child with that sharp-tongued shrew. If I'm careful not to jostle her, she shouldn't wake up. When we get to the marshal's office, I'll put her on the bench just inside the door. She'll be

163

comfortable enough there."

Brianna wanted to attack him from behind as he bent over her daughter. Instead, she clung to the tattered threads of her self-control, assured herself that the judge and marshal would take her word over his, and stepped to Abigail's apartment door. With a quick knock, she summoned her employer, explained as briefly as possible that she would be gone for a half hour, and then listened to the woman rant about her leaving for the second time that day.

"I expect a certain amount of production, Mrs. Paxton. You've accomplished very little during this shift."

Brianna opened her mouth to defend herself, but then she remembered the mistake she'd made on Mrs. Pauder's dress. It was true that she had accomplished little. "Today has been a deviation from the norm. I will do better on the morrow."

"I shall hold you to it," the proprietress snapped. "Otherwise I will be reviewing the other applications for this position, madam, and you shall be replaced."

# CHAPTER FIVE

Sunlight was giving way to gloaming as Brianna exited the dress shop behind David Paxton. Cradling Daphne in his arms, he paused while Brianna turned to lock the door and then fell into step beside him as they angled across the street. The first smells of the supper hour drifted on the cold breeze. Normally, Brianna experienced a yearning sadness at this time, wishing that she and Daphne could end each day together at a nicely set table, sharing a hearty meal that had been lovingly prepared. But tonight she was far too distracted and filled with anxiety to covet cheerful window curtains or a warm, aromatic kitchen. Instead she was acutely aware of the man who loomed beside her. He had a loose-hipped stride that he shortened considerably to accommodate hers. His spurs chinked with every step. Each time the sleeve of his duster brushed her elbow, she nearly parted company with her skin. She didn't dare think about that book and the awful suspicions that had formed in her mind. She was afraid she'd go to pieces right there in the street. She wanted to snatch the sleeping child from his arms and run as fast as she could. But that would be beyond stupid. To get Daphne safely away, she needed to hire a horse.

As Brianna stepped up onto the opposite boardwalk, Paxton shifted Daphne into the curve of one arm and caught hold of Brianna's left hand, drawing her to a halt as he examined her wedding band. With an arch of his burnished brows, he said, "I don't recall putting that on your finger, so I'm guessing I didn't."

Brianna's legs felt like stumps, and invisible weights seemed to have settled on her shoulders. She saw nothing to be gained by wasting her energy on yet another exchange. As it was, she was sounding like a phonograph stylus stuck in a groove.

With a jerk of his head, he indicated the door of the marshal's office. "Before we go in, you need to understand that I *know* this is my daughter, and I won't be leaving Glory Ridge without her. You can choose not to go with us. That's your decision to make. But I'm not about to let Daphne live like this, sometimes eating food you find in trash barrels. My daughter deserves better, and I intend to see that she gets it."

A sizzling retort leaped into Brianna's mind, but it died en route to her tongue. He couldn't know about her taking food from trash barrels unless Daphne had told him, and Brianna wouldn't call her child a liar when it was the truth. She'd sunk pretty low over time. No man had put that ring on her finger. Paxton was not her real surname. Daphne wasn't even her child. But she still had standards, lines she refused to cross.

She tugged her hand from Paxton's grasp. The touch of his hard fingers had seared her skin like a brand. Searching his clear blue eyes, she saw no sympathy, only grim resolve, and she knew in that moment that he meant to do precisely what he said: establish his paternity of Daphne and then abscond with her.

Brianna would never allow that to happen. *Never.*

With Brianna scurrying to keep up, David opened the door and carried Daphne into Marshal Bingham's dingy office. A lighted lantern hung from a ceiling hook in one corner. The place contained only one barred cell, appointed with two narrow cots, both presently empty. The lawman, a paunchy fellow with brown hair and eyes whom David had guessed earlier to be about fifty, sat across the battered desk from a gentleman David presumed to be Judge Afton. At least a decade older than the marshal, with a bald pate ringed by nearly white hair, he wore a shabby black serge suit flecked with dandruff across the shoulders. Pipe smoke wreathed his head and drifted away from him in layers of misty gray that hovered in the room like thick winter fog.

David set his jaw when he saw that the two men were playing poker. A small pile of coins and silver certificates lay between them. A half-empty jug of whiskey sat off to one side, and both men nursed tall drinks, the deep amber of the liquor indicating that they were downing the stuff straight. David carefully deposited the sleeping Daphne on the bench just inside the door, put his saddlebags beside her, and strode over to the desk. These men were well into their cups even though it was only half past five. If anyone in his office had pulled this stunt, he would have been out of a job as fast as David could yank the badge off his shirt. David was no puritan, but he never drank while on duty. Apparently Bingham had no underlings to take over while he imbibed —

or Glory Ridge was so small that little trouble ever occurred. Given the tight, defensive look on Brianna's face, David figured that tonight would be an exception. She'd go down fighting, no quarter asked — or given. Damn, but he had to admire that about her. He appreciated courage and grit, even when they came wrapped in an infuriating package.

Afton glanced up and flashed a bleary smile. "You must be Mr. Paxton."

David extended a hand. "Correct. And I'm guessing you are Judge Afton."

The older man put down his cards and set his pipe in a green dish caked with a thick layer of ash to give David a limp, clammy handshake. Then he belched and grinned again as he grabbed a gavel at his elbow and rapped the desk with a sharp report. The sound momentarily awakened Daphne. From the corner of his eye, David saw Brianna hurry over to soothe the little girl back to sleep.

"That's me, the Honorable Judge Afton, at your service, and as you can see, I've come prepared to give you audience and make a ruling." He lowered the gavel to pick up a brass stamp from atop a smeared and dented tin box that David guessed contained an inkpad. "I can't quite recall what your problem is, but if you'll hold on a minute, I will allow you to refresh my memory." He gathered his cards, glanced at the marshal, and slapped a dollar onto the ante pile. "I call, Barton. I think you're bluffing."

Glancing over the judge's shoulder, David saw that he held two pairs, sevens over deuces. In David's opinion, it was an okay hand, but not good enough to warrant such a large bet. Marshal Bingham anted up and showed his hand, and the magistrate swore, not even bothering to lower his voice as he barked the obscenity. "Three of a kind? You've become quite the cardsharp since we played last Friday, my friend."

The marshal took a large gulp of whiskey before raking in the cash. "I've also become a mite richer, Daniel. Read 'em and weep."

David was about to take both men to task for agreeing to meet with him and Brianna when they'd clearly planned to play cards and get wet to the gills. Judging by their conversation, Friday was their poker night. Before he could get a word out, though, he changed his mind, deciding that he might use this situation to his own advantage. He motioned to Brianna.

"Now that you've played out the hand," David said to the judge, "I hope you'll take a break from the game to give me and this lady your full attention."

The judge rocked back in his chair, tried to focus on Brianna, and blinked, clearly beset by blurry vision. Had the man gotten this drunk in only a few minutes or had he been tipping the jug all afternoon? "Good eventide, Mrs. Paxton. How are you faring?"

Brianna stepped forward. "I'm extremely distressed at the moment, Your Honor. This man has shown up out of the blue claiming to be my daughter's father, and I assure you, he is *not*."

The judge blinked again and rubbed the bridge of his bulbous nose. "He's not?"

"No, Your Honor, he's definitely not. I've never seen him before in my life!"

The judge tugged on the front of his jacket, his double chin canting off to one side as he tipped his head. "That, madam, doesn't make a lick of sense. If you've never seen the fellow before, how the hell did you wind up married to him?"

It definitely didn't make any sense, David thought. Score one for him. He'd keep his mouth shut and let her hang herself. Brianna launched into a feverish recitation of her harebrained tale about there being another David Paxton in Denver. "My husband is a miner there, Your Honor, not the marshal of some little town!"

The judge frowned. "No real mining takes place in Denver these days, young woman. What's he mining for? Fool's gold? Are you sure this husband of yours prospects there?"

Brianna paled and clasped her hands, her stance rigid. "I've received recent correspondence from him, Your Honor, and as before, the letter came from Denver."

The judge held out a hand. "Fine. Let me see it, please."

Brianna's green eyes sparked fire at the question. "My word on the matter should be good enough!"

"So you can't produce one of the letters?" David inquired.

"I threw all of them away!" she cried.

The judge took another swig of whiskey and glanced longingly at the abandoned playing cards. "My good woman, you've lived here in Glory Ridge for — what? — six years. You've always gone by the name Mrs. David Paxton. If you can't produce a letter from this *other* husband you claim to have, can you at least present marriage documents to prove he exists?"

For the second time that day, Brianna felt as if the floor had vanished from beneath her feet. She grabbed at the edge of the desk to keep her balance, jerking away as Paxton reached for her elbow. That rattlesnake! She couldn't *comprehend* that the judge and the marshal were questioning her word. Scratching at her thoughts like a chicken for remnants of grain, she said, "I had marriage documents, Your Honor, but when I left Mr. Ricker's employ, they were lost during the move."

Slurring his words slightly, the judge said, "I must make decisions based upon the evidence brought before me, Mrs. Paxton." He fixed a glassy gaze on David, who was quickly becoming the bane of Brianna's existence. "Apparently, Mrs. Paxton has no evidence to verify her story, Mr. Paxton."

Marshal Bingham muttered a curse under his breath, and then said, " 'Mrs. Paxton' and 'Mr. Paxton,' and the two of them aren't married? This is too confusing by half."

Brianna wanted to kick the man. "Perhaps part of your confusion is caused by overindulgence in spirits, Marshal." She returned her gaze to the judge. "And this isn't a *story* I've dreamed up!" She lifted her hands. "Why in heaven's name would I lie about such a thing?" She jabbed a finger in Paxton's direction. "I've never clapped eyes on this man in my life, I tell you! He is not my husband, and he is *definitely* not my daughter's father."

The judge motioned for silence. "You wouldn't be the first woman to find herself in an unhappy marriage and try to solve the problem by running off. If that is indeed the case, it is your misfortune that your husband has found you. I sympathize greatly with your dilemma, ma'am, but the law is the law. You shouldn't have fled with the child."

"I didn't flee with the child!" Brianna heard her voice going shrill. She took a deep, shaky breath, trying to compose herself. "You're making snap judgments, based upon the fact that I've lost my marriage documents and lacked the foresight to save my husband's letters. I mean no disrespect, Your Honor, but why is the burden of proof being placed on me? I haven't heard you ask Mr. Paxton what evidence he can produce to verify *his* story."

The judge arched an eyebrow. "That's true, Mr. Paxton." His paunch jerked with another burp, which he unsuccessfully attempted to squelch by swallowing. "Have you any evidence to present?"

Marshal Bingham interrupted to say, "So far, he hasn't told us his side. She's done most of the talking."

Brianna wanted nothing more than to tell

the lawman to shut his mouth. "As well it should be," she said instead. "As the judge pointed out, I've lived here for nearly six years, and my reputation is above reproach. This man is a complete stranger. You've no reason to believe a word he says." Brianna dragged in another breath and blurted on the exhale, "In fact, I have reason to believe he may be a lawless miscreant from Deadwood, South Dakota, bent on absconding with my daughter so he can sell her to some wealthy old Mexican across the border! Blondes sell for very high prices, and little girls Daphne's age are in high demand!"

Bingham snorted with laughter and rocked on his chair, so incautious with the shift of his weight that he nearly went over backward. He planted a hand against the rear wall to catch himself. Over Judge Afton's wheezing mirth, the marshal managed to say, "Dear God, woman, you've obviously been reading that trash my wife so dearly loves! I saw the book about slave trading. It's a bunch of stuff and nonsense. Deadwood is a tamed community now. Crimes are still committed there, of course, but the place is no longer solely a hideaway for lowlife scoundrels wanted by the law."

Brianna bent closer to bore the marshal with her gaze. "I've read the book, sir. It's a recent publication. I am sure the author must be required by his publisher to keep his facts straight. Criminals are *still* absconding with girls and selling them into slavery in Mexico. And I am convinced that is this man's plan. I don't think his name's David Paxton at all, and I don't think he's a lawman. He could have stolen that badge. How can you take his word over mine?" She flung a hand at the man under discussion. "Just *look* at him. What respectable lawman dresses like a — like a roughrider?"

The judge chuckled. "My dear girl, the comanchero slave trading was brought to an end back in the seventies. Let us refrain from making outrageous accusations."

Brianna clasped her hands, digging into her flesh so hard with her jagged nails that she felt the sting. "Well, then — supposing that's true — it in no way eliminates the possibility that this man is here for nefarious reasons. Unless, of course, both you and the marshal are so out of touch with modern-day crime that you've convinced yourself it doesn't exist." She pointed at a collection of Wanted posters on the wall behind the desk. "What are those, if not notices that those men are at large and dangerous?"

"Mrs. Paxton, this gentleman's likeness

does not appear on any of those posters," Afton pointed out. "And I'm not claiming crime no longer exists. I'm only saying it's highly unlikely this man intends to steal your daughter and sell her across the border. I believe he is here with honest intent. Misguided, perhaps. If you'll desist with your chatter and let me interview him, I'll be better able to determine the validity of his claim."

Her *chatter?* "There *is* no validity to his claim," Brianna retorted. "He just showed up, saying Daphne is his daughter, and I'm here to tell you he's lying!"

Bingham sighed and scratched his jaw. "Why would any man in his right mind lay claim to a child that isn't his?" He winked at Paxton. "I've got six, five still eating me out of house and home. If you're that eager to be a daddy, I'll give you a couple of mine."

The judge drained his glass and sloshed in more whiskey. "Order in the court!" He brought down his hand on the desk, sending cards flying. "What evidence of paternity can you produce, Mr. Paxton?"

Paxton went to collect his saddlebags. "I can produce no *official* evidence of paternity, Your Honor, but I can submit documents to show that I am an officer of the law and

177

*inarguable* proof that no other David Paxton exists in the Denver area."

Brianna watched with mounting dread as Paxton withdrew letters, paperwork, and two telegrams from a bag and tossed them on the desk. Using his index finger, he separated the offerings, pointing to the letters first. Brianna's heart felt as if it plunged into her stomach when she recognized her own handwriting on the envelopes.

"These are letters from Mrs. Paxton," David said. "They were addressed to me general delivery at the Denver post office. Please note that this one" — he pushed that letter closer to the judge — "is postmarked nearly six years ago." He slid the second missive over. "And this one is postmarked only five months ago. Countless letters — far too many for me to bring them all — were sent to me in between those two dates, but I never received them until a little over a month ago because I have never lived in Denver or picked up my mail there."

The judge rubbed his temple. "Why would Mrs. Paxton have sent mail to you in Denver if you never lived there?"

Paxton ignored the question and offered the judge both telegrams. "These were sent to me by the sheriff in Denver."

The judge squinted to read the messages.

"He says that no other David Paxton exists in Denver or in any of the other mining districts anywhere near there."

"Precisely," Paxton agreed. "I telegraphed the sheriff when I initially received Mrs. Paxton's letters, which requested, again and again, that I come to Glory Ridge for her and my daughter." He flashed Brianna an apologetic look. "I have no wish to offend Mrs. Paxton by being indelicate, Your Honor, so I'll just say that I tended to drink pretty heavy in my younger days when I visited Denver, and I have no clear recollection of ever having met this lady, let alone marrying her. That said, I'm not a man to shirk my responsibilities, so I not only asked the Denver sheriff to look into the matter for me, but I went there myself, launched my own investigation, and found no trace of another David Paxton within a hundred-mile radius of the city. I finally concluded — and not happily, I might add, because I do have a life in No Name that suits me just fine — that I'd done the unthinkable while I was intoxicated and taken liberties with some unfortunate young lady, leaving her in the family way. When I drank that heavy, I often had no recollection of what occurred the previous night. I believe I consorted with Mrs. Paxton, woke up the next morning, and departed for No Name. In short, I left her high and dry, with no idea how to contact me when she realized she was carrying my child."

"That *isn't* what happened!" Brianna practically screamed. She felt her eyes bugging and thought for a second that she might actually attack him. "I'm married to another man, I tell you. You know me, Judge Afton." She directed an imploring gaze at Bingham. "So do you, Marshal! Have I ever been anything but a proper lady? I am *not* in the habit of consorting with drunken strangers and never have been."

The judge opened one of the letters. Since she'd written it under duress, Brianna had kept it short. Ricker had been very exacting with his dictates as she penned the words, and she couldn't clearly recall what she'd said in any particular missive. Afton quickly scanned the sentences and tossed the letter back on the desk. "We all make mistakes, dear."

Brianna felt lightheaded. A cold sweat broke out all over her person. This was like one of those awful dreams where everything went from bad to worse, and she couldn't wake up. "I never made *that* mistake. This man is delusional."

Just then, Paxton drew something from

his wallet and tossed it on the desk. It was a small, tattered photograph of a lovely woman who, in gray and white, looked to be blond. Brianna sucked in a breath. The image could have been Daphne if not for the vast difference in age. In fact, the resemblance was so striking that Brianna leaned closer, amazed at the similarities. In that moment, her brain went like mush.

The judge studied the image with a frown. "Mrs. Paxton, it's no secret in Glory Ridge that you struggle to make ends meet," he said softly. "You should be grateful that this gentleman has the honor and integrity to come forward and offer to shoulder his personalities." He scowled. "Responsibilities, I mean. I don't understand why you aren't jumping for joy."

"I shall jump for joy when my true *husband* shows up and not before!"

The judge picked up the telegram from the Denver sheriff. "That photograph shows an amazing family resemblance, Mrs. Paxton. This wire also proves that this man's name is David Paxton, and that he is, indeed, the marshal of No Name."

"The wire proves nothing!" Brianna almost shouted the words. "He could have sent the telegraph to himself, planning in advance to use it as proof of his identity!"

As if she hadn't spoken, the magistrate flicked the edge of the desk with his fingertip, ran a liver-spotted hand over his hair, and sighed. "This is a most preculiar situation. Peculiar, I mean. I honestly don't know how to rule. You have no proof that you're married to another man, Mrs. Paxton." Directing a sympathetic look at Paxton, he added, "And your version of events is suppo" — burp — "supposition. Neither of you has offered any tangible proof to argue your case, although even I must admit that photograph is a bit stupefying." He guzzled more whiskey. "Very remarkable resemblance. Yes, remarkable, indeed."

"It's a photograph of my mother," Paxton said.

Daphne awakened just then. "Mama? Papa?" She sat up and rubbed her eyes. "Why is everyone yelling?"

Before Brianna could react, Paxton collected Daphne from the bench. Perching the child on his hip, he retraced his steps to the desk. To the judge, he said in a taut voice, "You say I have no proof? Look at her, Your Honor. Then look at me. Can you deny the family resemblance?"

The judge did as requested and then turned an unfocused, heavy-lidded gaze on Brianna. "The child does bear a remarkable likeness to him, and even more so to the woman in that phonograph." He took another swig of liquor. "In fact, the child looks more like him than she does you. How can you explain that?"

Oh, God. The judge was so intoxicated he couldn't formulate words, let alone rational thoughts. Brianna wanted to shout that any little girl with blond hair and delicate features might resemble an older woman with similar coloring and composition of countenance. But now that Daphne was awake, Brianna felt as if her tongue had been shackled. Her daughter wasn't yet old enough to understand precisely how babies were made, and Brianna didn't want her to be swiftly educated by two drunks and a lunatic. "The resemblance is a fluke, Your Honor."

"A *fluke?*" Paxton stepped closer to the judge and lifted Daphne's golden curls to expose the side of her neck. "Do you see this pink splotch, Your Honor? It's a birthmark that runs in my family. Practically every child is born with it." He jerked at the front of his duster and drew down his own collar. "*I* was born with it." He leaned over so the judge could inspect the evidence. "Mine's gone dark from the sun, right along with my skin, but it's still visible." He shot

Brianna a searing glance. "Explain that, Mrs. Paxton. How is it that this child is the spitting image of my mother and has the same mark on her neck as I do on *mine?*"

Brianna wanted to examine Paxton's mark more closely. It was dark, just as he claimed, and could be nothing more than a stain he had applied to his skin after seeing Daphne's strawberry splotch. This man was a schemer and clever beyond words. Even if he didn't plan to take Daphne over the Mexican border, he was up to no good. He had to be.

"Your Honor, that isn't a birthmark on my daughter's neck," Brianna lied. "She was splattered with hot grease as a baby. It's a scar, nothing more, and I suggest to you the very real possibility that this man duplicated it on his own neck with a smear of boot polish!"

Paxton rolled his eyes. "Where's some soap and water?" He met Brianna's gaze with smoldering intensity. "Or for that matter, a bleaching agent. I'll happily submit to a scouring. If you can remove this mark from my neck, I'll eat my hat."

Brianna wanted to jerk the filthy thing from his head and shove it down his throat. The tide was turning against her. She felt the shift and in rising panic cried, "Your

Honor, I request that you withhold judgment until morning when you've slept on it and can think more clearly."

The judge sat more erect. "Are you suggesting that I'm intoxicated, Mrs. Paxton?"

"No. *Yes.*" Brianna gestured at his glass. "You *are* drinking, sir. And quite heavily, I might add."

"I am still in possession of all my facilities." He paused, crinkled his forehead, and said, "Faculties, I mean."

"Then I beg your pardon, sir. But out of consideration for my child, I do submit to you that this meeting should adjourn and commence again when she is not present. There is subject content that is too mature for her tender ears."

"My ears aren't tender, Mama," Daphne chimed in. "I've never even had an earache."

Afton flapped his hand. At that point, Brianna knew that she was about to lose this battle of words and almost blurted out the truth. Terror held her tongue. As it stood, she still had maternal rights, and she wasn't sure she would retain them if she confessed that she was only the child's aunt. Besides, if they refused to accept that she wasn't married to this silver-tongued devil, why would they believe the real truth, which sounded so improbable even to her? Even if

185

she could convince the judge of it and Paxton was sent packing, Brianna would be left to deal with the result: a town full of holier-than-thou people who were all too ready to stand in judgment of others. Her life would be a living hell, and so would Daphne's.

Her mind swimming with disjointed thoughts, she decided that her wisest course was to stick with her original story — that she was married to another man named David Paxton. "Maybe," she cried, "my husband died, Your Honor, and I was never notified. Things like that do happen. Maybe he was killed in a mining accident quite some time ago! That would explain why *this* Mr. Paxton and the Denver sheriff can find no proof of his existence."

Paxton snorted, his expression heavy with scathing contempt. "Excuse me, but only a few minutes ago, you said you recently received a letter from the man. How does a dead person put pen to paper?"

David was fed up. He wanted to stuff cotton in his daughter's ears so she would hear nothing more. Better yet, he yearned to storm out with her and head directly for the stable to get his horse and mule, devil take the consequences. Let them come after him.

He didn't give a shit. Any men who volunteered to form a posse would probably be drunk. Now the fool woman was claiming that her husband was dead? She couldn't keep her story straight. Over the years as a lawman, he had seen others get caught up in their own lies, but this lady took the prize for inconsistency.

David was about to act on his impulse to skedaddle when the judge pounded his gavel on the desk, startling David and frightening Daphne so that she jerked.

"Enough of this poppycock!" he roared. "It is clear to me that no other David Paxton exists anywhere near Denver, and that being the case, the matter is simple enough to resolve. *This* David Paxton is clearly the father of the child. Since Mrs. Paxton has failed to produce marriage documents to the contrary, I will make an honest woman of her and be done with it so I can enjoy my poker night."

David still stood half-turned to leave. Those words snapped him back around. He stared incredulously at the judge. The inebriated fool roared, "By the power vested in me by the state of Colorado, I hereby pronounce you man and wife."

David couldn't quite credit his ears. Surely a judge couldn't slap his gavel on a desk and marry people.

"This is a farce!" Brianna cried. "And it isn't legal! I have not agreed to this, and I did *not* say 'I do'!"

The judge took another swallow of booze. "It's obvious to me, young woman, that you did more than say 'I do' at some point in time." Casting a meaningful glance at Daphne, he thrust out a hand to Bingham. "I need paper, Barton."

The marshal produced two pieces of parchment. The judge scribbled out a makeshift marriage document on each. When he finished writing, he shoved them toward both David and Brianna, saying, "Sign the damn things."

"Does that paper say I'm married to that — miscreant?" Brianna stabbed a finger at David. "I absolutely will *not!*"

"Wait just a second, Judge," David inserted. "As much as I want my daughter, there are certain laws we can't ignore. I think clear heads are called for here."

"Sign, I said!" The judge slapped the paper. "Refuse and I will find you both in contempt of court."

Brianna's mouth worked like that of a landed fish. "What *court?*"

The judge sneered. "*I* am the court, good lady, and I'm weary of this nonsense. You'll either sign or spend some time in jail."

"How *much* time?" she asked.

Afton grinned, his lips twisting lopsidedly. "That will depend upon my mood."

"You'll put us both in jail for refusing to agree to a marriage neither of us wants?"

"It's you who doesn't seem to want it, Mrs. Paxton," the judge replied. "I'm betting Mr. Paxton will agree to sign. If he does, and you persist in these theatrics, I'll lock you up and give him leave to depart for No Name with his child while you're behind bars."

David opened his mouth to protest. He shut it again. The judge had in effect ruled in his favor. It just bothered him that Brianna was right. This wasn't legal. He hadn't set out to force her to marry him. He'd only wanted to be a part of his daughter's life and make sure both mother and child were cared for properly.

Before David could decide what to do, Brianna stepped to the desk, snatched up the pen, and furiously signed her name at the bottom of each document. As she straightened, she shot David a look so searing it could have ignited waterlogged wood. David hesitated for only an instant, and then, shifting Daphne on his hip, bent to affix his signature below hers. Bingham added his John Hancock as a witness. The judge rolled his brass stamp over the pad and pressed the state seal onto both papers, making the union official. Then he signed as well. His plump jowls curving in a satisfied grin, he waved the documents to dry the ink, folded them, and handed one to David.

"For safekeeping, Mr. Paxton," he said with a rolling belch. "I suggest you guard it well. If Mrs. Paxton gets her hands on it, she will most likely destroy it." He fixed a narrowed eye on Brianna. "That would be folly, madam, for the marriage will become a matter of court record the first thing Monday morning." He tucked his copy inside his suit jacket. "You are rightly and truly married to the man now. All mistakes of the past are wiped clean. Rejoice in the fact that this upstanding gentleman has made an honest woman of you."

David collected his other papers from the desk and tucked the lot, along with the marriage document and photograph, into his bag. He moved Daphne to his opposite hip and draped the leather pouches over his shoulder. Before he and Brianna could turn from the desk, the judge sloshed more whiskey into his glass and invited the marshal to join him in a few more hands of poker.

David couldn't quite wrap his mind around what had just happened. In a haze of disbelief, he escorted his bride from the marshal's office. Deep twilight had descended. As they gained the boardwalk, a chuff of icy air buffeted them, making Daphne shiver in her cloak. Brianna drew her shawl close, her shoulders rigid, her face stark white in the faint light. David expected her to turn on him and let fly with furious accusations. He'd heard some pretty crazy stories about rigged hearings, but he'd never heard of any judge pronouncing a marriage valid without even performing a ceremony. Surely the union was illegal. Hell, Afton hadn't even bothered to call in a second witness off the street. But he wasn't about to tell Brianna that.

To his amazement, Brianna said nothing. Not one word. David was wondering about that when he realized her reticence was probably due to Daphne's presence. She didn't want to upset the child. David took his cue from her. He had a few things he wanted to say as well, foremost that Brianna had failed to voice to the judge the one objection that might have rung true — that she couldn't possibly agree to this marriage because to do so would be bigamous. In David's estimation, her failure to mention that was the strongest evidence yet that there was no other David Paxton and that she'd never been married until a couple of minutes ago.

So now what? David had the oddest feeling that he'd stepped over an invisible line, leaving reality behind. Legal or not, the marriage would be filed as such, giving him inalienable rights, not only as Daphne's father, but also as Brianna's husband. As badly as he felt about how it had all come to pass, he couldn't very well argue with the outcome. He'd set out to get custody of his daughter, and now he had it.

Brianna felt like a bug trapped in a jar gone wet inside with condensation. Her whole body dripped sweat. She wanted to rail at David Paxton, or whatever his name truly was, and then rip his hair from his head. But every word that tried to push up her throat was far too ugly to voice in front of Daphne. As soon as the child was no longer present, she would let the scoundrel have it, though. She could barely wait to tell him just how lowdown and unethical she believed he was.

"Mama?" Daphne said plaintively. "Does

this mean I don't get to be in my recital?"

The question jerked Brianna back to the moment. *The recital.* She'd forgotten all about it. "No, darling, no!" she crooned, holding her arms out to her daughter. "We'll hurry to the dress shop and get you in fine form posthaste!"

"I'll carry her," Paxton said. "You look ready to drop in your tracks."

Brianna wanted to jerk the child away from him. The satisfied curve of his lips told her that he believed he had won and now had complete control, not only of Daphne, but of her as well. Ha! This matter wasn't finished yet.

Feeling as if her throat might rupture with pressure from all the words she kept swallowing back, Brianna followed the blasted man back across the street to the dress shop. Once inside, Paxton helped tidy Daphne's hair and clothing while Brianna fetched the child's supper from a cloth sack in the trunk.

Paxton set Daphne on the sewing chair, pushed Mrs. Pauder's dress out of the way, and arranged what there was of the pathetic meal on the machine table. Then he plucked the half-finished bottle of sarsaparilla from the windowsill and set it beside the food. "There you go. Lay back your ears and dig in, sweetheart." He chucked the child under the chin. "Time's wasting. You can't be late for your recital."

As Brianna stepped from the cubicle, Paxton's spurs chinking in her wake, the door to the rear living quarters flew open and Abigail hove into view, her white apron smeared with food stains and the bib askew on her flat chest. "A half hour, you said! You were gone far longer than that!"

Before Brianna could speak, Paxton's voice, deep, resonant, and dripping charm, rang out from behind her. "Miss Abigail, I'm so delighted to see you. I figured that you had already retired for the night."

Abigail parted her pale lips to lace into Brianna again, but Paxton cut her off. "I'm so glad you're still awake. I wanted to tell you how deeply I admire your generous spirit."

Abigail blinked, clearly as bewildered as Brianna by that assessment of her character. "My *what?*"

"Modesty is becoming," Paxton said with a smile in his tone, "but in this instance, your kindness is so amazing that I can't help but marvel." He stepped abreast of Brianna. "Why I'm amazed, I have no idea. I knew the first instant I met you that a very tender heart rested under that pretty brooch you're wearing. Most employers would refuse to allow Mrs. Paxton time off this evening to attend the recital, but oh, no, not you. You understand how important things like this are to a little girl."

Abigail touched fluttering fingertips to the brooch, which was partly covered by an apron strap. "I was a child myself not so very long ago." She batted her lashes and blushed. "Naturally I have encouraged Mrs. Paxton to attend the performance."

"Even though the stop in production will affect your bottom line?" He shook his head. "That is beyond admirable, the mark of a truly fine lady. I only wish there were more like you in the world. It would be a better place."

If the events of the day hadn't been so horrid, Brianna might have laughed. This situation went beyond ludicrous, yet Abigail soaked up the praise like a thirsty sponge.

Paxton reached into his pocket and withdrew a silver money clip that sported a gold horseshoe on its front. Within its clasp was a thick fold of bills, more money than Brianna had ever seen in anyone's pocket, the uppermost a ten, with the corners of two twenties also showing.

"I would never intentionally offend a lady with your tender sensibilities, Miss Abigail.

But such generosity must be compensated. I won't sleep well tonight, knowing that your shop profit will suffer because of Mrs. Paxton's absences today, let alone tonight."

He caught Abigail's hand, closed her fingers around a substantial offering, and then lifted her bony knuckles to his lips. Brianna feared her boss might swoon on the spot.

"Please accept this token of my regard in the spirit it is given," Paxton insisted.

"Oh, no, I couldn't *possibly,*" Abigail said, gaping at the money on her palm. "A lady cannot accept monetary gifts from a gentleman, sir. It's inappropriate."

"Not a gift. Consider it to be compensation. Not many bosses are so kind. Besides, no one beyond this room will ever hear of it. I understand that a much-sought-after lady such as yourself has to guard her reputation. You must have countless admirers vying for your favor."

Abigail stuffed the money in an apron pocket and flattened a hand over her chest. "Not *that* many. It is a small town."

"With every available bachelor standing at your door?"

Abigail laughed and angled him a shy smile, looking almost pretty for the first time in Brianna's memory. "I don't suppose you are free tomorrow for supper, Mr. Paxton? I am renowned for my rack of lamb, and I would so enjoy your company for the meal, the most succulent lamb imaginable, with *all* the trimmings."

At that, Brianna truly did almost laugh. Judging by Paxton's expression, he'd just realized that he'd charmed his way into a very sticky corner and was rapidly searching his brain for a polite way out. "That sounds fabulous. I do have some appointments for tomorrow that may conflict, much to my regret."

"We can dine late," Abigail replied. "Say at six, after business hours?"

Brianna saw his Adam's apple bob. "That would be great. Like I said, though, I do have some stuff to take care of. If I don't stop by the shop by noon to confirm, please don't count on me."

"I *do* hope you'll endeavor to conclude your business well before six."

Flashing a sultry smile, Abigail executed a sweeping turn with a twitch of her narrow hips that was clearly meant to be seductive but instead put one more in mind of a scarlet-draped broom twisting in the wind.

When the door closed, Paxton said softly, "Well, I just saved your job."

Brianna pitched her voice low to spare

Daphne's ears. "And what of the rent next week? I must work all the hours I can to meet my expenses! Not to mention that when you fail to show up tomorrow night, she'll be sure to blame *me*."

He had the audacity to wink at her. "If you have any sense at all, you'll be well away from here by then and headed to No Name with me and our daughter."

"Pigs will fly first!"

Moving to a display case at the far end of the shop, Brianna waited for Paxton to close the distance between them, as she knew he would. There was nothing tentative about the man. When she heard his spurs chink to a stop behind her, she straightened her shoulders and directed her low-pitched words to him over her shoulder.

"I will despise you with a virulence to last a lifetime for your testimony against me tonight. You have destroyed my reputation. You've led two men who once respected me to think of me as a trollop. You've also cast into doubt the legitimacy of my daughter's birth. I will never forgive you for that, nor shall I *ever* forget."

Brianna wasn't sure how she expected him to respond. Certainly not with an apology, but as low as her opinion of him was, he still managed to shock her.

"Well, now, darlin', that should keep our marriage interesting. At least I know right up front that I'll never get bored."

# CHAPTER SIX

During the brief walk to the church, Brianna maintained a frigid silence she hoped David Paxton would notice. Unfortunately, he probably didn't get the chance because Daphne, perched on his hip, chattered like a magpie, clearly nervous about her forthcoming performance. As upset as Brianna was, she sent up a quick prayer that the child wouldn't get tongue-tied or forget her lines. Tutored at Charles Ricker's home by Brianna until February, Daphne had been totally unprepared for the cruelties inflicted upon her by other children when she was thrust into a classroom environment so late in the school year. The girls her age had already formed tight friendships, and Daphne, in her patched dresses, had made a perfect target for teasing. The torment had abated now that Daphne wore prettier frocks, but being ostracized for so long had damaged her self-esteem. Doing well tonight would go a long way toward rebuilding her confidence.

"You worried about forgetting your lines?" Paxton asked the child.

"A little bit," Daphne confessed. "But not as much as I would be if you and Mama weren't going to be there."

"We wouldn't miss it for anything," he replied. Then, angling a pointed look at Brianna, he added, "Would we, darling?"

Oh, how Brianna yearned to smack him. Her mouth was so dry that she couldn't have spat if someone yelled, "Fire!" But for Daphne's sake, she managed to push out, "No, I absolutely wouldn't! It's not every day that I get to watch my beautiful little girl give a solo recitation."

When they entered the church, Brianna drew to a stop beside Paxton. The dais at the front of the cavernous room where the pulpit normally sat had been transformed to serve as a stage and was brightly illuminated by strategically placed lanterns. Children stood off to each side, bunched into groups according to grade. Very few lamps had been spared for the rear of the church, where bisected rows of pews stretched back to the entranceway. Even in the dimness, Brianna determined quickly that every spot had already been taken. She saw the plump Mrs. Pauder sitting in a center aisle seat beside her gangly husband, Mike. Two rows ahead, the Wilson family took up nearly an entire bench, Charlotte looking pathetically thin next to her brawny husband, Mac.

"I'm late!" Daphne squeaked.

Paxton put the child down, tugged off her cloak, and licked his forefinger to wipe a smear of cheese from the corner of her mouth. "They haven't started yet, so you're only *fashionably* late," he said in a low voice as he straightened her hair ribbon. "All beautiful ladies try to be a tad late so every eye will turn to them as they make a grand entrance."

Daphne glanced behind her. "Does that mean everybody will stare at me?"

"Yep, but only because they'll be thinking you're the prettiest girl they've ever seen," he said. "Now, listen, okay? Don't run or let on that you're flustered. Walk like your mama does, slowly and gracefully, with your head high and your shoulders back."

Daphne nodded and cast Brianna a terrified look. "I can't remember my lines."

Determined to push from her mind all her worries about David Paxton, Brianna crouched down to take Daphne's small face between her hands. "You truly are the prettiest girl in town, dear heart. And you'll remember your lines when your turn comes. You've practiced and practiced. Mrs. Walton will be standing nearby, and she'll whisper reminders, too. You're going to do fine, I promise."

"What if I don't?" Panic tightened the child's expression.

Brianna saw Paxton fishing in a pocket of Daphne's cloak. He withdrew a shiny-bright copper penny, which he tucked into the child's right hand. "For luck," he whispered. "It's magic, remember."

Daphne grinned, pressed her fist to her heart, and nodded before tucking the coin into her skirt pocket. "It *is* magic. I forgot I had it!"

Daphne braced her thin shoulders and spun away, a swirl of multihued pink even in the dimness at the back of the church. Tears stung Brianna's eyes as she watched her daughter walk slowly up the aisle, clutching her skirt in one hand to mimic her mama even though the hem of her dress reached only to her shins. There was an innate dignity and grace about the child. Oh, how Brianna wished Moira could be there.

"Standing room only," Paxton said softly. He guided her to the left of the doorway, where they could watch with their backs to the wall. "Jesus. Are you as nervous as I am? She's placing way too much importance on this. It's only a recital, for Christ's sake."

"You are in a *church,* sir. Watch your filthy mouth."

He laughed softly. "Why bother when you watch it so good for me?"

She jerked with a start when he looped an arm across her shoulders in an unmistakably proprietary fashion. She looked up at him, drawing a hissing breath as his gaze sharpened on hers, warning her without words not to protest. As if she would dream of it. Pulling away from him in public would cause even more talk than standing there with his arm around her. She could see heads turning and heard a low-pitched buzz of conversation. She knew who was being discussed, and it wasn't Mrs. Walton, the teacher and mistress of ceremonies, now walking to center stage.

Daphne's group would perform fifth. The first skits were a blur to Brianna. She was mainly conscious of the weight of Paxton's arm and the rigid pressure of his sidearm against her hip. The older children sang a patriotic song she'd memorized as a child. All through the group recitation of the Declaration of Independence, her thoughts scurried about like a mouse in a rabbit warren. She had to think of a way to get away from this man. She could only pray that Daphne's remaining dress money would provide her with the means to hire a horse, reach the nearest railway, and purchase tickets to some town where she and her daughter could vanish like puffs of smoke.

Brianna mulled over the possibility that acting acquiescent might lull Paxton into a false sense of security. She would have to steal a good bit of food from the restaurant so she and Daphne would have something to eat while they traveled. Brianna detested having to pilfer bread and cheese. She left money on the counter to pay for it whenever she could, but this situation called for a complete lack of conscience.

She snapped to attention when two older boys on the stage erected a Maypole with colored streamers. Daphne's turn was coming. All the children danced around the staff, singing songs, and then Daphne came out onto the dais. An angel in pink, she searched the crowd with anxious blue eyes, finally spotted Brianna and Paxton, and blew them a kiss. Then she stepped forward.

In a tremulous voice, which she projected with a push of her thin shoulders, she said, "I am to recite to you 'Old Mother

Mitten.' "

Brianna's heart caught, and she sent up a silent Hail Mary, crossed her fingers, and then unsuccessfully tried to do the same with her toes. She felt Paxton stiffen beside her, which gave her cause to wonder if he actually was nervous. *Pshaw.* She'd seen how easily he charmed Abigail. The man had missed his calling to the stage.

" 'Old Mother Mitten and her pretty kitten took supper one night rather late. But they sat down to tea, and the dog came to see Pussy cut the meat up on her plate.' "

Daphne reached into her skirt pocket, undoubtedly to touch that blasted penny, which Brianna didn't believe was special in any way. Even so, the child's voice steadied. Brianna saw her release a breath and drag in another. She knew then that Daphne had overcome her fright and would recite her lines perfectly.

"She's amazing," Paxton whispered. "Such a beautiful, smart little girl. You've done a good job with her."

Brianna wanted to stay focused on Daphne's recitation, but that comment heated her blood. "Aside from feeding her from trash barrels, of course."

"Yeah, well, that isn't your fault. It's mine."

Applause broke out, and Brianna realized Daphne's performance had ended, apparently with a flawless presentation, judging by the enthusiastic clap of hands. She blocked out Paxton and watched Daphne step forward, as was her due as the soloist, and curtsy with her skirt held out at each side. Then the child straightened, beamed another smile, and said, "I have an important announcement to make! After a very long time mining in Denver, my papa finally came to see us today! Then tonight he and Mama visited Judge Afton and got married! Isn't that grand? I am ever so happy!"

For a horrible instant, Brianna thought she might faint. Though she grabbed for breath, her lungs refused to inflate. A collective gasp rose from the crowded pews, and a hum of censorious conversation ensued. Paxton snapped taut, withdrew his arm from around Brianna's shoulders, and said, "Christ on crutches!"

Before Brianna could guess what he meant to do, he handed her Daphne's cloak, shoved away from the wall, and strode up the center aisle, his greasy-looking duster flapping behind him. In this setting, he was like a weevil in the flour bin, a disreputable man in a building filled with pious, respectably garbed parents and grandparents.

Brianna cringed and wanted to close her eyes, but morbid fascination kept them open.

He made short work of closing the distance to Daphne. Once he gained the dais, he swept the child up into his arms and turned to face the audience. "Good evening to all of you," he said in a booming voice. "I'm David Paxton, Daphne's father. After our marriage several years ago, her mother and me were separated." He made a circular motion near his temple. "I guess you could say I lost my mind. I definitely got a maggot in my brain about striking it rich in the Denver area, and it took me a spell to get my head on straight and come here to collect my family. To celebrate our reunion, my wife and me decided to *repeat* our wedding vows. Judge Afton was happy to oblige." He stepped down from the dais. "This is a fabulous recital. I hope all of you enjoy the rest of it."

Brianna slumped against the wall. The man was hopeless. He'd done it again, using *me* when he should have said *I.* Even so, tears scalded her eyes as she watched him stride up the aisle, holding her daughter as if she were a precious gem. He'd just tried to save her reputation. It wouldn't work, of course. Tongues would wag with rampant speculation, and there would be people who would never forget, rekindling the scandalous gossip at every opportunity. Life as Brianna had known it in Glory Ridge was over.

She wondered if the polecat expected her to be grateful because he'd tried to salvage the situation. Hell would freeze over first. No doubt it would suit him just fine if she remained here and let him leave with Daphne. He had charmed the vinegar out of Abigail, but Brianna wasn't that foolish. With only one exception, she'd never met a man yet who hadn't tried to touch her inappropriately, usually with force, or do her dirty financially, oftentimes both. Paxton just hoped to depart with Daphne, leaving Brianna behind so he'd have only a child to deal with. A six-year-old was a lot easier to hoodwink than a grown woman.

David didn't know whether to laugh or cry. *Out of the mouths of babes.* He had heard his nephew, Little Ace, let fly with some revelations that had badly embarrassed his parents, but never had he said anything to equal Daphne's ecstatic announcement. *Holy hell.* The child didn't understand the ramifications, but David definitely did. He had tried to save the situation, but he knew it had been a pathetic attempt. His rebuttal had been received with disapproving glares and silence. If he had plotted and schemed for a month, he couldn't have lassoed Brianna more effectively. She couldn't possibly remain in Glory Ridge now.

As he collected his wife and guided her from the church, he could feel the brittle tension that radiated from her thin frame. Under the light pressure of his hand, her spine felt as if it might snap like a parched twig. Chin lifted, her face deathly white in the moon glow, she kept her eyes trained straight ahead, not even watching where she put her feet. The woman looked like she'd just seen a whole flock of spooks.

"Prairie-dog hole." David curled his fingers over her hip to steer her around the hazard. He felt her body jerk at his touch. Once the danger passed, he returned his palm to the small of her back. "Are you all right?"

She made no reply. Daphne didn't share her mother's reticence. "Papa, what did I say wrong? Everybody made funny noises like they were choking."

"Sweetheart, you didn't say anything wrong." David searched his brain for something more comforting to say. "Your mama and me are so *proud* of you."

"*I,*" Brianna snapped. "If you're going to talk to my daughter, you shall use correct English, sir."

David saw another prairie-dog hole and was sorely tempted to let the snooty little witch step in it. Instead he guided her around it and said to his child, "Your mama and *I* are so very proud. You never made a single mistake in your recitation! You totally outclassed Hope. The teacher had to remind her of her lines. Great job, darlin'!"

"Hope is the most popular girl in my class," Daphne informed him with a twinge of envy in her voice.

David couldn't understand why. Hope was a singularly homely child compared to his beautiful, sweet-natured Daphne. She had drab brown pigtails, unremarkable features, and a superior manner, as if she were God's gift to humanity. Were the kids in Daphne's class blind or just small-town stupid? David had never experienced the protective feelings of a father. They hit him like an ocean wave now. He wanted to knock little heads together. Wasn't that a fine kettle of fish? He couldn't browbeat his daughter's classmates into liking her. Ah, well, by this time tomorrow night, she'd be miles away from there, and if David had his way, she'd never see any of the narrow-minded little buggers again.

Brianna had been exhausted more times than she could count, but tonight she had moved beyond that to a muscle-melting weariness that made it difficult to lift her feet. This day had been the longest in her recent memory, and the worst part was, she couldn't look forward to dropping like a corpse onto her and Daphne's cot to grab a few hours of sleep. Though she now realized she couldn't remain in Glory Ridge, she still needed to go to the restaurant tonight, not for the wages she might earn, but for the food she could steal. She and her daughter couldn't take off on a hired horse with nothing to eat. They would languish from hunger and never reach their destination. She had no weapon to kill wild game. She doubted her knife, once used to discourage Charles Ricker's amorous advances and now hidden under the cot mattress, would do the trick. She couldn't run fast enough to catch a rabbit.

She glanced blearily at the Colt .45 that rode Paxton's hip, wondering if it was suitable for killing small game. Oh, how she wished she could slip it from the holster without his noticing. *Highly unlikely.* And even if she managed, she'd never been trained to use a firearm. She'd probably take aim at a fleeing hare and shoot herself in the foot.

Tangled thoughts scurried around in her tired mind as she contemplated her situation. The first order of business was to reach the attic room and quickly pack their possessions. Then she'd take everything, including her child, to the restaurant. With any luck, the establishment would be deserted. Sometimes the owner stayed late to bedevil her in the kitchen, but mostly on Friday nights, he stayed home, pretending to be a devoted husband. She'd remain there only long enough to pilfer sufficient food for a journey to another town. Then she'd walk to the livery to hire a horse. It would mean riding through the night to the nearest railway station. Hopefully, there would be no delay before they could catch a train. They needed to get away quickly, giving Paxton no opportunity to follow them. She sent up a quick prayer of thanks for what she'd saved of Daphne's dress money. If she spent it wisely, it might see them through until she found another job.

The entire day had been a blur of endless emotional upsets, probably magnified by her lack of sleep the previous night. How would she accomplish all that needed to be done? She wasn't sure riding a horse would be as easy as it looked. While growing up at the orphanage, she'd seen others riding in the park, but there had been no opportunity for her to take lessons. The one time Ricker had tried to get her in the saddle, the huge animal had stepped on her foot and then bitten her. She'd refused to go near a horse again. Milking the dratted cows had been bad enough, a skill that had taken her weeks to learn and had almost cost her the job. Then there'd been his infernal chickens. Every morning she'd gotten her hands pecked bloody by outraged hens when she went to collect the eggs. She'd finally learned not to apologize for the invasion in advance. Forewarned broody hens became viciously protective.

The thought brought Brianna back to awareness of the man who walked beside her, one hand pressed to her back while he managed Daphne's weight with his other arm. The cloak-draped child, apparently as exhausted as her mother, had looped her thin arms around his neck and fallen into boneless slumber, with her head lolling on his shoulder. *I am forewarned of the theft you hope to perpetrate,* Brianna thought, *and I will peck much more viciously at your stealing hands than any hen that ever lived.* Brave words. The way Paxton wore that gun conveyed that he knew how to use it. Not that he would need a weapon other than superior strength to overwhelm her.

In that moment, Brianna ached so badly and her limbs felt so leaden that she yearned to drop to her knees and fold her arms over the back of her head. But that wasn't going to happen. She was an O'Keefe, a descendant of at least one parent who must have been a stubborn, irrepressible rebel. She would *not* fold under pressure. She was made of stronger stuff.

They reached the dress shop, and Paxton slowed his pace to a halt.

David wasn't sure what came next. Thanks to Daphne's announcement at the recital, Brianna's choices had been trimmed down to one, their leaving for No Name. Yet how could he say that to her? He sensed that she needed to reach that conclusion by herself, and when he searched her eyes, shimmering like quicksilver in the moonlight, he glimpsed something that made him take notice. *Rebellious determination.* He'd seen it before many times in the eyes of people suspected of crimes. When backed into a corner, they had one thought: run.

Okay. He was ready for that and would foil any attempt she made to escape with his child. But, *damn,* he was tired. He'd been on the trail for three days. Judging by Brianna's expression, David knew he wouldn't be enjoying that soft bed at the hotel.

Gazing down at her, he was once again impressed by her grit. She looked even more played out than he was, yet she planned to bolt the moment he turned his back.

Though David knew he was wasting his breath, he said, "You look ready to drop in your tracks, and I'll bet part of the reason is you haven't slept in a comfortable bed for way too long. I'll happily rent you and Daphne a room at the local Taj Mahal. After a good night's sleep, we can discuss this mess in the morning."

"You know about the Taj Mahal?" she retorted. "That's utterly amazing."

David tried not to bristle. Maybe she talked fancier than he did, but he had a decent education. Way back when, Ace had paid David's tuition with his gambling proceeds, and the nuns at the parochial school hadn't allowed any slackers. "It took a thousand elephants to carry the construction materials to build the Taj Mahal," David informed her, "and it was embedded with precious and semiprecious stones that, to this day, make it seem to change colors, depending on the light. Some folks believe Shah Jahan did that on purpose, to reflect the changing moods of a woman."

Her chin came up a notch. "My moods may be mercurial, but my assessments of character remain rock solid. I wouldn't enter a hotel with you for any amount of money."

As weary as David was, he couldn't help but laugh. She was definitely a corker, a woman who'd keep him on his toes. A fleeting image of Hazel Wright flashed through his head, and he thanked God he had escaped that fate. He would have been bored silly. He appreciated a quick wit spiced with temper. Brianna was a lady he sensed would keep him entertained, both in bed and out of it.

"That being the case, sir," she continued, "I propose that we both find our rest in our respective places and meet in the morning." She withdrew her watch from her skirt pocket, popped open the case, and peered owlishly at its face. "Shall we say eight? The restaurant is in full service by then. We can discuss our next move over breakfast."

David knew damned well she had no intention of meeting him for breakfast. If he slept in until seven, she'd be long gone with his daughter. Telling her he knew that, however, would be a mistake. He'd dealt with plenty of runners during his career as a lawman, and he would keep his own counsel. Whether she realized it or not, she'd met her match.

So instead of arguing the point, David agreed to meet her for breakfast in the morning. After entering the dress shop with her, handing her the sleeping child, and collecting his saddlebags, he bade her good night and walked to the hotel, yawning along the way in case she was watching. He wanted her to get the impression that he'd fallen for her lie and planned to sleep like a baby all night.

Nothing was farther from the truth. Upon entering the hotel room, David gathered his things — shaving gear and soiled clothing — stuffed them into his saddlebags, and without a single backward glance at the bed, which had been calling his name ever since his arrival, left the hotel and walked to the livery stable. He found a shadowy spot behind the rattletrap wagon, sat on the ground with his back to the equally dilapidated building, and settled in to wait for his runaway bride.

■ ■ ■ ■

Brianna laid Daphne on a bench in the restaurant kitchen, which was blessedly dark, and straightened with an effort. Oh, how she longed to sink down beside the child and let exhaustion overwhelm her. But that wasn't an option. She had food to collect before going to the livery. Hopefully David Paxton was dead to the world by now.

Feeling her way to a counter, Brianna groped for the lantern and the book of Diamond matches that always lay near its base. Then, after fumbling to remove the glass globe and turn up the wick, she struck the phosphorous match head and ignited the lamp. When light bathed the room, Brianna barely glanced at the piles of dirty dishes and the food-smeared counters and stoves. She'd be donning no apron tonight. She drew a wadded pillowcase from the pocket of her skirt, snapped it open, and grabbed the lamp.

The pantry, a narrow room lined with shelves and iceboxes, was spooky at night with her shadow dancing over the walls. She set aside the lantern to begin foraging. An ache of guilt settled in her chest. She could almost hear Sister Theresa saying, "Thou shalt not steal." The preaching had fallen upon rebellious but fertile ground, and over the last six years, Brianna had never taken anything without praying for forgiveness. Ah, well, there was no help for it. She had to get away and rely on God's understanding that she was doing this for her child. Besides, she'd worked all week and had wages coming. She'd also put in countless extra hours without ever getting paid. Thinking of it that way, she found it easy to convince herself that this wasn't *really* stealing.

She selected two loaves of bread, a brick of cheese, and a goodly supply of meat — ham and bacon being her main choices because they wouldn't spoil as quickly as fresh chicken or beef.

A rattling sound made Brianna's heart catch. She froze and stopped breathing to listen, hoping against hope that it wasn't the restaurant owner. The tension eased from her shoulders when she determined that the sound was only a shutter flapping at a window. *Thank you, God.* It would be just like that filthy-minded old lecher to sneak in when he knew she was here alone. He considered it his privilege to corner her in the kitchen. Brianna detested the feel of his groping hands.

He'd probably never notice tomorrow that he was missing food. Keeping a proper inventory was one of his greatest failings. That would work in her behalf. The last thing she needed was to be apprehended by a Glory Ridge posse and incarcerated for theft.

Brianna picked up the lantern and bent to grab the pillowcase she'd packed with food. It was heavier than she anticipated. How would she manage to carry their possessions, the food, and Daphne to the livery stable at the same time? Only with the good Lord's help . . .

# CHAPTER SEVEN

Waiting had never been David's favorite pastime. He pressed his back against the livery wall and dug into the dirt with his bootheels to reposition his aching rump on the cold ground. *Jesus.* The instant that word shot into his mind, he winced. His days of talking any old way were over. In the church tonight, Brianna had made it clear that she disapproved of his speech. Okay, fine. He'd seen both Ace and Joseph cleaning up their language, strictly enforced by their wives. Nowadays, Ace, once the most feared gunman in the West, wouldn't say *shit* if he had a mouthful. Well, maybe sometimes when he was with the guys, he'd sin, but mostly he didn't, afraid his foul talk would rub off on his kids, shocking the teacher their first day of school.

Until coming to Glory Ridge, David had watched his mouth only when he was with his brothers' wives and kids and around ladies in town. Otherwise he had talked anyhow he wished. He guessed those days were gone forever. Brianna could go to the devil, but he'd be damned if he taught his daughter to speak like a cowpoke.

He heeled the dirt again, wondering if the earth here was packed clay. His ass — well, okay, his *behind* — ached like a son of a bitch. He tensed, realizing with a jerk of his stomach that he couldn't even manage clean language when he was thinking. How was he going to raise a daughter to be a fine lady? His ma had taught him right, and Ace had added ear cuffing as an incentive. David had just wandered away from good manners over time while overseeing rough-edged cowhands at his ranch and equally coarse deputies in town. When you were around bad language, you picked it up. It wasn't as if he was beyond salvation. With some practice, he'd do okay.

A rectangle of yellow spilled from the open livery doors, the source coming from a lantern hanging inside the barn. Occasionally, when the breeze let up, David could hear the hiss of the lamp. He stared up at the last-quarter moon, resembling a ball that had been cut in two. Judging by the moon's position, still rather low, it had to be around midnight. How long had he been there — three hours or more? Where was that infernal woman? He knew she planned to run tonight, and she struck him as being too smart to attempt a long jaunt afoot. She'd appear at the livery, sooner or later.

An awful thought occurred to him. Judging by her speech, she might hail from Boston, and even though she'd worked as a housekeeper and governess on a ranch for years, that didn't necessarily mean she'd acquired wisdom about the wilds of Colorado. What if she had it in her head to walk to some town? The thought scared David half to death. With a diminished moon, it was dark out there on the prairie, and the terrain crawled with dangers: a few rattlesnakes that were emerging from their dens with the coming of spring; hungry coyotes that had survived a long, hard winter; and, damn it, maybe even a stray mountain lion. Big cats didn't commonly frequent the prairies, but they had large hunting territories, and when the game grew scarce, which it might have done during the snow season, they went farther afield. Prairie dogs made a nice snack. A hungry coyote was also fair game. So was a damned fool woman, stumbling along in the darkness with a child. Her highfalutin manner wouldn't intimidate a puma. David pictured the confrontation, with Brianna braced for battle against a predator with lethal teeth and claws. He could almost hear her say, "I beg your pardon, *suh*."

David was about to leap to his feet when a shuffling sound reached him. He had needle-sharp night vision. Gaze routing through the silvery darkness, he picked out a shape moving toward him, a little over five feet tall and bulky, as wide at the bottom as at the top. As the figure came closer, he was able to see more clearly. It was a woman in skirts, carrying a child over one shoulder and two large bags in each hand. David relaxed against the barn. She shouldn't be carrying that kind of weight. It was what his ma called a lazy man's load.

Brianna stumbled, tripped on her skirts, and almost fell. Then, straightening from a weaving, bent-over stance, she regained her balance and plodded forward. David remained in the shadows, relief mingling with annoyance. At least the woman had sense enough not to set out afoot. Once again he had to admire her grit, although he deplored her actions. Here she was, planting one foot in front of the other even as her strength failed her. Damn her stubborn pride.

She staggered past him, never noticing him in the shadows, and entered the livery, stumbling to a stop just inside the doors. The child was double wrapped in both her own new cloak and what looked like her mother's cape, which left Brianna with no protection from the cold except for her threadbare dress. Where was her shawl?

"Hello?" she called as she stepped from David's sight. "Wake up, my good fellow! I need to hire a horse!"

Did she even know how to ride? David settled back, prepared to be entertained. He doubted the bloke who manned the night-shift would rent out the gentlest, or sound-est, steed in the stable to a greenhorn. Why offer good horseflesh to someone who wouldn't recognize it?

David heard plaintive grumbling and then a man's footsteps. The voice that rang out was not the livery owner's but that of a younger fellow. "How do, Mrs. Paxton. What brings you here at this hour?"

Brianna replied, "I need to hire a horse, sir."

"For what?"

"For transportation. Why else does one hire a horse?"

"Where you heading," the man asked, "and when will you be back?"

"I have no plans to return," Brianna replied. "I will be dropping the horse off at a livery in some nearby town."

The fellow laughed. The tone had a decidedly nasty edge. "We only hire out horses for round-trips. We can't have one of our mounts dumped off somewhere. We've got no way to get it back."

"Oh, well." David could almost hear Brianna's mental wheels spinning. "Then how much to *buy* a horse, sir?"

The stable hand took his time answering. "Well, now, a hundred and fifty dollars ought to do it. Unless you're feelin' accommodatin' and want to make a trade with me to lower the price. I just freshened the hay in our one empty stall. It's ready for use."

"I beg your pardon?" David had heard that note in Brianna's voice earlier and knew it didn't bode well for the guy on the receiving end. "Are you suggesting something inappropriate, sir? I will remind you that you are speaking to a lady."

David could see where this was heading and pushed to his feet to intervene. Before he came fully erect, he heard the stable hand say, "A lady, you say? The word is out now. Everyone in town knows your girl is the by-blow of some cowpoke who just rode into town and married you six years too late. From where I'm standing, I don't see no lady, just a gal with way too high an opinion of herself and up for the taking by any man who can pay her price. Hell, even that dress is indecent, so tight across your bosoms I can see your nipples plain as day."

As he stepped through the doors, David heard Brianna gasp at the insult. At a glance, he saw that she'd deposited the snoozing Daphne on a hay bale. Now she stood with the filled bags, old pillowcases judging by the looks of them, lying at her feet. Her slender body braced with outrage, she faced the livery worker with her chin held so high she was in danger of getting a crick in her neck. David stepped abreast of her, taking the other man's measure. Flicking back his duster to expose his Colts, he met the fellow's gaze, which went from hostile to cautious in a blink. The distinct smell of whiskey met David's nostrils.

"This *lady* is my wife," David said, keeping his voice level. "She needs to buy a horse and tack for a fair price. A hundred and fifty dollars is outrageous, and you know it. I could buy three fair to middling mounts, possibly four, for that amount."

The skinny, shabbily dressed employee paled visibly.

Startled by the sound of David's voice, Brianna whirled to face him, her expression incredulous. He noted with a glance that the stable hand was right. The cold night air had her nipples standing at attention like well-trained cadets. *"You!"* Words seemed to fail her for a moment. "What are you — ? You're supposed to be at the hotel asleep!"

"Or so you *thought*." David winked at her, which he figured was wiser than scowling. He didn't like it when people said they would do one thing and did another. "Never underestimate your opponent. You set yourself up for nasty surprises."

The stable hand's eyes flicked from David's implacable face to the guns he wore, and he appeared to shrink into his clothes. Gesturing weakly toward the nearest stall, he wet his lips and managed, "This one's an okay mount."

With one look, David noted that the gelding had a swayback and unsound knees. He rejected it out of hand. Aware that Brianna had retreated to curl an arm protectively over the sleeping child, he felt his temper flare. She acted as if he were an insane, murderous child abductor. The thought maddened him. He lived by his honor, and he expected others to do the same. On top of her failure to stand behind her word, she'd been about to embark on a fool's journey. It was one thing to endanger herself, quite another when it involved his daughter. Possibly she didn't realize how perilous her actions could have been, but he wasn't in any mood to consider both sides right now.

Two stalls down, David selected a nice-looking bay with far better conformation. He quickly negotiated a price, bearing in mind that the owner of the livery was a decent fellow and would be the one to take the financial hit if David bid too low.

Once the haggling was over, David began saddling the horses and his mule. At that point, Brianna finally found her voice to protest.

"Now that you've foiled my plans, Mr. Paxton," she said crisply, "I see no point in leaving in the middle of the night. We can postpone this madness until morning and travel by daylight like normal people."

Standing at the opposite side of Blue, David flipped a stirrup strap up over the saddle and shot his reluctant bride a burning look. "Your decision to take off tonight suits me just fine."

"Earlier, a journey on horseback was my only recourse, sir, not my chosen mode of transportation. If you're bent on taking us out of here, a stage would be far less taxing on both me and the child."

The lantern light cast dark hollows beneath her delicate cheekbones. Under her green eyes, the smudges of exhaustion had become so pronounced that they had the dark, purplish hue of bruises. David could see how played out she was, and he had no intention of pushing her too hard. However, he wasn't willing to return to the hotel and trust her to stay put until morning. She'd made that impossible, and she'd have to suffer the consequences. High time this feisty female learned that David Paxton said what he meant and meant what he said.

Kneeing Blue's belly and jerking on the cinch, David replied, "I'll make accommodations along the trail as comfortable as possible for you and the child."

"How magnanimous of you!"

Lowering the stirrup and patting Blue's neck, David tossed her a forced smile. "I'm not about to give you a second chance to sneak away. You'd drop out of sight, and I'd play hell trying to find you."

Two bright spots of guilty color touched her pale cheeks.

"We'll ride out tonight," David said with finality. "And we'll travel by horseback until you come to accept this marriage. If that means riding all the way to No Name, so be it. I'm not taking you into some strange town where you can start screaming that

I've kidnapped you and plead your case before another judge. Custody of my daughter hangs in the balance."

"She is *not* your daughter!"

David bit down hard on his back teeth. When he'd gotten a firm grip on his ire, he looked her dead in the eye and said, "I've got an order signed by a judge that says different. I'm not a man who riles easily, but if you say that one more time, I'm likely to get mad. I mean *really* mad. Needle me any other way, but no more about Daphne not being mine."

"And if I refuse to leave with you?" she challenged.

He shrugged. "Then I'll take my child and be on my way. I never said you have to come. Stay here if you like. You can keep in touch with Daphne by writing letters, and anytime you change your mind, I'll pay your way to Denver."

Sparkling tears beaded on her dark lashes, forming them into spikes that outlined her beautiful eyes with shimmering black. "You can't just *take* my daughter," she cried.

"Watch me." David patted one of the saddlebags. "The law is on my side. That document, signed and stamped by Judge Afton, says I'm your husband and the father of that child. I have every right to take her.

You can come, or you can stay. I don't give a damn which."

Brianna could barely contain her outrage. Not knowing which offense to address first, she blurted out, "A *proper* husband would have boxed that livery attendant's ears for saying such scandalous things to his wife!"

Paxton conceded the point with a nod. "A proper *wife* would never have put herself in a position to be on the receiving end of such a crack. What did you expect he'd think when you appeared in the middle of the night without your husband, wanting to hire a horse? He was out of line, but from the smell of him, he's been drinking. Alcohol scrambles the brains. Plus, I'm sure the news of Daphne's announcement tonight spread through town like a prairie fire." Looking over the horse at her, Paxton treated her to a slow once-over, followed by a deliberately insolent grin. "Any woman in a dress that displays her assets so noticeably has to expect a certain amount of unwanted attention from the opposite sex." He lifted one shoulder in another shrug. "If he'd taken it any further, I would have stepped in, but I'm not inclined to box a drunk man's ears for only looking and angling for a sample."

Blistering heat surged to Brianna's cheeks. She was well aware that she'd matured physically since her dresses had been made years ago. While in Ricker's employ, she had let out the seams to accommodate her increasing bust, but that hadn't helped much, and the side-seam inserts she'd added later while working for Abigail had only added puckers under the arms instead of solving the problem. She glanced at her cloak, which was wrapped around Daphne to protect her against the night air. One of their blankets would have served as well, but they'd already been stuffed in the pillowcases. Her shawl had been tucked into one of the totes at some point as well, and she'd been in too big a hurry to search for it.

Striding over to one of the packs now on the mule, Paxton lifted the flap and withdrew a denim flannel-lined jacket, which he tossed to her without a word of explanation. Grateful for the warmth and concealment that it offered, Brianna stuffed her arms into the sleeves, shrugged it on, and struggled with fingers gone numb from the chill to button the front. Once covered, she watched Paxton add her bags to the packs the mule carried and then check the load for balance.

*Come or stay,* Paxton had said. Taking stock of the situation, Brianna decided to postpone the battle for another time. She was up against a man who outweighed her by at least eighty pounds, every inch of him appearing to be overlaid with a steely layer of muscle. He also wore Colt revolvers and a hunting knife and had a rifle in his riding boot, plus a document in his saddlebag that branded her and her child as his property. The way she saw it, her options were few — if, indeed, she had any at all.

For tonight, at least, she would acquiesce and go with him, ever watchful along the way for an opportunity to escape. She would *not,* under any circumstances, stay behind. She couldn't be separated from Daphne.

After six long years of infrequent exposure to horses, Brianna's fear of the gigantic beasts had never diminished. Ignoring Paxton, who still fussed with the packs, she considered the daunting prospect of having to ride one of the horrible creatures. She had limped and favored her bitten shoulder for days after her only attempt to get in the saddle, and she didn't relish the thought of trying it again. Especially in front of David Paxton. Heart in throat, she forced herself to walk to the already saddled bay gelding. The animal grunted and nudged her in a friendly way, dispelling some of her trepidation and leaving a damp smear across her jacket sleeve.

Recalling the form of riders she'd watched, she assured herself that she could do this. It appeared that the stirrups hung too low for her, so she quickly readjusted them. By the time Paxton strode up behind her, she'd inched up both of her foot wells to what she felt was an appropriate height.

"Daphne will ride with me," he said. Then, piercing her with those sharp blue eyes, he asked, "You ever been on a horse? If not, speak up now. I don't want you falling off and getting hurt."

Brianna had suffered this man's superiority for too many hours to admit the truth. "I know what I'm about." She turned, grabbed the saddle horn, and bounced uselessly about on the ball of one foot while she tried, without success, to lift her other foot high enough to get it into the stirrup. She'd witnessed countless men in Glory Ridge mount with what had looked like effortless ease. How they managed it, she didn't know. It was like trying to scale Pikes Peak. "I have lived in Colorado for *years,* sir."

Paxton leaned around her to study the left stirrup. "Did you do that?" he asked.

"Did I do what?"

"Adjust the stirrups so high? I sure as hell didn't."

"They were too low for me."

"Christ on crutches, with them that high, you could set a supper plate on your knee."

"Can you *please* expend *some* effort to mind your tongue, sir?"

She heard him huff. He nudged her out of the way to readjust the stirrup straps. As he stepped around to the other side of the horse, he sent her a knifelike regard from under the shadowy brim of his hat. Even with the light of only one lantern, she saw his jaw muscle ripple and felt the sting of criticism in his gaze. Everything about the man unnerved her. It was difficult for her to think straight.

"Okay, here's how it goes. When you get on the damned horse, all I want you to do is to hold on to the horn and concentrate on keeping your seat. I don't give a shit what happens. Just keep your seat and let the bay do the rest. Horses are herd animals. He'll follow Blue Boy and Lucy. No worries."

"Are you suggesting I don't know how to ride this animal?"

His firm mouth quirked. In that moment, Brianna could no longer ignore the fact that he might be devastatingly handsome with a bit of cleaning up. In her mind's eye, she pictured him in a tailored serge suit with a fashionable felt fedora hat perched properly on his head. And with a haircut, of course. That long hair made him look like a scoundrel of the first order.

"I'm not *suggesting* anything. After getting to know me, you'll come to realize I never beat around the bush. I say what I think, and right now, I'm thinking you have absolutely no experience in the saddle." He circled the bay, came to stand front side of the readjusted stirrup, and bent at the knees to interlace his hands to form a cup. "Step up."

She stuck up her right foot. He released an audible breath. "Shit. With your *left* foot, Shamrock. You can't mount that way. It's physically impossible unless you go ass first onto the saddle and risk pitching over backward."

Brianna had never felt so humiliated in her life. She *knew* to use her left foot. It was just that he rattled her so badly she was making silly mistakes. "You, sir, have the filthiest mouth I have ever had the misfortune to come across."

"Because I said *shit?*"

Brianna winced. Had he no idea how crass

a word that was? He'd also said *ass.* She stuck her left foot into the cradle of his joined hands. With a push of his shoulders and arms, he lifted her with alarming ease, then caught her elbow to steady her as she jerked at her clumped skirts, trying to hide her knees. Sheer fright took precedence over modesty when she realized she was astride the horse. From where she perched on the saddle, it looked like at least a mile to the ground, and beneath her trembling body, she could feel the limitless strength of the gelding, which kept glancing nervously back at her.

"I can't believe the word *shit* puts you in a snit," he muttered. "Where I come from, we walk in it, we shovel it, and we use it to fertilize the garden. In fact, when I get up in the morning, I even *take* one. What fancy word do you use for it?"

She struggled to gather her wits. The very thought of traveling away from the safe environs of Glory Ridge with this uncouth, vile-tongued man unnerved her even more than being on the huge animal. "Excrement," she blurted.

*"What?"*

"In polite society, it is called excrement, or *feces.* And when the morning urge strikes people, they refer to it as 'a call of nature' or 'one's morning duty.' " Brianna shuddered and gave her head a slight shake. "I cannot *fathom* that we are engaging in such scandalous discourse."

"I take that to mean you don't like this conversation. Well, that's too damned bad. Where I come from, even ladies don't cringe at the word *shit.*"

"Well, sir, such females are not truly ladies."

"By your definition, not mine."

Brianna jerked and almost fell off the horse as he led it three steps forward. Following his advice, she grabbed hold of the saddle horn to keep her seat.

He stopped, nudged back his hat, and sent her an incredulous look. "The only positive thing about this trip is that at least you don't seem to be afraid of horses."

"Is being afraid of them a bad thing?" she asked in a thin voice.

"Sure as hell is. Horses can sense fear, and it spooks the daylights out of them."

Brianna's grip on the horn tightened until her knuckles ached. "Truly? Horses can sense if you're afraid of them? What . . . what do they do if they think you're afraid?"

"Well, shit. You *are* afraid. You're scared out of your wits to be up there, aren't you?"

She cast a nervous glance at the ground,

which didn't look any closer than it had a few seconds ago. "It is a bit unsettling."

"Just out of curiosity, do you lie about everything, Mrs. Paxton? I've heard tell of people who'd rather lie than tell the truth, but you take the prize. You say you can ride, but come to find out, you've never even been on a horse."

"I am capable of doing many things I haven't actually tried yet, sir. It is *not* lying to say I know how to do something when I've watched it done and feel that I'm able."

He sighed and hooked a hand over the crown of the gelding's neck to rub behind its ears. "Okay. Listen up. As you're riding, think about something pleasant. That should help get rid of your willies."

Brianna's favorite thing was to dunk a piece of chocolate in hot tea and suck off the melted part. But she didn't think it would calm her jumpy stomach to recall the taste of something she hadn't enjoyed for over three months. "All right," she agreed. "I'll do that."

He tucked the bay's reins around her saddle horn, then went to collect his animals and Daphne. Brianna had seen men riding many times in Colorado and knew they steered a horse with the leads. She didn't like the idea of being on an animal with no way to tell it which direction to go, so she collected the slender leather straps into the grip of one hand. The gelding threw his head back and she saw the whites of his eyes.

When Paxton noticed that she held the reins, his jaw muscle bunched. "You either have a hearing problem, Mrs. Paxton, or you're deliberately ignoring half of what I tell you." He gave her a long, hard look. "For once in your life, pay attention and do as you're told. If you're bent on holding the reins, you have to do it right."

"How do I do it right?" she asked, her voice thin with alarm. The bay looked a little wild, and she feared he was about to take a chunk out of her foot.

"Well, if you don't want him to rear, loosen your hold on the reins. Trust me when I say you don't want to be tossed. It's a long way to the ground." He watched her relax her clenched fingers. "A little more. You have to give him plenty of slack. Right now, you're pulling back so hard, he doesn't know if he should shit or go blind."

# CHAPTER EIGHT

As they rode from the livery, weak moonlight greeted them. Washed clean by the gusting wind, the town smelled of prairie grass and wildflowers. David smiled over Brianna's embarrassment when her skirts had bunched up. She'd been so bent on covering herself that she'd almost forgotten her fear of the horse. All he'd seen was her ribbed stockings — and, well, okay, the comely shapes of her calves and ankles. But she'd been as twitchy as an offended virgin. He repositioned the child in the crook of his right arm so she'd be comfortable, pleased to be hitting the trail even though his body screamed for rest.

Over his shoulder, David called, "There's no need for you to be nervous about that horse. He shows no signs of being spooky. My guess is that he's rock solid."

"My *life* may depend upon your *guess*, sir. Could you be so chivalrous as to reassure me in more definitive terms?"

Did she *always* talk that way?

"As long as you keep your seat, you have nothing to worry about," he said loudly because the wind snatched away his voice.

"And how does one keep one's seat, sir?"

"Pretend you're sitting in a rocking chair. Hold fast to the horn, relax with the motion, and press in tight with your knees."

Watching over his shoulder, he saw her attempt to follow his advice, letting her shoulders slump slightly. She loosened one hand from the horn to stroke the gelding's neck in an attempt to befriend the animal. When the town was well behind them, David circled back to ride abreast of her. She threw him a worried glance.

"You said I needn't worry about the reins, that my horse would just follow yours. How can he do that if you're back here with me?"

"I just thought it might be a good time for a little riding instruction."

"Oh, dear," she muttered. Then, with a nod, she said, "All right. Do carry on, sir."

"The name's David." He launched into an explanation of Western riding techniques and watched as she executed his instructions, stopping the horse, nudging it into a walk, and then reining left and right. "Good job. You'll be a horsewoman in no time."

"I doubt that," she retorted, but David heard in her voice that she was pleased. "Being a horsewoman is not one of my aspirations."

Even in the darkness, David noticed how rigidly she sat in the saddle now that he was next to her. He had a nasty suspicion that if he reached out toward her, she'd flinch away and fall off the horse. As if the bay sensed her fear, he snorted and swung his head around to sniff her foot. She jerked her toes back.

"He won't bite you. You can trust him."

"There are two species I will never trust, sir, and horses are one of them."

"What's the other one?"

"Men," she said flatly.

If any other woman had flung that insult at him, David would have chuckled, but for Daphne's sake, he needed to get along with this one.

"Sounds to me like you had a nasty experience with a horse at some point." And a man as well, but David decided now wasn't a good moment to broach that topic.

"Nasty? The horrid beast nearly bit off my arm, and then it stepped on my foot." A faint wash of moonlight broke through, giving David a glimpse of her pale face and flashing eyes. There were some lovely women in his family, but he couldn't recall ever having seen features as delicate or perfect as Brianna's. He couldn't look at that soft, full mouth without wanting a taste of it. "That was my first attempt to get on a horse, and until tonight, I swore it would be my last."

"I can't say I blame you. What fool tried to put you on a fractious mount?"

"My former employer, Charles Ricker. A few years later, I caught him putting Daphne up on the same beast. I grabbed her from the saddle and told him I'd slit his throat while he slept if he ever took her near that monster again."

"Good for you. Doesn't sound to me like he's any good with horses." Then another thought struck him. "Hell's bells, is Daphne scared of horses, too?"

"No. She's always loved them. And Ricker isn't good with any kind of animal. He has a vicious streak. I pity the woman who married him. She'll soon rue the day."

"Yet you stayed in his employ for almost six years?"

"Necessity is a pitiless dictator, Mr. Paxton."

Uncertain how to respond to that, David clicked his tongue at Blue and nudged him forward so he and Lucy could take the lead again. *Ricker.* Was he the bastard who'd made Brianna so wary of men? Had he been cruel to Daphne as well? The very thought made David draw the child closer. For two cents, he'd be tempted to return to Glory Ridge to give the fellow a ten-minute lesson on how to treat women and children. Somehow, though, David couldn't imagine Brianna standing meekly aside while her daughter was abused. As slightly built and skittish as the woman was, she still had a goodly measure of fight left in her. She'd be a hellcat if anyone threatened her child.

That certainty led him to wonder if he'd made a mistake by teaching her the rudiments of riding. She might use the knowledge against him and steal away from camp during the night. He set aside the worry. As exhausted as she was, she'd fall asleep the moment she lay down and wouldn't stir until he nudged her awake in the morning. He'd hobble the horses, so even if she did manage to saddle a mount, she'd be scratching her head, trying to figure out why the animal wouldn't run. With all that going on, she'd surely make enough noise to wake him.

Guilt assailed him. Brianna was right about one thing. Setting out on horseback would be hard on her and the child. If they had waited in Glory Ridge to catch a stage, they might have reached a railway in a day and could have traveled the remainder of the way to No Name in relative comfort. Unfortunately, the trains stopped at every Podunk along the way, and Brianna's determination to escape had weighed against his taking her into communities where she might prevail upon a well-intentioned stranger or a lawman to rescue her. No way. David would happily pay for train tickets, but not until Brianna resigned herself to the fact that he had inalienable rights as Daphne's father.

Meanwhile, David had decided to choose a route northwestward that would take them nowhere near any railroad tracks. He hadn't spelled that out for Brianna, but he'd hinted at it.

He'd make the trip as easy on mother and child as possible, and maybe at some point, Brianna would come to accept the situation. To that end, David stopped to camp only two hours out of Glory Ridge along the stream he'd seen early that day. When he shifted on the saddle to tell Brianna they were halting for the night, he saw that she was nodding off in the saddle and congratulated himself on his good timing. The last thing he needed was for her to pitch off the horse and get hurt.

David handed Brianna their sleeping daughter after she dismounted, and then he cared for the animals, pondering as he removed the packs from Lucy's back whether he should cook a meal. One glance over his shoulder had him vetoing that idea. Brianna slumped on the grass with Daphne cradled in her arms. He doubted either of them had the energy to eat. He'd wait until morning to fix them something. That decided, he set off to scavenge up the makings for a fire.

When he returned, he found Brianna stretched out on her side with her knees drawn up to protect the child from the wind. He tossed down the wood and dry cow patties he'd collected and went to forage through the packs for bedding. After he got them settled, he'd worry about laying the fire. He should have seen to his wife and daughter's comfort first.

Brianna came awake with a shriek when he touched her shoulder to waken her. David narrowly escaped a blow to his jaw by her flailing fists.

"Whoa, *whoa!*" he said, catching her wrists. "It's only me."

"Don't touch me," she cried, trying to break free of his grasp.

Daphne woke up and started to cry.

"Don't *touch* me!" Brianna shouted again.

David knew panic when he saw it. He quickly let her go and stepped back with his hands open and held out to his sides. "I meant no harm. Your beds are ready, and I just thought you'd be cozier in them than on the ground while I get a fire going."

She sat up, her thick hair loose from its pins and spilling over her shoulders. Even in the faint light, she was beautiful. Those eyes could easily grab hold of a man's heart and never let go. In the moon glow, they brimmed with emotions she probably didn't wish to reveal. To him, that made her seem vulnerable and in dire need of a strong arm to protect her. David would happily sign on for the job, but first he had to gain her trust.

As if she sensed his thoughts, she broke visual contact and turned to soothe Daphne. Then, without a thank-you, she carried the child to the two beds, rearranged them to create one, and retired under a double layer of blankets with the little girl locked in her arms. It occurred to David as he built a fire nearby that Brianna might still be thinking he was a slave trader, bent on stealing Daphne and selling her across the border.

He wished he could make light of her suspicions, but instead he had to applaud her savvy. What Afton and Bingham had said about the comanchero slave trade being a thing of the past was true, but they had their heads up their asses if they thought such dealings never happened anymore. Proof to the contrary often came across David's desk. Last month, a girl had gone missing from her parents' farm outside Colorado Springs, and because her body hadn't been found, the lawmen there believed she'd been kidnapped. David prayed not. There were some fates worse than dying, and for a young girl, being sold into slavery was one of them.

It was awful to think there were individuals in this world that would do something so horrible, but they were definitely out there. As long as mankind existed, there would be sick lechers who coveted pretty little girls and would part with almost any amount of money to get their hands on them. It was a terrible tribute to the nature of some men. But there you had it. Maybe Brianna was smart not to trust him.

Crouched over the fire, trying to coax it to life, David peered beyond the brightness to study his sleeping wife. He had no experience with skittish females, having always made it his practice to consort with only friendly ones. How did a man go about gaining a woman's confidence?

David hadn't a clue. As he shook out his bedroll, he decided he would be well-advised to sleep with one eye open in case Brianna woke up and decided to make a run for it. He wouldn't put it past her. He sighed as he stretched out, using his saddle as a pillow. Tipping his hat down over his eyes, he stared into the blackness of the bowl.

As a precaution, maybe he'd sleep with both eyes open.

Brianna awakened with a start to find Daphne gone. She jerked erect with dizzying abruptness and squinted her aching eyes against the bright morning sunlight. *Blast and blue blazes.* She'd slept not only through the night but well into the morning.

Her joints protested as she threw back the blankets and rose to her knees to shoot frantic glances in all directions. Still muddled with sleep, all she saw at first was the stream, rolling grassland, and wildflowers, and for a heart-hammering instant, she believed Paxton had made off with her daughter. She shot to her feet with a scream rising into her throat. It died to a squeak when she spotted the saddles and packs.

Weaving on her feet, Brianna ran in first one direction and then another, scanning the distance for her child. Her knees were still watery with fright when Paxton's blond head bobbed into view on the horizon like a marble bouncing on green carpet. Next his shoulders and chest appeared. He wasn't wearing the duster, and his shirt was almost the same blue as the sky behind him. She staggered toward him with lurching steps, her fists clenched for battle. Where was her daughter? What had he done with her?

She slipped and soaked one shoe while jumping across the stream. As she struggled for balance, Daphne materialized beside the man. Even at a distance, Brianna could hear the musical lilt of her voice. She was chattering nonstop and gazing up at him with a rapturous glow on her face. In her hands, she held his upturned hat.

Brianna drew to a halt, resentment sizzling through her veins like acid. He'd had no right to take her child from camp without telling her. And, oh, how it galled her that he'd won Daphne over so completely. Well, he wouldn't find her mother as accommodating.

As she waited for them to reach her, she thrust a hand into her skirt pocket to finger the handle of her trusty knife, which she'd kept under the mattress until last night. The blade was buried in a raw potato from the restaurant pantry, a trick she'd devised early on while in Ricker's employ so she could carry the weapon for protection without accidentally cutting herself. More than once, she'd held Ricker off with the instrument when he tried to press his unwanted attentions upon her.

When Daphne saw Brianna, she broke into a run, her pink dress whipping in the wind, her golden curls bouncing. She held the hat out in front of her, keeping it carefully balanced, as if it were filled with precious gems. Watching her, Brianna felt as if a strong hand closed around her throat. The child was absolutely beautiful, well worth a thousand dollars, if not far more, across the border. Was it Paxton's plan to lure Brianna far away from Glory Ridge and then leave her stranded while he made off with Daphne?

"Look, Mama!" Daphne cried as she covered the last few feet between them. "Papa found us all manner of things to eat! He says we're going to feast like royalty!"

Brianna glanced at the filthy collection of roots and leaves. Did the man have bats in his belfry? Many plants on the prairie were poisonous, even deadly. The Indians knew which ones were safe because they'd lived off the land for generations, but most white men didn't have that knowledge.

As Paxton reached them, he said, "It's all good fare. My mother's hobby is studying plants, and she taught me all she knows."

Without the filthy duster, he looked less intimidating in some ways and more so in others. As Brianna had suspected yesterday, he was strongly built. His shirt collar lay open to reveal the sturdy column of his sunburnished neck, and the blue cloth, flattened against his torso by the breeze, showcased broad shoulders and well-muscled arms.

"Mama, did you know tea made from blue-eyed grass can cure a fever?" Daphne asked. "And if I get an earache, Papa can make it go away with white milkwort!"

An awful thought struck Brianna. What if the man hoped to feed her something that would render her senseless so he could head south with her daughter without any protest from her?

"I brought plenty of food, dear heart," she said.

Brianna plucked the hat from her daughter's hands and shoved it at Paxton. "You'll enjoy your feast alone, sir. We will eat safe fare, and I will cook it myself."

He shrugged and then winked at Daphne. "More for me, I reckon. Maybe when your mama sees I live through it, she'll let you have some of my rabbit stew tonight."

Daphne sent Brianna a rebellious glare that swept her back in time to her childhood. She'd treated the nuns to that same look more than once, then done as she pleased.

Thirty minutes later, Brianna discovered that learning to cook over an open fire presented more challenges than she'd realized. First off, she had to collect fuel. Touching dry cow manure was disgusting, and carrying it in her raised skirt was even worse. Then she couldn't get her fire to ignite. Paxton had already rinsed his prairie finds and was halfway finished cooking his breakfast before Brianna even had flames. There was also the wind to foil her efforts. Ever constant on the prairie, it made the fire's heat a frustrating variable. One minute, her bacon was burning, and the next, it barely sizzled in the pan David Paxton had lent her.

*Why did I not think to bring a frying pan?* She'd procured plenty of food but nothing to cook it in. The oversight might have been laughable if it hadn't been so indicative of her rattled thought processes while she prepared to run. Even worse, the fabulous aromas drifting from Paxton's fire made her mouth water. He'd killed a rabbit shortly after sunrise, and now he was frying it while roots and God only knew what else boiled in a pot. He made meal preparation out on the prairie seem effortless.

Recalling her first weeks at Ricker's, when learning to cook on a woodstove had nearly gotten the better of her, Brianna felt sure she could master almost anything if she set her mind to it. Just then, a huff of wind blew out her fire, and she almost cursed. She stared gloomily at the half-raw bacon and belatedly decided that she and Daphne would fare well enough with hunks of bread and cheese. At *least* she'd had the presence of mind last night to bring along some fare she didn't have to cook.

Daphne settled in beside Brianna to eat, her small face drawn into a scowl. "I have to eat this every single day," she complained. "I hardly ever get vegetables."

Brianna, who'd been going without food as much as she could, thought the cheese and bread were delightful. She took a sip of water from the dented tin cup — another thing she'd had to borrow — and sighed. Her belly, so long deprived, already felt full, but she determinedly sank her teeth into the bread again. She needed to regain her strength. Even at her best, she'd be no match for Paxton physically. She would have to depend on her wits, and without nourishment, her brain had grown sluggish. The smell of the frying rabbit called to her. How long had it been since she'd eaten meat?

"Mama," Daphne said, shooting her a sweet smile. "Papa is eating all the plants we found, and he isn't getting sick. Won't you please let me have some?"

Brianna stared at Paxton. He was wolfing down food from a tin plate balanced on his knees. Plates were yet another thing she hadn't thought to bring. Not that the restaurant had tin ones, but she might have grabbed some china and protected it in the folds of their blankets. She'd forgotten forks and spoons as well. Her mouth spurting saliva, Brianna watched him go after a rabbit leg. She wanted some so much that she couldn't blame Daphne for feeling the same way.

"All right," she relented. "But you can only have some meat, none of the other stuff."

Daphne shot to her feet. Brianna grabbed her arm. "Look at me."

The child dragged her gaze from the rabbit to focus on her mother.

"You *will* do as I say. There are all manner of poisonous plants on the prairie. Mr. Paxton may *believe* he knows what is safe to eat, but there's every chance that he's wrong. You may have some of the rabbit and nothing else."

Daphne wrinkled her nose. "Mama, why do you call Papa Mr. Paxton? Myrna Hepplewhite's mother calls Myrna's daddy James."

Caught off guard, Brianna couldn't think how to answer. "You just do as I say, young lady, and eat only some rabbit." She released her hold on her daughter's arm. "Your promise, Daphne, or I shan't allow you to go."

Daphne released a theatrical sigh. "All right, Mama, I promise. But if he doesn't sicken before supper, can I have some of his rabbit stew?"

Brianna considered the question for a second. "If he remains well until supper-time, yes, I'll let you have some stew."

Daphne left the remainder of her bread and cheese on the napkin Brianna had spread between them, the one useful thing she *had* thought to bring. Bouncing away to the other fire, she cried, "Papa, Mama says I can have some of your rabbit!"

Paxton handed the child a plate, forked her up some meat, hooked a hand behind her neck to kiss her on the forehead, and said, "Lay back your ears, darlin', and dig in."

As Daphne did just that, Brianna settled a thoughtful gaze on Paxton. The events of yesterday had cemented into her mind that he was up to no good, but his actual words and manner didn't support that. When he looked at Daphne, his chiseled features softened with affection. He touched her with incredible gentleness.

Though it unsettled her and made her question her sanity, Brianna had to wonder if he wasn't precisely what he said he was, a small-town marshal named David Paxton.

*Poppycock.* The smell of his fried rabbit was addling her brains.

# Chapter Nine

After the breakfast mess was cleaned up and the bedding was repacked, Paxton fetched the horses and mule, which he had left where the grazing was better. Standing a few feet away, Brianna pretended to watch Daphne as she gathered flowers, but she was actually observing Paxton as he saddled the geldings. It was a task never required of her at Ricker's ranch, and just in case Paxton had nefarious plans, she'd need to know how to do it in order to get Daphne away from him.

She thought she was displaying just the right amount of disinterest when, toward the end of the process, he flashed a grin at her over the bay's saddle and touched the brim of his hat. "Did you get that? Or should I unsaddle them and start over?"

A flush of embarrassment flooded her cheeks. Did the wretched man miss nothing?

"I'd be happy to teach you how to saddle a horse. There's no need to stand back and pretend you're not watching. It's a skill everyone in this country should have."

For the second time that morning, Brianna wondered if the man had bats in his belfry. He had to know she was desperate to get away, and here he was offering to teach her a skill that might enable her to do that. Of course, he could have an ulterior motive. Was he planning to take off with Daphne and had conscience enough to make sure Brianna could get back to civilization safely?

She wasn't taking any chances where Daphne was concerned. He wouldn't wiggle an eyebrow today without her noticing.

"Come on," he said, when it became evident she wasn't going to answer him. "Let's go. We've got a lot of ground to cover today."

Brianna stepped to the bay's side, ignoring Paxton's outstretched hand, and took hold of the saddle. Hoisting a foot, she aimed for the stirrup and succeeded only in jabbing the horse in the stomach. The animal turned its head and looked at her in mild protest. She tried again. She couldn't get her left foot high enough to reach the stirrup.

Paxton watched her hop beside the horse

for another try or two, then he gave her a crooked smile that lent his rugged features a boyish appeal. "I'll give you a boost up if you'd like."

*I'll just bet you would.* She wasn't sure if his offer was only an excuse to get his hands on a female, or if he truly wanted to help. She didn't care. The bottom line was that she needed to learn how to mount by herself. "I can manage quite well, thank you."

Turning so that her backside was away from Paxton's gaze, Brianna tried again. She'd been taught to be grateful for the gifts God gave her, but she'd never wished more than now that those gifts had included a few extra inches. Her foot grazed the edge of the stirrup and jabbed the horse again. The animal heaved a patient sigh. Glancing up from the bedraggled bouquet in her hand, Daphne gave Brianna a curious look, then returned her attention to a clump of pink flowers.

"This is ridiculous," Paxton said after Brianna had bounced about several more times. "When we get to my ranch, I'll build you a mounting block, but for now, you'll have to settle for using a rock or my hands. I see no rocks, Shamrock, so you're stuck with me." He laced his fingers and stepped forward. "Come on. A lot of people aren't long enough in the leg to mount without an aid. It's nothing to be ashamed of."

Brianna sent him a look that she hoped made his ears burn. A gentleman never referred to a lady's lower appendages or called them by name.

Still offering her the cradle of his locked fingers, he said, "Stop being so prideful, Shamrock. God made you a little on the small side, but so what? You're put together right fine. Better than fine, actually."

Brianna gasped. "Were you born and raised in a barn, sir?"

Frowning slightly, he straightened and settled his hands on his lean hips. "What have I said wrong this time?"

"You refer to my lower appendages, assess and comment on my person, address me with a rude name, and you can still ask that question?"

He chuckled and shook his head. With sunlight playing over his chiseled face, she had to admit he was an exceptionally handsome man. "Don't tell me you're one of those prudish types who thinks every piano should be skirted so its legs won't show."

Brianna couldn't see the humor. "It is not prudish to have good manners, sir, and it is *not* mannerly to mention a lady's body parts. I am not a piano!"

Paxton looked her up and down in a way that made her skin burn. "No, ma'am, I can see that. I meant no offense. Where I come from, it's okay to recognize that women have legs, just like men, and a lady is flattered when she receives a compliment. And just for the record, I was born on a gorgeous plantation in Virginia."

"Really?" Brianna edged the question with a dubious note.

"Yes, really," he replied drily. "My father, Joseph Paxton Sr., was a Southern gentleman of some wealth. In addition to raising crops, he bred fine horses. During the war, he lost almost everything. With the little he had left, he purchased some land outside No Name, pulled up stakes, and moved us west. Right off, he learned the land sale was a swindle and his deed of ownership wasn't worth the paper it was written on. It's a long story, and we need to be on our way, so I'll just say he ended up swinging from the limb of a big oak tree on that land, punished for a murder he didn't commit, and thereafter it was up to my mother and my older brother, Ace, to raise me and my siblings. Maybe you don't think they did a good job, but I sure as hell do."

It sounded like a plausible story. Many

well-heeled Southerners had lost everything during the War between the States. Brianna felt a twinge of guilt for having blistered his ears. Not everyone had grown up in a convent as she had. Perhaps he was right, and she was a bit of a prude. It was just that nearly every word out of his mouth shocked her. Was that because of her up-bringing, or simply because she couldn't stand the man? Everything he said or did ir-ritated or alarmed her, or both.

She finally had no choice but to accept his offer of a leg up to mount the horse, and the instant her nether regions settled on the saddle, she whimpered, unable to gulp back the sound. Little wonder she'd hurt all over when she first stirred awake and had barely been able to walk. She felt bruised and rubbed raw in places that, until this moment, she hadn't even realized she possessed.

"You saddle sore, darlin'?"

With a supreme effort of will, Brianna straightened and gathered the reins. *Darlin'?* The man defined the word *audacious.*

"I've got some liniment in the packs that'll take care of it right quick," he informed her. "If you've got sore spots you can't reach, I'll happily rub you down."

Cows with angel wings would appear in

266

the sky before she accepted that offer. "I am perfectly fit, sir. Let us be on our way."

Once again, Daphne rode with Paxton, chattering almost nonstop. It was a bright, sunny morning, and Brianna yearned to shed the jacket, but given the man's comments about her threadbare gown and how revealing it was, she decided she'd rather be hot than take off the coat. Paxton would get no more free shows from her.

Riding two lengths behind the mule, Lucy, Brianna could hear little of what was said between her daughter and Paxton, but judging by Daphne's chortles of laughter, she was greatly enjoying the exchange and falling head over heels in love with her papa. Anxiety mounted within Brianna. Nothing good could come of this. If Paxton was actually on the level and believed he was Daphne's sire, he was bound to learn the truth sooner or later, and at that point, he would renounce the child, just as any man in his right mind would. Daphne might never get over the heartbreak.

Every few minutes, Paxton stopped the horses to dismount and collect vegetation. After going to great lengths to inform Daphne of each plant's common name, its medicinal properties or lack of them, and how it could be cooked, he stuffed the find into a drawstring canvas bag that dangled from his saddle horn. Brianna caught only snatches of the dialogue, which frustrated her no end. Did the man know what he was about, or was he filling her daughter's head with a bunch of nonsense that could very well end in her death?

Worse, simply sitting there with nothing to distract her but miles of grassland in all directions, Brianna found her gaze drawn repeatedly to Paxton's lean, muscular frame. He moved with an easy grace for such a powerfully built man, swinging effortlessly into a crouch and then pushing erect, and exhibiting speedy reflexes that she found altogether unsettling. Determined not to watch him, she gazed off across the prairie.

On this rolling terrain, she supposed there might be railroad tracks out there somewhere, but thus far they hadn't come across any. That struck her as odd. They'd ridden a good distance, though probably not as far as her aching backside indicated, yet she hadn't seen a sign of civilization. Was Paxton deliberately avoiding people? She suspected he was. He'd made it clear last night that he would not use public transportation until she came to accept this situation.

But what if he had some other reason for

avoiding people? Suspicion gnawed at her again. The man had her teetering back and forth like a seesaw.

He and Daphne finally mounted back up, and they were off again. How, Brianna asked herself, did Paxton know which way to go? The prairie all looked the same to her. She'd never had a good sense of direction. She knew that the sun rose in the east and set in the west, but right now it was almost overhead, which told her nothing. And she had no idea how to find her way after dark. As a youngster, she'd studied the constellations and how to use the North Star to navigate, but she'd long since forgotten how to find it in the sky. Such knowledge had not been necessary at the convent orphanage. The dear, wonderful nuns who'd raised her never left the convent grounds because it was a rule of their order to remain cloistered. As a result, Brianna had spent much of her life behind the convent walls, her only outings chaperoned by responsible ladies of the parish who volunteered to organize day trips for the children. Brianna had enjoyed those brief glimpses of the outside world, but they'd been rare, and the women driving the buggies had found their way through the city using street signs.

On the high prairie there *were* no signs.

With a sinking sensation in the pit of her stomach, she had to accept that she had no idea where they were. Was Glory Ridge behind them or off to her left? She felt almost certain the town lay on this side of the stream, but she wasn't sure. She'd been so exhausted during the ride last night that Paxton might have crossed it with her none the wiser. It was terrifying to swivel her head in all directions with no idea which way to go if she decided to run.

When the sun was high overhead, Paxton stopped along the stream for lunch. Brianna barely managed to keep her feet when she slid off the horse. Paxton unsaddled the geldings and relieved Lucy of her packs. Then, to Brianna's acute dismay, the man engaged Daphne in gathering handfuls of grass with which to rub the animals down. Brianna knew a single kick from one of those powerful beasts might seriously injure or kill her child. She limped — yes, *limped,* because every part of her lower body was afire with pain from riding for so long — over to the horses to voice her objections.

"I do *not* want my daughter near these unpredictable creatures, Mr. Paxton!"

Daphne left off rubbing Lucy's flank, which was as high as she could reach. "But, Mama, they're sweet. Come see. Papa is teaching me how to be safe around them."

*Papa.* If she heard her child utter that title one more time, she was going to tear at her hair and shriek. "As nice as they may seem, Daphne, each of them weighs a thousand pounds or more. If one steps wrong, even by accident, your foot could be injured." Brianna glanced at the child's patent leather slippers, which were too insubstantial to protect her feet. They were also nearly ruined now. She needed some thick, sturdy boots — preferably reinforced with steel in the toes. Brianna wished now that she'd thought last night to exchange the cute shoes for Daphne's sturdier play footwear.

Paxton paused in grooming Blue. Meeting Brianna's gaze for a tension-packed instant, he said, "You heard your mama, Daphne. If she doesn't want you messing with the horses, her word is the law. Maybe over time, she'll relax a bit and lift the ruling."

Brianna shot him a startled look. He was always in control, never giving away an inch of his authority, and yet he relinquished it now. He met her gaze with a humorless glint in his. Had she ever seen eyes that blue? *Yes.* Daphne had his eyes — a deep, summer-sky azure. The mental comparison had Brianna doubling back. Daphne did *not* have his eyes. What was she thinking?

271

Paxton turned his preparation of the noon meal into an occasion. Daphne joined him at the creek to wash their finds from the morning ride. He referred to their search as a "trip to God's general store," which delighted the child. She hung on his every word about the fabulous foods their Maker had provided for them.

"I travel light on the trail," he told Daphne as they crouched near the fire. "I bring some staples so I can make flatbread, corn cakes, or flapjacks. A little salt, sugar, and bacon are always nice to have. But I'm not like many men I've met who carry eggs in bags filled with sawdust and load their poor mules down with all manner of canned goods. If I get a hankering for eggs, I go out to find them if the season is right. If not, I do without. As for canned goods, I've got no use for them. The world around us is filled with the makings for salad, soups, and stews if you know how to find them."

"And I'm learning how. Right, Papa?"

Brianna swung away, wincing at the pain radiating from her hips to her toes. As she walked, searching for bits of wood and those revolting dry cow patties to fuel her own fire, she nearly groaned. Her rump felt as if she'd bounced repeatedly on a boulder. Her inner thighs burned. The least movement made her leg muscles scream in protest.

When Brianna returned with her skirt filled, Paxton left his fire to saunter toward her with that well-oiled, lazy shift of his hips and long legs that she found so unsettling. Didn't he ever get saddle sore? Everything about him struck her as being supremely masculine.

"Hold up," he said. "No point in building a fire only to have it blow out again."

She noticed that he held a short spade. Dropping to one knee, he treated her to a display of rippling muscle across his shoulders and back as he began digging a pit. He was built like a log-splitting wedge, wide across the chest and narrow at the waist.

"In this country, where there's no windbreak," he explained, "you protect your fire with a lip of earth. As long as you insist on cooking your own food, I'll dig you a spot."

Job completed, he sat back on one bootheel, nudged up the brim of his hat, and gifted her with a smile similar to the one he'd used on Abigail to rob her of her wits.

"I'm hoping you'll come around soon, though, and eat my fare. If ever a female needed fattening up, it's you. If a hard wind came along, it'd blow you away."

Brianna had often thought the same thing

about Abigail, and for an uncomfortable moment, she wondered if Paxton thought she looked like a broom. Then she reminded herself that she didn't care what he thought. He might be on the fiddle, a seafarer's term for men who stole extra rations that Brianna had learned as a child growing up near the Boston harbor. On ships, supper plates had a raised edge called a fiddle, which helped to prevent spillage on stormy seas, and those who took more food than was their share had servings that rode that edge. Over time, "on the fiddle" had become a term to describe crooks who stole or committed other reprehensible deeds, and she'd be foolish to forget David Paxton might be of that ilk until he proved otherwise.

She would not be lured in by those melting blue eyes or that crooked grin that always creased his left cheek, making her wonder if he'd once had a dimple there similar to Daphne's that had deepened and become elongated by exposure to the sun.

"I brought food aplenty. I'll not have my daughter consuming dangerous plants."

He shook his head and pushed to his feet. His greater height reminded Brianna once again that he had the physical advantage. Whatever would she do if he decided to exercise his conjugal rights? The marriage last night hadn't been legal, Brianna felt certain of that, but he still carried the stamped document in one of his bags, which officially made him her husband whether she wanted him to be or not. She was fairly certain he wouldn't try anything with Daphne sleeping beside her, but what would happen if he caught her alone? Common sense forced her to recognize that she was far too small to fight him off.

"I'd never offer my child anything poisonous to eat," he assured her. "And the same goes for you. I know what I'm doing."

"So you say."

"If I didn't know what I was doing, I'd have been dead long ago."

Brianna didn't answer that, but the sardonic twist of his mouth told her that he knew precisely what she was thinking — that his sudden demise wasn't a completely unwelcome possibility.

Brianna attempted to walk normally as she went to retrieve her bag of food from the mule packs. Crouching to sort through the contents brought tears to her eyes. Clearly, her body wasn't fashioned for horseback riding.

"The liniment is in there somewhere, a dark brown bottle wrapped in a white towel. Anytime you'd like to use it, feel free."

Brianna had rejected the offer earlier, but now she was so miserable that using his potion sounded like a fine idea. Perhaps she could take the bottle to bed with her tonight and apply it to her sore parts under the cover of blankets.

Paxton served the remainder of the breakfast rabbit for lunch, along with a green salad and some sort of cooked tubular. Brianna made Daphne sit with her at the other fire, where they dined on charred ham, cheese, and bread, again sharing a borrowed tin cup filled with water so they might sip as they ate.

"The food we found isn't making him sick, Mama. Can't I *please* have tiny tastes?"

Brianna's mouth was watering for some of that salad. She couldn't remember the last time she'd eaten fresh vegetables. Last summer, she guessed, when she'd harvested them from Ricker's kitchen garden. In the off season, the only green food on their plates had been snap beans, which Brianna had preserved each autumn. Paxton had even brought a few lemons in his packs, the juice of which he squeezed over the mixture of leaves and blossoms. Every time he forked some into his mouth, he closed his eyes as he chewed, his expression conveying that the taste was sublime.

"Please, Mama?" Daphne pestered.

Though Paxton seemed to be suffering no ill effects, Brianna was still reluctant to allow her daughter to eat any of that stuff. Just one poisonous plant in the mix could make the child deathly ill. "Just finish your dinner, Daphne. You've got ham. That's a lovely treat."

"But we found small-flower alyssum, and wild onions, and asparagus, and begonia, and field bindweed! Papa watches to be sure I pick the right things. Sweet alyssum is bad for us, but the other kind isn't. Did you know we found bitter rubberweed? Papa says it's poisonous to livestock, so he won't let our horses or Lucy anywhere near it. That's how come he hobbled them last night where it was safe for them to graze."

Brianna always hated having to tell Daphne no, but in this case, she felt it was in the child's best interest. Drat the man for making the little girl yearn for foods she shouldn't have. Daphne had been perfectly happy with bread and cheese up until last night, and now she was turning up her nose at ham.

"When you've finished eating, I want you to change into your play frock and sturdier shoes. I'll help you dig them out."

Daphne took a bite of ham and chewed as

if she had a mouthful of leather. Even Brianna had to admit that the meat was scorched and dry. The smell of Paxton's freshly boiled coffee drifted to her on the breeze. Coffee was yet another item that she'd forgotten, and she yearned to ask him for a cup. Her pride prevented her from doing so. She and Daphne would get along just fine with the rations she had on hand.

For the remainder of the meal, Brianna pondered the gravity of the situation. So far, Paxton had tried nothing underhanded. He'd been pleasant all morning, and he'd been unfailingly wonderful with Daphne. But she was a long way from being convinced that he had nothing nefarious in mind.

She rubbed her forehead. He seemed so sure Daphne was his. She kept remembering that absurd audience with the judge last night when Paxton had displayed that photograph of a female he claimed was his mother.

In Brianna's mind the question was: Could he be believed? The woman might be his mother, but he could have stolen the picture. Only, if the latter were true, how had he managed to come by an image that so closely resembled Daphne when he'd never even clapped eyes on the child?

Trying to sort her way through this maze was giving Brianna a headache. Each time she reached a conclusion, another thought made her oscillate. Was Paxton precisely what he presented himself to be — an honest man who truly believed Daphne was his child? Or was he a no-account, incredibly clever scoundrel? Brianna was coming around to giving the man the benefit of the doubt. His obvious affection for Daphne didn't mesh with his taking her across the border.

And if Brianna took that leap of faith, accepting that Paxton was for real, she had to somehow disabuse him of the notion that Daphne was his. The little girl was falling wildly in love with him, and the longer Brianna let this situation continue, the worse it would be for the child when he finally learned the truth.

Brianna shifted, seeking a more comfortable position. No matter which way she sat, either her muscles howled in protest or something raw rubbed against the hard ground. She stifled a sigh. He hadn't believed the web of lies she'd told him yesterday, but she couldn't really blame him. She was a hopeless liar, and she knew it.

If she told him the real story of Daphne's birth, what were the risks to her and the child? Glory Ridge was far behind them now. There might still be a chance that the authorities would take Daphne away from her because she wasn't the biological mother, but it loomed far less likely now than it would have last night. If she came clean with Paxton, he would have nothing to gain by exposing her. Instead, he'd probably just wash his hands of her and Daphne, dumping them off in the nearest town to fend for themselves. That would suit Brianna fine. She'd managed before, and no prospective employers could be as bad as Ricker or Abigail.

She watched Paxton with nervous, uncertain regard. If he was up to no good, then nothing she said would have any bearing on the situation. He'd simply carry through with his original plan. But if he was actually David Paxton, marshal of No Name, the truth might convince him to end this insanity now. So far as Brianna could see, she had nothing to lose by talking to him. Perhaps he would recognize sincerity when he saw it.

When the dinner dishes had been rinsed and put away, Paxton dug in the packs and tossed Brianna a couple of blankets. "I always like to take a nap after my midday meal," he said. "Call me a pansy ass if you like, but I need a break from the saddle."

Clutching the blankets to her chest, Brianna watched him saunter away. Did he do something special to rope his body with all that muscle? She'd never seen a man so strong, yet limber. He didn't look tired. In fact, she would be willing to bet he could ride all day and well into the night with no ill effect. Her throat went tight. Was he calling for a rest period on her behalf? She guessed maybe so, which was completely contrary to the caliber of character that she'd assigned to him. He stretched out on the bare ground, using his saddle for a pillow and his hat to shade his eyes. Brianna stood gaping at him for a moment. Then she turned to make a napping pallet.

Brianna snuggled her daughter close. Daphne thrust her hand into the pocket of her skirt and withdrew the coin that Paxton had convinced her was miraculous. The child held it up to the sunlight, twisting it this way and that.

"See it winking at me, Mama? It truly is magic. Last night, it helped me remember all my recitation."

Brianna wished that Paxton hadn't filled the child's head with such nonsense. It was just an ordinary penny. If Daphne continued thinking the coin had magical properties, she was bound to be disillusioned.

"You should put all your hope in God, dear heart, not in worthless objects."

"It *isn't* worthless," Daphne said fiercely. "You don't understand."

Brianna decided to let the subject drop. "Put it back in your pocket, then, so you don't lose it while you're napping."

Daphne gave the penny another turn and did as she was told. Within minutes, her breathing changed, and Brianna felt certain she was asleep. A *pansy ass?* Just when she thought Paxton could say nothing more to shock her, he plucked another crass expression out of his hat. Under her breath, she muttered, "He may be a good man, but he has the filthiest mouth I've ever seen."

It had been a hard day for Brianna, and she yearned to follow the child into slumber. Instead she kept her eyes wide open, waited a few more minutes, and then carefully slipped from the bed. If she meant to tell Paxton the *real* truth about Daphne's parentage, she needed to do it while the little girl slept. In time, when Daphne grew old enough to understand what had happened without thinking Moira had been in any way to blame, Brianna would tell her the story, but for now she felt it was best kept a secret.

Arms crossed over his well-padded chest

and booted feet hooked at the ankles, Paxton appeared to be sleeping when Brianna reached him. "Mr. Paxton?" she said softly, so as not to awaken Daphne.

He didn't jerk with a start, which told her he either had nerves of steel or he'd heard her approach. Nudging up his hat, he fixed her with a penetrating gaze and said, just as softly, "The name's David. Don't you think our daughter is going to find it a bit odd if you don't use it?"

"That's just the problem. Don't you see? Daphne truly isn't your daughter." Seeing him tense, Brianna threw up a hand. "Please don't lose your temper. I know you warned me not to say that again." She was so nervous, she caught herself wringing her hands. "I — um — need to talk to you, Mr. Paxton. Everything I told you yesterday" — Brianna glanced over her shoulder to be sure Daphne hadn't stirred — "was mostly lies, you see. You guessed right about that. Now, rather than let this situation continue, I feel compelled to tell you the actual truth, a story I've never told another living soul."

Well, now, this sounded interesting. David sat up and righted his hat. He'd seen some nervous women in his time, but Brianna looked ready to shake apart at the seams.

His jacket, which swallowed her, quivered around her thighs. She kept interlacing her fingers, digging in hard with her nails, and then giving her wrists a twist to pop her fragile knuckles. His made a loud sound when he did that. Her tiny bones made dainty little clicks.

"Not *here,*" she implored as she sent a glance over her shoulder. "I can't risk Daphne overhearing. Would you stroll down the stream a ways with me?"

David pushed to his feet and stabbed his fingers under his belt to tuck in his shirt-tails. If she meant to tell him the absolute truth, why was she so all-fired het up about it? His first thought was that she'd dreamed up another tall tale, hoping he'd believe her this time. Not a chance. He could see a lie coming from a mile off.

Even so, he agreed to walk downstream with her. With every step she grew more fidgety. He wasn't sure if it came from being alone with him, out of Daphne's earshot if she screamed, or if she dreaded having to launch into her story.

She stopped at a bend in the waterway where the grassy banks closed in on a spread of pebbles to create a musical trickle. To their right, a large rock jutted up from the earth, its top as smooth and round as a cornmeal muffin. Folding his arms, David waited for her to start talking. She stared into the frothy brook, both hands flattened against her waist, her throat working as she struggled to push out the words.

"Well, Shamrock, are you going to say something or chew on it until tomorrow?"

She glanced up, and David saw with a clench of his guts that her green eyes swam with tears. Her mouth, which had tempted him from the start, quivered and drew down at one corner. If this was an act, she should have pursued a stage career.

"When I was born, I had an identical twin," she finally blurted.

Okay, David could buy that. He hadn't met many twins, but he knew they existed.

"Our parents left us on an orphanage doorstep when we were infants." She closed her eyes, sending a silvery trickle down each pale cheek. "They left only a note to tell the nuns our names, Brianna and Moira O'Keefe." She pushed at her hair, which had long since escaped the prudish chignon. Her fingers shook. "Most of the nuns were Irish, and they knew our given names and surname were of Irish origin. Moira —" She broke off, as if speaking of her sister pained her. "Moira and I truly were identical physically. Even the nuns had trouble telling us

apart. We made a game of it, Moira and I."
She gazed across the prairie, her face twisting even as she smiled wistfully. "It was
great fun when we were little, tricking the
good sisters. But they always found us out
because although we looked exactly alike,
Moira and I had different personalities. She
was" — she gestured helplessly with a limp
hand — "*sweet* and ever so dear, a lady
through and through, even as a small child.
I don't believe I ever saw her get angry or
sass the sisters. She always did as she was
told, and she did it cheerfully. She was the
closest thing to an angel on earth that ever
walked. But I" — she gulped to steady her
voice — "I was just the opposite, always in
trouble, always rebelling, always craving attention the nuns had no time to give me. In
short, I was *difficult.*"

David could definitely believe that. She
was *still* difficult. The most infuriating
female he'd ever dealt with, anyway. And
he'd been right about her being Irish.

"It was a cloistered order." David had
been schooled by nuns in San Francisco, so
he understood what that meant. "The
sisters never left the convent grounds, and
only two nuns, Mother Superior and an assigned underling, dealt with tradesmen and
other outsiders. We children rarely went

beyond the orphanage walls. I was thirsty for knowledge of the world outside, while Moira was content to be isolated from it."

Okay, it sounded credible so far. But only so far. His experience with this female had been the kind that would make him doubt her word if she told him Christmas fell on December twenty-fifth. And she was awfully tense for someone who was telling the truth. He expected the tale to turn into a whopper at any moment.

He steeled himself against her tears and tremors. He'd seen women who could open the floodgates on a whim and be very convincing. So far, he felt positive this particular female had done nothing but lie to him. He had no reason to take her at face value now.

"And?"

"When we turned eighteen, we were supposed to leave the orphanage. The nuns had tried to prepare us for the outside. They did their best, really they did, but Moira and I were more suited to remain in the cloister, too innocent of worldly ways to survive on the streets. The nuns gave us the duty of doing business with tradesmen and other outsiders in Mother Superior's stead, unless it involved the induction of a child, in which case she took over. We did routine things like accepting, checking, and paying for deliveries. It allowed us to learn to deal with outsiders, plus we were required to work in the kitchen, helping with food preparation. The nuns did the actual cooking, and afterward we cleaned up. It gave us a way to support ourselves while remaining in the safe confines of the orphanage. Mother Superior hoped that our exposure to tradesmen and delivery people would gradually prepare us for the real world."

David was growing impatient.

"Anyway, the kitchen produce and some of our meat was delivered fresh, every other day, by a local farm on the outskirts of Boston. The — the deliveryman was the farmer's son, a young man named Stanley with blond hair and blue eyes. He came often, bringing huge boxes of vegetables and meat. Being the recalcitrant one who yearned for the *real* world, I found him fascinating. One afternoon we were going over a bill when he took my hand and asked me to meet him in the gardens after he left the kitchen."

Okay, David sensed where this was going. She was going to tell him she'd gotten pregnant with another guy who had blond hair and blue eyes. Likely, wasn't it? In the first place the story was too pat, and in the second place he couldn't imagine Brianna responding to advances with anything but a well-placed kick.

Even so, he listened without reaction, letting her spin her latest yarn.

"Being the unruly one, I said yes." She bent her head, and David actually saw tears drip to the dirt. "To my eternal regret, I said yes." Her shoulders jerked. "After that, I met him in the garden several times. Nothing improper happened. Not that he didn't want it to. I flirted, dodged his advances, and had great fun. To me, it was only a game. He'd try, and I'd keep just out of reach. Sometimes he got angry, but for me that was part of the fun. I knew he had the — the potential to try force, but it never occurred to me, truly it didn't, that a well-raised young man would ever go that far. But the slight chance of danger was exciting. I teased him out of his pouts and looked forward to sneaking off to meet him again."

David scuffed at the grass with his bootheel. "Okay, so get on with it. I'm presuming there's an end to this story and a reason you're telling it to me."

Her green eyes looked bruised and hurt. He searched them deeply and refused to let himself believe what he saw there. She'd lied through her teeth yesterday, fighting him tooth and nail before the judge. At this point, he had no idea what confounded claim she might make next, but punctuating her tale with tears and sniffles wasn't going to induce him to believe a word of it.

"Go on. I meant for this to be a rest break, not a grand stage production."

She flinched as if he'd slapped her, and her gaze slid away. Aha. He had her.

"So one day," he continued for her, "you met the jackass in the garden, and his potential for violence became a reality, right? He threw you down, forced his oafish self upon you, and got you pregnant." He paused for effect. "How am I doing so far?"

A shudder ripped through her and she sank down on the boulder beside the stream. Clutching her elbows with her hands, she doubled over as if in pain. Slowly, she wagged her head from side to side. David's eyes narrowed slightly. Either he was underestimating her acting ability, or she was really having a rough time with this. He strongly suspected the former.

"No," she whispered, so low that he could barely hear her.

He hunkered down beside her and saw the tears hanging on her lashes. She kept her gaze fixed on the ground. He was familiar with that tactic. When people lied, they never wanted to look him in the eye.

"One afternoon, Moira was asked to prune the rosebushes in the garden and collect bouquets for the dining tables. He — he found her out there and mistook her for me. Moira knew I'd been meeting him. She'd never had a beau. She thought it would be fun to trick him into thinking she was me, like we had once done with the nuns. That afternoon —" Brianna put a hand to her throat. "Unlike me, my sweet sister didn't know how to dance away or tease him out of his sulk, so he dragged her into the conservatory and he —" She gulped. Her knuckles went white with the force of her grip on her skirt.

"He what?"

She shivered again, though the day wasn't cold. "Oh, God, can't you guess? He raped her. She fought him. He beat her and choked her and left her for dead."

Before he could speak, she rushed on. "You have to believe me, Mr. Paxton. I'm telling the truth. Daphne isn't your child. She isn't even *mine.*" The words were pouring out of her now. "The nuns pressed charges, but the boy came from a good family. It was his word against Moira's. He denied any wrongdoing, and his father, who believed him, hired a lawyer and prepared for a fight. The sisters tried to raise money to engage him in court, but they couldn't get their hands on enough. In the end, that young man got off scot-free.

"The sisters couldn't have a pregnant girl at the orphanage, not because they didn't love and want to support Moira, but because it would have made tongues wag. They had to think of the other children and the reputation of the institution. The homes for unwed mothers were full. Moira was sick right from the start, bleeding if she was on her feet for too long, so the nuns did everything they could to keep her with them so they could care for her. They got her on a waiting list at three homes for unmarried mothers, praying that an opening would come available before her condition began to show. It didn't happen, but still the sisters allowed her to stay, tucking her out of sight when ladies from the parish or other outsiders visited. I thought for a time that Moira might be able to have her baby there, but when she was about six months along, a deliveryman came unannounced, and his eyebrows went up when he saw Moira in the kitchen. He left the orphanage and immediately started blabbing his mouth.

"The sisters had no choice then. Tongues would wag, and they had to get Moira out of there. I understood but I couldn't let her go alone. I was the *strong* one. I was the *responsible* one. It was my fault. What happened to my sister was *my fault!*" She practically screamed the words, then caught herself, took a shaky breath, and continued in a more controlled voice. "The nuns gave us our things and all the personal money they had. Sadly, they take vows of poverty, and their small monthly stipends often don't cover their own needs. They promised us more the next month by unanimously voting to cut their food budget by going without breakfasts and lunches. Even so, we left with our clothing and little else. I was the only one who could work. I found a small room in a tenement building and turned my hand to any toil I could find to keep food in Moira's mouth."

David had heard enough. It was a touching story. Under other circumstances, he might have gone for the bait. But as convincing as Brianna had been, Daphne's physical appearance trumped her mother's acting ability. Her sweet little face. The birthmark. The slight frowns that pleated her forehead. Dear God, the girl was the very picture of his mother. He couldn't deny what his own eyes told him, damn it. The child was his.

He shifted his weight onto one bootheel.

The emotion that twisted Brianna's delicate features looked like grief, but it could just as well be guilt for piling lie upon lie.

"Ah," he said. "So the rest of this story is that poor little Moira died in childbirth. Right? And you have devoted all of your life since to being a saint, fabricating a make-believe husband, finding a position in Colorado, and raising her daughter as your own. That means Daphne isn't my child. She's the daughter of some nameless bully who can't be located to verify the story. Convenient. That lets me off the hook and gives you your out. Gotcha."

The next thing he knew, he lay sprawled in the damp sand. For a stunned instant, he couldn't think what had happened. Then, as his senses cleared, he realized she had slapped his face. Only *slap* didn't begin to describe the force she'd put behind the blow. Even hunkered down on his heels, it took a lot to throw David off balance, much less knock him flat.

Face still smarting, he rose to his feet and glared down at her. He couldn't quite believe she'd struck him with that much strength, and yet his scrambled brain told him that she had. Schooled from childhood not to hit back when he dealt with a female, David jammed his hands into his back pockets. Were there no limits to what this woman would dream up to get rid of him?

"Well, now, that's quite a right hook. Next time, double your fist, and maybe you'll give me a bit of a jolt."

Instead of retreating, she leaped to her feet, clutching a handful of sand and pebbles. She threw it at him, and her voice held a thread of hysteria under the wild anger that throbbed through it.

"Damn you to eternal *hell,* Mr. Paxton. I've told you the truth, a truth I've never told *anyone,* and every word was wrenched from my heart. Yet you stand there and *mock* me? A *curse* on you!" She actually swept up her right arm and pointed a rigid finger at his temple. "May God strike you dead!"

# CHAPTER TEN

Uncertain whether to laugh or kick dirt, David watched Brianna limp away. To calm his temper, he took a deep breath of the prairie air. The noon sunlight bore down on his fleeing bride, gilding her and the grassland in shimmering gold. In the bright light, her dark hair flashed fiery red. He could almost picture her in her Irish homeland, a youngster skipping over the moors, lighthearted, carefree, and lovely beyond measure. Sadly, he'd never seen her happy-go-lucky. She'd either been born with a dash too much vinegar in her veins, or life had kicked her in the teeth too many times.

Every step she took seemed to be a struggle. She obviously needed to use the liniment. But, oh, no, she was too stubborn by half — and a gifted liar, to boot. Disheartened, David crouched by the water. It wouldn't do for him to return to camp just yet. He couldn't trust himself to hold his tongue in front of Daphne.

The tale Brianna had just entertained him with was the most inventive she'd spun so far. He could believe that she and her sister had been raised in an orphanage. Well, it was a stretch, but he could reconcile it in his mind, at least. And he could have swallowed that her sister had died in childbirth, leaving Brianna to raise Daphne as her own. Shit like that happened. Hell, a variation thereof had occurred in his own family when his father had been wrongfully hanged, leaving Ace, the oldest boy, to support his mother and three half siblings, with Eden, yet another mouth to feed, on the way.

Where David dug in his heels with Brianna's story was Daphne's undeniable resemblance to him and his mother. He also found it difficult, if not impossible, to believe that she'd supposedly, quite by accident, chosen David Paxton as the name of her dreamed-up husband and placed him in Denver. *That* was completely incredible. David was a common name, but Paxton wasn't. No, sir, he didn't buy that little twist. It gave the word *coincidence* a whole new meaning.

He'd definitely done the deed with her and gotten her with child. So why did she so obstinately resist working out some kind of arrangement with him? She and the little girl had been living in penury. David offered her an escape from that. He'd also treated her kindly. Unlike a lot of men might, he hadn't tried to take liberties, as was his husbandly right. Most females would find that reassuring and come to respect him for it, if only a little. But not her. It seemed to him that the farther they got from Glory Ridge, the more panicky she became. Maybe her experiences with other males had been so horrific that she simply couldn't bring herself to take him at face value and accept the circumstances.

Well, he wasn't exactly happy about them, either. He could have stayed in No Name and married Hazel Wright, who at least found him pleasing and looked forward to spending her life with him. He'd said goodbye to that plan with only mild regret, and he'd stepped forward to shoulder his responsibilities. The least he deserved out of this unexpected union was a wife who bore him some measure of respect and affection. Granted, he'd made a bad mistake, and both Brianna and Daphne had suffered for it. But there wasn't a person alive who didn't mess up at some point, and at least he was trying to make amends. Why couldn't she see her way clear to do as he was, accepting the situation and trying to make the best of it for their daughter's sake? It wasn't as if he'd gotten himself a prize for a wife. Not only was she the human equivalent of a prickly pear, but she was also the most straitlaced female he'd ever come across. How could a man make headway with her? With his cheek still smarting from the slap of her hand, he wasn't even sure he wanted to try.

Brianna made it to her fire and sat gingerly beside it, locking her arms around her shaking knees. David Paxton was, hands down, the most infuriating man she'd ever met. He'd *mocked* her. Telling him the real story about Daphne's birth had been one of the hardest things she'd ever done. With every word, she'd felt as if her heart were being lacerated with sharp knives. How could he fail to believe her when she'd so obviously been telling him the truth? Even more humiliating, he'd cut her off short, rejecting her account with that sarcastic crack about devoting her life to Daphne and living like a saint. Oh, how she *hated* him. Maybe her curse would work, and God would send a lightning bolt from the sky to strike him dead.

Daphne stirred and got up from the pallet. When she dashed away to meet Paxton at the stream, Brianna couldn't gather the energy to call her back. The prairie wind caught her hair and whipped it across her eyes. She stared through the auburn blur, her shoulders leaden with defeat. She'd been so hopeful that Paxton was on the level, a misguided marshal with only good intentions. Ha! She wouldn't be foolish enough to skip down that merry path again. He'd just proven to her, beyond any reasonable doubt, that he was up to no good. *Misguided, my foot.* He knew precisely what he was doing. He'd come to Glory Ridge with a plan to gain control of Daphne. Now he had it, and all Brianna could do was pray that she got an opportunity to get her daughter away from him before he made his next move.

Brianna rested her chin on her knees to collect her composure and organize her thoughts. Her only hope lay in using her head and beating Paxton at his own game. In the book she'd read, it said slave traders usually worked in teams. Was that why Paxton was avoiding civilization, because he had arranged to meet his partners somewhere out here? Then what? Maybe his job had been only to procure and deliver Daphne, and he would be paid for his efforts when he handed her over to the other men, who would then transport her south.

Brianna's heart picked up speed. That made perfect sense, and Paxton's apparent lack of hurry played into that scenario. He planned to meet his cohorts to deliver the goods. She'd seen that wad of money in his pocket clip. Well, no honest marshal drew enough in monthly wages to carry around that much loot. Paxton was on the fiddle, no question about it. It was the only conclusion that made any sense. A man didn't get that rich by keeping the peace in a small town and raising a few scrawny cattle.

With a sickening squeeze of her stomach, Brianna decided she needed a plan, only she couldn't think of one. Maybe once the day waned and after Paxton fell asleep, she could quietly saddle a horse, collect Daphne and some food, and make a getaway. She had no idea which direction to go, but she'd worry about that when the time came. Until then, she would pray that Paxton's meeting with his partners wasn't to take place until tomorrow.

*But what if the assignation is scheduled for today?* The ham Brianna had eaten tried to come back up her throat. In that event, both she and Daphne would be in terrible danger. Brianna doubted that they would take the child and kill the mother simply to get her out of the way. At twenty-six, Brianna knew she was no longer young and fresh, but she was still a female and halfway acceptable in appearance. Perhaps it was Paxton's plan to sell her as well. Thinking of what the future might hold for her and Daphne increased Brianna's nausea. She held it at bay by glaring at David Paxton and wishing him dead.

David was jerked from his musings by the approach of his daughter. The wind snapped the skirt of her green play frock around her thin legs. Her white stockings were streaked with dirt and grass stains. She planted a tiny hand atop her head to anchor her ribbon, her flying hair shimmering around her like spun gold.

David dredged up a smile for her, determined to protect her from all the ugliness transpiring between him and her mother. "Hey, pumpkin, I thought you were sleeping."

She shrugged. "I wasn't tired." She thrust her fist at him. "Will you take our lucky penny for safekeeping? I'm afraid I might lose it when I'm asleep."

David tucked the coin into his shirt pocket. "When we get home, I'll drill a hole in it and get a chain from the jeweler. Then you'll be able to keep it all the time."

"It's half yours, so get a chain long enough for you to wear."

"Good idea. Every once in a while, I could do with a little luck."

Her brows drew together in a frown so reminiscent of his mother's that his heart caught. She nibbled her lip the same way Dory did when she was choosing her words carefully. "Papa, I have something of a delicate nature to discuss with you."

David's forced smile deepened into a real one. No other six-year-old he'd ever met talked quite the way Daphne did. He supposed it came from being around Brianna. The woman could wrap her tongue around a fence post and still waggle it at both ends.

"Shoot," he said.

Daphne's frown grew more pronounced. "I beg your pardon?"

David chuckled and hooked an arm around the child to pull her onto his knee. "Shoot," he repeated. "That means go ahead and spit it out."

Daphne still looked bewildered. "I've nothing in my mouth to spit out, Papa."

David rested his cheek against her flyaway curls. They felt as fine as silk against his jaw. "You've got words in there, don't you? Spit those out."

She giggled, burrowed closer, and hugged him. Her arms were a hair too short to encircle him, but it was still one of the best hugs he'd ever received. "I want to offer you something on loan," she said hesitantly, "but I'm afraid it will hurt your feelings."

It was David's turn to frown. "My feelings aren't all that easy to hurt, darlin'. Shoot."

He felt her lips curve against his shirt and knew she was smiling. "You talk funny, Papa. Are you aware of that?"

"Where I come from, I talk normal. You'll be the one who talks a little funny there."

"Truly? Will the other children tease me, do you think?"

David hoped not. He wasn't sure he'd be able to stop himself from knocking pint-size heads together. "Nope. By the time we get home, I'll have you trained to talk normal, just like me."

Daphne giggled again, then sighed. "Are you sure your feelings aren't easily hurt?"

"Positive. What is it you'd like to lend me?"

"My toothbrush. It's almost new, and we can take turns using it if we each wash it good when we're done."

David hadn't seen this one coming. A toothbrush? He owned one and used it morning and night. He tongued his front teeth to check and felt no film on his pearly whites. Did he have bad breath, maybe? "I have my own toothbrush, pumpkin. Thanks for offering me the use of yours, but I really don't need to take you up on it."

"Hmm." Her murmur was laced with concern. "If that's the case, then perhaps you should use yours more."

David tongued his teeth again. He'd eaten salad for dinner. Did he have greens caught between his chompers?

"It isn't that *I* think you need to. It's just — well, Mama says you have the filthiest mouth she's ever seen, and maybe she'll like you better if you brush more often."

It was all David could do not to snort with laughter. Brianna had been complaining about his filthy mouth, had she? His amusement flashed out. He'd made a special effort all morning not to use coarse language. He hadn't used his favorite phrase, *son of a bitch,* even once. What had he said now to get her bloomers all in a twist?

To Daphne, he said, "Thanks for the tip, pumpkin. From now on, I'll go after cleaning my teeth like I'm killing snakes."

"Up and down. That's the most efficient way to brush, according to Mama."

David had always brushed up and down, the way his own mother had taught him, but from now on, he'd go back and forth just to spite the woman.

Late that afternoon, as the sunlight began to wane, Brianna began keeping her eyes peeled for a large boulder near the stream they were following to use as a mounting block. She'd seen several earlier in the day and kept her fingers crossed that she'd see another one soon. How she meant to induce Paxton to camp by it, she didn't know. Given the tension between them, he'd probably find it highly suspect if she suddenly displayed friendliness or any level of enthusiasm. Ah, well, she'd think of something when the moment came.

Crossing one's fingers didn't work much better for her than praying had recently. Just as full dusk descended, Paxton brought his gelding to a sudden stop and said, "Low and behold, Daphne, do you see what I see?"

Brianna saw nothing to be excited about, but Paxton swung off his horse, lifted Daphne down, and led her to a patch of green growth at a bend in the stream. Dismounting with painful care, Brianna inched closer to see what the fuss was all about.

"Normally they haven't come up this early

in the year," she heard Paxton say. "This is one of the best times to eat them, when the shoots are young and tender." He turned to inform Brianna, "This is where we'll stop for the night. There's no way I'm passing up a spring crop of broadleaf cattails. They taste so good my eyes roll back in my head."

Brianna fixed an appalled stare on the vegetation. He meant to eat *cattails?* The man truly was a lunatic. Brianna didn't care if they were young, mature, or at any point in between. She absolutely would *not* eat them, and neither would her daughter.

Wheeling away, she scanned the area, praying fervently for a boulder. But of course there wasn't one. For the last two days, her formerly productive communication with God had somehow been cut off. He didn't seem to be hearing her anymore. Either that or he was answering her requests with an unequivocal no.

Like it or not, she was up the creek without a rock.

Brianna got a crazy urge to laugh at her twist on the phrase, but she feared she might never stop if she let loose with a single giggle. Instead of giving in to hysteria, she went in search of fuel for her fire, imploring God with every step. *Hello, God, are you up there? I'm in a world of trouble down here. We've been abducted by a mania-cal man who plans to sell my child to slave traders. This is no time to be turning a deaf ear. Do something. Please, do something.*

When she returned to camp, no bolt of lightning had zigzagged from the sky to strike Paxton dead. Judging by the heaping tin plate beside his blazing fire, he and Daphne had already washed what they'd collected over the afternoon and were now harvesting the cattail shoots. Their excitement suggested that they'd stumbled across countless gold nuggets. *Correction, wrong husband.* It had been her *pretend* spouse who'd had the gold fever. *This* fellow had a penchant for making his fortune the easy way, by stealing little girls for a handsome profit.

Panic mounting, Brianna forced herself to focus on meal preparation. If she failed to produce a halfway-edible supper, Daphne might stage a revolt and eat Paxton's offerings. The child had taken after Brianna in that way and had a rebellious streak, a cause for ceaseless worry. She didn't want her daughter to make the same mistakes she had. She tried to set a good example for Daphne by emulating Moira, who'd always been calm, ladylike, and absolutely proper. It made Brianna feel stifled sometimes, but for Daphne's sake she kept trying. A mutinous nature led to misfortune, disaster, and regrets that never dimmed. She was glad Daphne hadn't witnessed her lapse in behavior after dinner. Blast David Paxton, anyway. He brought out the worst in her.

Brianna shuddered as she passed his fire to dig through the packs in search of the spade. Cattails? Just the thought of biting into one made her want to gag. Once she found the dratted spade, she set herself to digging a pit. When Paxton spoke from behind her, she jumped as if she'd been stuck with a pin.

"I said I'd do that for you. Why the hell must you be so infernally stubborn?"

According to Sister Theresa, her middle name was stubborn. She glanced over her shoulder. He stood with his feet spread and his arms akimbo, the very picture of masculinity, prepared to overtake and subdue. The setting sun came from behind him, casting his face into shadow and veiling his eyes. She could see his jaw muscle ticking, though, which told her he was clenching his teeth. She hoped it gave him a toothache.

"I've managed on my own for years, sir. I see no reason to change my ways now."

"I'll give you a good one. You're so sore you can barely walk. Digging your own fire pit is silly. My ma would say you're cutting off your nose to spite your face."

"Your *ma* is not here. If she were, she'd wash your mouth out with soap." Not that Brianna believed he had a mother. Monsters like him hatched from rotten eggs. "Please, just leave me to it. I've had quite enough of your mocking humor for one day."

"My *what?*"

"Your *mockery.*" Brianna dug furiously with the spade. She glanced up to make sure Daphne was out of earshot. "I told you the truth — at no small cost to myself, I might add — and you *laughed* at me."

He swung to walk away. Over his shoulder, he said, "Lady, you wouldn't recognize the truth if it ran up and bit you on the ass."

Minutes later Daphne whined, cajoled, and pleaded until Brianna finally gave the child permission to partake of Mr. Paxton's rabbit stew. It smelled divine, and so far, their abductor had shown no ill effects from eating all the questionable fare. She remained by her own fire, assuring herself that she was entirely happy with burned ham, over-crisp bacon, a hunk of bread, and water. She stiffened when she saw Paxton saunter-ing over. He carried a tin bowl and cup. With a sigh, he hunkered down beside her.

"A peace offering," he said huskily. "At noon, during story hour, maybe I was a little too hard on you."

*Story hour?* She yearned to smack the bottom of the bowl and send hot stew all over him. As if he sensed her thoughts, he set the bowl of stew and the cup, brimming with aromatic coffee, on the ground between them.

"I've had time to mull it over all afternoon, and maybe I'm a bit too stuck on people always telling the truth." He rested his elbows on his bent knees, broad hands dangling. "I put you in a hell of a position seven years ago — and then there's the mess I've got you stuck in now. I never meant to herd you into a marriage." He shoved back his hat. In the feeble light coming from her fire, his eyes looked like liquid silver shot through with sunlight. "I've tried to think how you must feel, out here alone with a man you don't know. I think you're afraid half the time and frantic the other half. I need to get it fixed in my mind that anyone might lie in some situations — that it's not really a reflection of your character, but more something you're doing out of desperation."

Brianna couldn't argue. Desperate was precisely how she felt. His expression looked convincingly sincere, and oh, how she wished he were exactly what he pretended to be, a misguided man determined to do the right thing.

"Anyhow." He looked into the fire and chafed his hands. "I know nothing I say is likely to ease your mind. Truth is, you *are* stuck, and so am I. I have no doubt that Afton will record our marriage at the courthouse Monday morning, making it official. We can't undo that unless we get a divorce." His features tightened. "I'm willing to give you one, but first, for Daphne's sake, can't we at least try to make this work?"

Brianna studied his profile. As suspicious of him as she was — and God knew she had reason to be — he didn't appear to be lying. And if he wasn't, she had it all wrong.

"You don't have to decide tonight," he added. "Just rest assured that I have no intention of forcing myself on you, marriage or no marriage. I've never used my strength to have my way with a woman, and I sure as hell don't plan to start now." He fell silent for a second. "I know there's a lot about me to criticize, Shamrock. I'm no namby-pamby with fancy manners. My ma did her best to teach me right, but then I came to Colorado, lived with my brothers for a spell, got a spread, and most of my polish wore off. I still have a few good traits, though. I'm not inclined to be overly bossy. I slick up and go to church almost every Sunday. I don't make a habit of drinking too much, and when I gamble, I'm cautious with my bets. I think, if you'll give me a chance, you'll find me halfway tolerable. I have plenty of money to support you and Daphne. In addition to my wages as a marshal and the profits from my ranch, my brother Ace encouraged me to invest. He's sharp about stuff like that, and I've done well. You and my daughter will never want for anything within reason."

Brianna couldn't think what to say. He was either as innocent as a newborn babe, or he was the most accomplished liar she'd ever had the misfortune to meet.

"I'll leave you to chew on it," he said, pushing to his feet. "Don't be afraid to eat the stew. I ate it. That should be proof enough that there's nothing bad in it."

Brianna glanced down at the bowl. The aroma made her mouth water.

"I don't know how you like your coffee, but I'm thinking it's probably been a spell since you got to enjoy anything sweet, so I added two chunks of sugar. I hope it suits your fancy, and if you want more, make free. The pot will stay hot sitting at the edge of the fire. You can fill your cup as many times as you want, and I left the sugar out."

Tears burned in Brianna's eyes. She had an awful feeling that she might have misjudged this man and his intentions.

He started to walk away and then swung back. "Um, one more thing. Daphne approached me during our midday rest stop. She offered to lend me her toothbrush."

Brianna stiffened, bewildered for an instant, then swamped with dismay.

"She told me you say I've got a filthy mouth." He chuckled, swept off his hat, and smoothed a hand over his long, wind-tousled hair. "You've said the same straight to my face, so I knew right off you weren't complaining about my personal hygiene. Anyway, how about if we strike a bargain? You allow me my little bywords — shit, hell, and damn, stuff like that — and I'll do my best to leave off saying anything else you find offensive. Does that sound at all workable?"

Brianna's throat had gone so dry, her larynx felt as if it were stuck.

He held up a finger. "Ass, I forgot ass. I've got a bad habit of using that word. I'm going to kick one, or shove something up one, or — well, you probably already know it's one of my favorite expressions. I can try to break myself from using it, but quite honestly, I think I'd have more luck trying to pick a sliver out of a porcupine's tail."

Brianna found all of his cursing objectionable, but she was in no position to make stipulations. "I dislike having my daughter hear talk like that."

"Me, too." He slapped his hat back on his head, worried the grass with his bootheel, and then sighed. "I want her to grow up to be a fine lady." In the dimming light, it was difficult to read his expression. "I mean really fine, like her mama."

Brianna was trying to think how she could respond to such a stellar compliment when he added, "Your only real fault is that habit you've got of lying, right and left. It'd be real fine if you could work on correcting that. I've got a problem with dishonesty, and I think it's just as bad for Daphne to hear her mother spouting falsehoods as it is for her to hear me cussing." He rubbed his jaw. "You've also got a hair too much starch in your drawers to suit me, but I reckon I'll get used to that over time."

Brianna stifled a smile. She didn't know how he'd managed it, but he had her wanting to laugh. "Is there anything else you think I should work on, Mr. Paxton?"

His forehead creased in a frown. "Since

you asked, yes, there is one more thing. My brother brought me up to never strike a woman. In a marriage — or whatever the hell it is we've got going on here — I think that should go both ways. No hitting. If I make you mad, then spit, throw things, or express it with words. Don't take me on as if you're a man, because sooner or later, I might forget you're not."

Brianna could only vaguely recall that moment when she'd slapped him. His mockery of a truth that had been her greatest heartbreak for seven years had momentarily robbed her of good sense. "Point taken."

"Good." He shifted his weight from one leg to the other, his tan jeans hugging the flex of ironlike muscle in his thighs. Then he inclined his head, turned to walk away, and called back, "Real good."

After he left, Brianna took a sip of the coffee and nearly groaned with pleasure. Sugar had been a luxury she couldn't afford for far too long. She drank nearly half the cup before turning a dubious gaze on the bowl of stew. It probably had cattails and all manner of other horrid things in it. She wasn't a cow or goat, happy to eat any old sprig she came across in a field.

After long consideration, she decided she could spoon out bits of rabbit and enjoy those. But she found it impossible to get none of the juice with the meat, and the flavor was so divine, she was soon pressing her spoon against the surface to slurp it down. Then she accidentally got a bite of onion. From that moment, she was lost. She positioned the bowl just beneath her chin and scooped the concoction into her mouth, moaning low in her throat. Definitely onion, she decided, and little bits that tasted like pepper, and oh, sweet Lord, asparagus.

After she emptied the shallow bowl, she wondered if she'd just eaten cattail shoots. Then it occurred to her that she didn't care. The one thought prevalent in her mind was, *More.* She glanced toward Paxton's fire, which burned brightly only a few yards away. To her mortification, he was crouched at its opposite side, his face well-defined in the light, watching her with a suppressed smile.

He beckoned her over. "Come on, Shamrock. There's plenty. Help yourself."

Her pride tried to assert itself, but the needs of her body won out. She struggled to her feet and walked hesitantly toward his camp, knowing with every step that she was telling him he had won. Given their noon conversation, she half expected him to rub it in. Instead he patted the grass beside

Daphne, who sat with a bowl cradled on her lap and ate as if tomorrow might never come. Before Brianna could sink down onto the assigned spot, Paxton relieved her of the bowl and cup and filled each again. He handed her the stew and then broke sugar into the coffee, giving it a brisk stir before presenting it to her.

"Thank you," Brianna said.

Daphne grinned, her mouth ringed with stew juice. "Lay back your ears, Mama, and dig in."

Helping with supper cleanup was difficult for Brianna. Her abused posterior and legs protested with every movement, and her body, long deprived of enough food, now screamed for her to collapse like a well-fed pig to sleep. When all the dishes had been dried and stowed in the packs, Paxton positioned his saddle near his fire, spread a blanket, grabbed Brianna by the elbow, and steered her toward it.

"Sit," he commanded with a smile in his voice. "Lean back and let the saddle seat support your back. It's time for another story hour."

Brianna didn't miss his reference to her confession earlier that day, which he still believed was a pack of lies, but her abused limbs overcame her inclination to reject the more comfortable seating. Daphne perched on the blanket beside her, and David — oh, dear, it was becoming all too easy for her to think of him as David — stretched out on the ground at the opposite side of the leaping flames.

"I'm first," he said. "I got a story that'll flat raise goose bumps. My brother-in-law Matthew told it to me."

Brianna shot him a warning look, but he was busy positioning his elbow and propping his head on the heel of his hand. Chewing on a piece of grass, he said, "I reckon neither of you has heard of Ten Mile Creek. It's over in Oregon somewhere, probably not too far as a crow flies from where my sister Eden lives now with Matthew Coulter. Back when this occurred, it was still Oregon Territory and a fairly wild place."

He went on to tell a hair-raising tale about several men who'd gone hunting along Ten Mile Creek. All but one of them was never seen alive again. "Nobody will ever know what happened up there in that camp. When the hunters didn't return, searchers went out to find them. Their horses began acting up about a half mile away." He paused to take a sip of coffee. "Horses can sense things, and they knew what those men didn't, that something really *evil* was up there by that creek. The men tried to make the horses keep going, but they bucked and fought and refused to cooperate."

Brianna spoke up. "This sounds as if it may be a *scary* story, Mr. Paxton."

"Of course," he said with a wave of his hand. "What good is a campfire story if it isn't scary? Anyhow, the men finally left the horses behind and went up on foot. They were all brave fellows, and they knew the guys they were looking for were just as unflappable. So what they found in that camp made their hair stand on end. Every single man in that hunting party, with the exception of one, had apparently sat by the campfire, feeding it until they ran out of wood, terrified to leave. Their horses were gone. Each man held a gun at the ready, but every single one of them had stayed by that fire pit, long after their wood and food ran out. They were frozen in position, just as they'd died, staring off into the woods with expressions of stark terror on their faces, the forefingers of their right hands curled over the triggers of their rifles."

Daphne gasped. Brianna curled a comforting arm around her shoulders. It was a silly, made-up story. Brianna had no doubt of that. "Mr. Paxton, perhaps we should —"

"Anyhow, for reasons nobody will ever know, those men were so afraid to leave their camp that they just sat there and *died.*" He sat up and chewed solemnly on the blade of grass. "The searchers meant to bury their bodies, but as they worked, they got spooked. Really spooked. Before the job was finished, they took off running the half mile to their horses, only to find that their mounts had gotten the hell out of there and raced for home. They had to walk all the way back, and when they arrived, the sole survivor of the hunting party had staggered into town. He was babbling mad and his hair had turned snow-white. He died shortly thereafter — the doc couldn't figure out why — and that poor fellow, the only one to survive whatever was up there at Ten Mile Creek, was never able to tell anyone what happened. To this day, nobody can ride a horse up there. The animals buck and go crazy, sensing the evil in those woods."

Just then a coyote wailed in the darkness and Daphne leaped to her feet. Instead of going around the fire, she took a flying jump over it at Paxton, who was unprepared for the impact of her weight. He went over backward and then caught her to his chest.

"Hey, now," he said. "What's this? It was only a silly story. Haven't you ever sat around a fire at night and told scary tales?"

Daphne shuddered and pressed against him. Brianna, frozen in place on the opposite side of the fire, saw darkness seeping onto Paxton's tan trousers and realized with mounting dismay that her daughter had just wet herself and the man holding her.

"Well, Jesus H. Christ," he said.

So much for limiting himself to a few favorite bywords. Brianna struggled to gain her feet, fearful that the man would explode with temper. But instead of growing angry, he smiled with unmistakable chagrin, tightened his arms around the child, and rolled to sit up.

"Pumpkin," he said huskily, "that was only a story, you know. I don't think it ever really happened. Your uncle Matthew —"

"Who?" Daphne's voice was muffled against his shirt.

"Your uncle Matthew. He's married to your aunt Eden. That's another long story, and you don't even know who Aunt Eden is, but I guarantee that when you meet her you'll love her on the spot, and she'll love you."

Daphne remained stiff in his arms. "I never want to meet her if she lives near Ten Mile Creek!"

David laughed. Brianna, no longer fearing

his reaction, sank down again to brace her back against the saddle. Foolish man, telling a child such a hair-raising tale. Even so, she wanted to smile. It was just — well, so very like him to speak before he thought.

Brianna felt suddenly uncomfortable, not physically, but way deep down. This man confused her terribly, making her think he was a lowdown snake one second and then, as he was now, forcing her to wonder if he wasn't the kindest, most caring person she'd ever met. Did he deserve to wear that badge? Did the family members he referred to so easily actually exist? Did he really have an older brother who'd raised him up never to hit women and a mother who'd taught him better than to use coarse language?

Brianna didn't know. She no longer trusted her own instincts. This man had come into her life like a tornado. He even made her wonder if what Judge Afton had said had any merit — that the books she loved to read were filled with dated tripe.

After talking with Daphne, trying to soothe away her fear, David announced that it was time for them to wash. With a glance at Brianna, he said, "We'll rinse her things to dry by the fire tonight. But for now she'll need another dress and underclothes."

Muscles protesting, Brianna scrambled to

collect her daughter fresh clothing. She braced herself for the worst as she stumbled through the moon-silvery darkness to the stream, half expecting Paxton to be naked in the water with her child. But, no. He crouched fully clothed next to the stream, bathing Daphne. The prairie wind had an icy bite, so he made a quick job of it, and then wrapped the little girl in a blanket from his own bedroll. Clearly, he felt better able to withstand the damp than they could.

"We'll dress you by the fire. It's colder than hell out here, unfit for man or beast."

At camp, Brianna helped dry off her child and stuff her into fresh garments. Then Paxton found sticks, which he drove into the ground to fashion a makeshift clothes-line. Even after all that, Daphne still jerked every time a coyote howled.

Paxton announced that it was time to bring out his fiddle. Brianna had long since judged him to be "on the fiddle," but it had never once occurred to her that he might know how to play one. He removed the fragile instrument from its case. In the flickering light, the wood gleamed red and gold, as reflective as polished glass.

"That's a beautiful piece," she said.

"The front is spruce, the back and sides maple. It was my father's, and Ma passed it on to me. She claims I ruined her hearing as a boy while I was learning to play it."

Brianna had cringed more than once herself when one of the children struck a sour note on the orphanage violin. "I'm surprised you bring it into the wild."

"The case protects it, and music makes good company when I'm traveling alone."

He sat by the fire, making the slender bow dance over the strings, creating music that drowned out the sounds of the night. Daphne forgot to be afraid of the evils lurking in the darkness and danced around the flames, singing songs at the top of her lungs. When she grew weary, Brianna tucked her in. The fire was dying by then, so she softly bade Mr. Paxton good night and joined her daughter on the pallet.

Exhaustion blanked out her mind the moment she closed her eyes. Her last thought was to wonder if Paxton would bathe in the creek before changing into fresh clothes.

When Brianna awakened the next morning — right at the break of dawn this time, the sky streaked with breathtaking hues of rose — she found her daughter once again missing from the bed. She sat up with a start to see David hunkered by his fire, pouring a cup of coffee. When their gazes met, he indicated his bedroll with a jerk of his head. She peered through the gloom and saw her daughter curled up in his blankets.

"Coyotes," he called softly. "She got scared, I think."

Brianna struggled to her feet — and it was indeed a struggle. From her waist down, she felt as stiff as an old woman. When she reached his fire, the only source of warmth, he poured her some coffee and laced it with sugar. She accepted the offering, relishing the warmth of the tin in her hands and the slide of hot pleasure as she took a first sip.

"You make wonderful coffee."

"Ah." He smiled slightly. "Secret ingredient, taught to me by a wily old cowpoke. When it rolls to a full boil, you toss in a dash of salt."

She tasted no salt, but the brew was still superior to any she'd ever made. Studying him, she noted that his hair drifted in the breeze as if it were freshly washed, and the whiskers he'd sported last night had vanished to display a clean-shaven jaw just now sporting new nubs. He must have bathed last night after she fell asleep, she decided.

She yearned to sit on the grass and absorb the warmth of the fire, but when she glanced at the ground, her sore body discouraged her from making the attempt. Getting down there would hurt, and standing back up would be even worse.

He set aside his cup and left the fire. Moments later he returned with her blankets, folded to make a cushion, and relieved her of the coffee cup, which he set on the turf. Extending his hands, he said, "Grab hold and lean back. I promise a soft landing."

Brianna extended her arms. His fingers enfolded hers, the breadth of his hands encompassing the whole of hers. As she leaned her weight against him, she felt the ironlike anchor of his strength and had no fear that she might fall. He lowered her gently onto the thick fold of blankets.

"Ah," she said with a sigh. "This is lovely."

He bent to retrieve her coffee. As she accepted it, he said, "No work for you this morning. You're about played out. I'll take care of everything. Before we ride, I strongly suggest you give that liniment a try. It'll sting a bit right at first if you're rubbed raw in places, but that goes away pretty quick, and then it works its magic."

Brianna definitely needed a bit of magic before she could climb back on a horse. "I surrender, sir. At this point, I'm willing to try almost anything."

He chuckled and resumed his former position at the opposite side of the fire. After taking a sip of coffee, he said, "That child was scared senseless when she crawled in bed with me. Next time I start to tell one of my campfire stories, tell me to shut my damn mouth."

Brianna nearly choked on a mouthful of brew. She sputtered and waved a hand in front of her face. She saw that he was grinning — not sarcastically now, but with genuine humor.

"I've never been around a six-year-old as an adult," he confessed. "Little Ace, my brother's boy, is still only knee-high to a grasshopper. He can't sit still long enough to listen to a story, so I honestly didn't stop to think the one I told last night would frighten Daphne that bad." He shrugged. "It's a bunch of nonsense, that tale, with maybe a smidgen of truth tossed in. Us boys used to tell Eden spooky stories when she was still little, and she never reacted that way. I figured it'd add a touch of adventure to the evening."

"It certainly did accomplish that, sir."

"Yeah." He shook his head. Then he angled her a serious look from under the brim of his hat. "I'm going to need some help to be a decent daddy. I checked while giving her a bath, and much to my dismay, there are no instructions printed on her butt."

Brianna almost laughed. It wasn't often that she got the urge. "Right after she was first born, I felt exactly the same way, wishing she had come with an instruction booklet." In the early days, when Daphne had suffered with colic and cried incessantly, Brianna had been frantic more times than not. "Know-how comes with experience."

"Kind of like cooking over an open fire?"

He'd done it again, made her want to laugh. "Precisely."

"Well, I'll teach you if you'll return the favor."

He spoke as if they'd be raising Daphne together for many years to come. Brianna knew that wouldn't happen. He wasn't the child's father. But somehow, over the course of last night, she'd come to accept that he believed he was. "I still make my mistakes with her, but I'll share what knowledge I have."

"That'll do."

Just then, Daphne stirred awake. "Mama? Papa?"

Darling in her rumpled brown-and-gold dress, she scrambled up from bed, rubbing her eyes. Stumbling sleepily, she went to David. He held his coffee out to one side, sat cross-legged, and drew her onto his lap. "Good morning, Sunshine."

"Morning." Daphne snuggled against him, twisting her small fists in her eye sockets again. "I was scared last night. There were evil things out there in the dark, Mama."

"Coyotes aren't evil, pumpkin." David pressed a kiss to her tousled hair. "They're God's creatures, same as us. They were only singing to the moon."

"I didn't like their songs."

"Ah, well," he said. "We can't understand what they're saying, but they do. They were probably trying to find a rabbit for supper, and they were powwowing back and forth about how best to catch one."

Daphne yawned. "Do you think they got one?"

"I reckon so. Rabbits are plentiful here. Speaking of which, I need to go get us one for breakfast. Why don't you cuddle with your mama while I go see what I can find?"

Daphne came to sit beside Brianna, huddling close within the circle of her arm. As they watched David walk away, the child whispered, "Papa makes me feel safe. Does he make you feel that way, too?"

Yesterday Brianna would have shuddered at the question. This morning, she nuzzled

330

her daughter's hair and softly replied, "Yes,
I believe he does."

# CHAPTER ELEVEN

The second day on the trail went pretty much as the first one had except that Brianna used the liniment before mounting up, and after the first sting of it wore off, she felt considerably better. She declined to join Paxton and her daughter on their foraging expeditions, still too sore to get on and off her horse frequently, but from a distance she enjoyed their antics. Daphne squealed as if they'd just come across a priceless jewel when David pointed out a plant they might eat, and they returned from each jaunt with his hat partly filled with plunder from the prairie floor.

During their dinner stop, Brianna found that she was still wary of David, but not nearly so much as she had been. She gave up on building her own fire and instead helped cook over his. When their fingers accidentally touched, her heart did a funny little dance, and a tingling sensation shot up her arm. No man had ever elicited that re-action from her, and though she was at first puzzled by it, she soon came to accept that it was physical attraction. She'd heard women whisper and titter about how certain men made them feel, but for Brianna, it was a new experience.

Even so, her blood went cold when she caught David watching her with a gleam of interest in his eyes. During her short stint as a barmaid in Boston when Daphne was an infant, she'd learned firsthand how strong men were, and he was more muscular and solid than most. It made her intensely uneasy to think that he might go back on his word and decide to exercise his conjugal rights. She tried to stay close to Daphne during the rest break, convinced that only a completely unconscionable person would force his attentions upon a woman in the presence of a child.

She no longer considered escape to be an option. The farther they rode, the more harshly it was driven home to her that she lacked the know-how to survive out there. She and Daphne would wander in circles until they starved to death. When she thought back to that first night when she had tried to hire a horse, she was almost glad her plan had been foiled. Never mind that David had the look of a scoundrel. Thus far he'd proved himself to be a good man, and he'd been kindness itself to Daphne. Unless he suddenly showed her a different side to his nature, she had to gamble that she and the child were better off in his company than they would be on their own.

Shortly after they'd enjoyed their midday meal and gotten back on the horses, Brianna saw three riders on the horizon ahead of them. Paxton held up a hand to signal her to stop. Then he dismounted and carried Daphne back to her.

"She can sit with you for a spell. I'm going to ride out to meet them alone."

After settling Daphne on the bay in front of her, Brianna cupped a hand over her eyes and squinted into the distance. "Who are they, do you think?"

David ruffled Daphne's hair. "I have no idea, but when I'm out like this, I prefer to introduce myself to strangers when my favorite ladies are a safe distance back."

For an instant, Brianna recalled her fear that Paxton meant to meet his cohorts out here and hand Daphne over to them. Panic bubbled into her throat, but then she met his steady, deep blue gaze. He'd seemed so sincere last night and again by the fire this morning, projecting himself as a man who planned to deal fairly with her and wanted only to be a good father. She had been on an emotional seesaw since meeting him, thinking him to be a devil one moment, then questioning her own reasoning the next.

Calling upon her practical nature, which had always stood her in good stead, she elected to set her doubts aside. She had nothing to lose. If those men riding toward them were his partners, she and Daphne would be in terrible trouble no matter what she did. She needed to keep a clear head and put her faith in David. If he meant to betray her, then he might at least suffer a twinge of guilt afterward for breaking her trust.

David checked his Colts to be sure they were loaded, and then he drew his Henry rifle from the boot to do the same. He could feel the tension that rolled off Brianna. Well, he didn't want to alarm her, but better that than to get caught with his guard down.

He almost mounted back up, but something, a feeling deep in his guts that defied explanation, suddenly made him decide against it. Brianna would have a far better chance of getting away and finding a town if she was on trusty old Blue.

Retracing his steps to the bay, he said. "Brianna, I want you to switch horses." He pointed to a nearby rock. "Use that as your mounting block. Put Daphne on his back first, then you get on behind her."

"But *why?* Blue is your mount."

Again, David felt reluctant to frighten her or the child, but she needed to do as he said. "You'll be better off on him if we get separated. Lucy's tethered to his saddle, so you'll have all the supplies with you." He glanced at Daphne. "It's just a precaution in case those fellows get any shady notions into their heads. Most likely, they won't."

He handed Brianna the Henry. Her lips went as white as sun-bleached bed linen. "I haven't a clue how to use this."

"You'll figure it out right quick." He smiled for Daphne's sake. The child's eyes had gone round with alarm. "I'm going to mosey ahead on foot to meet them. Keep an eye out. They're probably friendly fellows, but if not —" He broke off without finishing, but he saw in Brianna's eyes that she understood. "No worries," he added. "I'll be right back. If something happens, go and just keep going. Leave the bay behind, and I'll catch up with you. Okay?"

She nodded, her green eyes clinging to his. "All right."

"Once you get well away, give Blue his head and tell him to take you home. He'll make a beeline for No Name, but in the doing, he'll come across railroad tracks. When he does, follow them. They'll lead you into a town." He jerked a thumb over his shoulder at the roan. "Our marriage document is in the saddlebag along with plenty of money. Book passage on the train to Denver. Make sure the animals are comfortable in a stock car. When you get there, you'll find contact information and a telephone number for my brother Ace in the same bag. He's a good man, and you can trust him. If you've never used a telephone, somebody in Denver will show you how. Tell Ace you're my wife, and he'll send a couple of railcars to pick up you and the animals."

David yearned to tell her more — first and foremost that she'd need to ride for a goodly distance before she relaxed, and even then she'd need to keep looking over her shoulder, but he had to think of how his warnings might impact the child. He'd also run out of time. The men were closing in at a fairly quick pace.

As he turned to meet the oncoming riders, Brianna called out, "Be careful, David."

He spun to walk backward a moment. "I'm always careful. Hurry up and switch horses, Shamrock. I want you ready, just in case."

David's guts squeezed when he'd walked far enough to get a good look at the men. He'd been right to be cautious. They were a rough-looking trio. He hoped Brianna was on Blue and prepared to bolt. This could get ugly. He felt sure he could take three fast guns, but he also knew more than one man had gone to meet his Maker thinking that.

The riders drew up twenty feet away, taking close measure of David as he stepped off another five feet to get within talking range. One was a huge man in bloodstained leathers that stank so badly David's nostrils burned. The other two wore ordinary garb, equally filthy and streaked with crimson gone dark with time. Maybe they had skinned and gutted an animal, but David suspected their victim or victims had been the two-legged variety. They were bearded and yellow toothed, their eyes as hard and shiny as wet agates. Each was well armed, with rifles and side shooters. He knew their kind, ne'er-do-wells who'd sell their sisters for two bits and slit their mothers' throats for a dollar.

"Howdy," he said, trying to muster a friendly tone.

All three men looked behind him at the woman and little girl. The big lout in leather licked his lips. A tingle of warning shot up David's spine. He weighed his chances and decided he'd dive and roll if this went south. His only hope was to become a moving target and count on his Colts to do the rest. Ace had made him practice with six-shooters for hours, and David knew he was accurate and lightning fast — no brag, just fact. They might take him, but at least two of them would go down in the attempt.

"I don't want any trouble," he said. "I'm just passing through with my family." He flipped back the tails of his duster so they could see his badge and his guns. "Name's David Paxton, marshal of No Name."

He saw each man study his stance, and then they looked him dead in the eye. A man showed his colors when visual contact was made. If David blinked or acted nervous, they'd figure him to be an easy mark. With long practice, he had learned to keep his gaze steady and his body relaxed. A gunman with any sense realized then that he wouldn't give up without a fight. Men like these, seasoned to violence though they were, usually had a yellow streak. If they decided he could take at least two of them out before he went down, they might ride on and toss the dice another day.

"We ain't lookin' for no trouble, neither," the big guy said. He gave Brianna another long stare. "Mighty fine-lookin' woman you got there. Mighty fine."

David saw no point in denying the obvious. "Yep, and any man with a wife that fine doesn't hesitate to put his life on the line to protect her."

The hulky one, apparently the leader of the group, leaned sideways to spit in the dirt next to his sorrel's front hooves. "No need for that. Like I said, we don't want trouble."

David turned as the men nudged their horses forward. "Cut my family a wide berth. I've got an itchy trigger finger."

They nodded and crossed the narrow stream to ride in a broad circle to the south. David stared after them until they disappeared over the rise, which happened pretty fast. Then he strode back to where Brianna waited with Daphne on Blue.

"Is all well?" she asked.

Concern filled David when he saw that she had tears in her eyes. As for her question, he couldn't answer with any certainty. Those lowlife bastards had made his skin crawl. He also knew the prairie and had seen a whole herd of bison suddenly appear out of nowhere. Three men could just as easily remain hidden to stage an ambush. Brianna wasn't an accomplished rider yet, but she'd managed to keep her seat for the last two days. He decided to let Daphne remain with her on Blue.

"You can put the rifle back in the boot for now. If you need it later, it'll be handy there. I'll take the lead and ride the bay."

"You don't want Blue back?"

David didn't want Daphne to be in a dither all afternoon so he kept his response short. "What I said earlier still stands. I prefer that you stay on Blue."

The remaining color in her face drained away. She studied the horizon. "Whatever you say. You'd be better with the rifle, though, in case it's needed."

David wanted to keep his hands free, and there was no boot on the bay's saddle. Besides, if those no-accounts came back and she had to make a run for it, she'd require a weapon to protect herself and the child. "You keep it. I'll have no way to carry it."

David mounted the bay. He was concerned about letting Daphne ride double with someone as inexperienced as Brianna, but if those sourdoughs came barreling at them from out of nowhere, he'd be hard put to fight them off with a child in his arms. Not to mention that David had a bad feeling the polecats would be aiming for him, not the females. He didn't want his daughter to be caught in the line of fire.

Brianna accepted his decision without protest, but David saw the doubtful look in her eyes. He had to leave her wondering. If he spelled out his concerns, Daphne would be frightened all afternoon. For a long moment, they just locked gazes, then David clicked his tongue to the bay, determined to cover as much ground as possible before the light waned. He heard the clip of Blue's hooves fall in behind him and bit back a grim smile. His Shamrock had the makings to be a fine life partner — as smart as a whip, with twice the bite if you crossed her. She'd be a good woman to have at his back once he taught her how to shoot that Henry and hit her target.

Brianna caught herself squeezing her arm too tightly around Daphne. David rode just ahead of her now, Lucy bringing up the rear. She was acutely conscious of the rifle in the boot just behind her right hip. She stared at David's broad back. At this distance, even a novice with guns would be unlikely to miss such a large target. Surely he realized that, yet he'd insisted she keep the weapon.

If she lived to be ninety, she'd never forget that moment when he'd left her in charge of the horses, the mule, and all his possessions. He'd given her the opportunity to run. She could have left him afoot and unable to give chase. He wasn't a stupid man. He must have considered that possibility. Yet he'd put his faith in her, not because she'd done a thing to deserve it, but because he'd been willing to die to keep her and Daphne safe. No woman with good sense could fail to be touched by that.

Brianna also felt deeply ashamed. She had been suspicious of this man at every turn, thinking the very worst of him. And all the while, he'd been a fine man with good intentions who simply had his facts all wrong. She wouldn't be forgetting that anytime soon. Maybe she hadn't earned his trust, but he'd definitely earned hers.

"Are those bad men going to come back and try to hurt us, Mama?"

Daphne's voice was little more than a squeak, a telltale sign of how scared she was. Brianna gave her a quick hug. "You have nothing to worry about, little miss. Papa will keep us safe." With a start, Brianna re-

343

alized she'd just referred to David as the child's father, something she'd tried to avoid doing the entire trip. For reasons beyond her, it felt right. "He's a marshal. I think he's fast with those guns and knows how to handle bad men. We both need to remember that and do exactly what he tells us if anything happens, all right? No questions, no arguments. Will you promise to do that?"

"I promise," Daphne replied, her voice a bit stronger. "But what about you, Mama? You haven't minded him very good so far."

"Don't you worry about me. From now on, when he says jump, I'll ask how high."

Daphne giggled. "Papa will be very surprised!"

Keeping his eyes peeled, David settled back in the saddle, hoping against hope that they'd seen the last of those slime suckers. But a prickle at the back of his neck told him otherwise. He couldn't explain it. It was just something he felt — as if the air around him was fraught with lightning that might strike at any moment. He scanned the horizon as he rode and kept a sharp watch on the bay's ears. Horses had monocular vision — blind directly ahead but with a clear view off to the sides as far back as their rear haunches. If the gelding caught movement, he'd give a sign. David just hoped all that came near them were prairie creatures, not three ruffians in bloodstained clothing.

David still felt itchy as the sun started to set. He picked a camp spot by the stream, making sure there were rocks for Brianna to use as mounting blocks in case she needed them. He considered leaving Blue saddled and Lucy bearing the weight of the packs so Brianna could make a quick getaway. In the end, though, common sense won out. If those bushwhackers circled back, there would be no time for her to reach a horse. And the animals had worked all day and deserved a rest. Otherwise, they'd be played out tomorrow. David hated to make them suffer simply because he had a hunch there might be trouble.

He began doing the tasks that came habitually, thinking about what to fix for supper as he cared for the animals and then led them to the stream for a well-deserved drink. No hobbling them, not tonight. He'd already checked the species of grass and plants that grew nearby and had seen nothing poisonous. Better to merely ground tie the horses and mule so they'd be able to run if anything happened. David had seen some gorgeous horseflesh gunned down during a fracas, and he didn't want Blue or Lucy to get hurt. Not the bay, either, so far as that went. He was proving to be a good old boy.

Supper posed a problem. Normally David went out about this time to get a rabbit, but he was reluctant to fire a weapon. The sound could travel, and if those scoundrels were out there, doing their damnedest to track him, a shot might bring them into camp. All afternoon, he had ridden in a zigzag, crossing the stream and circling out, then angling back to the opposite side. Unless those yahoos were fine trackers, they'd play hell following him on grassland. On the other hand, if they were halfway smart — and he had a feeling the big fellow might be — they'd figure he'd stay near water unless he had headed west to reach a town. David hoped they decided he'd done the latter, because he didn't have the heart to put a woman and child through the rigors of a dry camp.

As for the evening meal, he had bacon in the packs, and Brianna had brought ham. They'd fare well enough with that and the plants he and Daphne had found that morning.

When he walked back up from the stream, he saw that Brianna had already gathered tinder for a fire and was working with the spade to dig a pit. She was sore to the bone, but she was still doing all she could. The lady definitely had what it took to be a Paxton. His clan cut a high standard, but she had it in her to meet or exceed it.

He hunkered beside her to take the implement from her hands. "We need to talk," he told her softly. "Preferably out of Daphne's earshot."

Daphne joined them at the half-dug hole. "Papa, shall we wash our vegetables? We found quite a few this morning before you stopped searching."

David had been too edgy that afternoon to keep an eye out for anything but two-legged predators. "We'll do that here in a bit, pumpkin. First let me get a fire going. I think your mama could do with a hot cup of coffee laced with lots of sugar."

While he finished digging the pit and coaxed the flames to life, he was unable to shake the feeling that those lowlifes were somewhere close, maybe even watching them. He didn't want to say anything that might scare Daphne, so as soon as the coffee was on, he took her to the stream to wash their vegetables. Once back at the fire, he assigned her the job of putting them into the pot to boil.

"I've never done the cooking part."

"You've watched me. I think you're ready." David got her the salt. "Don't add too much, now, and you need to stir constantly." Stirring steadily wasn't necessary, but he wanted to keep her busy while he laid out the hard facts to her mother. He handed the child a long-handled wooden spoon. "We don't want our vegetables to scorch, now, do we?"

Her small face solemn, Daphne said, "I'm a good stirrer. I won't let them burn."

"Mind your cloak and skirt," David told her. "Keep them tucked under your knees so they don't flutter up into the flames."

Daphne anchored her clothing. David nodded in approval. "While you're cooking supper, your mama and me are going for a short walk." He pointed. "We'll be over behind the elder and boulder, within hollering distance if you need us."

As recently as this morning, Brianna would have felt uneasy going off alone with David out of Daphne's line of sight, but the events of the day had convinced her that he was an honorable man. When those miscreants had appeared on the horizon, he'd put his life on the line to protect her and the child. His actions had spoken more loudly than a million words.

Her nerves prickled as she and David stepped behind the boulder, but she knew that feeling was due to her experiences with other men and had nothing to do with David Paxton. She turned with her back to the rock and foliage. He stepped around to face her, his burnished features drawn into an expression grim with worry. Placing his hands on his hips, the tails of his duster hooked back over his wrists, he sighed and searched her face. Then, without preamble, he said, "My gut tells me they may come in on us tonight. I need to know you'll sleep with an ear cocked and one eye open. We also need to huddle up. If anything happens, I don't want you and Daphne between me and them."

Fear trickled like ice down Brianna's spine. "Wh-what do you think they want? If it's money and valuables, can't we just hand them over and be done with this?"

David toed the grass. When he glanced back up, he shook his head. "They'll take the money and valuables after they finish me, but I don't think that's all they want."

"What, then?" Brianna's first thought was Daphne, and the possibility that those horrible men might get their hands on the child made her blood go cold.

"You," he said softly.

Brianna jerked taut. *"Me?"* She knew some men found her attractive, but she'd been so focused on Daphne's safety that she'd only fleetingly considered the dangers to herself.

He arched a tawny eyebrow. "Shamrock, this may come as a big shock to you, but you're a fine figure of a woman. Any man would want you." He held up a hand. "That doesn't mean a sane man will act on it. You're in no danger from me."

Brianna already knew that, and the assurance was no longer necessary.

"That big fellow — well, he had his eye on you. To him, at least, you're the main attraction. Daphne will be a bonus. She's worth a lot of money in certain circles."

"Down in Mexico?"

His mouth twisted in a ghost of a smile. "Mexico doesn't have a corner on evil, Shamrock. There are men everywhere who have a sick liking for little girls. Only a few, mind you."

Brianna shivered even in the heavy jacket. She cared about what might happen to herself, of course, but her main concern was still Daphne's safety. "What — what'll we do?"

"If there's trouble, you won't have time to reach a horse. I'll keep their attention on

350

me. I want you to stay out of my line of fire, grab Daphne, and run like hell. Go as far as you can. When you get tired, slow to a walk, but keep going until your legs give out. Carry her if you must. Unless they're good trackers, they won't find you. The grasslands will help hide your footprints. Come sunup, head north. Eventually you'll come to a railroad track." From his trouser pocket, he drew the wad of money she'd been so impressed by that first night. "There's plenty here for train fare and food when you reach a town." He tucked the cash into her hand. "Once you reach Denver, find the sheriff and tell him you're Ace Keegan's sister-in-law. He'll help you contact him."

"Ace *Keegan?*" Brianna's mind tripped on the surname. "*The* Ace Keegan?"

"He's a fine man. You can trust him."

*"Papa!"*

The child's cry, laced with urgency, brought Brianna spinning around. David caught her arm and held her back. "Stay here. If there's trouble, I'll send her to you."

David took off for camp, only a stone's throw away. Brianna stepped out from behind the scraggly tree and boulder, searching for her daughter. What she saw nearly made her heart stop. Those men had ridden into camp, and their horses were hemming Daphne in at the fire. David drew to a halt on the opposite side of the flames, spread his feet, and flipped back his duster, his hands hovering just above the butts of his revolvers.

"Daphne, go to your mama," he ordered.

With a frightened yip, Daphne skirted the fire and came barreling toward the rock. When the child reached Brianna, they grabbed hands and turned to flee. The prairie, blanketed with the gray of twilight, stretched before Brianna like a yawning mouth. *Run like hell,* David had said. Clutching her skirt in one hand, she lurched forward, pulling Daphne behind her. *Run. Don't slow down.*

Brianna did precisely what David had told her. Legs scissoring, her pulse hammering like a sledge, she raced across the grassland, her feet hitting the ground with such force that she felt her teeth snapping. Daphne, shorter of leg, was a weight at the end of Brianna's arm, which she held extended behind her.

"Hurry, dear heart. Show me how fast you can run!"

Daphne picked up speed. To Brianna's terrified gaze, the earth passed beneath them in a dizzying blur. Her lungs started to burn. She felt Daphne's pace slow, and then she began to lag behind. Then, without warning, the child caught her toe on something and pitched forward into a headlong sprawl, breaking Brianna's grip on her hand. *Carry her if you have to.* There was no time to see whether Daphne was hurt. No time even to think. She clutched her daughter in her arms and ran as if the devil were at her heels.

# CHAPTER TWELVE

Legs churning to cover ground, Brianna struggled to keep the sobbing child in her arms and realized with a skip of her heart that she'd lost her bearings. She stumbled to a stop. Had she been running that way? Or had it been *that* way? With no time to spare, she turned in the direction that felt right and broke into a lope. *Go until your legs give out.* The wad of money in her skirt pocket weighed next to nothing, but it felt like a ten-pound weight. David wouldn't have given it to her if he'd believed he was going to remain alive to escort them to No Name.

As Brianna ran, every word he'd said in those last few seconds became scored onto her brain. He'd known he might die, but even so, his only concern had been for her and their daughter. *Their* daughter? Oh, God. He'd walked out to face death, protecting a little girl who wasn't even his.

Remembering the tender gruffness of his voice and the look on his face made Brianna go blind with tears. *Shamrock.* She'd hated that nickname. Now she sent up frantic prayers that he'd live to nettle her with it again.

Daphne grew heavier, making Brianna's arms quiver and cramp. Worse, trying to run carrying the extra weight was exhausting her. Her breathing became labored, her lungs hitching. A stitch pierced her side. It became harder and harder to lift her feet.

Brianna's legs gave out. David had told her to run as long as she could and then slow to a walk, but as she staggered to a stop near a rock, she was so exhausted and winded that she couldn't take another step. He'd said to head north come dawn, but what if it was overcast? Without the sun clearly visible, she might go too far east or west and wander around on the prairie until they perished. Grabbing for breath, she stood there, arms trembling to support Daphne. The child was sobbing, her tears wetting the jacket. In that moment, Brianna had no energy left to kiss scraped shins or elbows. She had no more strength, period. The thought barely filtered through her mind before she crashed to her knees. With Daphne's added weight, her landing was hard, but the sharp, bone-bruising pain seemed dim, hovering just beyond the edges of her panic.

Just then, the rock exploded, its jagged top splintering like glass, pieces going in all directions. Something hit her at the corner of her eye. Then, a fraction of a second later, a gunshot rent the air. *That isn't right.* The report was supposed to ring out before the bullet struck. Or was it the other way around? Her thoughts swam. She felt as if a horse had kicked her in the head. Then, as if her brain were a pot of soup that had just been briskly stirred, the eddy of confusion began to slow, allowing her to think — if not clearly, at least in fits and starts.

*Down,* she needed to get down. She blinked, got her vision back into focus, and caught a glimpse of something bright yellow in the deepening shadows. *The fire.* Oh, dear God. She'd lost her bearings when Daphne fell, and now they were back near the camp. She was kneeling in plain sight, and Daphne was wailing and blubbering.

She dove to the ground, using the stone as protection as she shielded the child with her body. "Shush, baby, shush," Brianna whispered frantically, tapping her fingertips against the little girl's wet lips. "Those men — they'll hear you. Quiet, quiet!"

More gunfire erupted, cutting through the prairie gloaming with stutters of silence between the reports. *Oh, God, oh, God, oh, God.* David had ordered her to run, and she had, but somehow, she had circled back. If she stood up right now, they'd see her.

*They.* Those horrible creatures. There was no way David could come out of this alive, not when he was up against three gunmen. The shooting stopped. Brianna held her breath, hoping to hear another exchange, but the prairie had gone deathly quiet. Even the wind seemed to hold its breath. Brianna clamped a hand over the nape of Daphne's neck, warning her without words to stay low and not lift her head.

Straining her ears for the sound of voices, Brianna heard nothing except the frightened whicker of a horse somewhere in the distance. She guessed that the animals had fled when the fight started. *David.* If he was dead, she and Daphne were on their own, and soon those awful men would sweep out from camp, searching for them. Horror chilled her skin. This close to the fire, she didn't dare dash for safety. They would spot her and Daphne right away. Her only hope was to wait for full darkness.

It seemed as if an eternity passed. Occasionally she thought she heard movement in camp, but she couldn't be sure. The twilight had deepened to charcoal gray. In a few more minutes, the cover of night would descend to give her and Daphne an opportunity to run again. She waited, afraid to even take a deep breath for fear they would hear her. Daphne whimpered. Brianna clamped a hand over the child's mouth.

*A footstep.* Brianna tensed, her pulse slamming, certain she'd heard something. And then it came again — the soft, almost imperceptible chink of a boot spur. She shrank closer to the ground, terrified to look over the rock to see how close he was. *Be quiet, Daphne, please, please be quiet.* Had only one of them survived? If all three were alive, they'd be out here in force, sifting through every blade of grass. A picture of David's face swam in her mind. Oh, how she regretted now that she hadn't realized sooner what a good fellow he actually was. In that moment, she would have given almost anything to hear his voice, even if he was cursing.

"Son of a *bitch!*" A hand closed over Brianna's right arm, and she was jerked to her feet as if she weighed no more than a feather. "I told you to *run,* God damn it! As fast as you could go and as far as you could go! And I find you hiding only a few feet from camp!"

Brianna, about to let fly with both fists, went limp. *"David?"* she whispered incredulously. "You're *alive?* Oh, thank God!" She threw her arms around his neck. "Oh, thank God. David! I thought sure they'd killed you."

He grasped her by the shoulders and held her at arm's length. "Don't you *David* me!" He gave her a shake that rattled her teeth. "You willful, stubborn, *ungrateful* little brat!"

The next instant, his hand closed around her wrist, as relentless as an iron manacle, and she was jerked half off her feet as he turned back toward camp. "Daphne, come along," he barked.

Brianna's foot tangled in something in the dark. David caught her from falling and drew her abreast of him. "You — you have this all wrong!" she cried.

"Shut up!" There was a snarl in his voice. Even in the dim light, she could see that his lips were peeled back, stretched thin over his white teeth. "Don't test my temper right now. I've a good mind to turn you over my knee and give you such an ass warming, you won't be able to sit for a week!"

Still wailing, Daphne ran ahead of them toward the fire. Brianna was relieved to see that the child seemed to be unharmed. Unfortunately, it was the only thing she could be glad about. In a temper, David Paxton was a fearsome man. She wanted to explain to him what had happened, but she was afraid to say another word.

When they reached camp, he pushed her, none too gently, down onto a rock. Then he loomed over her, one forefinger rigidly extended to punctuate every word he blasted her with. "You *deliberately* disobeyed me! I walked in here, willing to die so you and Daphne would have a chance to run, damn it! And instead you stayed within throwing distance, putting not only your own life at risk, but my daughter's as well! Do you have any idea what those bastards would have done to both of you? *Do you?* If I hadn't prevailed, the party would just now be starting." He jabbed his finger at Brianna's nose. "And *you,* my fine, high-minded lady, would be the main source of entertainment!"

Daphne, who had finally stopped crying, tried to interrupt. "Papa?"

"Not right now, Daphne," David snapped. "This is between me and your mother. Go check the damned vegetables to see if they scorched."

"But, Papa, she's *hurt!*"

"I don't care if she's —" David broke off and grabbed Brianna by the chin, moving slightly to one side so his shadow, cast by the fire behind him, no longer hindered his view. "Oh, shit." He went down hard on one knee. "Oh, *shit!* Were you hit?"

Brianna remembered something striking her at the corner of her eye and started to reach up to investigate. He grabbed her wrist. "Don't touch it. If there's lead lodged in your skull, you might push it deeper."

She could feel him trembling, which was altogether frightening. "I think it was a piece of rock, not a bullet."

"Rock?"

Daphne broke in with, "The rock in front of us blew up, Papa."

David hauled Brianna back to her feet, encircled her waist with one arm, and half carried her closer to the fire. As he deposited her carefully on the grass, he said to Daphne, "Toss on some more tinder, pumpkin. I need better light."

As the flames flared, he tilted Brianna's face to examine her injury. The next thing she knew, he pulled his knife from the sheath that rode on his trouser belt. She flinched away. "Rest easy," he told her. "I've got to sterilize it first." He thrust the blade into the coals. "Daphne, can you get another pot out of the packs and run get me some water?"

While he wasn't looking, Brianna carefully fingered the wound. The flesh around it felt tender and ached dreadfully, but she discovered nothing sharp. Her hand came away covered with blood. "It's only a cut, David. A piece of rock flew up and got me."

He turned, saw her crimson-streaked fingers, and clenched his jaw muscle. "Will you *ever* do as I say? I told you not to touch it!"

"It's my face. I guess I know if there's a bullet in it or not. And I *tried* to do as you said. It's not my fault nobody ever taught me my directions."

He slanted a burning look at her. "What do you mean, your directions?"

"North, south, east, and west — *those* directions. All I know is right and left, unless you count forward and behind."

His stony expression turned incredulous. "Right and left?"

Brianna flung out her arm. "That is right." She flung out her other arm. "And *that* is left. It's useful enough knowledge, I suppose, but it isn't much help out on the prairie."

As sharp as finely honed blades in the flickering light, his blue eyes pierced hers.

"I ran, just as you said, truly I did. But then Daphne fell and rolled. By the time I managed to pick her up, I'd gotten turned around. I wasn't sure which direction I'd been going, so I did an eenie-meenie-minie-moe."

"Jesus H. Christ."

Brianna saw Daphne returning from the creek. Now that he seemed to have control of his temper, she dared to say, "Mind your tongue, sir."

David drew his knife from the fire. The metal glowed red-hot.

"You'll *not* touch my face with that thing, either. All I need is a bit of cleaning up."

He waved the blade to cool it. Daphne set the pot on the fire, then hunkered with her skirt and cloak tails drawn over her knees, minding David's warning not to let the cloth flutter into the flames. "Where are those men, Papa? Did you scare them away?"

David studied the cooling knife blade. "Let's just say they made a bad choice and soon saw the error of their ways."

Brianna had all but forgotten the other men. She glanced uneasily around. The recently fueled fire cast its light afar. She saw what looked like blood on the grass in several places, and there were also drag marks in the earth, leading off to a small copse of brush about fifty feet away. Had David killed all three men and then hidden their bodies so Daphne wouldn't see them? Or had the ne'er-do-wells run for their lives? Their horses were gone. But, then, Blue, Lucy, and the bay weren't there, either.

"Did you give them what for and whip them, right and proper?" Daphne asked.

Brianna waited for David to speak. He'd stood strong against three armed men and had every right to brag a little. Instead, he said, "Sometimes trouble comes calling. You don't invite it, and you try to avoid it, but it comes anyway. When that happens, you do what you have to do, and if you're real lucky and God is watching out for you, you live to feel sad about it, and then try to put it behind you."

"Are you feeling sad, Papa?"

David settled a warm gaze on the child. "Heck, no! I'm feeling very glad that all of us are safe. I think it calls for a party."

"It's fortunate that you have our penny in your pocket. I bet that's why you won."

That stupid penny again. Brianna wanted to tell Daphne that it had been God, not the coin, that had kept David safe, but she didn't want to stir that hornet's nest again.

David reached inside his duster to rest his

hand over his shirt pocket. "By Jove, you're right, pumpkin. Maybe our lucky penny helped save the day."

"For certain sure," Daphne cried. "It's the luckiest penny *ever.*"

"Did our vegetables scorch?" he asked.

Daphne looked in the pot and beamed a grin at him. "Nope. The water almost cooked away, and I think they're way too done, but they didn't burn."

"Well, then, after we get your mama's face doctored, we'll have ourselves a meal fit for royalty. I'm a fair hand at making corn cakes over the fire, and we've got plenty of sugar to spare. You ever had corn cakes drizzled with syrup?"

"Not for a very long time."

"Well, it's on the menu tonight."

"Yum!" Daphne exclaimed, the fate of the men forgotten. "Where's the cornmeal? I'll run get it."

David told her which pack it was in. As the child ran off, he shifted in his crouch and slipped the cooled knife back into its sheath. "I'm sorry I lost my temper like that," he said softly. "It's one of my worst faults, yelling and getting mad when I get a bad scare."

What Brianna found utterly amazing was that she'd never once feared he might strike her with his fists. She'd worried momentarily about the future of her backside, of course, but in her experience, a paddling could be survived with only a bit of soreness. Being knocked flat — having a man's hard knuckles connect with her cheek — well, that was quite another thing, and she never wanted to live through it again.

"I understand." She watched her daughter, who was barely illuminated now by the flames as she dug through the packs. She'd taken to this lifestyle as if she'd been born to it. "Those men. They're dead, aren't they?"

"Dead as doornails. I'll take care of them later after Daphne's asleep."

Brianna couldn't express with words how grateful she was to him for shielding her child from that kind of ugliness. "And the horses and mule? Are they — dead, too?" Brianna had detested four-legged beasts of burden for six long years, but she'd grown unaccountably fond of David's animals. "Did you hide their bodies as well?"

David laughed. "It'd take six men and a boy to drag a horse. All the animals are fine. When the gunfire broke out, they used the good sense God gave them and ran. Blue will round them up. That's why I wanted you on him today. Unless he stepped into a prairie-dog hole and broke a leg out there, he'll find his way back to me."

His tone when he spoke of Blue told Brianna he loved the horse deeply. Two days ago, she might have questioned his sanity, but tonight she gazed off into the darkness, hoping Blue was okay and that he'd bring Lucy and the bay safely to their camp.

She realized she was trembling like a leaf just as David reached out to grasp her shoulder. "You okay, Shamrock?"

It had been such a close call. She'd never been so scared in her whole life, but right then, she needed, almost desperately, to move forward and not think about it. "I'm fine," she pushed out. "Just a bit shaken up. When I realized I'd run in a circle, I was frightened half to death. I ran and ran and didn't go anywhere."

"How's the head? It looks as if the bleeding has stopped."

"I had almost forgotten about it." Touching the spot, she added, "It's definitely nothing urgent. Let's wait until Daphne has settled down before we clean it up. It's only panging a bit. I've endured far worse."

"When?"

That was a question she didn't care to answer. So instead she changed the subject. "Twice today, you said I should tell Blue to take me home." Brianna searched his face, admiring the chiseled cut of his features, delineated by the firelight. "Would he truly have headed for No Name? That seems a bit far-fetched. It's a long way, isn't it?"

David lifted the coffeepot and moved it to the edge of the fire. It seemed to Brianna that a lifetime had passed since he'd put it on to boil. The brew was probably as thick as sludge. "That's a trick every smart rancher teaches his horse. The dangers are many out on a cattle spread. You can get gored by a bull, or fall and break a leg. If you're so badly injured you can't guide the horse, you need him trained to take you home while you try to stay on his back. Blue is smart and well trained and has the homing instinct of a pigeon. He would have headed straight for No Name, just like I said."

Brianna searched the darkness, her throat going tight. She couldn't believe she felt like weeping over a stupid horse. But, oh — he wasn't just *any* horse. "I do hope he's okay, David."

He shrugged and swallowed. "If he doesn't come in, I'll look for him come morning and do what I have to do."

Brianna shivered. A broken leg usually meant certain death for a horse.

Just then, a joyous hee-haw cut through the night. Daphne leaped to her feet and shouted, "Lucy!" She went streaking out into the darkness, making Brianna's heart jerk.

But David only pushed calmly to his feet, hollering, "Mind your horse manners, Daphne!"

The child's voice came trailing back to them. "I will, Papa!"

As David struck off after the child, Brianna forced her exhausted body erect and plodded after him. "What, precisely, are horse manners?"

He slowed and curled an arm over her shoulders. The contact startled her, but his hard, warm hand cupped her opposite arm, holding her fast. "Easy," he said, his voice pitched low. "You can't see shit in the dark. I just don't want you to fall. As for horse manners, I'll teach you, but first we need to work on your directions. You can't find your way out here if all you know is left and right. Where'd you grow up, anyway, in a barn?"

Brianna bit back a startled laugh. "So you're holding that against me, are you?"

"Nah, my feelings aren't that easily hurt."

She almost reminded him that she'd grown up in a convent, not a barn, but her memory of his past reaction to that information had her biting her tongue. Instead she peered with strained eyes through the darkness for a glimpse of her daughter.

David apparently saw Daphne long before she did, for he strode forward without hesitation, his thigh riding her hip, his gun pressed so firmly against her that she might have been wearing it herself. The heat of his body radiated over her. She felt his strength, his hardness, and for the first time in her life, she found them soothing. Well, a little alarming, too. He made her feel things she wasn't at all certain she wanted to feel. She could finally understand why so many women were so foolish as to marry.

Soon Brianna saw her daughter and the equivalent of a small herd of huge beasts taking shape in the darkness. Daphne moved among the animals, patting them and rubbing their noses. The child had become particularly fond of Lucy and went up on her tiptoes to put her short arms around the mule's neck as Brianna and David reached her.

"Take care, Daphne," Brianna called out.

"I am, Mama. But Lucy won't kick me or step on me as long as she knows where I am. It's only when they get startled that they do things like that. She's a dear heart."

"Watch and learn," David whispered,

drawing Brianna to a halt. "Until you have learned, stand clear. Even the best horse might kick if you're standing in a blind spot."

A blind spot? Brianna had no idea what that meant, so she decided to err on the side of caution, watching David and Daphne move through the group of four-legged monsters. In the gloom, she picked out three extra mounts belonging to the miscreants, all saddled and blowing hard. Blue had done his job, gathering all of them up and bringing them home. Well, not *home,* exactly, but she had a feeling the roan considered David to be his safe place.

David was quickly becoming that for Brianna as well — his strength, his fierce protectiveness, and his love for her daughter were a combination difficult to resist. It bothered her to feel that way. She disliked being dependent upon anyone. When you trusted people, you gave them an opportunity to do you dirty.

"Good job, Blue," David said, patting the roan's shoulder and then scratching him behind the ears. "I can always count on you. You're a good fellow." He moved over to the bay. "And who's this? A loyal man like you deserves a name. Daphne, that can be your job. Tonight while we fix supper, come up with a proper handle for this guy."

"I already have one!" Daphne said proudly. "Except for his black tail and mane, he's close to the same color as an acorn."

"He is the color of an acorn, isn't he? Hmm. I like that. Acorn, it is."

Once back at the fire, David left the animals untended while he cleaned the cut at the corner of Brianna's eye. He'd ripped up a shirt and dipped a piece into the boiled water to dab at the wound. As he cleared away the blood, he saw that the gouge, which did resemble a bullet wound, was only superficial. She'd have a shiner come morning, but he doubted the cut would leave much of a scar. Surveying her face, he was damned glad of it. It would be a sacrilege for such perfection to be permanently marred.

"Well?" she asked when he tossed the bit of cloth onto the fire. "Do I have a bullet working its way into my brain?"

David bit back a smile. A lot of women would play it up for sympathy. All Brianna cared about was being proved right. "I think you'll live to bedevil me another day. It's a nasty cut, but there's no debris to pick out. It should heal nicely, and over time, you'll probably have no more than a pockmark to remind you it ever happened."

"As if I'm worried about a scar. As long as I'm able to work and care for Daphne, I'm happy."

David realized that this woman truly didn't realize how pleasing her countenance was. It was little wonder that Daphne was, hands down, the most gorgeous little girl he'd ever clapped eyes on. She'd taken after her grandma Dory in looks, but she had her mama's fine bloodlines, too. David knew the day would soon come when he'd be knocking horny young bucks off his doorstep to keep them away from his daughter. And, gazing at Brianna's lovely face, he wondered if he was any more trustworthy than green, passion-driven boys. Looking at her gave him physical urges he suspected would send her screaming into the night if she knew he had them. Thank God she wore that damned jacket, night and day. Otherwise he'd be drooling and licking his lips like that big, leather-clad lout he'd killed earlier.

But he'd seen Brianna's curves before he'd lent her the coat, and his memory served him well. Maybe it was a reaction to his close brush with death, but he suddenly needed to celebrate life, and for him, sex was high on his list of favorite pastimes. His britches felt a shade too tight in the inseam as he tended to all the animals and then cooked supper, bantering with Daphne and giving her the job of simmering their syrup. They feasted on overcooked vegetables, ham, and hot johnnycakes drizzled with sweetness. Afterward, Brianna helped wash up, trying to conceal her stiffness. David pretended not to notice and began to play his fiddle to drown out the cries of the coyotes while she sneaked off to the packs, procured the liniment, and wandered off to the stream to apply it in private. He sure did wish she had some sore spots she couldn't reach, but even if she did, he knew she'd never ask him to rub her down. Just the thought of providing that service had the crotch of his jeans pinching him again.

As he moved the bow over the fiddle strings, watching his daughter dance, David knew he had waded into deep shit. He needed to get his head on straight because the feelings he was coming to have for Brianna might never be returned. She'd been treated badly by some fellow, or his name wasn't David Paxton, and sometimes a woman could never work her way past that to trust again. All the same, they were married. She hadn't entered into the union willingly, and neither had he, but regardless, they were hitched in the eyes of the law. Was it wrong of him to hope they might make something of that — something good and lasting, maybe even something wonderful?

For Daphne's sake, they needed to try.

# CHAPTER THIRTEEN

When the after-supper festivities ended and all of them were bedded down, David lay awake, waiting to be sure Daphne was asleep before he went out to take care of unfinished business. He had three men to bury. No matter how far they had wandered from righteousness, they'd been human beings, and he needed to respect their remains, making sure scavengers didn't drag them off.

Bone weary, he didn't look forward to all that digging with a short-handled spade. But he couldn't wait until morning. Daphne might see the men, and they hadn't died pretty. David guessed no one did, but the aftermath of a violent death was something no child should witness. Hell, he was a grown man, and sometimes the things life had thrown at him still haunted his dreams.

When David felt sure the child slept, he slipped from his bedroll, donned his hat, and went to get the spade. He had good night vision, so he needed no light. He'd have to cover the graves with rocks. Otherwise, coyotes would sniff out the corpses and have easy digging. Collecting stones would be the hardest part. He guessed he could leave that for morning. The important thing now was to cover the bodies.

Determined to be finished before Daphne awakened, he went to work, consoling himself with the thought that he could sleep late in the morning. Digging with a short spade was always a back breaker. David couldn't put much of his weight behind the blade. It was all arm and shoulder work, but with grim determination, he dug the holes — not as deeply as he would have with a proper shovel, but deep enough to satisfy the Lord.

That accomplished, he turned his attention to the men. He'd shot one of them right between the eyes, a fine piece of work, nasty as the result was. He had Ace to thank for that. If not for all those hours of practicing with six-shooters as a boy, he'd be the one going into a hole. No gladness lifted his heart. He had killed before and probably would again, but there'd never be any joy in it for him. Although these men had made the decision to come after him, and he'd had no choice but to fight, there was a lump in his chest, making him feel as if he'd swallowed a rock. Long ago, Ace had tried to explain how being a gunman had eaten at his soul. David hadn't understood back then, but over time, he'd come to feel exactly the same way. Each time he took another human life, something way deep within him felt as if it died, too.

He crouched over the big fellow's body, his nostrils burning at the stench. He needed to relieve each man of his personal effects. Maybe in the doing, he'd learn their names and could notify their families.

The fire had burned low by the time Brianna slipped from bed, carefully repositioning the blankets over her sleeping child. Then she crept to the copse where she knew David toiled, digging graves. It was slow going for her, walking over uneven ground in the dark. Maybe he could see like an owl at night, but she couldn't. Even so, she wanted to help.

When she pushed past the bushes to reach the area where he'd dragged the bodies, she stood frozen until her eyes adjusted and she was able to see more clearly.

"What are you doing here, Shamrock?" he asked matter-of-factly, telling Brianna that his hearing was as sharp as his vision. "This is no sight for a lady."

*Shock.* Brianna had seen only one corpse, her sister's, but Moira had been as beautiful in death as she had been in life. These men — oh, dear God. Even blurred by shadows, the damage done by the bullets was hideous. The back of one man's head looked as if a huge animal had taken a bite out of it. Her stomach lurched. She swallowed convulsively. So very much blood. The smell of it, along with the stink of the men's unwashed bodies, hit her nose. It took all her self-control not to gag. A sweet, metallic odor prickled on her tongue and gathered at the back of her throat.

Not wishing to embarrass herself by vomiting, she shifted her gaze from the bodies, sprawled in unnatural angles on the grass, and focused on David. Stunned disbelief washed over her in waves. He was emptying the dead men's pockets.

"Wh-what are you *doing?*" she cried.

He jerked — with guilt? — and turned to look at her. "What's it look like I'm doing?"

"You just killed those men, and now you're going through their pockets?"

"Go back to camp, Shamrock. I don't want you seeing this."

"These men, you mean? Or that you're

relieving them of all their valuables?"

"They'll have no need for any of this where they're going," he said calmly. "Go back to camp, Brianna, like I said."

"But you're — this is despicable, the lowest, most immoral thing a man can do. You're robbing *corpses!*"

He looked up at her again. "I'm *what?*"

"You heard me." Brianna swung her hand at the piles of valuables. "I thought — well, I was starting to think —"

He sat back on his bootheel. "You were starting to think what?"

"That you were different! That maybe, at long last, I'd finally met a man I could trust! And now this? It's worse than grave robbing! These men died at your hands."

He pushed erect and took one step toward her. "Is that what you think? That I'm stealing from them? It's been one hell of a day, Shamrock. I'm exhausted and in a sour mood. Don't speak before you think. Do I look like a thief to you?"

Brianna bit down hard on her lower lip. In her skirt pocket, she still had the money he'd given her earlier. She *had* spoken without thinking. He'd proven to her in countless ways that he was a good man and as honorable as could be.

Before she could backtrack and try to

recall her accusatory words, he bent to sweep all the loot into his hands and then advanced on her. Grabbing for one of her jacket pockets, he stuffed everything inside — money, coins, watches, and other things she couldn't identify in the dimness.

"Take it! You need it a hell of a lot worse than I do. Maybe it'll save you from digging through other people's garbage to find morsels of food after I dump your ass off in Denver!" Even with night blindness to hinder her vision, Brianna saw the angry flash of his eyes. "Oh, yeah," he went on with a snarl in his voice. "I'm finished. I've done everything I can to prove myself to you, even putting my life on the line tonight. If you're still not convinced my *stratum* is good enough, to hell with you. Did it ever once occur to you that I'm looking for identification? And that if I find some, the money and valuables will go to these men's families? No! You'll always think the worst of me."

Brianna felt as if he'd given her a double punch in the stomach. He meant to leave her in Denver? Not that she could blame him. She'd had no business saying such an awful thing to him.

She swallowed hard and found her voice. "I'm sorry. I was wrong to accuse you."

With trembling hands, she collected the things from her coat pocket and pushed them back at him. Coins and a watch plopped at her feet. "I have no need of these valuables."

Brianna swung away, caught her foot on a stone, and staggered to right her balance. Then she marched from the copse, blinded now, not by darkness but by tears.

"Son of a *bitch!*"

David kicked furiously at the dirt. For him, it had been an evening filled with regrets. When he'd found Brianna huddled behind a rock just outside of camp, he'd jumped to the wrong conclusion and acted like a complete ass, even threatening to turn her over his knee. *Christ.* In a temper, he had mush for brains. And to add insult to injury, he'd just jabbed at her about once being reduced to foraging in garbage barrels for food. He *knew* how prideful she was, and yet he'd thrown the reminder in her face anyway. *Again.* It wasn't right to use one of a person's worst moments in life as a weapon to draw blood. But had he hesitated? Hell, no, and when he'd thrown the words at her, she'd flinched as if he'd slapped her.

He bundled the valuables in a handkerchief, no longer caring what had come from which man. If he could learn who they were, he'd divide the proceeds evenly among all three families, which seemed fair enough. The bastards had been partners, after all.

So what if Brianna had accused him of robbing dead men? That was probably how it had looked to her. He had accused her of speaking without thinking, so why hadn't he kept his temper in check until he'd had time to think? And then, to make him feel even worse, she'd been the one to apologize.

God, he disgusted himself sometimes. Now she was probably huddled under the blankets with Daphne, battling tears. He made fast work of dragging the dead men over to the holes he'd dug and dumping them in. After he'd shoveled and kicked dirt over the bodies, he jerked off his hat and tried his damnedest to say something reverent over them. Only what? If David had made a single mistake during the lead-swapping contest earlier, he'd be dead right now, and Brianna's screams would be piercing the night. Maybe these fellows had once been decent, but somewhere along the way they'd veered way off course.

He settled for reciting the Lord's Prayer, then clamped his hat back on his head and jerked at the brim to turn it just right. That was as good as he could do for the bastards. He turned and left the copse, surprised to see that Brianna had kept the fire going and was sitting near the flames. *Great.* Now he had to dig deep for an apology, a chore he would have preferred postponing until morning, when his brain wouldn't be foggy with exhaustion and sorrow. Killing was ugly business.

When she heard his footsteps, she leaned forward to fill a tin cup with coffee. "I kept it hot for you. After doing such a despicable chore, you might welcome some coffee laced with sugar. It boiled too long and got a little strong, but it's drinkable."

David sank onto the grass cross-legged beside her. He accepted the cup and took a sip, hoping the sear would clear his throat so he could speak. Only thing was, he needed some words to say, and he'd never been real handy with them. "Brianna —"

"Me first," she interrupted. "It was despicable of me to accuse you of stealing from dead men. I'm sorry I said it, even sorrier that I thought it, however briefly, and I don't blame you a bit for wanting to dump me off in Denver."

David almost groaned. "After I had a minute to think about it, I could see why you thought what you did. I was going through their pockets. It must have looked bad. Just know that wasn't my purpose. Even polecats have families. It'll be good if I can notify their next of kin about how they met their end and where they're planted."

"And send them the valuables," she finished for him. "I can see that now, David. I'm sorry I didn't right away. Men like that — well, their relatives may be poor. A few dollars here, a gold watch there — that might be very welcome if their families are struggling to get by as I have in the past."

"On that subject." David set aside his coffee and rested his elbows on his upraised knees. He pressed his forehead against the heels of his hands, wishing he'd been smart enough to keep his tongue on a leash earlier. "I'm sorry, too, about the trash barrel thing. I took aim at the one thing I knew would cut you the deepest."

She turned her face from him to stare off beyond the flames, her shoulders tense, as if braced for another blow. David detested himself for making her feel that way.

"Once and for all," he said gruffly, "let me set the record straight on how I feel about you foraging in trash barrels to find food for our daughter. I *admire* you for it."

She threw him a startled look, her eyes shimmering in the flickering light. "What?"

"I hold you in the highest regard. No matter how hard it got, you never gave up. You went without sleep to work at any job you could find, and when that wasn't enough, you got creative. Daphne is a beautiful, healthy little girl, and that's all on account of you. You've got more sand than an ocean beach, and I think you're one hell of a lady."

Looping her arms around her knees, she smiled slightly and relaxed. She'd folded back the jacket sleeves because they were too long, and in the amber glow, her hands looked dainty and fragile. It was difficult for David to imagine her digging through garbage with those slender, delicate fingers. He was happy to note that the cut near her eye showed no sign of bruising yet. Maybe she wouldn't have a shiner, after all.

"Only you could compliment a woman and manage to stick *hell* into it."

Caught off guard, David laughed, and he was finally able to relax, too. "Just so we're clear. I'm very glad my child's mother has mettle. You've taken such good care of her, and you've raised her right in the bargain. She talks like a walking dictionary, her manners are perfect, and like her mama, she's too pretty by half but doesn't have an excessively favorable opinion of herself."

Brianna stared fixedly into the fire. "Those

moments weren't proud ones for me, David. The garbage ones, I mean. My child was hungry, and I didn't have a choice. I worried that what I found might make her sick. I took to watching people's back stoops to see when they took out their trash, but even then, I couldn't be sure it was fresh."

David tried to imagine what that must have been like, and he hated himself for ever having put her in such a fix. "I'm so glad now that I came." He swallowed hard. "When that fellow from Denver brought me that bag of letters, I thought about pretending I'd never seen them. Not for long, but I did consider it. I had my life all planned out. I didn't want to believe I had a child in some Podunk place called Glory Ridge. Daphne's letters smote my conscience, though, making me wonder if she might really be mine. She couldn't spell a lick, but she got her message across, that she and her mama were in dire straits."

"Oh, David." She shook her head and closed her eyes. "You shouldn't have come. It saddens me to think you upended your whole life for a child that isn't yours."

"Are we back to that? She's *mine*. Here I thought we were starting to get along."

"We are." Her lashes fluttered up, thick, curved at the tips, and so long they almost touched her brows. "Just remember, when the time comes, I won't hold it against you if you decide to wash your hands of us."

"Jesus H. Christ, Shamrock, leave it alone."

"Just remember." She fixed an imploring gaze on him. "You're a fine man, and you've got a big heart. Perhaps too big for your own good, with plenty of room to love a little girl simply because you feel obligated to."

David threw up his hands, so aggravated that he was about to get up when she reached out to clutch his wrist. "Don't go. I've said my piece. I'll keep my mouth shut now. I just need to know that you'll remember what I just said."

"All right, fine. It's stamped on my brain. Are you happy now?" He sighed and settled back. "Sometimes, Shamrock, you're like a chigger that's worked its way under my skin. I have an unholy urge to give you a swat."

She giggled. David wasn't sure if he'd ever heard her actually laugh. It was a musical sound, soft and sweet. He turned to stare at her. "I'll be damned, Shamrock. I think you have a sense of humor buried in there somewhere."

"By now, my sense of humor has become a bit twisted, but I do still have one. Sometimes I find humor in the strangest things. Last night, I was frantic to spy a rock I could use as a mounting block and somehow convince you to camp near it so I could escape while you slept. Then you came across those *damned* cattails and completely foiled my plan. I thought, 'Well, I'm up the creek without a rock,' and I almost burst out laughing."

David shot her another long look. "Did I just hear you say *damn?*"

"Yes. Your foul mouth is rubbing off on me. Be warned. It will rub off on my daughter, too."

"*Our* daughter."

"Fine, *our* daughter. Just mind your tongue or she'll soon be talking like you do, which would be unbecoming for a young lady. That isn't to say it's becoming in you."

"Jesus H. Christ. You are the most nettlesome woman I've ever met."

"Ach! You just took the Lord's name in vain. What must I say to drive home to you that you can't talk that way around her?"

Sparring with her took his mind off the men he'd just buried. "The H in there makes it okay to say. Do you think the Lord's middle name was Herbert or something?"

She fixed him with an incredulous look.

"Is *that* how you justify it?"

"Absolutely. It's not the Lord's name. It's a byword phrase. I don't say *Jesus* by itself. Well, I do, but I've been trying not to the last couple of days."

"Jesus H. Christ is *not* on your list of allowed words."

"True, but you prick my temper and make me forget what words we decided on. I'm hoping I remembered to tack on *son of a bitch.* It's one of my favorites. When I'm mad, I can work it all different ways and put a lot of emphasis into it."

"That isn't on your list, either."

"Well, damn. That was a serious oversight. It's not really such a bad phrase. *Son* is an ordinary word, and *bitch* is a female dog. I happen to like dogs a lot. If I were to say my bitch was due to whelp, you wouldn't get your drawers all in a twist."

She giggled again. David decided he truly did *love* that sound.

"You, sir, are *impossible.* Where is the soap? I'm going to make you take a bite."

David remembered a few times when his mother had done exactly that, and the thought sobered him. He enjoyed giving Shamrock a hard time about his cussing, but underneath was a serious problem. Using coarse language had become habitual to him, almost as instinctive as breathing. "I really am trying, Shamrock. You haven't heard me *say* 'son of a bitch,' have you?"

"Yes," she said flatly. "You yelled it when you found me behind the rock tonight."

David remembered only being scared. "I did?"

"You did."

"Well, hell, I guess I'm hopeless."

"That is only an excuse. If you plan to be around *our* daughter, you *will* clean up your mouth."

"I will," he said. "But I have to tell you it isn't easy."

"Raising a child is never easy. If you're so eager to be a father, then work on doing it right."

David studied her from the corner of his eye, and he liked what he saw. She no longer assumed a brave posture, pretending she wasn't afraid of him. There was a touch of color in her cheeks, and she didn't hold herself stiffly with her chin lifted high.

"Are you over being upset with me about the garbage comment?" he asked, no longer wanting to tease.

"Are you over the corpse-robbing accusation?"

David thought about it. "Not all the way."

"Well, there you have it, then. It stung,

and I'm still smarting just a little."

"You know those men I was robbing tonight?" He reached down to pluck a blade of grass to chew on. "I'm guessing they never did an honest day's work their lives. You *did*. And I also think you often went without food so Daphne would have more."

"So?"

"So? Shamrock, you're extraordinary."

She sighed and tipped her head back to stare at the stars. David noticed that her hair was in a furious tangle, she had a grass stain on her cheek, and she looked so exhausted a puff of wind could knock her over.

"I'll put it behind me if you will."

"We've got a deal."

She sighed again, and he knew he should send her off to bed, but since he planned to sleep in, he decided he could keep her up for a few more minutes. After she conked out, she wouldn't wake up until he started stirring around in camp.

"Shamrock, I've got a bad feeling about you."

She blinked and stifled a yawn. "How so?"

"Well, I get the distinct impression that you've been badly treated by some other man. Am I right?"

"I have a bad feeling about you as well,"

she said, instead of answering. "You killed three men, hid their bodies, and then you made the evening special for Daphne. How could you act as if nothing happened?"

It was a legitimate question, and David considered his answer. He didn't feel as if nothing had happened, and he didn't want her thinking of him that way. His heart was heavy, and he yearned to stumble down to the creek for a good wash. He had blood on his hands, even though no one else could see it. Sadly, it was the kind of taint he'd never be able to scrub away. Ace had tried to explain that to him once and done a poor job of it. David didn't figure he was any more gifted with words — less so, in fact. Ace could quote Shakespeare, and all David knew were childhood riddles.

"Please don't think I take lives with no regret. That isn't the case at all. I wish those men had ridden on and left us alone. But they didn't, and it came down to them or us. I knew what they'd do to you and Daphne if I went down. It's as simple as that, and I saw no reason to burden a little girl with the awfulness of it, so I tried to make supper festive.

"I take no pleasure in killing. As I buried those polecats, I felt regret, not so much for what I had to do, but because they went so bad at some point in their lives that they came in on us, forcing me to shoot them." David didn't know if that had made any sense, but he figured she could sort her way through it. "I'll go scrub up here in a bit, and when I'm clean and wearing fresh clothes, I'll try to forget about it."

"So in the morning, you'll just wake up, face a new day, and not think about it?"

Oh, how David wished he were made that way. "Nope. In the morning, I'll go out for a rabbit, and I'll wonder about the salvation of my soul because I'll feel more regret about killing a small creature than I did tonight while killing three men. That'll make me worry about what kind of person I am."

Brianna fixed shimmering, pained eyes on him. "Rabbits are such harmless little things. I can understand why it makes you sad to kill them. At the same time, my stomach welcomes the meat."

"Mine, too. It's a sadness of life. They just want to nibble on grass and clover and go back to their warrens. They are the least of us, victimized by humans, coyotes, and hawks, even though they never ask for it. Those men came after us like we were rabbits, Shamrock. But we aren't. Here's how I figure my way through it and move on. Life throws piles of shit at me sometimes, and when it does, I either slog on through or drown in it. My choice, and when it comes down to dying or fighting back, there really isn't a choice. So I'll scrub up and go to bed tonight, hoping to sleep without nightmares. If I do wake up in a cold sweat, I'll remind myself that I'm no rabbit. I'll think about you and Daphne, and what might have happened to both of you, and I'll be damned glad my every roll and pull on the triggers was timed just right. In the morning, I'll sip a cup of coffee and savor the taste, glad that I'm alive to enjoy it. And I'll pray that I was in the right and they were in the wrong, and that God forgives me for what I did."

Her eyes went bright with tears that never spilled over. "It's going to haunt you forever, isn't it? This night and what you did to save us."

"I would have done the same if I'd been alone. Don't go burdening yourself with that. I've shot fancy with my six-shooters before, and I'll do it again. Maybe next time, I won't be so lucky. That's up to God, I reckon. All I know is, I've never pulled the trigger unless the man at the other end of my Colt gave me no choice."

She dipped her chin in a nod. "Thank you, David. You went out there, prepared to die, and you saved me and Daphne from untold suffering." When she looked over at him, her eyes were so deep and beautifully green that he could have dived in headfirst. "I can't express my gratitude with words."

David thought a kiss might do it, but he figured now wasn't the time to make that move, even though he allowed himself a long look at that sweet, tempting mouth. "Express your gratitude by answering my question. Clever evading, Shamrock, but I'm not dumb as a post. Who made you so wary of men?"

Her face drew taut. He saw her larynx bob. "It wasn't only one man, David. It has been nearly *every* man. Except for an elderly fellow who helped me once, I've never met one yet who wouldn't do me dirty if he got the chance."

David studied her lovely features and searched the shadows in her eyes. He sensed that he'd taken her as far as she could go until she knew him better. "Oh, yes, you have, Shamrock. Yes, you have."

She blinked and peered up at him. "I'm sorry? I'm not following."

He dipped his head and pressed his lips to her forehead. "You *have* met a man who won't do you dirty. You've met me."

He decided to leave it there, let it simmer

in her mind. He pushed to his feet and turned to extend a hand to her. "Up you come. It's long past bedtime for both of us."

He half expected her to struggle erect by herself, but instead a slight smile curved her mouth and she placed her hand in his. Maybe he was out of his mind, but for him, it was one of the sweetest gifts he'd ever received. Her trust. Even though he knew it came with limitations, it pleased him. He braced to lift her slight weight, held on until she caught her balance, and resisted the urge to kiss her forehead again even though what he really wanted was a long, deep drink from those soft, moist lips.

"Good night, Shamrock. Sleep easy. I've got a very lucky penny in my possession. I have it on good authority that it saved my ass tonight. I guess it can again."

She glanced heavenward. "We should place all our hope in God, not objects."

"I totally agree," he told her, then patted his shirt pocket. "But it never hurts to have some reinforcement. I don't think there's any harm in having a little magic in our lives. A penny that means nothing can add some sparkle to this dreary old world."

He started to turn away, but she reached out to grab his hand. David turned his palm to fold his fingers over hers. To him, the touch was electric. He couldn't tell by her schooled expression how she felt, and he guessed she wanted it that way. She was clearly unsettled by the physical attraction building between them, and maybe she always would be.

"In your dreams, remember how grateful I am to you for protecting us tonight," she whispered tremulously.

He gave in to his earlier urge and bent to press a quick kiss to her lips. Honeyed sweetness came away on his mouth. "Shamrock, it was my honor. And if it comes down to it, I'll do it again."

As David watched her move away, he realized that he'd never given anyone a more heartfelt promise.

# Chapter Fourteen

The morning brought warmth and sunlight that pooled on the rolling grassland like puddles of melted butter. Brianna was miserable in the hot, heavy jacket, but modesty made her hesitate to take it off. She didn't complain or mention her discomfort, so she was surprised when David approached her with his last clean shirt.

"Take off the coat and wear this today. It's not much, but it'll give you cover."

"But then you'll have nothing clean to wear."

Dark blond hair lifting in the breeze, he shrugged off her protest. "I can get our clothing washed in town. Even if there's no real laundry, there are usually a couple of women who make extra money doing people's wash."

Brianna sent him a wondering look. "Town?"

He patted one pocket of his duster. "A

place near here called Clapboard Flats. I have some business with the marshal there." His blue gaze held hers. "If I take you and Daphne along, can I trust you not to cause me trouble by demanding to see a judge or telling some stranger I kidnapped you?"

Only desperation had made her consider doing that. Now that she knew for certain he had no nefarious plans, the biggest problem she faced was his steadfast belief that he was Daphne's sire. Until he came to accept the truth, he had the upper hand legally. The marriage document in his saddlebag gave him inalienable rights, not only as Daphne's father, but also as Brianna's husband, and her chances of prevailing against him in a custody battle were slim. She couldn't provide the little girl with a home, and she presently didn't even have a job. Any judge would assess her situation and rule in David's favor. Her smartest course of action was to accept the present circumstances and wait until David came to realize his mistake. Until then, she had nothing to gain by causing trouble and everything to lose, namely her daughter.

"You needn't worry on either count, David. I give you my word."

Brianna expected him to say her word wasn't worth much, but instead he merely nodded. "Good. A real bed will be welcome, and the animals deserve a rest, too."

Brianna glanced at the horses. "What will you do with the extra mounts?"

"If I can learn the identity of those men, I'll try to sell them and split the proceeds between their families. If not, I'll see if the livery stable will take them, I guess."

"I found another one!" Daphne called.

Brianna turned to see her daughter emerge from a thicket holding a rock almost larger than she was. David loped over to relieve the child of the burden. "Sweetheart, don't lift rocks this heavy. You'll hurt yourself. Besides, we've found enough."

Daphne scampered after him as he lugged the stone over to the copse. "But, Papa, it's extra pretty with red in it! It'll make our monuments more special."

Brianna stripped off the coat and donned David's shirt, which was red with a stand-up collar and white buttons down the front. *Monuments. What would that man dream up next?* Rather than upset Daphne with the truth — that he'd killed three men — he'd told the child that he wanted to build monuments to commemorate how lucky all of them had been last night. Now, according to David, whenever they passed this way, they'd remember how God had watched over them and kept them safe.

Brianna followed them into the small clearing. To her, the mounds of rock looked like graves, not monuments, but David had the child thoroughly convinced. In time, Daphne would think back and recognize it for the gargantuan lie that it actually was, but for now, David was protecting her from the harsh realities.

"Not *there*, Papa. Put it here."

David narrowed an eye at the child. "It's heavy, and I'm not moving it again."

"I'm sure." Daphne beamed a smile when the rock was situated to her liking. Then she stepped back to survey their handiwork. "That is *perfect*." She turned a sparkling gaze on Brianna. "That one's yours, Mama. After lengthy debate, we decided you should have the prettiest rocks because you're the prettiest of us all."

Brianna suppressed a shudder. "How thoughtful," was all she could think to say.

A slight frown pleated the little girl's brow. "Papa, why did we hide our beautiful monuments behind these bushes?"

Thrown by the question, David sent Brianna an imploring look. She came to his rescue with, "Because these monuments are our special secret. We don't want just any old body to come along and see them."

"Oh." Daphne brightened again. "I like having a special secret!"

Minutes later, they had broken camp and mounted up. Daphne once again rode with David. Lucy and one of the extra horses were tethered to Blue's saddle. Brianna brought up the rear on Acorn, with the other two surplus animals trailing behind him.

David cut across the stream. Brianna had no idea what direction they were going. Judging by the position of the sun, she guessed north. It didn't really matter to her, though, not anymore. She would never be truly lost with David as a guide. He seemed to possess some unerring instinct to find his way that she sorely lacked.

When they came upon railroad tracks, they followed them. In what seemed like no time, they rode into Clapboard Flats. The community was larger than Glory Ridge, with two short business streets surrounded by houses on small plots of land. Clothing flapped on clotheslines. A black and white dog tore out from his yard to bark at them but kept a respectful distance from the horses. Shielding her eyes from the sun, Brianna saw two hotels, a restaurant, a bath-house, and the usual stores. David drew their small caravan to a stop in front of the marshal's office. Leaving Daphne on Blue, he looped the reins over the hitching rail, employing a peculiar knot Brianna had never seen.

When she tried to duplicate it with Acorn's leads, she ended up shrugging in defeat. David stepped over to do it for her. She tried to pay attention, but the breadth of his hands and the grace of his thick fingers distracted her. His wrists were nearly twice as wide as hers, dark brown from the sun and dusted with gold hair. Remembering the strength of his grip, she got a funny, fluttery feeling way low in her belly.

"You got it?" he asked.

What Brianna *got* was that she'd somehow waded into trouble up to her chin. She didn't mind coming to admire and respect David Paxton, but these other feelings — silly, female feelings — were unwise. Eventually, he would want his freedom to resume that life he'd told her about last night. She had a very bad feeling that it included a woman. David was . . . well, extraordinarily handsome. It hit her every time she looked at him. She surely wasn't the only female to have recognized it.

Oblivious of her mental turmoil, he said, "It's a simple, quick breakaway tie. Pull on this, and you're ready to go." He demonstrated the technique, the reins fell away from the post, and then he redid the knot. "If the horse pulls back, it tightens." He jerked on the leather, and sure enough, the reins cinched on the wood. "You'll see men throw a double loop without tying any kind of knot to really secure the animal. I think that's foolish and unsafe for the horse." He fixed his gaze on her face. "You okay, Shamrock?"

Brianna couldn't think how to respond. She was wishing she could perfect that knot to keep him tethered. They'd reached civilization now. Probably sooner than later, he'd investigate her story about Boston and learn that every word she'd spoken by the stream had been the absolute truth. The thought of watching David walk away, of never seeing him again, filled her with inexplicable sadness.

"I'm right as rain." The moment she spoke, Brianna realized she was even starting to talk like him. "Just a bit tired, I suppose."

He went to lift Daphne from the horse, swung her into Brianna's waiting arms, and then led the way into the lawman's office. The marshal, a young fellow with a shock of sandy hair, glanced up from his desk. Brianna barely glanced at him. Her gaze was glued to the Wanted posters affixed to the wall behind him. David, she realized, was looking at them, too, and the tick of his jaw muscle told her she'd guessed right. Three of the likenesses were of the men he'd killed last night. Each of them, wanted dead or alive, had a 250-dollar reward on his head.

"Well, well," David said softly as he flipped back his duster to reveal his badge. "I'm Marshal David Paxton, out of No Name." He reached across the desk to shake the other man's hand. "I had a run-in last night with those three gents."

The lawman turned to look. His expression went grim as he returned David's regard. "You kill 'em?"

David glanced meaningfully at Daphne. "Let's just say they realized the error of their ways and hightailed it to a better place." He reached into the pocket of his duster and plopped a knotted blue handkerchief on the desk. "You got any idea how to get in touch with their next of kin?"

The other marshal nodded. "I know where they harkened from. It should be easy enough to locate family."

"Good." David patted the bundle. "Divide it three ways so their relatives can divvy up their shares." He hooked a thumb over his shoulder. "I've got their mounts and gear outside. Nice animals. You know anybody in the market for good horses and tack?"

"I reckon I can find some interested parties." The marshal of Clapboard Flats arched both eyebrows at David. "Normally, before I send a telegraph for reward money, I require —" He broke off and slanted a thoughtful look at Daphne, perched on Brianna's hip. "Proof, I guess is the word, that they did indeed hightail it off to a better place."

David leaned over the desk, grabbed a piece of paper and pencil, and jotted something down. "There's the location if you're bent on proof. You'll find three beautiful monuments there." Winking at Daphne, David added, "But keep it a secret. My little girl doesn't want just any old body to know where they are." Hooking a thumb over his shoulder, David went on to say, "Personally, though, a man's horse, saddle, and personal possessions are usually enough proof for me."

"Point taken."

David nodded. "I'll trust you to handle everything. I'd like the reward money sent to their families as well. When the horses are sold, same goes."

"You have my word. It's a fine thing for you to do. Most folks would want the rewards for themselves."

"I have no real need of it, and their families might." David turned to take Daphne from Brianna's arms. "We'll head over to the livery. I'll cover the costs for the extra three horses tonight, but you'll need to make other arrangements with the owner until they're sold. He can take the cost of boarding them out of the sale proceeds, I reckon."

Brianna followed David from the dim office out into the bright morning. Birds sang sweetly from the eaves of the buildings. A light breeze carried the scents of grass and wildflowers. Her eyes burned with the sting of repressed tears. She wanted to grab David's arm and apologize to him once again for the accusation she'd made last night. He was no thief. He'd kept nothing from those men for himself, and he'd even turned down the reward money, which, in her opinion, tallied up to a small fortune.

As they walked toward the livery, Brianna saw several nicely dressed women pause on the boardwalk to stare at her with stark disapproval. She glanced down at herself and realized she must look a fright, with David's bright red shirt calling fast attention to her appearance. Heat crept up her neck. She met those women's gazes with haughty disdain and judged their gowns to be only passable. Ready-made clothing from Montgomery Ward, no doubt, or the products of their own pathetic attempts at a sewing machine. She swept by them with her chin held high, too proud to let them see her embarrassment.

David spent more than an hour at the livery getting all the horses settled in. After traveling with him, Brianna wasn't surprised that he insisted on seeing to every detail himself. He was a man who not only valued animals but also appreciated their hard work. Before he saw to his own comforts, he would see to theirs. Brianna almost sat on a hay bale to wait him out, but that struck her as being lazy, so instead she went with Daphne to care for Lucy and Acorn. At Ricker's, Brianna had learned how to man the business end of a pitchfork. She tossed fresh straw into the stalls while Daphne filled the water buckets and struggled to dump two leaves of fresh hay into the troughs. They were weighty burdens for a little girl to manage.

Watching her daughter, Brianna felt her heart swell with pride. She was fast becoming quite the horsewoman. Lucy adored her, and Acorn nuzzled the child appreciatively, as if he sensed that their relationship would be one of long standing.

When David was satisfied that the animals would fare well for the night, he led Brianna and Daphne from the stable. Brianna expected him to head directly for one of the hotels. She yearned for a bath, and then she wanted to stretch out on a real bed. But David grasped her elbow and veered left toward the town's dress shop.

"Daphne and I need something fresh to wear while our clothes are being laundered," he said, his voice laced with underlying firmness. "For now, something ready-made will do us, so while you're in this shop, selecting a couple of nice dresses in your size, I'll take her shopping."

Brianna dug in her heels before he could open the door. "I can't afford two dresses. I can't even afford one. All I have is what remains of the money you sent Daphne."

"You have that roll of bills I gave you last night. Spend some of it." His blue gaze bore into hers. "Don't hike your chin up at me like that. New clothing, from the skin out, plus a pair of decent shoes and a nice cloak. No wife of mine is going to be snubbed by the wives of a bunch of clod busters. When you leave this shop, I want you looking like a lady of substance."

Brianna parted her lips to protest, but David had already turned away. Daphne, clutched in his strong arms, flashed Brianna a grin over his right shoulder. "Buy some pretty dresses, Mama! If you don't, Papa will be angry." Brianna, still wanting to protest, started to call out, but Daphne forestalled her with, "You said you'd ask how high. Remember? He just told you to jump!"

David made fast work of finding clothing for Daphne that would do her for the night while her scanty wardrobe was laundered. He also bought himself a change of clothes. Before leaving the dry-goods store, he stopped to buy his daughter a lollipop, which she promptly poked in her mouth. Holding her hand, he carried the bundle of purchases under his left arm as they angled across the street to the dress shop.

David plopped the package on a bench just outside the door and lifted his daughter to sit beside it. "You stay here and enjoy your candy. Okay? I want to help your mama choose some dresses, and most dress-shop owners frown upon sticky little girls."

Daphne tucked the orb of candy into her cheek. "I'll be fine. I'll watch passersby."

"Just don't leave the bench." David glanced up and down the street. It seemed like a quiet town, but he didn't want his daughter off by herself. "You understand?"

"I won't move," she promised.

David pressed a kiss to her forehead, and then entered the dress shop to find Brianna shoving a dress back at the clerk, a slight, white-haired lady with spectacles perched on the end of her bony nose. Right off, David liked her a lot more than he ever had Abigail Martin. She had a sweet smile and kindly gray eyes.

"That's far too much money," he heard Brianna say, "and the color is too bold for me. I prefer subdued tones."

David took in the dress. It was emerald green, almost the exact same color as Brianna's eyes. "If it fits, she'll take it."

Startled, Brianna whirled to face him, her expression taut with admonishment. "I beg your pardon, sir? I'm quite capable of selecting a dress for myself."

David almost chuckled. She only addressed him as "sir" when her temper flared. His Shamrock had an explosive disposition under all that control. She constantly struggled to keep it under wraps, but it bubbled to the surface despite her efforts. That bothered him. Why did she try so damned hard to smother her true nature? She was a spitfire with a mean right hook, yet she pretended to be a meek lamb.

"*A* dress?" he popped back. "I told you to get four."

Her cheeks went crimson. "You most certainly did *not!* You said *two,* and I judge even that to be grossly extravagant."

David didn't like being overbearing with a lady, but with her pride as an obstacle, he could see no way around it. He winked at the dressmaker. "You've got a good eye. That color would be perfect on her. Do you think it will fit?"

The old lady knew a source of profit when she saw one. A twinkle lighted her gray eyes. "Close enough. I can do some quick alterations to make it perfect for her."

David waved his hand. "Try it on, wife."

Brianna sent him a look that put him in mind of Bess in No Name — green fire meant to obliterate anything it touched. "This dress is outrageously overpriced!"

"I don't care how much it costs," David informed her.

"You, sir, are impossible."

David didn't care if he was being impossible. He never again wanted to see her cheeks go hot with shame when she met better-dressed women on the street. She was his wife, damn it, and she would take second seat to no one.

During the trying-on stage, David stepped outside frequently to check on Daphne. When her lollipop disappeared, he took her up the street for a sarsaparilla and then parked her on the bench again while he went inside the shop to check on Brianna's progress. She stood before a mirror in the emerald green gown. Even with her hair in a tangle about her shoulders, she was so beautiful that she nearly took his breath away. The gown hugged her upper torso, showcasing her generous bust and slender waist, the skirt puffing out from there to shimmer over her hips, the slight bustle accentuating her delightful posterior. So far as David could see, the gown fit her perfectly.

"Sold," he said.

"I am *not* taking this dress. It's shameless." She tugged at the décolletage, trying to cover the plump swell of her creamy breasts, which were delightfully exposed. So delightfully that David's manhood sprang to attention. "Forget it." She turned to the proprietress. "What else have you in stock that might fit?"

"Hold it." David strode over, doing his damnedest not to gape at the plump, ivory orbs of her generous bosom. "A bit of lace might work," he said to the shop owner. "My ma does that with gowns that are a bit too revealing."

"I have just the thing!" The little woman hurried behind a display case and set out several bolts of lace. David was no expert, but he had a good eye. Well, he knew what he liked to see on a woman, anyway. He bypassed a russet and then a bright gold, thinking they'd both draw the gaze directly to Brianna's breasts. Well, hello, he didn't want the attention of every man to shoot straight to her bosom. He pointed to a sturdy jet black with a scalloped edge that was dotted with little holes. "I like that one."

"Excellent choice. Eyelet is substantial enough to cover but delightfully intriguing to the male eye."

From the front, David decided the eyelet would cover Shamrock's attributes, but he didn't like that it was ruffled. He consoled himself with the thought that any man who got close enough to look down the flutes would be dead before he hit the ground. *Jesus Herbert Christ.* He was feeling jealous, and if that wasn't crazy, he didn't know what was. He was the only man present.

Brianna huffed. "My last desire is to wear anything intriguing to the male eye."

David seconded that sentiment but slapped his hand down on the eyelet anyway. "You'd be intriguing to the male eye in a flour sack. Just shut up and let her and me figure it out."

"She and I," she corrected.

David was in no mood for an English lesson. "Gotcha! You're wrong. It'd make no sense at all if I said, 'Let *I* figure it out.' "

Brianna gave him a heated look that could have wilted a healthy cornstalk.

He nodded to the woman. "Whip something up." He gestured at Brianna's astounding cleavage. "I want my wife to look fabulous, mind you, but I'd just as soon other men don't drool overmuch."

"Ah, a possessive husband. My Orville was a mite possessive back in the day. I, too, had to wear inserts with my more revealing gowns." The woman drew out a pair of scissors and cut a length of the black eyelet. "This will do perfectly with a bit of tacking."

David went to the dress rack while the two females fussed over the proper placement of the insert. He shoved aside a bright blue. Nope, not for his fiery-haired Shamrock. She needed colors that complemented her striking complexion. He came across a muted black silk. He liked that it wasn't shiny to distract from her skin, glorious hair, and fabulous eyes. Brianna didn't need adornment to make her sparkle. Oh, yeah, he liked this one. As he drew it off the rack, he pictured her in it. He stepped sideways to toss it on the counter.

"Let me see her in that one."

Brianna looked at the price tag and gasped. David ignored her. Though he hadn't yet told her, they'd be taking the train home to No Name, and he'd be pickled like baby cucumbers if he allowed his wife to be scorned by other female passengers. Hell, maybe he'd even buy her a bonnet all decked out with silly ornaments. Fake birds were the current rage, with feathers going every which way. He wanted her to look wonderful when he presented her to his family. His ma was a fine lady and put a lot of stock in dressing well. Dory would box his ears if his wife wore rags that were about to pop at the seams.

David came across a shimmery brown silk. When he held the dress up to the light, he caught flashes of green, bronze, and red as he twisted the hanger. *Perfect.* Looked at straight on, the dress was an unassuming brown, but on Brianna, it would be pure decadence, highlighting the red flashes in her hair and the deep green of her eyes, and offsetting her ivory skin with the touches of bronze. He tossed that one on the case as well.

And then he came across a deep gold day dress with capped sleeves, a low décolletage studded with emerald beads, and a waist sashed with shimmery jade silk. She'd look like a sultry angel in it. With a flick of his wrist, it joined the pile.

David figured he had probably offended Brianna's delicate sensibilities enough, so he went outside to collect his daughter. After a spit bath, he judged her to be passable for a dress shop. Once inside, Daphne instantly became his ally, oohing over this and applauding that. David saw Brianna's shoulders slump and smothered a grin. Victory had a nice taste, but nothing, he thought sourly, could ever compare to the honey of Brianna's mouth, brief though his savoring of it had been. He wanted to sneak another quick kiss. Then she stepped out in the brown silk, her breasts plumping up like mounds of whipped cream over the scoop neckline. He forgot all about her lips, and his mouth went dry. On her, the dress went from ordinary to astounding, a shimmery rainbow of subdued color and lightning. His manhood went instantly hard.

He sat on one of the two chairs against the wall, settled a boot on his knee, and flipped his duster over his crotch, not wanting his daughter to see him in such dire straits. Brianna was enough to drive any man over the edge.

An hour and a half later, Brianna left the shop with the emerald green gown, which had quickly been tucked, tightened and let out where needed, and altered with a bit of black eyelet across the low neckline. In the sacks David carried were underclothes, three changes in all, the memory of which made his mouth water. Picturing Brianna in lacy underthings was nearly his undoing. Trudging beside him, she still wore her rags, but over them a new black cloak of fine wool rode her slender shoulders, its folds encasing her body to protect her from the wind, which had grown cool with the late afternoon. They'd pick up the other dresses tomorrow.

David assessed the two hotels and led his little tribe toward the newer looking of the two. At the desk, he signed in, ordered three hot baths, two snack plates for one room, one for his, beverages for his girls, and a fifth of Irish whiskey for himself, plus two cigars. While he soaked up to his chin in hot water, he meant to indulge in booze and smokes. He ignored the censorious spark in Brianna's eyes. She could go whistle Dixie and learn from experience that he wouldn't get roaring drunk, that he'd wash off the stench of the cigars and present himself at dinner sober and smelling nice. In the meanwhile, he would enjoy a manly bath. She and Daphne could do the female version. To that end, he ordered scented bath salts, leaving Brianna to choose what she wanted. She looked so startled at first by the suggestion, and then so troubled by the choices offered her, that he suspected she'd never used bath salts or oils.

She finally settled on a rose scent. David loved roses, and imagining her in that emerald green gown, smelling like a rose garden, made him go hard again. *Jesus,* he was in trouble. She wasn't ready for any advances from him. Maybe she'd never be. He needed to get his head screwed on straight or he'd come in his trousers during supper.

After her bath, which had been so luxurious she'd never wanted it to end, Brianna got dressed. Daphne, already scrubbed clean and wearing her new store-bought clothing, sat on the bed, oohing over Brianna's lacy underclothes and then clapping her hands when Brianna donned the emerald gown.

"Can you do me up in back?" Brianna asked.

Daphne stood on the bed to fasten all the

buttons; then she sighed as Brianna stepped away. "Oh, Mama, you look like a princess!"

Brianna felt a bit like royalty. A hotel employee had already taken their soiled clothing downstairs for laundering with a promise that everything would be returned before checkout time at eleven the next morning. She was unaccustomed to being catered to. It felt decadent.

Smoothing a hand over the green silk, she smiled at her daughter. "I've never possessed anything this fine. I still can't believe he spent so much money!"

Nibbling her lip, Brianna wondered how she would ever pay David back. The day would come when she'd have to settle up with him. The thought dampened her mood considerably. He had started to grow on her in more ways than she cared to count. The way he sat a horse. The cocky tilt of his hat brim. The scruff of whiskers that appeared each afternoon even though he shaved of an evening. The slash that creased his cheek when he grinned. The way his blue eyes warmed and started to twinkle before any hint of a smile touched his mouth, and how lines appeared at its corners when he gazed off into the distance. And, oh, how it touched her heart to watch him with Daphne as he taught her string tricks at night by the fire, ruffling her hair when she grew frustrated, and playing his fiddle to distract her when she was frightened by coyotes.

Last night, he'd risked his life to protect them. And for the first time since leaving the orphanage, Brianna felt safe, no longer a woman alone in the world with no champion to defend her. It was such a comforting feeling, and when their so-called marriage ended, she would miss it.

*Stuff and nonsense,* she chided herself as she stepped over to the mirror to check her hair. Would David think she looked pretty? The thought no sooner zipped through her mind than Brianna wanted to give herself a good, hard shake. Why should she want David to think she was pretty? The man had turned her life upside down, and he could still take Daphne away from her. Even worse, when he finally realized the truth, that he wasn't Daphne's sire, he would promptly wash his hands of them. She couldn't allow herself to have these feelings. Only a foolish woman walked down such a thorny path, knowing that heartbreak waited at its end.

A light tap came at the door. Daphne bounced off the bed to answer the summons. David poked his head into the room, his blond hair still damp from his bath. He wore blue jeans with a just-off-the-shelf crease in each leg, a white shirt, and his boots, which appeared to have been wiped clean with a wet cloth. His badge winked above his left breast pocket. The Colts rode his hips, the wooden grips gleaming in the lantern light.

To Daphne, he said, "Never open the door without asking who's there. It isn't safe." Then he shifted his gaze to Brianna. "Well, now, don't you look prettier than sunrise, sunset, and everything betwixt and between."

Brianna thought he looked awfully nice, too. She recalled the first time she'd seen him, how intimidating he had seemed to her then. Now he made her feel a host of different emotions, but fear wasn't one of them. He moved his gaze slowly over her; then, as if realizing a beat late that he was staring, he looked at Daphne.

"Am I a lucky fellow or what? Not every man receives the honor of escorting two of the prettiest ladies in the world downstairs for a sit-down supper." He caught hold of Daphne's hand and offered Brianna his arm. "You ready?"

Brianna left the lamp low. Fishing the room key from her skirt pocket, she tucked her hand over his bent arm and stepped out into the hallway with him. Daphne was so excited she was dancing on her tiptoes.

"I've never had a sit-down supper in a restaurant," she cried.

David locked the door for Brianna and slipped the key into his trouser pocket. Brianna took his arm again as they walked along the hallway. At the landing, Daphne fell in behind them to go down the stairs. Brianna felt unaccountably tense. She assured herself it was because she'd only ever worked in a restaurant and had never been a patron, but deep down, she knew her nerves were leaping because of the man beside her. He made her feel feminine and beautiful.

At the bottom of the stairs, he turned right toward the eating establishment, which adjoined the hotel lobby. The wonderful smells coming from the kitchen made her stomach growl. Startled, she touched a hand to her waist as a flare of heat crept up her neck. David didn't seem to notice. He grabbed Daphne's hand again and said, "I don't know about you ladies, but I'm so hungry, I could eat the south end of a northbound jackass."

Caught off guard, Brianna giggled before she could swallow it back. "Mr. Paxton, pray mind your manners."

He flashed an irreverent grin. "You worry too much about manners, Shamrock. Relax and have fun for once."

Refusing to have fun with David was nearly impossible. He was becoming more difficult to resist with each passing moment. He selected a round table near the bank of front windows. With a flourish, he seated Brianna first, and then, with equal fanfare, he pulled out a chair for Daphne. The child stared with round eyes at the artfully folded napkin that held court at the center of her place setting. She fingered the white linen tablecloth as if it were made of spun gold. David took a seat between them and signaled the waitress, a plump woman in a blue day dress with capped sleeves and an out-of-fashion bustle that ballooned behind her.

"What can I get you, mister?"

David winked at Daphne. "This is my daughter's first sit-down supper in a restaurant, so I'd like it to be special. She'll have a chilled sarsaparilla in a wine goblet as her before-supper drink. My wife and I will share a bottle of wine if you have any."

The woman smiled. "We have a nice red. Customers say it's quite good."

David nodded. "And what do you have by way of whore dervies?"

Brianna, in the process of taking a sip from her water glass, nearly choked.

"We have fresh fried potato chips with a mayonnaise dip and we also offer a relish plate."

"We'll have both," David said. "We'll munch on those while we look at the menu."

"Our special tonight is fried chicken, mashed potatoes with gravy, sweet peas, and a green salad. Hot bread fresh from the oven is served on the side with sweet cream butter — or if you'd rather, you can ask for biscuits."

David glanced at Brianna. "That sounds wonderful," she told him.

Daphne piped in with, "I haven't had fried chicken in a long, *long* time."

With a grin, David said, "No menus are necessary, I reckon. The special sounds good to me, too."

Gazing over at him, Brianna realized that though he was still the most rugged, dangerous-looking man she'd ever met, he was also unnervingly appealing. The warmth of his smile, the deep drone of his voice, the enticing scent of his bay-rum facial invigorator — everything about him played upon her senses.

Daphne was a chatterbox all during the meal, raving about the potato chips, her wineglass, and then her supper, which she claimed was the best she'd ever tasted. David insisted that the child have a tall glass of milk, and while waving her hands as she talked, Daphne sent the tumbler flying. Before Brianna could react to stop the flow with her napkin, white liquid spilled across the tablecloth and funneled down a drape in the linen directly onto David's lap. She was aghast.

"Oh, dear heaven!" Brianna skirted the table to mop frantically at his lap. "Brand new jeans, and now they're soaked." She turned a censorious gaze on Daphne. "You have been taught better, young lady. For shame, bouncing about on your chair and waving your arms at the table!" Dab, swipe, dab. David's trousers were ruined. "I've a good mind to box your —" Brianna felt a hard rodlike swell beneath the now drenched napkin and froze with her hand cupped over it. "Oh. I'm sorry!" She jerked the sopped linen away. "Pardon me. I didn't mean to —"

David met her startled gaze and winked at her, his blue eyes dancing with mischief. "I can't recall ever having enjoyed a spilled glass of milk quite this much. You can mop me up all you want."

Brianna straightened her spine and turned

toward her chair, only to bump into the buxom waitress, who'd come running with a towel. They both tried to circle, but in the same direction, and collided once again. Brianna's dignity had suffered a severe blow by the time she collected herself and resumed her seat. The waitress, wiser than Brianna, handed David the towel to dab his wet lap by himself.

"Thank you," he told her as he returned the crumpled linen. "Another glass of milk for my daughter, please."

As the waitress walked away, Brianna drilled Daphne with her gaze. "And you shan't behave like an ill-mannered street waif and spill this one. Do I make myself perfectly clear?"

Daphne's eyes went bright with tears. "I didn't mean to knock it over, Mama. It was an unfortunate accident."

Just then a pea struck Daphne's cheek. She jumped as if she'd just been hit by a bullet. Both she and Brianna turned startled gazes on David, who had his fork poised for another volley. "That'll teach you to dump your milk in my lap. I don't get mad; I just get even." With a flip of the tined flatware, he nailed the child again. This time the projectile struck the tip of Daphne's nose. "You just gonna sit there and take that, or are you going to fire back?"

Daphne's cheek dimpled in an impish grin and she grabbed her fork, balanced a pea on the tines, and fired away. Brianna gasped. David laughed when the pea splatted his white shirt and left a green smudge.

"Ho!" he said with a deep, vibrant laugh. "You're going to get it now!"

Brianna compressed her lips and watched in mounting horror as little green projectiles flew back and forth. "You are making a terrible *mess!*" she cried. "We'll be asked to leave!" Her objection earned her a pea in the face, launched at her from David's fork. "David Paxton, I *swear,* you're the most imposs—"

Another pea hit her on the neck and rolled down into the valley between her breasts. Face burning with mortification and no small amount of outrage, Brianna dipped her fingers under the insert of black eyelet and plucked the squishy thing out. When she had the pea between thumb and forefinger, temper overcame her good sense, and she threw it at David, hitting him dead center on the forehead.

He looked so startled that she snorted with laughter — actually *snorted.* Where were Sister Theresa and her ruler? This was no way for a lady to behave in a restaurant.

Only two other tables were occupied, but the other customers had to be gaping at them.

"I have *never,* in all my days, been so embarrassed," she whispered.

David's response was to launch another pea at her. The absurdity of it was too much. Brianna snorted again, and then went for her fork to fire back. Soon Daphne was chortling, David was chuckling, and Brianna found herself laughing so hard her sides ached.

When they finally ran out of peas, she sank weakly back on her chair, feeling dazed and more than a little incredulous. She couldn't recall ever having had such a good time. "Now what?" she asked him, her voice faint from the drain of unbridled hilarity. "There are peas *everywhere.*"

David settled back and silently toasted her with his glass of wine. As he took a sip, he frowned. A pea floated on the surface. He fished it out with his spoon. "The waitress will clean up the mess. I'll be sure to leave a hefty gratuity."

That was his answer? They'd all just behaved like orangutans that had escaped from a city zoo. "Such deplorable shenanigans are unacceptable in a public place," Brianna told him, trying to regain some semblance of dignity. "Is this how you want our daughter to act in an eating establishment? We are duty bound to teach her better."

"We're also duty bound to show her how to have a good time." He winked at Daphne. "Don't forget your milk, and make sure to get it *inside* of you this time."

Daphne grabbed her glass and took several gulps. Her big smile was ringed with white. Brianna was about to scold when the child daintily wiped her mouth with her napkin. "I'm sorry if we embarrassed you, Mama."

"Your mama can do with a little embarrassment," David said. "She places far too much importance on manners and not enough on joviality. We all had fun, it was a great supper, and my jeans will dry. No harm done."

After Daphne finished her milk, David signaled for his tab. The waitress picked her way through the peas on the floor to bring it to him. "Sorry about the mess. We got a little carried away." David lifted a hip to fish in his jeans for his money, then gave Brianna a look filled with humor. "You've got my clip."

"Oh." Brianna reached into the pocket of her skirt, found the roll of bills, and handed it over.

David peeled off enough certificates to cover the bill and then topped it with a dollar. "To make up for the extra work we've caused you. I do apologize for the mess."

The waitress gave him a wide-eyed look. "That's *very* generous of you, sir. Thank you so much."

Brianna studied her daughter, whose cheeks had gone rosy. It had been far too long since Brianna had heard her daughter laugh with such abandon. It was a special gift, she realized, all wrapped up in a bow and presented to her by a charming desperado whose badge had winked at her every time he flipped a pea at the child.

He pushed up from his chair. "Ladies, I think we've done all the damage we can for one night." He helped Brianna scoot back her chair and then offered her his arm. "We're all due for a good night's sleep, I think."

Once upstairs in the hallway, Brianna shooed Daphne into their room to prepare for bed. As soon as the door closed, she turned to David. "Thank you so much for the lovely meal. It was made all the more special by the projectile entertainment, and I'm sure Daphne will remember it for a long while."

David, standing with his hands at his hips

and his feet slightly apart, moved toward her. His big, work-hardened hand cupped her chin. "I'm your husband," he reminded her in a voice gone husky. "There's no need to thank me for the meal. As for the entertainment, it was my pleasure."

He dipped his head. Brianna's breath caught, for she knew he meant to kiss her. It had been years since she'd allowed such a liberty, and even then, she'd engaged in only quick pecks, never a real joining of lips. David had given her a quick peck last night, but she had a feeling that wasn't his usual habit. His face blurred in her vision. His breath, sweet with the scent of recently sipped wine, wafted over her cheek. She didn't know what to do with her hands, wasn't sure she even wanted this to happen. But David wasn't asking. He moved in with easy certainty, tipping her head just so as his lips settled lightly over hers. At the contact, all the breath rushed from her lungs. His mouth caressed hers like warm satin. Her eyes drifted closed. Her hands finally found anchor on the front of his shirt, her fingers clutching a bit frantically at the cloth as a delicious, tingling sensation swirled deep into her core.

When she felt the tip of his tongue trace the seam of her lips, she jumped with a start. He drew slightly back, his blue eyes sharpening on hers. A quizzical expression settled on his dark face. Then he smiled slightly.

"Sweet dreams, Shamrock." He tucked her room key into her hand and curled her limp fingers around it. "Lock up tight. If you need me, I'm only one room away."

Brianna's knees felt watery. She sank against the portal behind her for support, her lungs still hitching from the sensations he'd ignited within her. He paused outside his room, watching her expectantly. She realized he wanted her safely inside her chamber with the door secured before he sought his own rest.

She turned to fumble with the doorknob, her hands shaking. When she spilled inside, Daphne sat on the edge of the bed brushing her hair. She wore only the new shift David had bought her at the general store. Brianna had trouble fitting the key into the hole. When she finally got the mechanism to turn, she pocketed the apparatus and stood with her shoulder blades pressed against the door.

"Are you all right, Mama?"

Brianna wasn't certain. Her bones felt like candle wax that had softened from too much heat. "I'm fine." Her voice sounded as if it belonged to someone else, faint and far away. "Just fine."

David kicked off his boots and shucked the damp jeans before flopping down on the bed to stare sightlessly at the shadowy ceiling. The smell of sunlight and spring breezes drifted up from the linens and blankets, telling him they were clean. He also caught the scent of beeswax coming from the furnishings. He was no stickler when it came to hotel accommodations, but he did like to know he wasn't using bedding that had been soiled by a stranger.

Troubling thoughts circled in his mind as he considered Brianna and that brief kiss. She'd kept her lips clamped closed like an untried schoolgirl, and he'd felt the jolt of surprise that shot through her body when he tried to breach the barrier with his tongue. Then, when he drew back, her cheeks had been as red as California apples, and she'd been so flustered that he doubted she could have strung three words together. Strange. All his instincts told him that the woman had never been properly kissed. But how the hell could that be? She'd borne him a child, and David, drunk or sober, always kissed a woman before he took things any further. Maybe, he decided, she was just sorely out of practice.

He sighed and let his eyes drift closed, his body yearning for sleep. But he had no sooner shuttered his peepers than he lifted his lashes again. Another thing about that kiss deeply troubled him. He'd felt no sense of recognition when he tasted her mouth. It was a very sweet, intoxicating mouth, and it amazed him that he had no recollection of having kissed her in the past. Granted, he'd locked lips with countless females, and he didn't remember every single one, but it seemed to him that engaging in that kind of intimacy with a beauty like Brianna should have stuck in his mind.

How drunk had he been that night, anyway? Pretty damned drunk, he guessed. The thought shamed him. He twisted and punched his pillow. A feather escaped the ticking and stuck to his lower lip. He sputtered and scrubbed it away with the back of his hand. Then he sank into the down beneath him, determinedly closed his eyes, and willed himself to fall asleep.

In the next room, Brianna, too, stared blankly at the ceiling. She'd just turned off the lantern, and it still made a slight hissing sound. Beside her, Daphne had already snuggled down to snooze, her breathing deep and even. Exhausted, Brianna yearned for rest, but she was too upset to relax. So David had kissed her, and yes, it had been delightful, but what kind of ninny was she to go weak at the knees over it? She had to keep her wits about her with that man.

He felt honor bound to be a father to Daphne, and Brianna had to bear in mind that she was merely part of the package. He hadn't kissed her because he felt attracted to her. He was simply taking stock of the situation, and being a practical man, he had decided that a marriage of necessity might be more tolerable for both of them if they engaged in physical intimacy. Well, she wasn't about to be bamboozled by a handsome marshal with a weighty amount of guilt and obligation riding his shoulders. He was a good man. She'd come to sincerely believe that. But she wouldn't accept his affections when he offered them only out of a sense of duty. It was humiliating enough that she had succumbed so eagerly to that one kiss.

*Never again.* She'd all but swooned. To melt like that when the man kissing her had only been pretending made her cringe with shame. Pigs would fly before she let it happen again. The next time David Paxton tried to kiss her, she'd set him straight in no uncertain terms.

Willing himself to sleep didn't work. David tried counting sheep, but he remained wide-awake, reliving that kiss. It had been incredible, at least for him, so much so that he'd almost lost it for a second. As arousing as it had been, though, he couldn't shake his impression that it had been one of Brianna's first.

Baffled, David recalled Brianna's story about having a twin sister and growing up in an orphanage. What if she was telling the truth? *Nah.* Daphne's looks negated that possibility. She was definitely a Paxton. Still troubled, David drifted off to sleep and dreamed of the wonderful sound of his daughter's giggles. Then the dreams changed, and he jerked awake in a sweat, aroused by images of Brianna, naked and willing in his arms. *Vivid images.* Maybe, he decided, he did remember her in some dark corner of his mind.

# CHAPTER FIFTEEN

Because David now felt certain that Brianna would get no harebrained notions about trying to escape, he stuck to his decision the next morning that further travel on horseback was unnecessary. Leaving her and Daphne to linger over breakfast in the hotel restaurant, he walked up the street to the tiny train station to procure tickets to Denver, and then arranged traveling accommodations for the horses and mule. The train was due to depart at noon, so David went to the livery to collect the animals, enlisting the help of a stable hand to bring the riding tack, packs, and plenty of feed over to the stock car. All the gear, except his saddlebags, which he'd left at the hotel, was stowed in the baggage compartment.

When he got back to the hotel, checkout time had come and gone. He found his wife and daughter waiting in the lobby. Brianna had gotten a key to his room, and his saddlebags, plus hotel-stamped totes containing their laundry, rested at her feet.

"You could have just waited in the room," David told her.

She waved away the suggestion. "They were going to charge you for another night. I don't think they're full, so I thought we could let more rooms if you decided to stay."

She looked beyond beautiful in the emerald gown with the black cloak draped over her bent arm. Daphne was equally lovely in her yellow and brown frock and patent leather shoes, which had taken a beating out on the prairie but were still presentable. David drew out his watch to check the time. They had only forty minutes to collect Brianna's other dresses and accessories from the shop.

David carried their belongings and herded his small flock out of the hotel and up the street. The dressmaker had finished the alterations and packaged the garments, leaving out only a black drawstring reticule and a brimmed black hat adorned with a mass of emerald green bows at the crown. While Brianna donned the bonnet, securing it with hatpins, David paid the bill, collected their things, and then allowed his ladies to carry the parcels as they hurried out onto the boardwalk. Dodging women shoppers and businessmen in trousers and frock coats, they all but ran to the opposite end of town. They had only five minutes to spare when they reached the closet-size station. Wearing a black suit and billed cap, the conductor yelled, "All aboard!" Then he shouted the names of the towns where stops would be made. David wondered why. There were no other passengers that he could see getting on in Clapboard Flats.

He juggled his saddlebags and bundles of laundry to dig the tickets out of his duster pocket, then boarded the train behind his wife and daughter. The passenger area, a far cry from the plush interiors that Ace had designed for his private train cars, was nearly empty. An older couple sat at the far end, and a lone gentleman sat at the middle right. David indicated a front compartment with a nod of his head. While Brianna and Daphne took places facing each other, he stowed all their stuff under the child's seat.

"As we get closer to Denver, more travelers will join us," David told them. "For now, let's enjoy having the car mostly to ourselves."

Brianna fanned her face. "My goodness, such a rush! I'm breathless."

So was David, but not from exertion. Just looking at Brianna robbed his lungs of oxygen. The gown and fancy hat had transformed her from shabby to elegant. The cut at the corner of her eye was healing nicely and scarcely detracted from the perfection of her countenance. The insert of black eyelet, designed to conceal her cleavage, performed its job, but nothing save a cloak could hide the generous swells of her breasts above the ruffles.

Daphne wiggled on her seat, reminding David of a worm squirming on a hook. She was so excited when the whistle blew and the train shuddered forward that her eyes danced with delight. He sat back, content to let her expend all her energy quickly so she'd fall asleep before the car filled with passengers at future stops. He needed to have a long, private talk with Brianna.

Daphne took two hours to wind down. Brimming with questions, she kept both David and Brianna busy. What made the train move? How fast did it go? When the conductor left the car, what did he do? Where were Blue, Lucy, and Acorn? Did they have food and water? David figured the animals were more comfortable than they were. There was a dining car, but in his experience the food would be pretty dismal. When the train stopped to refuel, they could go to a restaurant, but it would be a mad dash. The train wouldn't wait for any passengers late getting back.

During the first leg of the journey, David couldn't help but admire Brianna for her determinedly cheerful attitude. Though her nether regions were still saddle sore, she didn't complain about the hard bench seat, and she was patience itself when Daphne grew cranky. David loved the kid, but her constant chatter started to wear on his nerves. He wanted her to pipe down for five minutes and give his ears a rest.

Finally, the child slumped in the window corner of her seat, her blond head lolling against the glass. David nearly groaned with relief. He glanced over at Brianna.

"Blessed silence at last," he whispered.

"All this is so exciting for her. She was only an infant when I brought her out West."

David decided to ignore that. He'd barely slept last night, and if Brianna started in with her convent story again, he wasn't sure he could hold his tongue. It was time for her to accept their situation and move ahead.

"Now that she's asleep, we need to iron out a few things. Once we reach Denver, it'll be late at night, possibly the wee hours of morning. I'd like to make some decisions now while we're still rested and thinking clearly."

"About?" Brianna arched a dark eyebrow at him. "If you still intend to dump me off in Denver, you'd best understand that you'll not be leaving me there without my daughter."

David deeply regretted that remark. "I was angry when I said that. I didn't mean it."

She folded her hands primly in her lap, only the white glow of her knuckles revealing her tension. "So what do you plan to do?"

"I considered setting you up in your own dress shop," he ventured. "Denver would be an ideal location, with lots of wealthy ladies who might become patrons." He saw her stiffen and added, "But brief as our acquaintance has been, I've come to realize you'll never be happy living away from Daphne. It's only a morning's journey by train from Denver to No Name, though, so if you're interested in the idea, we could work it out. You could see her on weekends. There are plenty of bedrooms at my ranch. And during the summers, she could stay in Denver with you, and I could do the commuting."

Her green eyes sparked with outrage. "I will *never* live apart from my daughter, sir."

David had pretty much figured that out

already. "All right," he said, striving to keep his tone calm and soothing. "We'll work something else out. Just understand that I've been thinking about all the possible alternatives, and they're problematic."

"I don't care how *problematic* they may be. I will *not* be separated from my child. If anyone is going to live apart from her, it will be you."

"I said we'll work it out, Brianna. Just calm down."

She drew a shaky breath and relaxed her shoulders. "So what are our options?"

David took a moment to gauge his words before replying, "Well, for starters, I'm as determined as you are to be a full-time parent. I've missed six years of her life, and from now on, I want to be a proper father to her. Surely you can understand that."

She indicated that she did with a slight nod.

"Anyhow," David went on, "I can't see how I can accomplish that if I don't live under the same roof with her."

Brianna's eyes went round with apprehension. "But if I am bent on living under the same roof with her, and you feel the same, where does that leave us?"

David could think of no easy way to say it, so he just spit it out. "It leaves us living together." He held up a hand. "Think about it before you let that Irish temper get the better of you. I suppose we could maintain separate residences and share time with our daughter, but think how that would look to the people of No Name. Nobody would understand why a man and wife would choose to be married and live apart."

"Frankly, I don't care what the people of No Name think or say."

"You will about the time it starts hurting our daughter. The gossip might affect Daphne more than us."

"Oh, dear," she said softly.

"Divorce isn't unheard of," David went on, "but it's still considered to be scandalous. Vicious tongues can draw blood, and I don't want it to be Daphne's. The way I see it, we are responsible for her existence, and that means we are the ones who should suffer the consequences. For her sake, I think we need to make every possible attempt to appear to be a happily married couple."

Brianna stared with glistening eyes at their daughter, who was still deeply asleep. She said nothing.

"There's a dress shop in No Name," David told her. "It has living quarters on the second floor. I've never been up there, but judging by the lower floor plan, I suspect the apartment is roomy. The proprietress is an older woman and often wishes aloud that she could sell out and go to live with her son in California. I'm pretty certain she'll negotiate with me if I offer a fair starting price. You've always wanted your own dress shop."

She fixed him with a bewildered look. "How did you come by that information? That I want my own dress shop, I mean."

"Daphne. When we're riding together, she talks nonstop."

Brianna sighed again. "That child needs a sock stuffed in her mouth sometimes."

David chuckled. "Ah, well, in this case, the information came in handy. So what do you think? Should I pursue the dress-shop idea? As marshal, I divide my time between town and my ranch, often spending nights in the jail. It would be just as easy for me to sleep on a cot in the dress-shop apartment. On the surface, it would appear that we're a happily married couple, recently reunited. No one will think it strange if I continue to spend some nights at the ranch to oversee my hired hands and do the books."

"Well, I must say I find this proposition more appealing than having to live in Denver so far from my daughter. But practically speaking, how can you and I make a

447

charade like that work over a long period of time?" Her gaze clung to his. "I agree that Daphne's happiness is of the utmost importance, but what of *your* future? As far as our marriage goes, we both know the union may not be legal. In fact, I'm fairly certain it isn't."

David couldn't argue with that. Brianna hadn't given her consent, there'd been only one adult witness instead of the required two, and the whole mess had taken place in the very worst kind of kangaroo court. "Your point?"

"Have you considered an annulment? If we both went together and filed for one, it would probably be easy to get."

It was David's turn to stiffen. "And?"

"Until you realize the truth, that Daphne isn't yours, I would be willing to live with the child in Denver so you might see her regularly." When David started to speak, she held up a hand. "Hear me out. You spoke the other night about having your life all planned before you got my letters. I believe those plans involved a woman. Am I wrong?"

David stared beyond her out the window, the passing scenery nothing but a blur. "No, you're not wrong. There was a woman, but it wasn't —"

She cut him off to say, "With the marriage annulled, you would be free to marry her, David, and have other children. You're so wonderful with Daphne. You'd be such a fabulous father. Even if it makes you furious with me for mentioning it again, I can't help but feel I must out of fairness to you. She is *not* your child. And when you finally come to realize that, you're going to resent me and *her* for ruining your life."

A burning sensation crawled up the back of David's throat. "Are you finished?"

She searched his gaze. "Yes, quite finished. Just never let it be said that I have withheld the truth from you or that I set out to hoodwink you."

He laughed, the sound bitter even to his ears. "God knows I'll never say that. You've told me your *truth* a dozen times. Enough. All it does is infuriate me. I'll never believe that child isn't mine, and I'm not about to have her live in Denver. So get that idea out of your head. I've offered you an alternative. Take it or leave it."

"Pretending to be a happily married couple? What if I say no, David? What if I believe such a charade will never work?"

"All I know is, I'm not parting company with my daughter."

"And neither am I."

Disgruntled, David shifted on the seat, moving his hat from one knee to the other. "Then we're at loggerheads. If you can accept the No Name dress-shop idea and a pretend marriage, maybe we can work at making it a real marriage over time. In the end, it will be best for Daphne if her parents are able to give her a real family."

Still embarrassed about the kiss they had shared last night, Brianna watched the passing landscape for a moment before speaking. "On the subject of working toward making this a real marriage, I must warn you that I want no part of marital intimacy. Without love or at least some measure of genuine desire on both our parts, it would be debasing. I will never be with a man simply to keep up appearances."

He said nothing, and his continued silence finally forced Brianna to look at him. His eyes twinkled with humor, which was at least an improvement on the anger she'd seen in them moments ago, but she had the uneasy feeling the joke was on her.

"May I ask what is so funny?"

His firm mouth tipped into a grin as if he harbored a hilarious secret he wasn't willing to share. "You have my word that I will never press you for intimacy unless there is love or at least some measure of genuine desire on both our parts. With that agreed upon, can we move ahead with the dress-shop idea and *pretending* for a while?"

Brianna couldn't see that she had another choice. "So long as we both agree on the intimacy stipulations, I suppose we can give a life of pretense a try," she conceded.

Satisfied with Brianna's response, David stretched out his legs and settled back with his hat over his eyes to take a nap with his daughter. Problem was, he couldn't sleep. Brianna wanted there to be love in the relationship, and he wasn't sure anymore what love was. He'd definitely enjoyed that kiss last night and would happily go for seconds, but that was only lust. Or was it? She was a beautiful woman. More important, though, she challenged him at every turn, amusing him one moment, infuriating him the next, and at times filling him with tender feelings he'd never experienced with a female.

All his adult life, David had clung to the hope that he'd one day find a woman who brought pure magic into his heart, someone who elicited all-consuming emotions within him — someone with whom he could laugh and cry — someone who could fill his world with love and contentment. Was it possible that he might find that magical something with Brianna when he'd failed to find it with Hazel Wright? David thought maybe so. Brianna was like spiced wine, heady and tempting in a way the schoolteacher wasn't.

*Maybe I'm losing my mind.* The thought made him grin into the bowl of his hat. On the surface, Brianna was the epitome of a well-bred lady, but under that cool, oh-so-proper exterior, she was stubborn, willful, and hot tempered. He'd always hoped to find a malleable, tractable woman — someone sweet and easy to get along with. Life with Brianna would be like riding on a runaway stagecoach, one dip and jostle after another. And when she wasn't in a temper, she was so damnably decorous all the time, the type to freeze a man out during and after a quarrel instead of giving vent to her true feelings. Last night, he'd pushed her into giggling and acting silly, but that wasn't the norm for her, and, damn it, there was more to marriage than having sex. David wanted a wife he could laugh with, someone who wasn't afraid to cut loose and forget about propriety sometimes. He wasn't sure Brianna could do that without a lot of prodding, and over time, prodding her constantly would get old.

Even so, he found himself growing more attracted to her with each passing second. And if that wasn't a fine how-do-you-do, he didn't know what was.

Sitting across from her daughter, Brianna sought sleep as well, with no more luck than David was having. Her thoughts were centered on the problems that could arise in a sham marriage. More than once, she'd glimpsed masculine appreciation in his eyes when he looked at her, and she would never forget that kiss last night. He seemed perfectly willing to keep his hands off her right now, but what if he changed his mind later? The marriage document in his saddlebag would make his taking of her legal. Having been single all her life, Brianna was no expert on the baser natures of men, but she suspected that their physical needs were far more urgent than those of women. How could he hope to be happy and content in a platonic relationship?

Emotionally drained, Brianna removed her hat and fingered the looped emerald ribbons at the crown. She'd never possessed anything so fine. In the convent, colorful garments had been forbidden, and all but the most subdued pieces of jewelry had been frowned upon. *Adornments,* the nuns had called them. Proper young ladies wore nothing ostentatious. As a girl, Brianna had yearned for a bright red dress and patent leather slippers studded at the toes with diamonds. That seemed so silly to her now. As an adult, she'd come to appreciate just having clothing, no matter how drab it was.

Even so, she loved this emerald gown. Slipping her palm over the fine-grained silk, she smiled dreamily, wondering for a fleeting moment if God hadn't guided David to Glory Ridge. Whether he was Daphne's father or not, he offered the child everything that Brianna had always yearned to give her. Would it be so evil of her to simply accept this good fortune and say nothing more to David about the truth? He grew furious each time she brought it up, so why couldn't she simply acquiesce and keep quiet?

Because she felt so guilty, she decided. He was revamping his whole life around a child that wasn't his, possibly even forsaking marriage to a woman he really loved. She'd tried several times to be honest with him, though. In the end, when the harsh truth smacked him between the eyes, he wouldn't be able to say that she'd been anything less than forthright. *Let it go,* a small voice whispered in her mind. *Pray about it, have faith, and all will be well.* Ah, Sister Theresa, whispering to her again, Brianna thought. A very wise woman, that nun, for no matter how Brianna circled it, the dress-shop idea had its appeal and would be the best arrangement for Daphne.

It would, in fact, be nearly perfect. With David as her father, she would have a family — a grandmother, uncles, aunts, and cousins. She'd be loved and never want for anything. David had become her father in every way that counted. Daphne adored him, and he adored her.

With a sigh, Brianna settled back on her seat and let her eyes drift closed. There were so many possible pitfalls in David's plan, though. What if someone in No Name discovered that their marriage was a sham? That would be utterly devastating for Daphne. And it would be wearing on both Brianna and David to live a lie, day in and day out. He would be consigning himself to a loveless future without a real wife to warm his bed. And when he discovered that he wasn't really Daphne's father, what would become of her and Daphne then?

It was a bridge she would cross when she came to it, she supposed. She and Daphne had survived before and they could do it again. Until then, Brianna would be like a leaf, blown this way and that by a wind over which she had no control. *Pray about it, have faith, and all will be well.*

Their train pulled into Denver at half past three in the morning. Brianna, nearly blind with exhaustion, was relieved beyond measure when David decided they should get rooms at the hotel and postpone the last leg of their journey to No Name until the next day. Using the hotel telephone, he called Ace to arrange for their transportation. They were to be at the train station by noon, which would give them at least a few hours to rest before leaving the city.

David went to a saloon up the street to see if he could get food because all of them were hungry. He returned with steak sandwiches and a quart bottle of apple juice, which they could drink from water glasses in their rooms. Brianna answered his knock, gratefully accepted the cold fare, and bid him a hasty good night. She had learned her lesson the previous evening and didn't linger in the doorway, fearing he might kiss her again if she gave him an opportunity.

Because it was so late, there was no hotel staff on duty to bring up tubs, so she and Daphne settled for spit baths. Brianna made short work of getting herself and the child dressed for bed. Then they sat on the edge of the mattress to eat. Brianna had just taken a bite of sandwich when a tap came at the door.

She set aside her food and crossed the room. "Who is it?"

"David. I forgot to get some juice."

"Oh." Brianna quickly opened up. "I'm sorry. I didn't think."

He stepped in, holding an empty water glass. Brianna poured him a measure of apple juice and then stared up at him, uncertain what else to say.

He smiled slightly. "Thanks. The sandwich is dry with nothing to help wash it down."

She followed him back to the door and watched as he stepped out into the hall. "Good night again," she said.

"Good night. Be sure to lock up tight."

After finishing her meal, Brianna turned off the electric light, which was a novelty to her, and then joined her daughter in bed. Her last thought as exhaustion blacked out her mind was that on the morrow she would accompany David to No Name and meet his family. She had no doubt that they would welcome Daphne into their fold, but how would they feel about her — a wicked woman from David's past who'd gotten pregnant with his child out of wedlock?

She was too tired to worry about it. David

could deal with his family, blast it. She was only a leaf blowing in the wind.

# CHAPTER SIXTEEN

Brianna was awestruck by the sumptuous appointments in Ace Keegan's passenger car. The seats with curved armrests were upholstered in dark green, cushiony leather that felt as soft as butter to the touch. Instead of planks, intricately patterned rugs of green, burgundy, and deep gold cushioned the floor. At one end, a hand-carved mahogany bar was stocked with different kinds of spirits, soft drinks, glasses, and an icebox filled with chilled snacks. Daphne enjoyed a sarsaparilla, slices of cheese, and an orange before curling up on the sofa for a nap. Sitting beside David in one of the armchairs, Brianna sipped a glass of sherry while he partook of a fine whiskey.

"Your family must be very influential in No Name," she observed.

"I guess you might say that."

The realization struck her that David was a powerful man in his community, undoubtedly as respected in his own right as he was well connected. She stared for a moment at his badge, which represented authority and dominance few men attained in their professions. As much as she'd come to trust him on the prairie, she knew things would be different now. What if he changed his mind about their agreement and insisted on a real marriage? She would have no one to turn to for help.

"You feeling okay, Shamrock? The motion of the train isn't making you sick, I hope. With fewer cars, there's a little more movement, I reckon."

"No, no, the car is lovely. I've never traveled in such luxury."

"Ace doesn't spare coin when it comes to comfort," he told her. "His home is simple in layout, just a ranch house, but it's got all the conveniences possible. Joseph and I have followed his lead. Esa is still toying with the idea of modernizing his place."

Brianna suddenly remembered her question to David right before his shootout with the three ne'er-do-wells, and to distract herself from other, far more unsettling thoughts, she decided to follow up on that. "I've read stories about a gunslinger named Ace Keegan," she said, forcing a smile. "Surely we're not discussing the same man."

David turned his tumbler, studying the amber contents. "Will you fall over in a dead faint if I say we are?"

Brianna did feel momentarily lightheaded. If David wasn't joking, then his family was far more than simply influential; at least one member was downright dangerous. "The Ace Keegan I read about once killed three men with one bullet."

"*That* was a freak accident. He shot the first guy, and then the bullet ricocheted to kill the second one. I think Ace fired another shot to kill the third fellow, but I could have my facts wrong. We don't pay those novels much mind because they're usually so far-fetched. The truth of what happened never makes for quite as good a story."

Brianna set aside her glass of sherry. "So your older brother is *the* Ace Keegan."

"Yes, gunslinger and gambler turned family man. He never wears his Colts now unless he's forced to. He's a good man, Brianna. I think you'll like him. Just know up front that nothing nettles him more than the outrageous stories told about him in those damned dime novels."

"Thank you for the warning. I don't believe it would be wise to nettle Ace Keegan."

David threw back his head and barked

with laughter. "You can nettle him all you like. He'd never harm a hair on your head, and that's a fact."

Once in No Name, David rented a buggy from the livery to drive them out to Ace's ranch. Brianna had hoped to postpone meeting the Keegan and Paxton clan until tomorrow, but David nixed that with, "No way. They'll all be gathered at Ace's place, and the women will have a huge meal prepared to welcome you. If we don't show up, they'll be sorely disappointed."

Brianna was unaccountably tense. Out on the prairie, she'd been completely alone with David, except for Daphne, and she'd come to trust him in ways she'd never trusted another man. But this was different. He was taking her into *his* world, he was her spouse, and at the back of her mind, she kept returning to the reality of her situation, namely that husbands had absolute power if they chose to exercise it. They were the kings of their households, and in many cases, wives were treated with little regard. She didn't believe David would turn suddenly autocratic or consider her to be a possession, but way deep down where she couldn't rationalize her way past it, she felt uneasy and vulnerable.

Daphne bounced on the buggy seat between Brianna and David, so excited to
meet David's family that she was nearly
beside herself. Brianna supposed that for
the child it was indeed a momentous occasion. Daphne had never had relatives, none
that acknowledged her, anyway, and now
the little girl suddenly had a host of them.
It was Grandma Dory this, and Aunt Caitlin that, and she pestered David relentlessly
to go over the names of everyone else so
she wouldn't forget.

When Brianna saw buildings in the distance, she turned to straighten Daphne's
clothing and tidy her hair. "Remember your
manners, now. Wait until you're properly
introduced before addressing the adults,
and once inside the house, you mustn't ask
for anything. If you're offered something
and you'd like to have some, what do you
say?"

Daphne wrinkled her nose. "I say please,
that sounds wonderful, and thank you very
much for offering."

David flashed Brianna a grin over the top
of the child's head. "Shamrock, you're in
for a big surprise. We aren't a family that
stands on ceremony. Just relax, okay? None
of them bite."

Brianna couldn't relax. She was about to

meet people who had every reason to stand in judgment of her and might also resent her for ruining David's life. As the house came into view, she made tight fists in her skirt, straightened her shoulders, and lifted her chin. No matter what they said or did, she would face them with pride.

A little dark-haired boy Brianna guessed to be a bit over three was the first to spot the buggy. He tore across the front veranda, shouting, "Unco David, Unco David!"

"Little Ace," David said. "Going on three and a half, and full of mischief."

Brianna thought he was adorable, with olive skin, shoe-button eyes, and a shock of pitch-black hair. He was dressed in a blue pullover shirt, denim knickers bloused at the knees, black stockings already smeared with dirt, and sturdy little black boots.

David drew the buggy to a halt, looped the reins, and set the brake. Lucy, tethered to the back of the conveyance with Blue and Acorn, let loose with a happy hee-haw. The mule clearly recognized her surroundings and knew she was almost home. The geldings joined in with shrill nickers to voice their excitement, too.

Just then an extremely tall, jet-haired man in jeans and a blue chambray shirt stepped out onto the porch, holding the screen ajar behind him to offer passage to a beautiful, slightly built redhead in a blue-checked gingham day dress. In her arms, she held a raven-haired little girl who was chubby and darling in a lacy pink frock.

"Ace, his wife, Caitlin, and their youngest, Dory Sue, named after my ma," David supplied. He leaped from the buggy and circled the matched set of blacks to come around and help Brianna down. "And there comes Joseph with his wife, Rachel, and Little Joe."

Brianna was so startled by the sight of Joseph, who from a distance appeared to be a dead ringer for David, that she lost her footing on the step. David caught her around the waist to keep her from falling and swung her easily to the ground. At his touch, Brianna's breath caught. Was it only her imagination, or was David acting more proprietary than he ever had before? "Calm down, Shamrock. It's just my family, you know? They're happy to have you here."

Brianna wasn't so sure about that. Though Ace wore no weapons, his stance and air were of a man who could look death in the eye a thousand times and never blink. Brianna didn't miss the way he assessed her from head to toe with his dark eyes. His fiery-haired wife came down to stand at the left of the front steps with him, and Joseph and his wife took their positions to the right. It was almost as if they'd rehearsed the greeting and stood off to each side to make way for a queen.

And then she appeared, an older lady in a lavender housedress with perfectly coiffed blond hair shimmering with streaks of silver. Brianna froze, staring at her with fascinated incredulity. In another fifty years, it could have been Daphne standing on that porch. The resemblance was astounding. No, no, Brianna corrected herself, it was downright unbelievable. Little wonder David remained so fully convinced that Daphne was his. The little girl truly was the spitting image of his mother.

Dory Paxton remained on the porch for a moment, her slender hands pressed to her heart. Even from many feet away, Brianna saw her blue eyes, the same color as Daphne's, go bright with tears. Then, with her skirt lifted in one hand and exquisite grace of carriage, she came down the porch steps and cut across the patchy front yard, her gaze never wavering from the child still sitting in the buggy. She bypassed David and Brianna, stepped between the iron wheels, and lifted her arms.

"Hurry, hurry," she said with a laugh. "Come give your grandmother a hug."

Daphne launched herself into the woman's arms. Dory Paxton caught the child fiercely close, swayed side to side for a moment, and then beamed a smile at David, her lovely face streaked with tears. "She looks just like *me.* I can't believe it! Just like me! What a lovely gift to bring home to your mother!"

"Ain't she something?" David laughed and curled an arm around Brianna's shoulders. She stiffened under the weight of his hand on her upper arm. *Not my imagination,* she decided. He was letting everyone present know that she belonged to him. "I almost fainted when I first saw her."

Dory stepped over to touch Brianna's hand, then leaned forward to kiss her cheek. "Forgive my appalling lack of manners, dear, but a grandmother does have her priorities." She cricked her neck to study Daphne's face again and beamed another smile. "My, my, such a grown-up girl you are, Daphne." She turned so the child could see her other relatives. Pointing, she introduced them. Daphne seemed particularly taken with Little Joe, Joseph's son, who would celebrate his first birthday in only a few weeks.

Little Ace ran up to tug on Daphne's slipper. "Get down, Daffy, get down! Come see our kittens! We got lots and lots!"

"Hold on for just a moment, Little Ace," Dory said. "First let your uncle David introduce his wife to everyone."

The introductions passed in a blur for Brianna. The famous Ace Keegan stepped forward first, gave her a firm hug, and said, "Welcome to our family." To Brianna, he seemed as tall and sturdy as a tree. Next she was being embraced by Caitlin and treated to a wet, open-mouth kiss on the cheek from Dory Sue. Upon closer inspection, Brianna confirmed that Joseph was indeed a dead ringer for David, his mannerisms and speech nearly the same. He hugged her with a clench of strong arms, then set her back a step to survey her face. "She'll do," he told David with a smile. Rachel, still holding Little Joe, gave Brianna a shyer greeting, but it was nonetheless welcoming. She was a lovely woman, diminutive of stature, with large blue eyes, corn-silk blond hair, and an angelic countenance.

"Now can we go see the kitties?" Little Ace cried.

Dory laughed and set Daphne on her feet. "Mind the cow and horses, Little Ace! I don't want you getting kicked!"

The warning fell on deaf ears. The little boy was already racing toward the barn with

Daphne following in his dusty wake. Caitlin handed Dory Sue to her husband. "I'd better go supervise." She settled sparkling blue eyes on Brianna. "Would you like to come along to see our kittens?"

Brianna felt David's palm at the center of her spine, nudging her forward. The heat of his hand gave her a start. As she fell into step behind Caitlin, who was hurrying to catch up with her son, she heard Joseph's wife, Rachel, say, "You take Little Joe. I want to see the kittens, too."

Before Brianna knew quite how it happened, she was in the barn with two just-met women who called her by name and acted as if they'd known her forever. It was the oddest experience of her life. No sidelong looks of disapproval, no uncomfortable questions, no sense of separateness. Brianna felt overdressed, for both of her sisters-in-law wore cotton, not silk. She comforted herself with the thought that their simple gingham dresses were far nicer than the one she'd worn the day before yesterday, and she was glad David had insisted on buying her new outfits, inappropriate for the surroundings though they might be. At least she didn't feel humiliated beyond bearing.

Feeling absurdly overdone, Brianna removed her hat and hooked it over a stall post. The dim interior lacked the rank odor of manure that had always assailed her nostrils in Ricker's barn, which told her that Ace, like David, took excellent care of his stock. Lifting her skirts, she sat on the scattered hay with the other two women to watch the children admire the kittens. Daphne's face glowed as she lifted a tiny bit of tabby fluff to her cheek.

"Oh, Mama, I've always wanted a kitten!"

Caitlin, strikingly beautiful with her glorious red hair, refined features, and vibrant eyes, laughed musically. "Take your pick. When they're old enough, I'll send one home with you!"

Rachel interjected, "Oh, no, you don't! Daphne can come to my house and take her pick now. Mine are already old enough to leave their mamas."

"I offered first!" Caitlin cried. Then, grabbing Little Ace by the backs of his hands, she said, "No, *no,* you be gentle. Ears are to hear with, and eyes are to see with. If you poke, I'll give you a swat."

Little Ace immediately lightened his hold on the kitten and, following Daphne's example, held the bit of fur to his cheek. "Can I have one, too, Mama?"

Caitlin rolled her eyes. "I'm afraid you can have all of them except for the one

Cousin Daphne picks. Papa says we've plenty of milk, cream, and rodents to have a hundred cats. Aren't you a lucky little boy?"

"I am." Little Ace smiled at his mother. "I want this one. It's soft and smells good."

Caitlin ruffled his hair. "Mind that you are gentle, then."

Rachel lifted the mewling feline she held to admire its markings. "I stand corrected, Daphne. This is the one for you. A baby girl with a diamond shape on her forehead. If you take her, you'll always have baby kittens to love, too. Just make sure your papa approves and commits himself to supplying plenty of milk and food for your cat family."

Daphne took the kitten, her blue eyes round with wonder. Looking up at Brianna, she whispered, "Do you think Papa will let me have her, Mama?"

In that moment, Brianna would have believed anything was possible. "He might."

"I'm going to call her Diamond!" Daphne cried.

Dory entered the barn and came to sit on the hay with them. The circle was now complete. She admired Daphne's kitten. "I don't think Diamond is the right name for her," she said thoughtfully, her brow creasing in a thoughtful frown just the way Daphne's did. "See how the diamond shape is up between her little ears? I think she should be called Tiara."

Daphne took the kitten back to study her markings. "Like a princess, Grandma?"

"Absolutely," Dory said, dimpling her cheek. "My granddaughter deserves nothing less than a cat with royal blood."

Brianna stared stupidly at her daughter and Dory Paxton. The resemblance between the older woman and little girl wasn't only physical. They shared mannerisms and facial expressions. Watching them together and knowing that the two were not related by blood, Brianna could scarcely believe her eyes. Dory even had the same strawberry mark on her neck.

"Well," Rachel said, springing to her feet, "we can no longer count on Grandma Dory to be watching over dinner. I'd better get back before the men take over."

"Oh, lawzy." Caitlin jumped up, too. "Ace will start playing with Dory Sue and forget all about my bread."

Little Ace started to cry because he didn't want to leave the kittens. Caitlin quickly dispensed with his tears by saying, "Run, Daphne! I bet Little Ace can't catch you!"

And the race was on. Brianna fetched her hat. As she departed from the barn in the company of David's female relatives, she swatted at her silk skirts to dispense with the hay. "I think I need to visit the dress shop for some more practical gowns. I can see right now that silk will never do for everyday wear."

"The dress shop? You needn't do that." Caitlin grinned impishly. "Rachel and I both sew, and our husbands have supplied us with the loveliest sewing machines you've ever clapped eyes on."

Rachel nodded. "I have some yellow gingham that would look fabulous on you! I thought it would work for me, but when I got it home and held it up in front of a mirror, I looked like a yellow blob."

"And I have a length of pink!" Caitlin exclaimed. "I've always wanted to wear pink, but it simply isn't usually possible for me. It clashes with my hair something awful."

"You both sew?"

Dory, trailing slightly behind them, answered that question. "Sew? They are masters of the art."

"I have heaps of patterns," Rachel cried. "Just wait until you see. I've got all the latest fashions."

Brianna was delighted to have sisters-in-law who shared her passion for creating gowns. "Uh-oh. That won't bode well for a dress shop. David mentioned buying me the one in town. It doesn't sound as if I'll get much business."

Caitlin's eyes lighted up. "Are you a designer?"

Brianna considered the question. Normally she would reply with modest understatement, but these women made her feel as if she was one of them, and it didn't seem wrong to state the truth. "It is my aim to one day become famous for my originals. I've only had the opportunity to design a few gowns, with cost always a drawback because it was in a small town, but with what I had to work with, I feel that I created some smashing successes."

"Truly?" Dory stepped forward to lock arms with Brianna. "How lovely! The dressmaker in No Name is older and doesn't keep up with the trends. If I want something high quality and fashionable, I must go back to Frisco for fittings. It would be so much easier if I could do that here. Are you really that good?"

Brianna thought about it for a moment, and deep in her heart of hearts, where impossible dreams had taken root, she did believe she was. "Well, it's all very subjective, isn't it? What I can definitely say is that I'm talented at sketching and producing what I draw. So perhaps we could spend a day creating some lovely gowns on paper to see if we share the same vision."

"Oh, lands!" Rachel planted a hand over her breasts and spun in a circle. "I must ask Joseph to fill out a blank draft so I can go a little crazy. I'm due for at least *two* really fabulous gowns. My aunt Amanda is in Paris right now! She sent me some pamphlets of the fashions there. How lovely would it be to greet her when she gets home wearing an eye-popping Parisian look-alike?"

In that moment, Brianna felt as if she was truly a part of this family. It was a heady, wonderful feeling. There was only one fly in her ointment: the inescapable fact that she didn't truly belong.

The early supper, which Brianna helped to prepare, was mind-boggling to both her and Daphne. So much food for only one family! There was fried chicken and pork chops, mashed potatoes, green beans, canned corn swimming in butter, fabulous yeast rolls fresh from the oven, two huge pitchers of chilled milk, and salad, all the ingredients of which Dory had collected from the grasslands around Ace's house. Little Ace was perched on a stack of books on the side bench of the long plank table. The toddlers each sat at a corner in elevated chairs with swing-around eating trays that Ace had made.

Just as the family surrounded the table to say the blessing before sitting down, the front door swung open, and another man who greatly resembled David stepped inside, dusting his jeans with a brown Stetson and stomping his boots on the threshold rug.

"Sorry I'm late. Had a heifer go down while calving. She almost didn't make it."

David unfolded his hands and went to hug his brother. As he turned back to the room he said, "Brianna, my baby brother, Esa. Esa, my wife, Brianna, and my daughter, Daphne."

Esa, with his David-like face and blue eyes, pushed at his short blond hair and whacked his hat against his leg again. "I'm too dirty to shake hands, but I'm glad to make your acquaintance, Brianna." His mouth relaxed into a grin. "Hey, Daphne. It's good to finally meet you."

Ace, who loomed like a dark sentinel behind his chair at the head of the table, said, "Between kittens and dinner preparation, I've barely met them myself." Inclining his head at the one empty place setting, he added, "Go wash up. We'll wait for you if you hurry and don't let the food get cold. Just remember to scrub behind your ears."

"Jesus, Ace, I'm not a pup anymore."

Dory spoke up. "Another word like that, young man, and I'll be scrubbing your mouth with lye soap. You'll not take the Lord's name in vain in front of the children."

Brianna jerked her gaze to David's. His lean cheeks went a bit pink; then he winked at her. She ducked her head to hide her smile.

"Sorry, Ma." Esa paused before heading up the hall to the washroom, which Brianna had visited and knew held a commode, a sink, and a tub, all with piped-in hot and cold water. To her, those were incredible luxuries. Glancing at the children, Esa said, "Jesus and I are best friends, so I say his name real regular during prayer. I meant no disrespect." He plucked a small, leather-bound book from the waistband of his jeans. He wore a hand-tooled belt and also a gun belt much like David's, which sported a holstered Colt revolver at each hip. "My Bible," he said. "I plan to be a preacher someday soon."

"A *what?*" Ace asked.

Esa drew up his shoulders, met his older

brother's gaze with eyes that suddenly sparked like flint, and said, "You heard me. I'm going to be a preacher."

"Jesus H. Christ," Ace whispered.

Dory said, "Caitlin, where is your lye soap?"

"Ma," Ace said with a warning note in his voice. "This is no time for that. He's serious."

"The two of you are talking like sailors, and I won't have it in front of the children."

Brianna totally agreed and was mentally applauding Dory for speaking her mind when David broke out with, "For Pete's sake, Ma, Esa just said he's going to become a preacher." He gestured toward his younger brother with a spread hand. "You can't blame us for questioning his sanity. He's a gunslinger, same as we are. How in the hell does that make sense? He can't read from the Good Book and tell people how to live their lives when he's packing six-shooters."

Esa took a step back into the dining area. "Why the hell can't I? I can believe in the Good Lord and still wear guns. Where does it say I can't defend myself against violence and still be a Christian? You need to read the Bible, David. Jesus was no pansy ass. I'll wear my Colts and quote Scripture, and I'll reach people who are struggling to survive

478

in this harsh country, carrying a rifle in one hand and a shovel in the other."

"I don't think defending myself is wrong," David retorted. "But given the fact that I do defend myself and will continue to do so when I'm threatened, I don't think I'm fit to be a man of the cloth, and neither are you."

Brianna glanced at her daughter. Daphne's eyes were as round as supper plates. Returning her attention to the Keegan-Paxton family, Brianna decided that her arrival as a fallen woman, with a heretofore illegitimate daughter in tow, had just taken second seat. *Bless you, Esa.* He'd drawn all the attention away from her.

The next instant, Brianna wasn't so sure Esa was a godsend. Joseph, David, and Ace all surged away from the table in a wave of formidable masculinity to confront their youngest brother, who stood with his worn Bible clutched in one brutal fist. Brianna feared there might be a physical clash. Just the possibility had her racing around the table, grabbing up her daughter, and retreating to a far corner of the front room. To her amazement, Rachel and Caitlin never moved from behind their chairs, leaving their children in harm's way. Their only concession to the heated debate was to place their folded hands on the backs of their chairs, as if they were still waiting for a reverent blessing and eats.

"You don't have what it takes to be a preacher, Esa," Ace intoned firmly. "I'm with David. What the hell are you thinking?"

Joseph chimed in, "For God's sake, Esa, you cuss worse than I do. Some impression you'd make."

David capped it all by saying, "Son of a bitch. I bring my wife and daughter here for a first family dinner, and what does Esa do but make the announcement of the year and ruin everything! Do you always have to be the center of attention?"

Dory sent Caitlin a pointed look. Caitlin hurried into the kitchen and returned with a bar of soap in her hand. Dory caught hold of it, straightened her narrow shoulders, and to Brianna's horror, waded right into the middle of the fray, with men towering around her. She looked each of them directly in the eye.

"Enough! You're behaving like ill-mannered galoots!" She held up the bar. "You can continue with this foolishness and eat lye soap, or you can return to the table, bow your heads for the blessing, and dine like the gentlemen I raised you to be."

With a bit of groaning, the men returned to the table while Esa went to the water closet for a quick scrub. He returned with dampness darkening his blond hair. His face, ears, neck, and hands were free of dirt. Brianna repositioned herself and Daphne in their former places, and Ace, at the head of the table, commenced with the blessing.

As the food was passed, Brianna expected the men to remain silent, but before the mashed potatoes reached her, David said to Esa, "You aren't going to get all preachy, are you? I don't think I can handle having a holier-than-thou brother."

Esa swallowed, dabbed at his mouth with his napkin, and said, "That's where most preachers fail, by acting holier-than-thou. They set standards no normal human being can live up to, and then they become laughingstocks when they fail to do as they preach. I'll never claim to be without sin, and I'll never expect anybody else to be, either. We're all just people doing the best we can to live decent lives."

"Since when did you decide to wear a white collar?" Ace asked.

"I've been thinking about it for a while." He glanced apologetically at Caitlin. "I'd honor you by becoming a priest, Caitlin, but I'd like to marry and have children someday, so I don't think that's my calling."

Dory piped in with, "I, for one, am very pleased to hear that Esa is considering a religious calling. At least some of our Bible study at night rubbed off on one of you."

The remainder of the meal passed with mostly pleasant exchanges, the only exceptions being when the males of the family ribbed one another. At one point, Dory excused herself to collect her childhood scrapbook and show off a daguerreotype of herself at about Daphne's age. Brianna could only gape at the likeness when the book was passed to her. The resemblance to Daphne was uncanny. Upon closer inspection, however, Brianna determined that any blond little girl with fine features might resemble the image in the daguerreotype. Granted, the similarities were there; that was undeniable. But the Keegans and Paxtons were making more of them than was warranted.

"Daphne has Dory's chin," Rachel noted. "And she even has the Paxton birthmark!"

Caitlin remarked, "That dimple in the child's cheek is another dead giveaway."

Ace laughed and said to David, "That is one child you can't deny."

David beamed with pride.

Brianna went with the flow of conversation, nodding and smiling in agreement. What else could she do? Even if she blurted out the truth and convinced these people to believe her, it would destroy Daphne.

When it came time to clear the table, Brianna had started to relax around the men. The fearsome Ace Keegan was a gentle giant with his children and wife. Joseph spent more time holding Little Joe than Rachel did and was wearing a goodly amount of mashed potatoes by the time he'd finished trying to feed his son.

The men rolled up their shirtsleeves to clean the kitchen, which surprised Brianna. Ace washed, David dried, Joseph put away, and Esa took charge of the leftovers. The women were shooed out to sit on the veranda and visit.

*Here it comes,* Brianna thought. She'd be grilled with questions now, and she had no idea how to answer because she wasn't sure what her husband had told everyone. How did you meet David? Why did you never contact him when you realized you were expecting? How did the two of you finally reunite?

But the questions never came. Instead the conversation centered around Caitlin's newly planted vegetable garden, Dory's hobby of collecting wild edibles, the wildflowers presently in bloom, sewing, and Rachel's talent for crocheting and tatting. Dory Sue was just learning to walk, so Daphne held the child's hands and helped her totter back and forth across the yard while Little Ace galloped circles around them on an imaginary stallion named Spirit. Rachel nursed Little Joe and rocked him to sleep.

When David finally appeared on the porch to take his family home, Brianna was sad to see the evening end. Daphne was having the time of her life, playing with her little cousins, and the adult conversations had been stimulating. It had been a very long time since Brianna had been able to chat at length with other ladies. And once she left with David, they would be entirely alone again, save for Daphne.

As if David sensed her reluctance to leave, he said, "You'll see everyone often, Shamrock. All our ranches are a hop, skip, and jump away from each other."

Good-byes coupled with affectionate hugs followed, yet another ceremony Brianna had long been denied. Once back in the buggy with David and Daphne, she felt happy, sad, and tense, a confusing mix. As welcoming as everyone had been, she and Daphne were imposters who were being included on false pretenses, and it was anyone's guess how long it would be before the truth came out and ruined everything.

En route to David's ranch, which Brianna learned was named Wolverine Flats for the creek that angled through it, David talked almost nonstop, pointing out to her and Daphne where each of his brother's ranches were located. In Brianna's estimation, they were a lot farther apart than a hop, skip, and jump, but she supposed that, given the large tracts of land for each parcel, adjoining dooryards were impossible. In the fading light of day, she glimpsed oak trees, willows along the streambed, and wildflowers galore. It was beautiful country, a wonderful place to raise a child.

David's ranch proved to be an almost exact replica of Ace's, with a long entrance road that led to a large, tidy barn, sturdy paddocks, and grassland rolling out from the buildings for as far as the eye could see. Barking and growling in a friendly way, a yellow and white, long-haired dog bounced across the yard to greet the buggy when David stopped in front of the rambling one-story house.

"Hey, Sam!" David called as he swung out of the conveyance. He spent a moment ruffling the canine's thick fur and scratching him behind the ears. Then he lifted Daphne to the ground. "I brought you a new friend. Guard her with your life."

Brianna, exiting the buggy by herself, had to smile at that pronouncement because Daphne was already on her knees with both arms locked around Sam's neck. It was apparently love at first sight, for Sam returned the affection with wet doggy kisses and curious sniffs of the child's hair. A second later, girl and canine raced off to play.

A middle-aged man in jeans and a blue work shirt emerged from the barn. David waved hello and called, "Put them up for the night, would you, Rob? Rub them down good and give all of them an extra ration of oats. I'll return the buggy in the morning."

The man lifted his tan hat in greeting, his brown hair, trimmed neatly above the ears, whipping in the evening breeze. "Will do, boss. Welcome home."

David came around to grasp Brianna's arm. "You ready for the grand tour?"

Noting the edge of humor in David's voice, Brianna realized that he felt his house was far from grand, but to her, it was a veritable palace. A deep veranda swept the length of the front, accommodating two rockers off to one side and a swing at the other. She could picture herself relaxing there of an evening to watch the sunset. Two double-hung windows flanked the front door, which had been crafted with thick beams of wood, providing a safe barricade against intruders. It was a house with a friendly facade, unprepossessing but comfortable looking. Brianna had never had a real home, unless she counted the orphanage, and having recently lived in an attic room no larger than a closet, she doubted that David had any idea how lucky he was.

When Brianna stepped inside, a sense of homecoming filled her. The large living area served as a sitting room and dining room, with a spacious kitchen leading off from it at the far end. A leather sofa and two armchairs bracketed a stone fireplace to the right. David's long plank supper table, she noted with relief, was lined with high-back chairs instead of benches, which were difficult for a lady in skirts to manage.

"It's in sore need of some fixing up," David told her. "I saw to the basics, but I'm not much for decorating. I've been meaning to get curtains." He released her arm to rub beside his nose. "Maybe it's just as well I didn't. Ladies kind of like to do their own choosing when it comes to stuff like that."

"It's wonderful just as it is," Brianna said,

thinking to herself that she wouldn't be here long enough to worry about curtains. But, oh, what a fabulous place for any child to call home, even if only briefly. When Brianna had dreamed of getting a proper house for Daphne, she'd always pictured it tiny and furnished with wobbly, scarred things she bought secondhand. Never had she imagined anything this grand. "All it needs are a few touches of color here and there to brighten the rooms."

He showed off his kitchen, which sported a new cookstove with double ovens, a center firebox, dual warmers, and a sizable water reservoir. Open shelves lined with dishes and foodstuffs held court over varnished countertops and an oversize icebox. In one corner sat a washing machine, the likes of which Brianna had never seen.

As if guessing her thoughts, David said, "It's rigged up to drain through the floor, so you don't have to haul buckets of water outside to dump them. I got the idea from Darby, Rachel's uncle by recent marriage. Not so long ago, Rachel was housebound. Long story, that. Anyway, Darby had her all set up so she never had to step foot outside, and I copied some of his inventions to make it more convenient here."

David was about to give her a tour of the

water closet and bedrooms when a thump came at the front door. It was Rob, the hired man, arms laden with David's saddlebags and all their other possessions.

"Good man," David said, setting his saddlebags just inside the door and then relieving the man of the stuffed pillowcases and packages. "You see my daughter out there anywhere?"

"She's off with Sam, checkin' out the kittens in the barn. Judgin' by the way she's latched onto the yellow one, I got a hunch you'll have a new family member soon."

David was laughing as he closed the door. "I'd forgotten about little girls and kittens. My sister, Eden, loved them, and we always had two or three cats underfoot."

"Will Daphne be all right out there alone?" Brianna asked.

"Sam's with her. And Rob will be around." He sauntered toward her with the pillowcases, dumping the one filled with food at the kitchen entrance, then leading Brianna up the hallway. "I've got five bedrooms. Mine's at the far end. You and Daphne can take your pick of the others. The beds are all made up fresh."

Brianna peeked into the two rooms on the right but hesitated to step inside. "These will do," she said. "I like that they're next to each other. That way I'll hear if Daphne needs me."

David put all her pillowcases inside the door of the room closest to his and then turned to rest a muscular arm against the jamb. No lanterns had been lighted, so only dusky light from the bare window behind him played over the room. In the shadows, his eyes shimmered like polished pewter. She saw his jaw muscle ripple. For an instant, she feared he might try to kiss her — or more. Instead he only trailed his gaze slowly over her face. Beneath his thoughtful study, her cheeks started to burn.

"And she'll also be able to hear you. Isn't that what you're thinking?" He said it softly and didn't pose it as a question.

"Whatever do you mean?" Brianna's heart had started to race. It seemed to her that the breadth of his shoulders took up the entire doorway. She folded her arms at her waist. "All mothers like to be within hearing distance of their children at night."

"Don't try to bullshit me, Shamrock. You've been as jumpy as a long-tailed cat in a roomful of rockers ever since we got on the train in Denver. I'm thinking you've got some notion in your head that things are going to change between you and me now, that I'll suddenly decide to make this a marriage in fact."

Not knowing what else to say, she blurted, "You are my husband. You have papers to prove it."

He continued to search her gaze. She had the awful feeling that he could see clear to her soul. "Who did this to you? Where along the way did you start thinking that every man you're alone with is going to turn on you?"

Brianna's throat felt dry. She wasn't sure she could speak. Her voice came out crackly and weak. "You ask questions, David, but you don't like my answers. You say you're a stickler for the truth, but you don't want to hear it. My past experiences with other men are all intertwined with a story you believe is a pack of lies."

His eyes began to smolder.

"There, you see?" she challenged shakily. "How can you expect me to tell you my darkest secrets when all you're going to do is get mad?"

He followed her example and folded his arms. She had the uncomfortable feeling he did so to control himself — to make sure he didn't give in to the urge to put his hands on her. "It upsets me when you imply that Daphne isn't mine. You saw how my family reacted when they saw her. There is no mistake, Brianna. She's my daughter."

Brianna turned to move away from him up the hall to the front of the house. While he was in this mood, she wasn't about to enter that bedroom to sort through her and Daphne's things. He'd stand behind her and block the doorway.

"Before you run off, let me make one thing clear."

Brianna halted and turned to look at him. "What is that?"

"If I was of a mind, I could turn you every which way but loose with one hand tied behind my back." He inclined his head at her person. "You're half my size. You wouldn't stand a chance against me. Taking the room next to Daphne won't keep you safe. It's simple enough for a man to keep a woman from screaming while he does his worst to her." He thumped the jamb with the toe of his boot. "And there isn't a door in this entire house strong enough to keep me out if I want in."

A tremor ran the length of Brianna's body. "Are you threatening me, David?"

He smiled slightly. "Nope, just stating the facts and hoping to ease your mind."

"Ease my mind?" she asked incredulously. "By saying things like that to me?"

"Yep. I won't say I don't want you, Shamrock. It'd be a lie. But if I meant to take you by strength of arm, I would have done it by now. Who is there to stop me? It's not like you can go to the town marshal and say I raped you."

Brianna's stomach clenched and rolled.

"That's part of it, isn't it? Why you're all of a sudden nervous around me again. The situation has shifted. We're on my home ground, and I'm the law around these parts. That marriage document in my bag is playing real heavy on your mind."

"David, I —"

He held up a hand. "Don't deny it. I felt the tension in you as I helped you off the train. At Ace's place, when I put my arm around your shoulders, I felt you flinch away. When Caitlin invited you to go see the kittens and I nudged you forward, you jerked as if I'd stuck you with a pin."

"Yes," she confessed in a whisper. "We're married. Men have all the power. You're influential in this town. Of *course* I've had moments when I thought of all that."

He sighed and bent his head. When he lifted it, he said, "Shamrock, you'd be in no more danger here in this bedroom with me than you were out on the prairie. Feeling nervous and jumpy is a waste of your energy, not to mention that it's plumb foolish." He pushed erect and sidled toward her. When she put her back to the wall to let him pass, he stopped, moving his blue gaze slowly over her face, and then cupped her chin in his hand, trailing his thumb lightly over her cheek. "Maybe someday you'll tell me who the bastard was who made you so leery, maybe you won't, but always bear in mind one thing."

"What?" she asked thinly.

"I'm not that man." He released her and strode up the hallway, never looking back. "While you unpack, I'll go check on my animals. I'll corral Daphne while I'm out there and bring her back with me. You may as well settle in good and proper. When I return the buggy in the morning, I'll stop by the dress shop to talk with Clarissa Denny to see if she's interested in selling, but even if her answer is yes, negotiating a price and all the details may take a while."

Brianna sank limply against the wall, the tension in her body draining away. When she heard the front door slam closed behind him, she released a shaky breath. As crazy as she knew it was, she felt better. David had an odd way of offering comfort, but somehow it had worked. He truly was different from all the others. She was safe with him. She'd been foolish to let doubts slip into her mind.

She'd just pushed away from the wall when she heard someone reenter the house. The sturdy thump of a man's boots echoed through the sitting area and dining room. David reappeared at the front of the hall.

"It just occurred to me that the least I could do is make sure you have light to unpack by." He strode past her and into the bedroom. She watched as he struck a match and touched it to the wick of a lantern on the mahogany bedside table. A golden glow filled the room as he adjusted the brightness.

"I could have done that," she said.

"I don't mind doing things for you, Shamrock." He graced her with a crooked grin. "The way I was raised up, that's what husbands are for, to be helpful."

As he turned to leave, Brianna said, "David, wait."

He paused to regard her.

"I'm sorry," she whispered. Then in a stronger voice, she said, "I meant no insult. It's just — well, I've never known a man like you, and it's all too easy for me to take your measure by the behavior of others in the past. Does that make any sense?"

He nodded. "Perfect sense. Life can be a harsh teacher, and once lessons have been driven home, it's hard to change your way of thinking. It'll get easier with time. In the meanwhile, try to relax and have some faith in me. That marriage document is only a piece of paper. It has no bearing on who I am. I'm not going to slap it down on the table some night and change the terms of our agreement. If our relationship changes to something more, it will be because you want it that way, not because I insist on it."

After he left the room and closed the door behind him, Brianna stood with her finger-tips pressed to her lips, so close to tears that it was all she could do to blink them away. David Paxton stirred feelings and yearnings within her that she'd never felt for another man. Fear one moment, desire the next. And at every turn, just when she expected him to take unfair advantage of her, he proved her wrong. She'd lived all of her adult life trying to avoid men, ever distrusting them. Never in her wildest imaginings had she entertained the possibility that someone like David might exist.

He made her want things she couldn't possibly have. He filled her head with fantastical wishes and dreams. What a cruel twist of fate that everything between them was built upon a terrible misunderstanding.

# CHAPTER SEVENTEEN

David left shortly after breakfast the next morning to return the buggy and visit the proprietress of No Name's only dress shop. Daphne had pleaded to go, and Brianna didn't have the heart to tell her no. Sam joined them for the ride. Apparently the dog was David's shadow wherever he went and often accompanied his master on business.

Brianna found herself alone in the house for the first time, with a breakfast mess in the kitchen to clean up and soiled under-clothes to wash. The first chore turned out to be fun. She had thoroughly enjoyed preparing the morning meal, a part of her delighting in the fact that she could finally show David that she did indeed have cook-ing skills. His hired hands, five in all, had been pleased to receive heaping plates of food at the back door, and only the fore-man, Rob Atkinson, had failed to return his dishes. She had a feeling that the long plank table in the dining room had been built to accommodate not only David, but his men as well, and if she'd been staying on, she would have started inviting them to share meals at the house.

She found it difficult to remember that her time here would be temporary. With morning sunlight coming through the many windows, she could see that all the panes needed a good shine and that a thin layer of dust covered everything. She yearned to dive in and have the place spotless by noon, but she resisted. If David couldn't make arrangements to procure the dress shop, Brianna would have to find some other way to earn an income in town. Allowing herself to float along until this situation resolved itself was one thing; to do it on David's dime was entirely another. She at least needed to know she was paying her own way.

Oh, how she wished things were different. David, with his slow smile, protective nature, and gentle manner, had worked past so many of her defenses. For the first time in her life, she trusted a man and was developing feelings for him that she chose not to bring forth into the light of day. He made her — well, she'd be wise not to think how she felt when his eyes caught hers or when his thumb traced the curve of her cheekbone ever so gently, a sensation different from any other masculine touch she'd ever experienced. Better to keep those insane urges buried, to pretend they weren't there. Daphne's future was her biggest concern. The little girl had opened her heart, not only to David, but to everyone connected to him, even that silly dog, Sam.

Even though Brianna knew it was absurd, she allowed herself to pretend it *was* her kitchen as she washed and dried dishes. She envisioned the cheerful towels and hot pads she would embroider, and pictured herself in a gingham housedress, protected by a starched white apron. The house would smell of beeswax, bread hot from the oven, and meat simmering in a pot. She would be the mistress of Wolverine Flats, and when David came in from work, she would greet him with a plate of warm cookies and coffee made to his taste with a dash of salt. Swept away by the fantasy, she even found a stool so she could wash the window above the sink.

The fun ended when she faced the washing machine. It was a newfangled contraption, and she had no idea how to use it. She was about to rinse her and Daphne's underthings by hand when a knock came at the kitchen door, which led onto the rear stoop. Brianna opened the portal to find the foreman standing there. In his hand, he held a soiled plate, crisscrossed with a knife and fork.

"Sorry, ma'am. I got sidetracked with the animals and plumb forgot to bring this back so you could wash it up with the morning dishes."

"Oh, no worries." Brianna accepted the eating utensils. "I hope you enjoyed your breakfast."

"It was delicious. The boss, well, he's a good cook, but he's so busy with the ranch and his marshaling job that we hired hands usually throw something together over at the bunkhouse. It's been a long spell since I ate flapjacks that light and tasty, and the eggs were done to an easy turn, just the way us boys like them."

Pleased to hear that, Brianna said, "Would you care for a cup of coffee?"

"Oh, no, thank you, ma'am. I know you got chores, and so do I."

"I insist. Actually, Mr. Atkinson, I was wondering if you know how to work the washing machine."

His sun-weathered face creased in a grin. "You bet I do. I helped the boss rig it up, and us boys use it to wash our duds once a week."

He stepped inside the kitchen, and the instant he did, Brianna felt uneasy. Just because the man worked for David didn't mean he was trustworthy. She probably shouldn't have let him inside the house while she was alone.

Oblivious to her nervousness, Atkinson showed her how to fill the bucket at the sink and empty it into the washer drum. "For a full load, you only need three buckets and some soap, which is right yonder behind the machine," he told her, then moved on to demonstrate how to turn the agitator. "You crank on this until you reckon the clothes are clean. Then you flip this lever to drain the tub. All the water goes out through the pipe underneath. It works slicker than greased owl shit." He coughed. "Um, sorry, ma'am. For my language, I mean."

"Amazing!" Brianna was so fascinated by the washing machine that she forgot all about being uneasy. "And to rinse the clothes, you just add fresh water?"

"Yep, and then agitate some more, drain. Keep on until you see no more suds. Then you take the wet clothes out, put them in the bucket, and flip down this here thing, which is the wringer. It squeezes all the water out of the clothes right into the drum so you can empty out the water through the floor pipe."

"That is absolutely *brilliant.* What a work saver."

Atkinson chuckled. "The boss is right smart when it comes to things like this. Of course, he borrowed the idea from old Darby McClintoch, but he put his own twists on it to make it even better."

Brianna was so anxious to try the machine that she forgot all about the coffee she had promised Mr. Atkinson and ushered him out the door empty-handed. She went to collect soiled garments, so excited about her mission that she even invaded David's bedchamber to find his pile of laundry. The instant she stepped into the room, the smell of him surrounded her — the enticing scent of his face invigorator, his shaving soap, and the oiled leather of his duster.

The room was much larger than hers, with a reading corner appointed with two chairs that flanked a kerosene floor lamp. His bed, a sturdy four-poster, had been made up, testifying to his tidy nature. The coverlet was a lovely wedding-ring quilt Brianna decided must be the handiwork of his mother or one of his sisters-in-law. Feeling self-conscious, she stepped over to his washstand, lightly tracing the pitcher spout and the edge of the bowl. Then she trailed his shaving brush along her cheek, closing her eyes at the silky caress, which reminded her of his lips grazing hers. Her belly tightened and ached at the memory.

*What's happening to me?* This wasn't like her. She'd never been one with her head in the clouds or allowed herself to yearn for impossible things, the only exception being her deep longing to give Daphne the kind of childhood she and Moira had been denied.

Giving herself a firm mental shake, Brianna went into the adjoining dressing closet, where she found David's soiled clothing piled in a corner. Flanks of drawers along one wall held his clean clothing. More drawers lined the other wall, but they were empty. Her heart caught as she opened one after another and saw nothing. She guessed he'd built this dressing closet with a wife in mind, some nameless, faceless woman he'd once planned to wed. Only now that couldn't happen.

Oh, how that plagued her. Determined not to dwell on what she couldn't seem to change, Brianna gathered his soiled garments and dashed from the room.

■ ■ ■ ■

David decided to stop by Ace's place on the way home just to say howdy. He wanted Daphne to become well acquainted and comfortable with his family, Dory especially, as quickly as possible. As it happened, Dory was out in the field collecting greens for a dinner salad, and before David could stop Daphne, she was off to join her grandma, Sam racing at her heels. Ace sauntered out of the barn.

"Morning, little brother. How's married life treating you?"

David wasn't sure how to answer that question. He had Brianna settled in at his house in a separate bedroom. This morning she'd made breakfast, but that was as personal as it had gotten. "I feel like I've taken up squatting rights with a stranger."

Ace led the way over to a paddock fence, where they each hooked a bootheel over a lower rung and rested their arms on a rail. The sun hadn't quite reached its zenith, so the morning air, warm as it was, still felt a bit nippy when the breeze picked up. Sighing, David was taken back through the years to his boyhood, when he'd stood like this with Ace countless times to talk about his problems. It had become a ritual, he guessed, for he needed to do that now.

"You want a chaw?"

David cast his brother a wondering look. "I thought Caitlin cured you of using tobacco."

"She has — except when I'm off alone." Ace shrugged. "I rinse my mouth before I go in, she never knows the difference, and I enjoy my occasional chew. Not often, mind you, but at times like this, something to work my teeth on seems called for."

David accepted a bit of snuff from the can and started chewing and spitting. Ace was right. It helped to sort his thoughts. Haltingly at first, he filled Ace in a bit more on all that had transpired since he'd first ridden into Glory Ridge, including, in detail, Brianna's harebrained story about raising her dead sister's daughter. "I could believe the bit about the sister dying," David concluded. "It happens in families, and it's left to a close relative to raise the child. Hell, it even happened in our family when Pa was murdered. Where I get stuck is in the details — Daphne's looks, the birthmark on her neck, and Brianna swearing she just accidentally dreamed up a husband in Denver named David Paxton." David turned his hands to study the lines deeply etched onto his palms. "I'd like it to be a real marriage, Ace, but damned if I know how to take it there. I thought about kissing her again last night, and I think she knew."

"How'd she react?"

"She went stiff as a fire poker. Fact is, I think she was scared half to death of me."

"Hmm." Ace rubbed his jaw and scratched under his black Stetson, one of the few articles of apparel from his gunslinger days that he still wore. He'd sworn off the black clothing, but like most men, he was right fond of his hats and couldn't bring himself to wear the new one he'd bought, claiming Stetsons were like a pair of boots, uncomfortable until you'd worn them for a while. "When it comes to gentling reluctant women, I'm no expert, David. If you'll recall, Caitlin flooded my whole house and damned near burned it down before we came to see eye to eye."

David laughed at the memory. "Esa and Joseph and me — well, we mopped and mopped, fair choking to death on the smoke, mad because you'd chased off after Caitlin and weren't there to help. I'll never forget that night. I can't remember exactly what Caitlin said to us before she ran from the house — something about you always wanting to clear the air and calm the waters.

She told us to have fun doing both. She'd beaten on the handle of the cookstove damper until it was stuck closed, and we couldn't get the damned thing unstuck. Joseph was cursing and ranting. I'm glad it was you who found Caitlin, because Joseph was mad enough to chew nails and spit out screws. I think he might have smacked her."

"Nah, not Joseph. No matter how mad he ever gets, he'll never hit a woman."

Ace smiled at the memory and gazed off across the field at his mother and niece, who were racing about, collecting edibles. On the wind, Dory's exclamations of praise for Daphne's knowledge drifted to their ears.

"Caitlin and I, well, we had some rough patches," Ace admitted, "but we're happily married now. Anything worth having takes work and time, David."

"I know." It was David's turn to scratch under his hat. "I just can't, for the life of me, figure her out, Ace. Under all that proper behavior, she's a spitfire, but it takes a lot to make her lose control and reveal that side. I get this weird feeling sometimes that she keeps the real Brianna stifled and is pretending to be someone else."

Ace frowned thoughtfully. "There might be a smidgen of truth to that convent story she told you." At David's protest, he threw up a hand. "Hold on. I'm not saying her whole story is true. Anyone with eyes can see that child is yours. But I don't find it hard to believe Brianna was raised by nuns. She moves like one. She talks like one. Nuns have a way about them, and she's got all the mannerisms. Haven't you noticed that?"

David's feet felt suddenly cold. He recalled that first day when he'd watched Brianna stoop to pick something up, how she'd kept her rump tucked under and her spine straight, barely even bending her head. He'd thought at the time that he'd seen someone else move like that, but his mind hadn't taken him back to his schoolboy years when he'd been instructed by nuns. "Jesus Herbert Christ."

"Herbert?"

Still feeling dazed, David waved his hand. "I have to tack on Herbert or Brianna pitches a fit about my language."

"Sticking in an H isn't good enough?"

"Hell, no, she's a stickler on coarse language, just like a —" David broke off and swallowed hard. "Just like a nun, Ace. Why the hell didn't I ever pick up on that? You're right. She moves exactly like a nun. You remember how they always tucked their hands under the sleeves of their habits to hide them? Shamrock does that. It rang a

bell, but I never zeroed in on the chorus."
He waved a hand. "No habit sleeves, no
beads. The similarity is there, but without
the trimmings —" He broke off and met his
brother's gaze. "Dear God, what if she was
telling me the unvarnished truth, that
Daphne is her dead sister's daughter?"

Ace shook his head. "That child out there
in the field has Paxton written all over her,
right down to the family birthmark. I'm
guessing she told you part of the truth, but
in the end, the seed that sprouted that child
was yours. I'd go to the bank on that."

David's shoulders relaxed. "So it's up to
me to find out what part of her story is truth
and what part is fiction?"

"Pretty much. For reasons we don't know,
she doesn't want to tell you the whole of it.
The only way you may ever find it out is to
do some digging yourself."

David wished it didn't have to be that way.
He preferred to hear the real story from
Brianna. But for some reason, she wasn't
willing to level with him.

A horrible thought occurred to him.
"Damn, Ace, what if it was her sister Moira
that I fucked?"

Little Ace came dashing up to his father
just then. Ace swung the child up onto his
hip. "Watch the language," he warned.

David swallowed hard and nodded, his mind racing off in a half dozen different directions. That kiss at the hotel. It had been deep, sweet, and *memorable*. How in the hell could he have made love to Brianna, yet have no recollection of ever kissing her? An icy feeling of dread settled deep in the pit of his stomach. "I figured the orphan part of her story could be true, that maybe she traveled out West to be with distant relatives until she reached her majority. That happens all the time, and it follows that her relatives may not have looked after her properly at social events. If I was drunk, and she caught my eye —" David glanced at Little Ace. "Well, you get my gist. But what if both girls came west to Denver, and it was the sister I trifled with? And what if she actually did die during childbirth? Oh, God, it's suddenly starting to make sense."

"I'm not following," Ace said.

"Brianna would have been left with the baby. A young woman with a baby who had no husband. It would have been a nightmare in a city, Brianna trying to work while caring for an infant. Getting a live-in position was probably her only recourse, and highfalutin city folks may not hire a woman with a squalling kid."

Ace mulled that over. "I can see where

you're going with it, David, but what would have possessed her to take your name, raise the child as yours, and come back to Colorado, even going so far as to write you letters, asking you to come for her?"

"They were identical," David said softly. "Twins no one could tell apart. As children, they tricked people all the time. Maybe —" David shrugged and lifted his hands again. "I don't know. I'm just supposing, you know? Maybe she got the harebrained notion that she could take her sister's place and I'd never guess the truth." David turned slightly to better see Ace's face. "Think about it, big brother. If Brianna is only the child's aunt, and I'm the father, she has no right at all to the child. I could take Daphne and send Brianna packing. She adores that little girl. Maybe she thought she could carry it off until I showed up in Glory Ridge, and then she chickened out. At that point, naturally she would have lied, trying to convince me I'm not the father."

"Like you say, this is a lot of supposition," Ace inserted.

"Yes, but it makes more sense than her continually trying to convince me I'm not the daddy if she's the child's real mother."

"In that event — if you find out you're the father and Brianna's only the aunt, will you cut Brianna out of the picture?" Ace asked.

"No." David swallowed hard. "She's Daphne's mama in every way that counts. She's sacrificed everything, the best years of her life, to be a mother to that child."

"You're falling in love with her, aren't you?" Ace queried softly.

The question made David's guts clench, for he knew the answer was yes. But the hell of it was, that was all he knew for certain right then, except that Daphne had to be his. Everyone in his family saw that. *He* saw that. Only now David had to wonder which woman he'd trifled with to create her.

"What kind of man am I?" David wondered aloud.

"A good man," Ace replied.

"I got a young girl pregnant one long ago night in Denver. If distant relatives had taken her in, how do you think they reacted when they realized she had a bun in her oven? In a lot of families, that is an embarrassment not to be borne. They would have sent her back to wherever she came from to endure the shame alone. The nuns at an orphanage might not have taken her back in. Maybe she died in childbirth, maybe she didn't, but either way I was a lowdown skunk."

"David, don't beat up on yourself too much until you know the whole truth."

David knew that was sound advice, but it wasn't easy to follow. That day down by the stream, Brianna had cried, *I couldn't let her go alone. I was the strong one. I was the responsible one!* His stomach lurched. He stared hard at his boots. Had Brianna returned to Boston with her pregnant sister? If so, David hadn't destroyed only one girl's life; he had destroyed two.

"David?" Ace said his name softly. "Are you all right?"

David felt as if a high wind had just hit him broadside. "I don't know, big brother. I always thought I knew myself, but now I just don't anymore."

"Well, that's plumb crazy." Ace set his son down and told him to go check on the kittens. As the boy raced off to the barn, Ace settled those dark, piercing eyes on David's face. "David, you're a fine man."

"Am I?" David shot back. "Even stupid drunk, Ace? Am I a fine man then?"

Ace planted his hands on his hips. "A lot of people blame their bad behavior on drink. So far as I know, you've never been one of them. Before you hang yourself on a cross of your own making, you need to know the *real* truth, every damned bit of it, and while you're digging, remember this. I raised you right. Whatever happened, I'll never believe you knowingly did a young woman wrong. Maybe parts of Brianna's story are true, but don't leap ahead and start filling in the blanks until you have some facts to go on."

David gazed across the field at his daughter. "I got some business to see to," he told Ace. "Back in town. Some wires to send. I don't want Daphne with me. Can you, Ma, and Caitlin look after her while I'm gone for a bit?"

Ace nodded. "Of course I'll look after her. Go do what you have to do."

David whistled for Sam. The dog whirled at the sound. Even at a distance, David saw the struggle the canine went through. His master had called, but now the silly fellow's heart felt another tug, and the new tug won the war. Sam flapped his snubbed tail wildly at David as if to apologize, and then circled in close to Daphne, refusing to come. It was a first for Sam.

Ace chuckled. "Looks to me like that little bit of calico out there done stole your mutt."

David agreed, a bit disgruntled, but mostly glad. Even Sam recognized that Daphne was of his blood, and the dog had automatically assumed responsibility for her, just as any loyal, protective canine should. David approved Sam's decision. He could always get himself another dog, but he could never in a million years replace Daphne.

On the way home from the telegraph office, David stopped by Ace's place to collect his daughter and dog. Daphne rode home in front of him on Blue, stroking the gelding's neck as she regaled David with stories about her day with Grandma Dory, finding edible plants, and baking cookies with Aunt Caitlin, samples of which they carried with them in a bag.

David's thoughts were a hundred miles away. Correction. His thoughts were thousands of miles away, in Boston, where he'd just hired Pinkerton agents to investigate Brianna's background. It would take possibly weeks for him to get anything conclusive back from them, but in the end, David knew he would eventually learn a truth that Brianna had refused to share. Maybe she had been raised in a Boston orphanage, and maybe she'd had a twin sister named Moira. All David knew was that he'd impregnated either Brianna or her sister, and he held the result in the circle of his arm. As they trudged home on faithful old Blue, Sam ran circles around them.

As a lawman, David had learned to be patient as he ferreted out the facts. He'd be patient now and simply wait. Sooner or later, he would receive correspondence from the Pinkerton Agency, telling him what he needed to know. Until then, he would leave it be and move forward as planned.

Clothing flapped on the clothesline out back of the house, and as David rode closer, he saw Brianna struggling to unpin a towel, which kept snaking around her torso and catching on her auburn hair. He drew Blue to a stop to watch for a moment.

"What is it, Papa?" Daphne asked.

"I'm just thinking your mama is one of the prettiest ladies I've ever seen," David said huskily.

"Yes, she is," Daphne agreed. "Aunt Caitlin and Rachel are pretty, and so is Grandma Dory, but I think Mama is the prettiest one of all."

David remained there another moment, watching his wife and wishing the domestic scene were as real and lasting as it appeared. Then he clicked his tongue to Blue and proceeded on to the barn. He left Rob to tend the gelding and held Daphne's hand as they walked toward the house.

Brianna stood at the table, folding laundry, when David herded Daphne inside and closed the door behind them. "Howdy," he said, doffing his hat and hanging it on a wall hook to his right. "Looks like you had a busy day." He smelled beeswax and noted that all his furniture gleamed. The hearth had also been swept clean, and the delicious aroma of pot roast drifted in from the kitchen. Today Brianna wore the brown silk gown, inappropriate garb for housework, but she'd soon be a businesswoman with the tending of a ranch house far behind her. "The place looks great."

Pleasure pinked her cheeks. "I needed to keep busy. You were gone awhile."

David patted Daphne on the head. "I'm for some fresh coffee, pumpkin. Would you like a glass of chilled milk?"

Daphne danced ahead of him into the kitchen, then filled her own glass while David stoked up the cookstove fire and put a pot of coffee on to boil. Brianna disappeared for a bit, he presumed to put away clothes, and then came to stand behind him with her hips resting against the counter's edge. She belonged here, David thought, but he had no idea how to convince her of that. Brianna wasn't a woman to be wooed with deep kisses and fancy words.

"So what did Clarissa Denny have to say?" she asked.

David turned to see Daphne digging her hand into the bag of cookies. "Don't ruin your appetite for supper. It smells like your mama has a delicious pot roast on."

"I only have two."

Daphne took her milk and treats to the dining room. David was glad for the privacy. "Clarissa's daughter-in-law in California is having a rough confinement, and she'd like to be there well before the baby comes. There are three other youngsters, all little whippersnappers, and her son works long hours at his shop. Right now he's hiring a woman to come in, but he can't afford it."

"So she's willing to sell?"

David searched Brianna's lovely green eyes. "If Clarissa had her way, she would have been on a train for California yesterday. She's so eager to leave, she'd damned near give the place away." David crossed his ankles, resting more of his weight against the counter. Then he locked gazes with Brianna again. "I won't take advantage of that, but if I make her a fair offer, I'm sure she'll accept. Just say the word, Shamrock. If owning a dress shop and sharing a home in town is what you really want, it can be a done deal in the morning."

"What other recourse is there?" she asked, her voice slightly tremulous.

David glanced toward the dining room. "You could stay here," he said softly. "We could work toward making this a real marriage and have a real family."

Her eyes went bright, like emeralds polished to a high shine. "Without love, David?" She shook her head. "You deserve more than that."

David uncrossed his feet and then crossed them again. After folding his arms, he said, "What if I were to tell you that I'm developing feelings for you?"

"This is only the sixth day of our acquaintance," she reminded him.

"It was a long trip, Shamrock. Six days isn't much in most situations, but in our case, we've had plenty of time to take each other's measure. I admire you. I feel affection for you. It's my hope that you feel the same about me. We can build on that."

"Affection." She rolled the word slowly over her tongue as if to test its taste. "That isn't love, David. We need a stronger foundation on which to build a marriage. Besides, there are still things you don't know, things that may change your mind. It's only prudent to move ahead as we planned, leaving ourselves free to file for an annulment."

David had allowed a judge to railroad her into this marriage. He wouldn't force her to remain in it. If the time came when she wanted an annulment, he'd give her one, and then they'd have to figure out how both of them could be parents to Daphne. "All right, the dress shop it will be, I guess."

She nodded and even smiled, but her expression told David she wasn't really happy. He wished — oh, hell, he didn't know what he wished. That he could understand her better, he guessed, and that she'd trust him enough to tell him everything. If she was only Daphne's aunt, did she honestly think he would use it as leverage against her in court to take the child away from her?

"Just for the record, no matter how this shakes out, I'll never deny you the right to be with our child," he told her. "I know how dear she is to you. I'd never take her away from you."

She tipped her head to regard Daphne at the table. "In some ways, David, you're already doing that," she whispered.

"Doing what?"

"Taking her away." Her eyes glistened with tears when she met his gaze again. "She already loves you so, and your family is so wonderful. Ever since her birth, it's been only she and I. I was always the center of her world. Now . . ." She smiled tremulously and shrugged. "Now I feel like someone standing backstage."

David's heart caught. "That isn't so. She loves me, yes, and she's coming to love my family as well, but that takes nothing away from her love for you."

"Perhaps not, but it does drastically alter her relationship with me. Don't think I resent it, David, because I don't. I've always wished that Daphne could have a family. I couldn't give her one. You have. I'm not so selfish as to not be happy for her."

David's throat went tight. "I'm sorry you didn't have that as a kid."

"Ah, well, I did all right. I had many mothers to love me, and each of them, in her way, loved me very well."

The nuns again, he thought. Before, her references to the orphanage had infuriated him, but now he was no longer quite so sure that part of her story was a lie. "You have my family now. If we make this marriage work, you'll never be without family again."

She studied him for a long while, until the silence became taut and uncomfortable. Finally she said, "As tempting as your offer may be, I am not so selfish as to do that to you. You've dealt honestly and fairly with me, David. You nearly died to protect me and my child. How can I do anything less than deal honestly and fairly with you?"

After a wonderful supper, David cleaned the kitchen while Brianna got Daphne ready for bed. When the child was tucked in, David dried his hands and went to sit on the edge of her mattress to tell her a story and kiss her good night. Having learned his lesson about the uncomfortable mix of spooky tales and six-year-old girls, David conjured up a memory from his childhood when Eden had taken a walk in the woods near their house and gone missing. Daphne clung to his every word.

"And so you found her, safe and sound?" she asked.

"We did. Your grandma Dory spent hours with brush and comb to get all the sticks and tangles out of her curly red hair, but she was safe, and after that, she never took off into the woods without one of us boys."

"When you describe Aunt Eden, she sounds like Aunt Caitlin. Do they look alike?"

David drew the covers up to Daphne's chin. "They look amazingly alike, and well they should because they're half sisters."

Daphne frowned. "Then you're related to Caitlin?"

David realized he had waded into water

too deep for a child. "Nope. Caitlin is related to Eden, but not to the rest of us." At Daphne's frown, he laughed and forestalled any more questions by saying, "When you're older, I'll tell you that story, but it isn't one you'll hear tonight."

"How old will I have to be?"

With a smile, David said, "Oh, I don't know. A lot older than you are right now. How's that?"

He found Brianna waiting for him in the dining room when he reached the end of the hall. She sat with her arms folded primly atop the table, her slender hands tucked against her forearms. How often had he seen the nuns in San Francisco hold their hands just that way, hidden under the winglike sleeves of their habits?

He took a chair across from her. He had deliberately postponed giving her any more details about purchasing the dress shop, hoping — foolishly, he guessed — that spending the evening together as a family might change her mind. He sensed that she yearned to stay there, but for reasons beyond him, she refused to do it.

David had things he needed to talk with Brianna about, most important the story he and Ace had cooked up to explain David's coming home with a wife and six-year-old child, but he decided that could simmer until they actually moved into town. Instead he broached the subject he knew was of more interest to Brianna right then. "I reckon you're anxious to hear more about the shop?"

Behind her, the fire snapped and crackled in the hearth, forming a halo of flickering amber around her dark hair. "I am, yes."

David shifted to get more comfortable. "The long and short of it is, you can probably take over day after tomorrow. Clarissa wants to sell everything — the stock and equipment, the upstairs furniture, even the dishes and bed linens. She wants to walk out with only her personal things, clothing, toiletries, and family mementos. Her price is reasonable, and I have plenty in the bank to cash her out. She'll sign over the deed to everything in front of a notary public, and then it'll be yours. You can move in with your personal things and be ready for business the next morning."

Brianna shook her head. "I'd like a separate contract to be drawn up, David. I can't accept the shop as a gift from you. I'll want to make monthly payments to you, with the going rate of interest included, so the shop will one day be rightfully mine."

David hadn't seen that coming, but when

he considered how prideful Brianna was, he could only wonder why he hadn't. "All right. I'd prefer it to be a personal contract, drawn up privately between us and signed and countersigned behind closed doors. In the eyes of the townsfolk, we're married. It'll raise eyebrows if it's public knowledge that you're buying the shop from me."

She considered that idea for a second, and then nodded. "I trust you. A private contract will suffice." She drew in a shaky breath and slowly released it. "This is a longtime dream of mine, you know. I've always wanted to have my own dress shop."

The tension eased from David's shoulders at the reminder. Until now, he'd been thinking of the dress shop as a final blow to any possibility of a real marriage between them, but since it had always been her dream, he could never deny her the experience, marriage or no. Eden was as fast and accurate with a gun as David was, and though he and his brothers had always sought to shelter and protect her, they'd also realized long ago that she was a filly who would always fight against too much coddling and control. David had nothing against strong-willed, self-sufficient women. He'd be proud to have a wife who was a successful businesswoman.

"Are you excited about it?" he asked.

Brianna's eyes took on a sparkle as she considered the question. "Excited, yes, and nervous as well. I want to design, David. I want wealthy women as customers who will demand gowns that are high quality, different, and on the cutting edge of fashion."

David knew there weren't enough wealthy women in No Name to support such an aspiration, but there were plenty in Denver. "Are you that good?"

She met his gaze. "I believe I am."

"Well, then, we'll need to advertise your talent in Denver. Thanks to Ace, the railroad spur from there to here offers plush passenger travel. If we court the right ladies, they can travel here in style for fittings and be home that same night."

*"We?"*

David chuckled and held up his hands. "Don't worry. I won't interfere in the designing and sewing. But I do have a good head for business, and as your pretend husband, I don't mind offering my expertise. You'll need to branch out to a richer customer base. From what you say, I gather you'd like to be famous someday."

Her eyes went dreamy. "Famous, yes. Brianna Paxton originals will be coveted, and women will pay high prices for them."

"Well, honey, I think you're on your way. Tomorrow the shop will be yours. The rest will be up to you."

# CHAPTER EIGHTEEN

Brianna loved the dress shop. It was on the same side of the street and only three doors down from the marshal's office. Right next door was a milliner's shop, the proprietress an aging lady named Beatrice Masterson who wasn't quite ready to retire but might be soon. That would give Brianna a chance to buy her shop, knock out the adjoining wall, and have a truly spectacular business space.

Ah, but for now, she was so excited with the present shop that she would have spun in circles if not for the presence of David and Clarissa Denny, who was walking her through the downstairs area. Clarissa was a slender lady, around sixty, with graying brown hair and gentle blue eyes.

"As you can see, I've invested in the newest and latest that Singer has to offer, including a ruffle attachment on this machine." She ran her fingertips lovingly over the hand-carved case as she lifted the lid to display the equipment. "The one upstairs is the same model, but I haven't yet invested in a ruffle attachment for it." She turned from the work cubicle to show Brianna the display rods, the glass cases, and the dressing rooms, which sported three-way mirrors so customers could admire their new gowns from all angles. "Over there," Clarissa said, pointing to two cushioned armchairs, "is where husbands sit to view the finished products, or to simply be a part of it all when we're selecting colors, styles, and types of cloth."

Smiling, the older woman flipped a wall switch. "And you have electric lighting down here. It will be costly to wire the upstairs, so I was saving back for that. Perhaps you'll do well enough to take care of that soon. The clarity of light is so much better with electricity. It blinks once in a while, but mostly only at night when others in town are using the current, too. Mostly it's steady and bright." She pointed to a rear exit. "I do my wash in the back dooryard, weather allowing. In the winter, I bundle up my soiled things and take them up the street to Dorothy Chandler, a dear lady who also has the candle shop. Her husband is the town chimney sweep. An enterprising couple, the Chandlers. Jesse helps Dorothy in the laundry, and they do a fine job, in my opinion, for a fair price."

Brianna grabbed Daphne's hand as they ascended the stairs behind Mrs. Denny to see the living quarters. David's boots resounded on the steps just behind them. Clarissa opened the door at the landing and led the way into a spacious kitchen. A round oak table, placed in front of a window that overlooked Main Street, was draped with a pristine white tablecloth. A blue-patterned cream pitcher and sugar bowl flanked a narrow stem vase that contained a single silk rose. Frilly curtains hung in graceful swags across a solid pull-down blind that was presently rolled up to let in the sunlight.

Brianna took in the white cabinetry, the cookstove, and a large deep sink with faucets, which told her hot and cold water had been piped in. She fell instantly in love. The sitting room was small but adequate and beautifully appointed with a horsehair settee, two matching chairs that shared an ottoman, and gleaming cherry tables draped with tatted lace. The fireplace at one side of the room was faced with red brick and topped by a thick oak mantel. Never in Brianna's wildest dreams had she hoped to live anywhere so perfect. Small, yes, but ever so cozy and nicely decorated, and it even had a water closet — nothing so grand as David's, but serviceable, with a washstand, flushable commode, and space in one corner for an aluminum bathtub.

"It's lovely," Brianna said. "It must break your heart to leave here, especially with all your personal touches remaining behind."

"I want to travel light," Clarissa said. "If I took everything dear to me, I'd need several large trunks. And, quite honestly, I hope to live with my elder son. All my things would be superfluous, and I'd probably just have to sell them. I can't be bothered."

Daphne ran around the kitchen, opening lower cupboard doors. "Mama, there's pots and pans and all manner of things!"

"Daphne, mind your manners. Those are Mrs. Denny's things for now."

"Only for now," Clarissa rejoined with a laugh. "And I will not for a second regret my departure. Not that it hasn't been a wonderful place and served me well for years, but it's time now for me to move on. I lost my dear husband ten years ago. My boys are in California. At this age, I yearn to live near them and my grandchildren." She chuckled and rubbed her palms together. "I'm already packed to leave!"

Brianna laughed with her. "It appears,

Mrs. Denny, that the end of your dream is the beginning of mine!"

"And mine!" Daphne cried. "A dress shop, Mama. Your very own dress shop!"

"Clarissa," the older woman corrected, directing her gaze at Brianna. "I'm old, but I'm not *that* old." She led the way to the bedrooms, which were situated at the back side of the kitchen. They were small but, like the rest of the apartment, decorated with thought and care. Brianna instantly decided that the one done in shades of rose with floral print wallpaper would be Daphne's. "Well, young woman?" Clarissa eyed her expectantly. "Will I be catching the train for Denver this afternoon, or do you need more time to think about it?"

Brianna had barely been aware of David until then. He stood in the doorway behind her, one muscular shoulder resting against the jam. The toothpick he clenched between his teeth jutted out from one corner of his firm mouth. When she searched his gaze, he winked at her. "It's your decision, not mine. If you're ready to roll up your sleeves and get to work, I'm ready to write out a draft and call it done."

Brianna turned back to Mrs. Denny. "Godspeed on your journey to California, Clarissa. I'll take it!"

■ ■ ■ ■

Forty minutes later, David followed Clarissa Denny, his wife, and Daphne from the bank out onto the boardwalk. As Clarissa said farewell with hurried hugs and handshakes, anxious to catch the train, David fingered the deed to the dress shop, eager to present it to Brianna with a flourish.

When the elder woman dashed away, however, Brianna waved a hand and refused to accept the document. "Not until we've drawn up our own contract, David."

"Oh, bullshit." He winced as the word slipped out. He'd been working really hard at cleaning up his mouth around Daphne. "You're taking stubbornness a bit too far. We'll do that over the next couple of days, I assure you, but for today, it's time to celebrate!" He stuffed the papers into her hand and pressed her slender fingers around them. "You own a dress shop, Shamrock! And it comes with a really nice living area. For once in your life, can't you just let loose and shriek with happiness?"

She fixed him with a startled green gaze. "Shriek?"

"Okay, I'll settle for a jump and a skip. You own — no, you're *buying* a business.

Can't you just —" David did a little skip and jump himself. "Come on, turn loose and be happy."

"Yes, Mama!" Daphne grabbed Brianna's hand and started bouncing about on her tiptoes. "It's a beautiful shop, and now you have the keys! Let's be happy!"

Brianna's cheek dimpled in a small smile. "I can be happy without abandoning proper decorum."

David gave up. The lady had way too much starch in her drawers.

"Can we sleep there tonight?" Daphne asked as they turned back to the dress shop, only two doors away. "I want the pink room! You and Papa can have the blue. Okay? The blue one is bigger."

Brianna flashed David a startled look. He bit back a grin. Apparently she had just remembered that, for appearances, they would have to share a bedchamber. David planned to procure a cot from the jailhouse that he could sleep on, but he couldn't very well remind Brianna of that in front of the child.

He fell in behind his ladies, his gaze fixed on the play of Brianna's brown silk bustle. It was the new, less punctuated style, but the woman needed nothing to accentuate that ass. Just watching her walk made his mouth go dry. Her narrow waist, no doubt cinched in by a corset, filled his mind with images of settling his hands on her hips. Even better, he would have loved to loosen all those stays, strip her down to bare skin, and tug all that glorious hair loose to let it spill in curly clouds over her ivory shoulders and down her slender back. *Damn.* He had a bad itch, and for the first time in his life, he knew of only one woman who could scratch it.

Just then, he looked up the street and saw Hazel Wright marching up Main, apparently finished for the day at school. She wore a pretty pink dress with a white shawl draped around her shoulders. Even at a distance, her eyes bored holes into him. *Shit.* David had never run from a confrontation in his life, but the infuriated expression on Hazel's face told him she was fighting mad. She'd clearly heard that David had returned from his mysterious journey with a wife and child, and even he had to concede that she had every right to an explanation. He'd come damn close to proposing marriage to the woman and had even given her a costly necklace.

Problem was, he and Brianna hadn't agreed on the explanation that he and Ace had cooked up yet. Whatever he said to

Hazel would spread through No Name like wildfire, and his first responsibility was to protect Brianna and Daphne from public censure, no matter what. He jerked to a halt, noted the indignant angle of Hazel's head, and said, "Brianna, I just remembered some stuff I need to take care of at my office. How's about I do that while you and Daphne explore the shop and apartment again?"

Brianna turned, her eyes glowing with excitement. "All right. When you're ready to head back to the ranch, just tap on the door."

David lifted a hand in casual farewell and spun on his heel, hoping his wife wouldn't watch where he went. Instead of entering his office, where Hazel could follow, he walked a few more feet and dove through the batwing doors of the Golden Slipper. No lady who valued her reputation would even stand in front of the place, let alone enter it.

David took up a hiding position just inside the doors, his shoulder pressed hard against the plank wall. Seeing him, Mac called out from the bar. "Well, howdy, Marshal Paxton. Good to see you back! I heard you came home with some extra baggage."

David winced. He did *not* want his wife

and child being referred to as baggage. But right then he had Hazel to think about. She could be bold. What if she marched right up to the entrance and demanded to speak with him? He needed a story to tell her, and he didn't have one. Not one that had Brianna's stamp of approval yet, anyway. He didn't feel right about circulating it around town until she agreed to it. He and Ace thought it was a pretty rock-solid explanation, but Brianna might want to add her own embellishments.

He ignored Mac and edged out from the wall to peek around the doorjamb. Where was Hazel? He poked his head out over the batwings. Where had she gone? A woman couldn't just vanish off the street. *Oh, God.* David pictured her in the dress shop, lacing Brianna up one side and down the other. Hey, he could understand that Hazel's feelings might be hurt, but he didn't want her taking it out on his wife. None of this was Brianna's fault.

Just then a door slammed a short distance away, the impact so violent that the floor shuddered under David's feet. He cringed. Between the Golden Slipper and the dress shop were the marshal's office, the bank, and the milliner's shop. He couldn't tell by the report which door it might have been.

Easing his head around the corner of the jamb, he saw Hazel leaving his office. Her honey brown hair shone rich in the sunlight, her eyes flashed with tears, and even to a man who wanted to avoid her at all costs, she was undeniably a fine figure of a woman.

David would have settled for her once, but those times were far behind him now. Life with Brianna might be a rough ride some of the time, but by comparison, Hazel seemed as bland as flour-and-water gravy with no salt for flavor.

"You hiding from Hazel Wright, Marshal?" Mac asked with a lilt of suppressed humor in his voice. "I'm sorry for laughing, but you have to admit it's funny. I've seen you walk out and face gunmen on that street. How can one small woman make you huddle up and quail with fear?"

David straightened away from the wall. Marcy May, wearing a red dress, the bodice of which barely covered her nipples, came sashaying around a table toward him. With a sweep of his gaze, David noted that the saloon had no customers yet. He reckoned it was still too early in the day.

"Ah, now, Mac," Marcy crooned, "leave the marshal be. Miss Wright is in a fine dither. She had a nice fish on her hook, and he's wiggled free of the barb." Marcy May hugged David's arm, pressed close, and squished her half-covered breast against the side of his elbow. "No worries about me, Marshal Paxton. My hook is barbless. You can come nibble on my bait and then slip away without a struggle any old time. Looks to me like you got woman trouble, and I know just the cure for what ails you."

Right then, the last thing David figured he needed was another woman to complicate his life. Hazel had disappeared down the street. *Marcy May and her henna-streaked hair.* She was a fair one, and David suspected she did well upstairs, but he wasn't interested. That said, she was a sweet enough lady, and he didn't want to hurt her feelings.

"Well, now, Marcy May, that is a mighty appealing hook you're dangling in front of my nose, but I'm married, right and proper, and it isn't in my makeup to cheat on my wife."

Marcy was young in years but old at her trade. She just smiled. "I prefer married men. They know how to treat me nice." She flashed a saucy grin. "You'll be back to see me, Marshal. Appears to me your wife is one of them proper ladies, and they ain't no fun. I know how to show a man a good time. You just remember that."

David pulled away from her. She pouted her lips but didn't try to hang on. After checking again to make sure the way was clear, David slipped out of the saloon and practically fell into his office. Once the door was closed and locked, he wanted to jerk off his hat and mop his face. He had a bad feeling that Hazel wasn't going to let this go without a nasty showdown.

With a grunt, Sam got up from his napping spot behind the stove. David had left the dog in his office while they toured the shop and apartment. There was no sign of his deputy, Billy Joe, who was probably out making rounds.

"Hey, boy," David said, scratching the dog behind his ears.

A folded piece of paper lying on his desk blotter caught his eye. He opened it and read the angry slash of a feminine hand.

You are a low down, conniving, rotten, philandering skunk, and I will never forgive you for humiliating me the way you have. One way or another, I will see to it that you live to regret the day you were born.

"Whew," David said softly. Glancing down at Sam, he said, "She's in high dudgeon, that's for sure. How should I deal with this? You got any bright ideas?"

Sam lay on his belly, crossed his white paws over his eyes, and let loose with a mournful whine.

David didn't want to cut the fun short for Brianna and Daphne, so he and Sam stayed in the dress shop's viewing area for the next few minutes, waiting for the ladies to tire of their exploration of the upstairs rooms. From all parts of the building, he could hear exclamations of delight when they came across something that pleased them. It made David feel good. There had been few causes for celebration in Brianna's life.

When they moved downstairs to admire the store's stock, he yawned. He liked seeing females all decked out in pretty dresses with ribbons in their hair, but these bolts of cloth and gewgaws almost made his eyes roll back in his head. His time would be better spent working at his office.

Just as he was about to excuse himself, Brianna pulled out a bolt of yardage. "Oh, my, Daphne, just *look* at this fabulous taffeta. Isn't it sublime?"

David sauntered across the carpet to peer over her shoulder at a shimmery blue material. "Hmm, taffeta," he observed. "Maybe we should rename this town Taffeta Falls."

Brianna sent him a startled look. He searched her green eyes and winked at her. She clearly remembered plucking that particular lie out of her bonnet because a flush stole up her neck and flagged her cheeks. "Will you never let me live that down?"

David chuckled, and though she tried to suppress it, Brianna smiled slightly. "Are you about ready to head back to the ranch?" she asked. "You look bored to tears."

"It's up to you. I have things to do over at my office if you'd like to stay longer."

She patted the bolt of material. "Unless your work is pressing, we're ready to leave. Until we have our things here, we can't settle in."

"Would you like to do that tonight?"

"Tomorrow morning will suffice."

David drew his watch from his pocket to check the time. "Can I interest you in an early supper over at Roxie's? That'll save us from having to cook when we get home."

Daphne clapped her hands. Sam, who loved going to Roxie's, barked joyously. Brianna smiled demurely. "It appears we have a unanimous vote of approval, sir. An early supper sounds lovely to me as well."

David escorted his entourage across the

street to the restaurant. So early in the afternoon, there was only a handful of customers: two ladies at a window table having tea and pie, and two men at the counter sipping coffee. Red-checked tablecloths and matching napkins gave the place a bright, homey atmosphere. Sam was a regular customer there, and David guided his wife and daughter to a corner table where the dog could lie down in comfort without being underfoot. Roxie waved from behind the counter, her countenance rosy from the heat of the kitchen, her merry green eyes settling with unabashed curiosity on Brianna.

"Good afternoon!" she called as she circled the counter. "What can I get for you folks?" She smiled brightly at Daphne. "Would this young lady like a sarsaparilla and maybe a piece of my famous apple pie?"

David ruffled Daphne's hair. "She'll start with a sarsaparilla, but no pie until after supper." After introducing Brianna and the child, David added, "We're eating a little early today. What's the special?"

"Beef and sausage meatloaf." Roxie grinned. "It's the finest textured meatloaf in existence, served with clear dripping gravy, mashed potatoes, peas or corn, and my specialty sourdough bread with whipped butter on the side."

Just then the entrance bell clanged. David caught a flash of pink from the corner of his eye, and his stomach sank. *Hazel.* Had she followed them? Probably. He braced himself for a nasty confrontation.

Roxie, apparently sensing how the wind might blow, turned on the charm. "Miss Wright, what an unexpected pleasure!" She hurried over to take the schoolteacher's arm. "I have a special table in mind for you. Please step this way."

Hazel allowed herself to be led across the room, but, cricking her neck to look back over her shoulder, she sent David glares powerful enough to pulverize granite. The look she gave Brianna burned with undisguised hatred and resentment.

Brianna raised her eyebrows. In a low voice, she asked, "Who *is* that lady?"

"A former friend." It was all David could think to say.

"Oh." Brianna lowered her lashes and caught her lower lip between her teeth. As ill-timed as it was, David ached to taste those shimmery lips and do a little nibbling as well. His Shamrock was so damned beautiful and fine. On her best day, Hazel Wright could never measure up. "I'm sorry, David."

Why Brianna was apologizing, he didn't know. "Don't worry about it. Let's just enjoy our meal."

Everyone chose the special of the day, but with Hazel glaring at him from across the room, David didn't feel much like eating, and he noticed that Brianna picked at her food as well. Only Daphne and Sam, who was always served his own meal on the floor, seemed to enjoy the fare. David was relieved to pay the bill and leave.

Once on the boardwalk, he could breathe easy again. Hazel Wright had a nasty streak he'd never glimpsed when courting her. He had a bad feeling she meant to cause trouble, and for the life of him, he couldn't think how to handle the situation. David had unknowingly done the woman a serious wrong. He'd had good intentions, but there was no way in hell he could explain the situation without stirring up gossip that would embarrass his wife and hurt his daughter. As soon as he and Brianna moved into town, they needed to agree on the story they meant to circulate about their marriage, separation, and recent reunion. Then David would talk with Hazel and hopefully assuage her anger. That wasn't a discussion he wanted to have with Brianna tonight, though. It should be an evening of celebration, and David didn't want to spoil it for her.

Once in the wagon and headed for home, David had little to say. He knew Brianna was upset, and he couldn't rightly blame her. Daphne crawled in the back with Sam on some blankets David kept there to give the dog a cushioned ride.

"That woman," Brianna ventured in a low voice. "Is she part of that life you had planned?"

David sighed. "Yes. Her name is Hazel Wright. She's the new schoolteacher."

"Do you — ?" She made tight fists in the folds of her silk skirt. "Do you love her?"

Not wanting to answer too quickly because he needed Brianna to understand that he'd thought deeply about his answer, he finally said, "No. It wasn't like that between us, at least not for me."

"Of course you would say that." Tears sparkled in her eyes. "Oh, David, I feel terrible. Daphne and I — we've ruined everything for you, haven't we?"

"No, damn it, you haven't." David shifted his grip on the reins and clucked his tongue to the team. "I'm thirty, Shamrock. On the second of June, I'll be thirty-one. I kept waiting for the right lady to happen into my life. I wanted — hell, I don't know — magic,

I guess you could say, the kind of all-or-nothing love that Ace and Joseph have with their wives. But it just never happened. I've always wanted children. I started thinking about how time was wasting, and when Hazel came to town, I decided maybe that was as good as it was going to get."

"So you decided to marry her?"

David knew their whole future, if they even had one to look forward to, depended upon his answer. "Not exactly. I toyed with the idea, I'll admit, but when it came right down to it, something always held me back. I knew if I asked her to marry me, I'd be settling for second best. A part of me wanted to do just that, but another part of me wanted to wait."

"For what?"

"For —" David didn't want to scare the sand out of her, but at the same time, he wanted to be absolutely honest. "I didn't know what I was waiting for until I met you."

*"Me?"*

He slapped the reins against the horses' rumps. "Yep. One look into those green eyes of yours, and I was a goner."

"That is preposterous. Don't wax poetic with me, David Paxton. I've agreed to this absurd arrangement. There's no need to pretend with me in private."

David wasn't pretending, but she obviously wasn't ready to hear how he really felt. He'd bide his time, play the game, and then, when it felt right, he'd make her listen to him. Hazel Wright was a mistake he'd nearly made, and nothing more. Well, she was also a huge problem, but over time, maybe she'd settle down and accept the offer of some other man. God knew there were plenty standing in line to win her favor.

# CHAPTER NINETEEN

That night, David tucked Daphne into bed again and told the story about the time Eden and Joseph had gotten into a quarrel while cleaning the kitchen and broken nearly every dish in the cupboard. Brianna sat on the opposite side of the mattress, attending the tale, which pleased David because he'd noted her reaction to the heated exchange that had occurred during supper at Ace's house. Both his daughter and wife needed to understand that as vocal and volatile as the Paxton-Keegan clan could be, physical violence never took place.

"Was Uncle Ace angry when he had to buy all new dishes?" Daphne asked, her eyes round with worry.

"Well, he wasn't exactly happy, but he was making good money by then at the tables, so he could afford new dishes and wasn't what I'd call angry."

Brianna cleared her throat to get David's

attention. When he met her gaze, she said, "Remember that morning by the fire when you told me what to do if you told a spooky story ever again?"

David recalled exactly what he'd said, that she should tell him to shut his damned mouth, but the tale he was telling wasn't spooky. He went back over the details and realized Brianna didn't want her daughter to know about her uncle Ace's gambling.

"How did Uncle Ace make money at the tables?" Daphne asked. "Was he a waiter at a restaurant?"

David wasn't about to lie to the child, and he disagreed with Brianna's judgments. Ace's gambling profits had saved his family from poverty, and David was extremely proud of all the sacrifices his brother had made. To him, it wasn't a shameful thing that he wanted to hide from anyone, least of all Daphne.

"For a long time, Uncle Ace swept barroom floors and emptied spittoons to keep a roof over our heads. Grandma Dory helped by doing laundry and cleaning other people's houses."

"Just like Mama," Daphne said, snuggling deeper under the quilt.

"Yes, just like your mama." David met Brianna's gaze. "Your grandma Dory was brave and industrious. She did whatever she could to keep her kids fed. That's a very admirable trait in a lady. And Uncle Ace — well, he was only eleven when he had to start supporting us, so he had a lot of responsibility placed on his shoulders at a young age."

"I'm almost that old!" Daphne exclaimed.

"Yes, you are. In five more years, you'll be as old as Ace was when he became the man of the house." David chose his next words carefully. "Problem was, sweeping floors and emptying spittoons didn't bring in much income, and your uncle Ace was too smart to keep doing that for long. While he worked in the saloons, he watched the men play poker, and slowly but surely, he learned to be a professional gambler."

"What's a professional gambler?"

David met Brianna's gaze again. "It's someone who can shuffle cards so fast you can barely see his hands move, and he knows how to count the cards as well. Uncle Ace learned when he was still only a boy, and he started winning a lot of money playing poker. Before we knew it, we were living high on the hog. He bought us a beautiful house in San Francisco, and us younger kids went to parochial schools, where nuns taught us."

"What happened then?" Daphne asked.

David tugged the quilt up under her chin. "Well, when Aunt Eden and Uncle Joseph broke all the dishes, Uncle Ace had plenty of money to buy new, for starters. We were all very glad about his success at the tables. Before that, we had only beans to eat, sometimes with a ham hock in the pot to add flavor if we were lucky. When Uncle Ace started winning at cards, we had wonderful meals, nice clothes, went to fine schools, and had beautiful horses in our stable, just like my pa back in Virginia before the war."

Daphne searched David's face. "So how come do you look sad, Papa?"

David thought about that for a moment. "I guess because your uncle Ace gave up some of his life for us. All his younger years were spent taking care of his family, leaving him no time to think about himself, and the gambling life was a hard one that eventually led him to a way of living that he never would have chosen for himself."

"He's happy now, though. Right?"

"By the grace of God, yes, he is." After saying that, David remembered that he had something in his shirt pocket for his daughter. He plucked it out and held it up. "Surprise!"

Daphne gasped and jerked upright, her

blue eyes almost as bright as the copper penny that now dangled from a fine gold chain. "Oh, Papa! You went to the jeweler's!"

David chuckled. "I did. He drilled a hole in our lucky penny, and he made sure the chain is long enough for me to wear. It'll probably hang down to your belly button."

Daphne grabbed the chain and pulled it over her head. As David predicted, the coin hung low, but she squealed with delight. "I can wear it under my frocks. It will be our special secret."

David bent to kiss her forehead. Then he settled her back under the quilt. "It's time for a little miss I know to close her eyes now and go to sleep."

Daphne groaned, but she was smiling as she folded her small hand over the penny. "Thank you, Papa. What a lovely good-night gift."

"You're very welcome." Sam jumped up on the bed just then and sprawled beside the child. David chuckled. "It appears to me you've stolen my dog."

Curling her arm over Sam's neck, Daphne pressed her face against his ruff. "He's still yours, Papa. He just loves me a lot, too."

After studying the dog for a moment, David shifted his gaze to Brianna. "I suppose that's true. I'm learning that our hearts have a huge capacity for love."

After getting Daphne settled in for the night, David left Brianna to get ready for bed while he rode Blue back into town. It was late. The shops were all closed, and the houses surrounding Main Street were mostly dark. From the windows of Roxie's came only a dim glow, telling David that the place was now closed to customers while Roxie cleaned up and prepared for the morning rush. Only a few men were on the boardwalks, walking back and forth between the Golden Slipper and the Silver Spur in search of another drink, a luckier card game, or female company. The scent of cigar smoke drifted on the night air.

David had made arrangements for his deputies to handle the marshaling duties the last couple of days, so he knew Rory Eugene Cobb, his junior man, was either monitoring the saloons or doing paperwork in the office. The kid, half Mexican and as pretty of feature as any girl, had a tough edge and a good head on his shoulders for someone only twenty-one. Now that trouble occurred less frequently in No Name, David trusted him nearly as much as Billy Joe, who'd been with him much longer.

When David stepped inside the office,

Rory leaped up from the desk, his pitch-black, curly hair glistening in the newly installed electric lighting. "Marshal Paxton, what brings you here? I thought you were spending tonight out at the ranch."

David stepped over to the desk to shuffle through office mail he hadn't had a chance to open. *Nothing important.* To Rory, he said, "I just stopped in to borrow one of the extra cots."

"A cot?" Rory arched a thick brow. "What the hell do you need with a cot?"

David straightened away from the desk. "None of your damned business, son, and so far as you know, I never took one."

Minutes later, David was lugging the folded cot up the dress-shop stairs and struggling to get it through the doorway of the apartment. A good deal of cussing rent the silence because the spring mattress kept slipping off the frame. He regretted the lack of electricity on the second floor as he felt his way through the kitchen to the blue bedroom. Once inside, he slid the cot under the bed. He figured Clarissa Denny had extra bedding and pillows stored somewhere, but he'd hunt them up tomorrow night when he needed them. His and Brianna's pretend marriage was about to be put under a public microscope.

Daphne would have to learn to knock before she entered her parents' bedroom. That would give David time to collapse the cot and shove it under the double bed so his daughter never realized her parents slept apart. If she barged in unannounced, David would think up a quick white lie. Maybe he could say he snored and kept Brianna awake, so they had decided on separate beds. At six, Daphne would believe whatever he told her, just as she had when he'd collected rocks to cover those three graves out on the prairie. Not graves, in her mind, but special monuments.

The memory made David smile. He stepped to the window. The blind was up. With the back of his hand, he pushed away the frilly lace curtain to stare at the sky, a blaze of brilliant starlight against black velvet. When his gaze settled on one pin-point of brilliance, he was tempted to revert back to childhood and make a wish. But as a man who'd seen the shadows in Brianna's eyes, he knew it would take more than wishing to make things right between them.

The following day, David helped Brianna move into the dress-shop apartment. Brianna discovered the hidden cot right away, and later, when David entered the bedroom, he saw that she'd set out blankets, linen, and a pillow on the foot of the bed. It would be a pain in the ass to make up the cot every night, but there was no way around it.

During the child's nap, David sat with Brianna at the kitchen table to relate to her the story he and Ace had decided would be appropriate to tell everyone about his and Brianna's marital history. "When I called Ace from Denver, he needed something to tell our family, so we talked it over and came up with a fairly good tale."

"Which is?"

"We'll just say we had a serious misunderstanding shortly after our wedding and separated. Then, a few months ago, we started communicating by mail, realized that our parting was a mistake, and decided to meet to see if we could sort out our differences. Our love for each other prevailed, and now we're happily reunited as husband and wife."

Brianna nodded. "That sounds believable."

"Any changes you'd like to make before I go public with it?" he asked.

"Am I to understand that even your family was told this lie? Is that why the women asked me no questions, because they believe we were somehow married before Daphne was born?"

David rubbed a hand over his eyes. "I know that part isn't going to sit well with you, but I honestly think the fewer people who know the truth, the better."

"I don't feel right about lying to your mother and brothers, not to mention their wives," Brianna protested. "But apparently you took my vote out of the equation when you talked to Ace that night on the phone."

David reached across the table to take her hand. "If you're dead set on telling my family the truth, I'll abide by your wishes, but I think it'd be a mistake. I trust Ace to keep it under his hat. But when you tell a secret to too many people, someone is bound to let it slip sooner or later. No one in my family would ever do it intentionally, and I feel bad about lying to them, too. But our first concern has to be for Daphne. Neither of us wants our daughter to be hurt by the mistakes we made one long-ago night in Denver."

Denver, Denver, *Denver.* Until recently, Brianna had never even visited the town, but David remained convinced that he'd once met her there. He believed in that so strongly, in fact, that sometimes it was difficult for Brianna to keep the facts straight in her own mind. She had even caught herself thinking of David as Daphne's actual father. For a woman in her position, that was dangerous.

Last night as she lay awake, waiting for David to return from town, she'd found herself wishing that his version of her past was the truth. It would be so lovely to feel secure in this marriage, to know that the rug couldn't be yanked out from under her at any moment.

"I've never been a very good liar," she told him.

That brought a grin to David's face. "You're lousy at it, actually, but for Daphne's sake, we'll both carry it off."

"People are already whispering, I think." Brianna glanced down at the street, where shoppers scurried from one store to the next. "When I open the shop tomorrow, I fully expect a dozen women to drop in just to get a good look at me."

"Don't worry about that. People are going to talk. There's no avoiding it. But with me being the marshal and my family being so well respected in the community, the buzzing will die down pretty fast."

"And what about Hazel Wright?"

David frowned at her. "What about her?"

"Don't you think she'll be very upset, and

justifiably so, if she believes you courted her when you knew you were a married man?"

"Shit." He raked a hand through his hair. "You're right." His eyes went as dark as storm clouds. "Ace and I didn't think about that. What'll I tell her?"

Brianna considered the question. "Tell her that we had long been discussing divorce in our letters, and you thought you'd soon be free to marry."

The creases in his brow vanished. "That'll work. The last time we talked, I was getting itchy feet, so I said something about having to make plans before I proposed officially."

Imagining David about to propose to that woman put a bad taste in Brianna's mouth. "So we're agreed? We were going to divorce and changed our minds."

He nodded.

Brianna took a bracing breath. "So now it starts. As of today, we begin living a lie."

"Yes," David replied. The emotion in his blue eyes tugged at her and made her want to believe in magic again. "Who knows? Maybe if we do it well enough and long enough, it'll no longer be a lie. I'm coming to care for you. Maybe in time you'll come to care for me."

Oh, how Brianna wished it were possible for this to become a real marriage. This man had wormed his way past most of her defenses, and she was starting to fall in love with him. Rationally, she knew that was a mistake. The only reason David wanted so badly to make this marriage work was because he cared deeply for Daphne and wanted her to have a normal, happy childhood. He would do anything to protect his child — *anything,* even it meant sacrificing his own life. He'd proven that.

Gazing into his eyes, Brianna wouldn't allow herself to believe in what she saw there. He didn't love *her.* He loved Daphne because he thought she was his own flesh and blood. How would he feel when he learned she wasn't?

Immediately following his talk with Brianna, David went to sit in front of his office and wait for Hazel Wright to leave the school and walk the length of Main to her little house, provided for her by the town. He could face her now. Brianna had agreed to the story he and Ace felt should be told. He'd relate it to Hazel and try to assuage her hurt feelings, and hopefully they'd part as friends.

It wasn't long before David saw her trudging along the dirt thoroughfare. She wore a pretty green dress and a lacy shawl the color of whipped cream. When David stepped out into her path, she jerked to a halt and pierced him with a wounded gaze that made him feel like shit. He'd never meant to hurt her.

"Hazel, can we talk?"

"Yes." She swept past him. "At my place. I will not be humiliated out here on the street."

David felt like a dog trained to heel as he followed her home. Once inside her sitting room, he swept off his hat. Meeting her gaze dead on, he said, "I know I've got some explaining to do. Just please know I never meant to mislead you."

She stepped over to a round table at the end of her settee and opened a carved box. The next instant, David felt the sting of something hit him in the face. He looked down and saw the gold pendant he'd given her lying at his feet.

"You are a lying, faithless scoundrel!" she shrieked.

"Hazel, please. Just hear me out."

She disappeared into the kitchen. A second later, she reappeared with a broom. David realized she meant to hit him with it, and he had the option of ducking, but he'd hurt this woman and figured he had a hard lick coming. He braced as she swung. The broom handle caught him alongside the head, and for a second he saw stars.

"Get out!" she cried. "And take your lies with you!"

David nodded. "All right. I understand your anger. You're entitled to it. I just wish you'd listen and —"

She swung with the broom again. Until that moment, David hadn't realized that Sam had followed him into the house. The dog yelped as the broom handle connected with his back. He scrambled behind David, whining. David stared hard at this woman he'd once tried to tell himself he loved. Had he taken leave of his senses? He couldn't stand people who abused animals, and Sam had done nothing to deserve a wallop.

Head still smarting, David turned, flung open the front door, and nudged his dog out on the porch. *To hell with giving her an explanation.* As far as he was concerned, she no longer deserved one. Before he could close the portal behind him, Hazel took two more swings, nailing David on the knee and Sam on the head. That cinched it.

David rounded on her. "Take your anger out on me, but leave Sam alone."

She struck David on the arm. "A pox on you *and* your stinking dog!"

When she tried to hit Sam again, David

flung up his arm to block the blow. The broom handle snapped clean in two. Hazel stared at the broken wood. Before she could decide to stab Sam with a sharp end, David cleared the porch, ordering his dog to follow him.

So much for trying to do the right thing. From here on out, Hazel Wright could pickle in her own bitterness.

Over the next many days, Brianna's life with David fell into a pattern. He stayed above the shop a few nights a week and went back to the ranch the other nights. On town nights, they circled each other. Brianna felt like a splash of kerosene exposed to an open flame. To her the tension between them seemed so electrical that a mere touch of their fingers set off sparks, and she truly felt as if her very flesh might ignite. As she had out on the prairie, she often found herself watching him, admiring his physique. The play of muscle under his clothes fascinated her. From the corner of her eye, she enjoyed observing the way his thighs flexed as he moved. The rich sound of his voice made all her nerve endings thrill. She even liked how he looked in what she had come to think of as his "desperado" garb. In Boston, no one would ever mistake him for a gentleman, but she had come to appreciate his rough edges and strength, finding those traits far more appealing than tailored suits and manicured nails.

With David in the apartment, she felt protected against all outside dangers. Perversely, it was only David himself who presented a threat to her peace of mind. Sometimes when she caught him studying her, she saw a glint of desire in his eyes and knew he wanted to bed her and make their pretend marriage a real one. Brianna held firm, not because she still harbored any fear of him, but because consummating the marriage would be unfair to him. When the day came that he realized Daphne wasn't his, Brianna wanted him to be free to leave her and make a life with someone else. He was far too honorable a man to ever make that choice if he believed she might be pregnant or if they'd had a child together.

*No.* She would be strong for both of them. If he ever wanted out, there would be nothing to hold him back. She just hoped he didn't choose to be with that snotty Hazel Wright.

Hazel came into the dress shop nearly every day after school, and without fail, she was spitefully unpleasant. Though Brianna could understand Hazel's feelings of resentment toward her, she began to dread the visits.

"This satin is less fine than what Clarissa kept in stock," she said one afternoon. "You'll soon find yourself out of business if you try to sell gowns of lesser quality to optimize your profits."

Brianna, standing behind the display case, met Hazel's glittery blue gaze. "Actually, that particular satin was here when I bought the shop. Dorothy Chandler is delighted with the gown I fashioned for her from that bolt. It's so popular I'll need to order more soon."

Another time, Hazel bypassed the snide remarks and went right for Brianna's throat. "I've heard the story of your marriage to David, and I'm convinced it's a bunch of poppycock. He isn't the kind of man who would court me when he was married to another woman."

Brianna put down the child's frock she was hemming and stood to face Hazel. "You're free to think what you like, I suppose. The story you heard is the truth."

"So David is a conscienceless philanderer?"

"I didn't say that," Brianna replied. "David is a fine man. I don't believe he has it in him to do anything dishonest or unkind."

"Really?" Hazel studied a brooch displayed on velvet inside the glass case. "Well, he certainly had no problem being unfaithful to you. He courted me. He bought me gifts. He was about to propose marriage. If he's such a fine man, why was he contemplating bigamy?"

Brianna moistened her lips. "At the time, David and I were discussing divorce in our correspondence. David believed he would soon be free to marry. As it happened, though, we began sorting out our differences in our letters, and we changed our minds about ending the marriage."

Hazel brought the flat of her hand down on the glass with such force that the report was deafening. "You're lying! And mark my words, *Mrs.* Paxton, one of these days I will take great pleasure in exposing you for the trollop that you really are."

Brianna clenched her teeth to keep from saying anything in response. When Hazel left the shop, she hugged her waist, bent her head, and tried to stop shaking. David entered the shop just then. Brianna jerked and looked up.

"What the hell did she want?" he asked.

"She knows, David. She knows it's all a lie."

He strode over to grasp Brianna's shoulders. "She knows nothing for certain, Shamrock. Don't let her upset you this way."

"It's difficult to remain calm when someone is being so nasty."

David cupped her cheek in his hand. His touch sent a tingle all the way to her toes. She'd come to love the light caress of his thumb over her cheek, and it took all her strength of will not to lean into him right then and beg him to hold her close.

"You want me to tell her to stay away from the shop?" he asked.

Brianna collected herself and stepped away from him. "No. It's a place of business, open to the public. If we did that, we'd only be adding fuel to the fire."

David sighed and put his hands at his hips. "You're probably right. Maybe you should just ignore her. You're not obligated to talk with her about anything personal. If she makes snide remarks or asks questions she has no business asking, try pretending that you don't hear."

"I'll do that."

For David, his nights in town were a mixture of pleasure and torture. He greatly enjoyed the evenings above the dress shop, with Daphne chattering while they fixed supper and then entertaining them with stories of her day during the meal. With school out of session in less than a month, he was pleased to hear that the child was making friends. She particularly liked Kaylee Thompson, Brad and Bess's blond, green-eyed daughter, a bright little four-year-old who'd entered first grade a year early. Then there was Ralph Banks, Eva and Charley's son, a stocky boy, soon to turn twelve, who'd taken Daphne under his wing; and Donnie Christian, a jet-haired little pistol with mischief gleaming in his blue eyes, who would celebrate his eighth birthday in June. Daphne regaled them with tales of Donnie's latest pranks in class.

"So how do you like your teacher?" Brianna asked one night at supper.

Daphne wrinkled her nose. "She's all right, I guess. She's not mean to me or anything. I just don't think she likes me very well."

Brianna shot David a worried look. Later, as he helped her with the dishes, he tried to reassure her in a hushed voice. "Surely Hazel won't take out her anger on a child." He remembered Hazel's attacks on Sam and prayed he was right. Anyone who'd hit a dog without cause might mistreat a little girl. "I mean — well, I know she's doing a burn, but none of it is Daphne's fault."

"Let us hope." Brianna plunged her hands into the sudsy dishwater. "So far, I've detected nothing in that woman's character that I deem commendable."

Clutching the towel in both fists, David yearned to toss it down and encircle Brianna's waist from behind so he could nibble on the nape of her neck. Tiny dark curls had escaped her chignon to rest against her pale skin. He imagined nosing them aside, tasting her, breathing in the scent of her until he felt intoxicated. She had apparently purchased bath salts and was using them, for even at three feet away, David caught the light, heady fragrance of roses.

The yearning to hold her plagued him every night when he stayed in town. Small as the apartment was, he brushed against her in the kitchen as they worked, and each time, his body reacted. Later tonight, he knew he would lie awake on the cot, listening to the sounds of her breathing and turning over only a few feet away. And he would wish as he had a dozen times before that he could make those springs sing a different tune. She was his wife, damn it, and he suspected that she was as attracted to him as he was to her, yet she held him at arm's length.

When the kitchen was tidy, David sat at

the table with Daphne to help with her homework while Brianna sat in a corner rocker, hand stitching the hem of a gown for Tory Thompson, Tobias's wife. Though she'd placed a lighted lantern at her elbow, she squinted to see. It was time, David thought, to get the upstairs wired for electricity. There was a social scheduled for the first part of June, and a lot of ladies were ordering new dresses for the occasion. Brianna was even working on a gown for herself in her spare time, the cloth the color of burgundy wine. David couldn't wait to see her in it even though he had no idea what it would look like finished. *Burgundy.* Normally Brianna gravitated toward dark, drab colors. Her decision to wear something brighter and more striking gave David hope that she was beginning to relax a little in their marriage.

He didn't believe in making Daphne's study hours at night boring, so instead he tried to turn everything into a game. Tonight she was studying the presidents of the United States. Tomorrow for her test, she would have to recite their names in the order of their terms of office. To David it seemed a hard assignment for first grade, and he was thankful she wasn't required to spell them.

"So who is our president right now?" he asked.

"Benjamin Harrison," Daphne replied.

"No, sir!" David protested. "What happened to Grover Cleverhand?"

Daphne giggled. "Cleveland, Papa, not Cleverhand."

"I *know* his name was Cleverhand. I voted for him. He came into office right after Arthur Chester."

"No, you have it backward. His name was Chester A. Arthur!"

David turned to Brianna. "Tell her I've got it right."

Brianna smiled slightly. "You know very well you have it wrong. Why must every study session be a bunch of tomfoolery?"

David wanted to reply that she *never* engaged in tomfoolery, which was even worse. Brianna always held herself apart, watching and seeming to take pleasure in her daughter's laughter, but never departing from her ladylike behavior to join in. Why? The question bothered David continuously. He sensed in Brianna a great capacity for laughter and silliness, so why did she keep herself stifled and under strict control?

By evening's end, Daphne knew all the presidents' names and years in office. David tucked her in with a tale he made up about a big old tomcat that was terrified of mice. Toward the end of the story, Daphne fell asleep, clutching their lucky penny in her small hand.

When David returned to the kitchen, Brianna was still hunched over her sewing. He wanted so badly to jerk the gown from her hands, draw her into his arms, and kiss her senseless. Instead he bade her good night and went to bed on his lonely cot. Sleep evaded him. Being around Brianna so much had his manly urges in a constant stir.

An hour later when she entered the room, she closed the door and drew down the blind, plunging the room into total darkness, apparently thinking it would give her privacy as she undressed. Soon moonlight penetrated the shade, though, enabling David to see far more clearly than she realized. The pale glow of a slender arm, the roundness of a hip, the plumpness of her bottom. He squeezed his eyes closed, unable to watch for fear he'd leap from the cot and take her into his arms.

After she drew on a nightdress and got into bed, he waited to hear her breathing change. He waited — and waited. Finally he realized that she had the wide-awakes, too. Was she feeling the same deep yearnings for a physical relationship between them? *Yeah, right.* Sometimes when they bumped against each other in the kitchen, she gasped softly and jerked away as if his touch burned her.

On weekends, Daphne loved staying at the ranch with her father, and Brianna didn't have the heart to say the child couldn't go. They usually returned home early enough Sunday evening for Daphne to do her homework, bathe, and get to bed for a good night's sleep, but occasionally David packed Daphne a fresh change of clothes, toiletries, and her schoolbooks so they could come back Monday morning, just in time for the child's first class of the day.

Either way, the time alone seemed like an eternity to Brianna. She'd never been apart from her daughter, and the child's absences left her feeling empty and cast adrift. David always invited Brianna to go, of course, but she normally declined. David's family was almost as easy to love as he was, and Brianna saw no point in condemning herself or them to heartbreak. The truth was bound to rear its ugly head, and then Brianna and Daphne would no longer be considered a part of the Paxton clan.

Brianna worried about the outcome for Daphne. She had adored David from the start, and now she was becoming deeply fond of everyone else. Sadly, Brianna was powerless to prevent her child from opening herself up to future pain. Daphne returned from each visit with countless tales of Ace, Joseph, Esa, Grandma Dory, Rachel, Caitlin, and her little cousins. There were family suppers, cookie bakes, games in the yard, and horseback rides. She'd fallen so madly in love with David's dog, Sam, that David spoke of getting himself a new puppy.

On town nights, Brianna remained tense with David in the house. The most innocent of touches made her heart race. Was it longing she felt? Sometimes she caught him watching her with a speculative expression. More and more often, she found herself wishing that he would make the first move and put her out of her misery. Maybe, she reasoned, she'd find pleasure in his arms. Was she foolish to resist what was surely the only practical outcome?

No. David still believed Daphne was his daughter, but one day, he would realize she wasn't and might want out. As much as Brianna appreciated the life he had given her and Daphne — and as much as she might wish that it could go on this way forever — going to bed with David would be underhanded of her. She'd come to care too deeply about the man to entrap him.

Even so, when she lay awake at night, filled with yearnings both new and frightening to her, she knew they couldn't possibly go on like this. No man and woman could live under the same roof for any period of time, pretending to be married, without one or both of them developing physical yearnings.

Each night when she dressed for bed under cloak of darkness, she leaped if a floorboard creaked, thinking David had risen from his cot and was crossing the room. When she was finally able to sleep, she jerked awake if David so much as rolled over. Was he awake, too? Did he ache deep inside like she did? Sometimes she could have sworn she smelled his cologne and the musky, male scent of his skin. If he came to her, what would she do? Brianna greatly feared that one gentle touch of his hand would obliterate her good sense.

Some mornings David got up feeling as if he hadn't slept a wink. But not even exhaustion could dampen his mounting desire for Brianna. Nights became a torture for him, with his manhood as erect as a flagpole, the throbbing in his loins so pronounced that he ached in his lower abdomen. *This is mad-*

*ness!* He'd been crazy to think he could live this way. He wanted Brianna more than he'd ever wanted another woman. But how would he ever manage to convince her of that? She believed that his every show of affection toward her was born out of obligation. *Horseshit.*

Oh, how he wished he'd met her under other circumstances — that he could court her the way she needed to be courted. *Damn.* He felt like a kitten trapped in a burlap bag. And yet, when he looked at Daphne, he couldn't bring himself to wish she didn't exist. She'd become a joy in his life he'd never expected, and he loved her like the dickens. He just had to find a way to convince her mother that he'd come to love her as well.

Love. For years, it had been a mystery to David how grown men could act like fools over women. Now he finally understood it. When he looked into Brianna's beautiful green eyes, his heart actually hurt. He yearned to cup her chin in his hand and taste that delectable mouth again. He wanted to hold her in his arms and hear her whimper with pleasure. He wished she would open up to him and share her innermost thoughts, her dreams, and her secrets. And he wanted to make more babies with her, too.

Despite the sexual tension between her and David, Brianna's favorite time of day was in the evening when David came home from the marshal's office. When she wasn't in a rush to finish something for a customer, she'd taken to working after hours to update her own wardrobe. At the community social, she wanted to make a grand entrance in a fabulous gown to lure more customers into her shop. She sat in the rocker and did her fine stitchery by the light of the lantern.

"I can lend you the money to get this upstairs wired for electricity, you know," David offered more than once.

Brianna's answer was always the same. "I'm already in debt to you up to my eyebrows, David, and I don't want to borrow anything more."

"You're my *wife*," he would say.

Ah, but she wasn't, not really. She was only his *pretend* wife. "I will wire the upstairs as soon as I can afford it," she would reply. "I grew up with lanterns. I love the smell of the kerosene and the warm, cozy glow."

The poor lighting strained her eyes, but in truth, half the time, instead of stitching, she watched David and Daphne at the table, playing games or doing homework. David managed to make everything fun and had Daphne giggling even as she labored to perfect her cursive and learn her arithmetic. Oh, how the child detested doing her numbers, a trait Brianna knew came from her. Moira had loved math, but Brianna had always detested it. The nuns professed that it was Moira's thoughtful nature coming into play that made mathematics easy for her. Brianna was just the opposite, skipping steps in a problem, determined to do things her way. She'd been a dreamer, more proficient at art, languages, and sewing.

"Four plus four is —" David broke off and nibbled his pencil. "Hmm, seven?"

Daphne squealed and pushed at her father's shoulder. "Nuh-uh, it's *eight*."

Somehow the laughter and nonsense never prevented Daphne from learning her lessons, and soon they'd moved on to her spelling test. David, of course, misspelled words, right and left, keeping Daphne in stitches.

"Money," he said. "I know for a fact it's spelled m-u-n-n-y."

"No, it isn't," Daphne shouted. "It's m-o-n-e-y!"

"That isn't how you spelled it in your letters to me," David argued. Leaning over the child's shoulder, he said, "Hey, hold up, there. How come you're spelling hour with an H?"

"Because that's how it's spelled."

"In your letters, you spelled it o-u-r. How can you expect your papa to get his spelling right if you keep tricking me all the time?"

Working diligently on her scarlet gown for the social, sewing on one tiny seed pearl at a time, Brianna smothered a smile and shook her head. *The man is impossible.* It had become one of her most familiar mental refrains. But now she added a new one: *He is also the most wonderful father on earth.* When Brianna helped Daphne with her homework, she was all business, just as Sister Theresa had been. But David made it fun. He was a great tease who understood how difficult it was for an energetic little girl to sit still and study.

The realization took Brianna back in time to when she'd been the flighty, adventurous twin, always searching for a spark of excitement and the first to laugh until her sides ached. What had happened to that girl? Then she remembered Moira's white face as she lay dying, the weak, almost undetectable whisper of her voice as she pleaded with Brianna to raise her daughter as her own. Brianna remembered in detail that day when she'd walked across town to report Daphne's birth. En route, she'd sworn to abandon her flighty ways and be more like her angelic sister. *I have a daughter now. The best legacy I can pass on to her is to teach her how wonderful her real mother was, a veritable saint on earth.* In a twinkling, life for Brianna had become a job, and each night, she graded her performance.

Now she was what she'd aimed to become, a replica of her perfect twin. Oh, but how she yearned to join David and her daughter at the table. To be silly and giggle again. To participate in their games of nonsense. Sometimes she wanted it so badly that her limbs twitched and her fingers went stiff on the needle. David was bad for her, she decided. He made her want things she'd long since sworn to abandon. And deep down, Brianna feared that she could no longer tell herself she was merely falling in love with him. She'd already taken the plunge. She was so afraid he might glimpse the truth in her eyes that she had grown fearful of meeting his gaze.

# CHAPTER TWENTY

David often caught Brianna grinning as she watched them at the table in the evenings, and he wondered what it was that held her back. Female nonsense, he guessed. He only knew that he saw yearning in her eyes that told him she wanted to engage with them. It saddened him that she chose work over having fun.

The days passed, and before David knew it, all of May was behind them. The month was a blur of happy memories for him, times with Daphne at his ranch or with his family, but his favorite ones were of long spring evenings with his wife and child in the apartment above the dress shop when a cozy intimacy filled the kitchen and only the sounds of their voices or his fiddle broke the silence. In the mornings, he usually cooked breakfast while Brianna prepared for work. Daphne's favorite meal included flapjacks, which David made a show of flipping high into the air. One time, he even got a laugh out of Brianna when Sam took up sentry position near the stove to gobble up the pancakes David dropped. Life was good. It could have been even better if he and his wife had a real marriage, but even without physical closeness, he had never enjoyed a month so much.

He occasionally glimpsed Hazel Wright at a distance and marveled at what he'd ever seen in her. She was attractive enough, he supposed, but on her best day, she couldn't hold a candle to Brianna. Though it went against his grain, David avoided encounters with the woman. She'd been unreasonable when he'd gone to her home and tried to speak with her. She had even struck his dog. Since then, when he'd seen her at a distance, he had detected nothing in her expression or demeanor to indicate that she'd had a change of heart. Fiery glares, clenched fists, and a rigidity in her posture that suggested barely controlled anger. If David bumped into her in a public place, he had no idea how she might behave or what outlandish accusations she might make. Despite the gossip that had circulated around town after David's return with a wife and child, Brianna and Daphne were settling in nicely. He couldn't risk a nasty scene that might make tongues wag again. The way David saw it, he had tried to mend his fences with Hazel, she'd acted like a wild woman, and he owed her nothing more.

David's birthday fell on a Tuesday during the final week of school. Even though Little Joe's celebration would be on Saturday, Dory insisted that there had to be two separate parties. David's took place in the evening at Ace and Caitlin's place so Brianna could attend. David sensed that she was reluctant to go. But she put a bright face on it, engaged in the festivities, and even surprised him with a present — a blue shirt she'd made for him on the sly. It was a perfect fit and the color matched his eyes.

As David tried it on, he said, "Something this nice should be worn on special occasions. I think I'll save it for the social."

Brianna was excited when Friday of that week finally came because it marked the end of the school year. Normally when David went to the ranch over the weekends, Daphne accompanied him because she had no classes on Saturday or Sunday. Now that summer had arrived, Brianna hoped that the child would stay in town with her over the weekends because the shop was closed from noon on Saturday until early Monday morning. Brianna looked forward to spending time with her daughter and had planned all sorts of fun things to do.

"But, Mama!" Daphne cried when Brianna made the suggestion, "I *have* to go with Papa tonight. Tomorrow is Little Joe's birthday party."

Brianna's heart sank. "Oh, that's right. I'd forgotten." Quickly regrouping, Brianna said, "Well, perhaps your papa will bring you back into town after the party. I'll be off work tomorrow evening and all day Sunday. I thought we might —"

"Then I'd miss the cookie bake. Aunt Rachel got some new cutters, and we're even going to decorate them with icing and candies. And Grandma Dory is going to show me how to crochet."

"But, dear heart, what about *our* special times together? I thought, since school is out, that you'd start staying in town with me on the weekends. It seems like forever since we had a chocolate dunking party, and I hoped we could make a cake. And with summer coming on, we need to select some yardage and pick patterns for your new summer frocks. Wouldn't that be fun?"

Even as Brianna spoke, she knew she was being selfish. Daphne adored being at David's ranch. To the child, that was her *real* home, and the apartment paled in comparison.

Coming from Daphne's bedroom with a satchel filled with her clothing and toiletries, David said, "Your mother is right, pumpkin. Now that school is out, you should stay with her on weekends when she has time to do things with you. I can bring you back to town after the party tomorrow."

"Mama, *please.* Can't I stay with you another time?" Daphne's blue eyes swam with tears. "I want to be with Papa and do things with our family. I'll get to play fetch with Sam, and I want to curry Acorn. Papa says he's my horse now, and I'll be able to ride him when I get a bit older. If I have to come back here, I'll miss all that and I won't get to play with my cousins. I don't understand why you won't come so we can all be together. No customers will visit the dress shop tonight, and you could just keep it closed tomorrow morning! That way, you can be at Little Joe's party. Papa can have you back early enough on Monday to open on time."

Brianna had already endured one family celebration that week and had no desire to experience another one. She'd used work as an excuse not to attend Little Joe's. Being around David's family unsettled her. They were demonstrative individuals, always hugging, patting, or verbally expressing affection, and it was all too easy for Brianna to forget she didn't belong in their tight-knit circle.

Throat tight, she said, "I can't go tonight, darling. I have some dress work I must do." It wasn't really a lie. The social was scheduled for the following Friday evening, and with Daphne gone, she could devote herself to the beautiful burgundy gown she was making. As the local dressmaker, she needed to make a grand appearance at the event to establish herself as a superb designer of originals. Bending down to hug Daphne, she said, "You have heaps of fun, all right? When you get back, we'll pick out material for your summer frocks, and I'm thinking new slippers are in order as well. You're growing like a weed!" Brianna did her best to sound bright and cheerful. "Now that I've got a shop that brings in a steady profit, you'll never be in shoes that pinch those cute little toes again."

As Brianna straightened, she met David's gaze. Loaded down with his saddlebags and Daphne's paraphernalia, he stood by the door that led downstairs. His blue eyes held shadows she'd never seen before. Sadness or possibly regret? Perhaps he realized how wrenching it was for her to see Daphne choosing to go with him rather than stay behind with her.

"We'd really love it if you'd come. Like Daphne says, I can have you back bright and early Monday morning." He glanced at Sam, who lay at his feet. "He's going to miss being brushed morning and night."

Brianna had taken to grooming Sam twice a day to keep him from filling her shop with clumps of fur. The silly mutt loved the extra attention, especially when she ran the bristles lightly over his upturned belly and armpits. Or were they leg pits on a canine? With a jerk of her heart, she realized that she'd fallen in love with the dog, too.

"He'll have so much fun that he'll barely miss me," she said with a forced laugh. "The three of you go on." Flapping her hand, she said, "Hurry, now. I've work to do and you're keeping me from it."

Brianna kept the smile pasted on her face until they'd left and she heard the shop door downstairs jangle closed. Knowing David always locked up, she stood at the window to watch her daughter skip happily away with him and Sam to the livery stable. An awful pain clutched her heart. The tears in her eyes burned like acid.

Fighting the urge to sit at the table and

cry, she turned to her work the moment they vanished from sight. Weeping was a useless endeavor, and she'd learned long ago to set aside her feelings and push forward. Even so, the apartment felt empty and lonely. One of Daphne's hair ribbons lay on the kitchen counter. She'd kicked off her patent leather slippers just inside her bedroom. Everywhere Brianna looked, she saw evidence of her daughter.

She wandered downstairs, hoping to find something to distract her. Behind the center display case, Sam's hairy bed lay empty. In her sewing area, she found a wilted nosegay of wildflowers that Daphne had picked for her yesterday. She sat on her work chair and stared at the sewing machine. Her chest hurt so badly it felt as if someone had cut away a huge chunk of her heart. Without her daughter, she felt lost and alone in a way that chilled her very bones.

She couldn't spoil this time for her child. For however long it lasted, Daphne was getting to experience what it was like to have a real family. At least she would be able to look back on this period of her life and know firsthand how it felt to be surrounded by people who loved her.

Brianna had allowed herself to be selfish once. She'd broken the rules, sneaked away behind the good sisters' backs, and flirted with disaster — all because she'd enjoyed the excitement and been foolish enough to believe no one but she would ever suffer for it. Well, she'd been wrong. Moira had paid the price for Brianna's wildness.

Now it was up to Brianna to keep her promise to her sister and look after Daphne. And what was best for Daphne now? Glancing around the shop and envisioning the apartment upstairs, Brianna knew she could provide financially for Daphne, but at David's ranch something even better was being offered.

Crossing herself and then folding her hands, Brianna bent her head in prayer. For the very first time, she implored God to somehow prevent David from ever discovering that Daphne wasn't his. Brianna didn't ask this for herself. No, she said the prayer for her daughter's sake. *Please, God, let nothing happen to rob her of all this love.*

During the ride out to the ranch, David barely heard Daphne's constant chatter or saw the plants she pointed out to him. He felt the waning sunlight on his face and chest, but it didn't warm his heart. *Brianna.* If he lived to be a hundred, he would never forget the pain he'd glimpsed in her eyes when Daphne had begged to leave with him. He kept recalling that time in the ranch kitchen when he had assured Brianna that he'd never take her child away from her, and how she'd whispered, *You're already doing that.*

He was guilty as charged. He'd lured Daphne away from her mother with a dog, kittens, a horse, and all his family. At the ranch, the little girl raced from one exciting activity to the next until she fell into an exhausted sleep at night. David doubted she even missed Brianna.

Once at the ranch, David left Blue in Rob's capable hands. Daphne begged to curry Acorn and then walk him in the paddock. David needed to look over his accounts and do the books before he started supper. He couldn't take the time to watch her.

"Rob, can you keep an eye on her?" he asked his foreman. "I have some desk work to do that really shouldn't wait."

Rob grinned and ruffled Daphne's hair. "No problem. I'll keep a sharp watch."

Daphne flashed a huge grin and raced into the barn. David gazed after her for a moment, and then turned toward the house. It was dim inside, and the rooms smelled musty. As he settled at his desk and lighted the lantern, he made a mental note to open all the windows in the morning while he swept and dusted the furniture.

A stack of correspondence lay on the leather blotter. David guessed that Rob must have been in town and stopped at the post office to collect David's personal mail. Rob did that sometimes and then left it there for his boss to open when he came out to the ranch. Other times, David got it when he picked up deliveries for the marshal's office.

He was regarding the top envelope, something from the Colorado Cattlemen's Association, when Daphne burst through the front door, her green play frock billowing, her white stockings already streaked with dirt. "Papa, while I'm still too little to ride Acorn, can I have a pony? Mr. Rob says Charley and Eva Banks have a nice one that Ralph is getting too big to ride."

David rolled his chair back from the desk and patted his knee. His first inclination was to give Daphne anything and everything she wanted, but at the edge of his mind, he knew spoiling the child wouldn't be best for her in the end. Children, just like adults, needed to learn they couldn't always have everything they wanted.

Daphne bounced up onto his lap. "Can I,

Papa? *Please?*"

David was about to speak when the child shoved her hand down the front of her dress and plucked out their lucky penny. Before she could make a wish, David caught her small fist in his grasp. "Whoa," he said. "We have to be careful with our penny, Daphne. Wishing on it should be saved for very important things."

"Why?" Her blue eyes widened with anxiety. "Will it run out of magic?"

"It might if we abuse it by wishing for things that aren't truly important."

"But, Papa, a pony is truly important!"

David resisted the urge to smile. "No, darlin', a pony is just something you'd really like to have." He kissed her forehead. "The proper protocol for getting a pony is to ask your papa for one."

"But what if you say no?"

David couldn't look into his daughter's pleading eyes without feeling as if his bones might melt. He needed her mother here, he thought. Brianna would intervene with that no-nonsense manner of hers and quickly regain control of the situation. Left to his own devices, David was beginning to realize he had a problem denying the child anything.

"If I say no, then you won't get a pony."

Daphne glanced down at her fist, in which she still grasped the penny.

"Don't do it," David warned. Maybe, he decided, Brianna had been right all along and it had been a mistake to tell Daphne the penny was lucky in a very special way. He didn't want her to grow up thinking she could have anything she wanted simply by wishing for it. "Our penny is to be saved for very special, important wishes, and a pony doesn't qualify."

"But I *want* a pony."

David sighed. "All right, but you're going to have to earn one."

"How?"

"By doing chores, not only here at the ranch but also at the shop. Nothing worth having in this old world comes free."

David gave the child a list of tasks she could do in the barn that afternoon under Rob's supervision. Daphne bounced off his knee and raced for the door. "I'll work really hard, Papa. You'll see! I'm going to *earn* my pony."

David smiled as she exited onto the veranda and slammed the door closed behind her. He had a lot to learn when it came to being a good father. His grin faded as he leafed through the mail. He flattened his fingers against one piece in particular, a thick envelope addressed to him by the Pinkerton Agency: the report on Brianna's background.

His stomach clenched. He clamped his teeth together. A part of him wanted to pretend the missive hadn't come. But it had, and he couldn't ignore its contents. It was time for him to learn the absolute truth.

With shaking fingers, he opened the envelope, drew out the documents, and started to read.

As always, the late afternoon brought a brisk breeze. David sat atop a paddock rail, watching Daphne exercise Acorn within the enclosure. He was acutely conscious of the paperwork he had stuffed inside his shirt. Tears slipped silently down his cheeks. *What in God's name have I done?* The question circled mercilessly in his mind. As he watched his daughter, he felt as if his heart might break, for she wasn't really his. Brianna had told him the absolute truth that day by the stream. Recalling that conversation, David felt sick. She had bared her soul to him, and he'd discounted every word as a lie. And she'd been right to accuse him of mocking her. He had done exactly that.

Acorn's hooves kicked up dust as Daphne led him around the pen. The child glanced up at David and reeled to a stop. "Papa, what's wrong? It looks like you're — like you're crying."

David forced a smile. "Some dirt blew in my eyes, darlin'. That's all."

He kept his lips curved until the little girl led the horse away. Gazing after her, he realized he was still reeling with shock. How could the child not be a Paxton? She looked so much like his mother. How in the hell could that be? David had no answers anymore. He only knew for a fact that Daphne was not his daughter.

The orphanage had kept excellent records, and the documents the nuns had released to the Pinkerton agent chronicled the lives of Brianna and Moira O'Keefe, who had indeed been left on the doorstep as infants and grown up within the orphanage walls, cared for by the good sisters. The detective had spoken directly with Mother Superior, who remembered the O'Keefe girls well. Moira had been raped, choked, and beaten senseless in the conservatory by Stanley Romanik, a farmer's son. The violent encounter had left her pregnant. To the heartbreak of the nuns, their first responsibility was to protect the reputation of the orphanage, and they'd had no choice but to eventually ask Moira to move out. Brianna had gone with her sister. The two girls left with only a few dollars from the nuns and a knapsack of clothing.

From there, tracing the O'Keefe girls' whereabouts and activities had taken more investigative work. Brianna had rented a small room in a tenement building and worked at any job she could find to care for Moira, who was sick all during her confinement and hemorrhaged if she was on her feet. A midwife ordered complete bed rest to save the babe. The precautions worked; the infant lived, but Moira died only minutes after delivery. Shortly thereafter Brianna went to a nearby hospital to report the advent of Daphne Rose O'Keefe. The birth certificate named Brianna as the child's biological mother. The name of the father was omitted.

Tears still burned in David's eyes as he watched Daphne work with Acorn. *Sweet Christ.* She had such a way with horses, yet another Paxton trait. How was it possible that she wasn't his? That first day in Glory Ridge, Brianna had indeed lied, sticking to the story she had fabricated to attain the position as Charles Ricker's housekeeper years before. Looking back on it now, David figured Brianna had felt she had no choice but to cling to her original tale. He'd waltzed into the community, convinced himself Daphne was his, and then relentlessly waged war, determined that he would not leave that one-horse town without his little girl. During their audience with the judge, Brianna had fought with everything she had to keep her child. She must have been terrified. Far too often, the courts ruled against mothers in custody issues.

The regret David felt was so intense that his bones ached. He'd ridden roughshod over Brianna, forcing her to come with him to No Name, so damned determined to be a proper father that he could think of nothing else. And now, just look at the mess he'd created. Daphne loved David and his whole family. He'd done such a fine job of putting his own spin on the story that even Daphne believed she was a Paxton by birth. She often touched a finger to her cheek and said, "I've got Grandma Dory's dimple!" The child had a sense of belonging here. Even worse, Daphne now preferred to be with David and his family than to stay in town with Brianna. What had he *done?*

Simple answer. In his arrogant disregard for anything Brianna had said, he'd gone at being a great father as if he were killing snakes — spoiling Daphne, luring her in. Well, he'd succeeded, hadn't he? He'd stolen from Brianna the only thing in the whole world that mattered to her.

David was only vaguely aware of Daphne as she called for him to watch her do this or that. To him, the sunlight had blinked out. The grassland had vanished. In his mind's eye, he was in Boston a little more than six years ago, seeing Brianna at a younger age, impoverished, living in a tiny room, and hovering over a dingy mattress while her twin labored to give birth and then began to hemorrhage. He could see it all so clearly. Brianna dealing with her sister's death, then standing over a pauper's grave, probably in the rain or snow, with precious little by way of wraps to protect her and the baby from the cold and damp. He even imagined Brianna's stomach snarling with hunger, and the baby's thin wails for want of her mother's milk, which Brianna, despite all her love of the child, hadn't been able to provide. Then he pictured that younger, slump-shouldered Brianna trudging along the rain-slicked streets to keep her vow to her sister and claim the babe as her own.

A sour bitterness filled David's mouth. He could no longer delude himself. He wasn't merely *starting* to fall in love with Brianna. It was already a done deal. Thinking back, he couldn't remember exactly when he'd lost his heart to her. Maybe it had been that day by the stream when she'd slapped him with such pent-up fury that she'd knocked him on his ass. Or maybe that night when he killed the three sourdoughs and realized, in the height of rage, that she had been hurt during the exchange of lead. For several heart-stopping minutes, he'd believed she had a bullet lodged in her skull, and he'd been so afraid he had trembled.

Before he knew it, he'd been in so deep that he could never resurface, and learning the truth about Daphne's real father hadn't changed how he felt one whit. He loved Brianna, not only because she was the most beautiful thing he'd ever clapped eyes on, but because she was so damned brave. Thank God for that Irish temper she so ruthlessly controlled and her infernal stubbornness as well. It had been only the latter that enabled an impoverished girl to raise a babe not her own. It had taken a lot of grit for her to sneak food from the restaurant and garbage barrels to feed her niece even as she weakened with hunger herself. Had she never yearned to stuff some of that sustenance into her own mouth? David had experienced hunger, so he knew the strength it had taken for her to leave her belly empty in order to fill Daphne's.

Now what? David watched Daphne lead Acorn in figure eights, stopping after each pass to praise him and give him treats, undoubtedly supplied by Rob. Was he going to shatter that little girl's whole world by recanting now and telling her she wasn't his?

He couldn't do that. It was time for a powwow with Shamrock. Time for them to dispense with all the bullshit that had created such a wall between them. Time to start dealing honestly with each other. *The truth, and nothing but the truth.* He would beg for her forgiveness, on his knees if necessary, because he'd done her a horrible injustice.

"Hey, Daphne!" David called. He leaped off the fence rail and strode out to where his daughter stood with the horse. Yes, by God, *his* daughter. "How would you like to stay overnight with Grandma Dory, Uncle Ace, Aunt Caitlin, and your cousins?"

Daphne glowed at the suggestion. The wind caught her golden curls. *Paxton gold.* Even now, David looked at her and saw the striking resemblance to his mother.

"Are you staying overnight there, too?" she asked hopefully.

"I can't, pumpkin." David crouched down.

"I have some unexpected business in town. Will you be okay without me? Sam can stay there with you."

Daphne grinned, showing off the new tooth that had appeared recently to partially close one of the gaps in her smile. "I *love* it there. Maybe Grandma will show me her scrapbook again and tell me more stories about when she was my age."

"Maybe so. Or maybe you can get Aunt Caitlin to make fudge."

"Fudge?" Daphne giggled. "I wish Mama had come. She *loves* fudge."

Two hours later, David guided Blue into the livery stable south of town. Chris Coffle, a stout man of short stature with black hair and brown eyes, met David before he could dismount. The aging bachelor, who wore his everyday outfit of blue dungarees and a checkered work shirt, took Blue's reins. He flashed David a grin.

"I been at this long enough that I know the routine. Rub him down, give him the best hay I got, and a ration of grain. Yes, the water will be fresh. Yes, I'll be here all night. And, yes, I'll make sure no fool comes in here with a lighted cigarette."

David had to laugh even though his heart felt like a lead weight in his chest. "I guess you know my horse is mighty important to me." And so was his daughter. David trembled inside when he thought of the upcoming conversation with Brianna. "Take good care of him for me."

As David left the stable, he took a deep, bracing breath. He thought about stopping at one of the saloons for a couple of stiff whiskies. *False courage.* He wouldn't face her liquored up. He'd need to be sober and thinking straight. He stared at his feet as he walked. His boots sent up puffs of dust, heralding the end of spring and the arrival of summer. David could only hope that was a good omen, that this evening would mark the beginning of things for him and Shamrock, not the end.

He went first to his office to place the Pinkerton report in his desk drawer. He would tell Brianna that he'd hired investigators back East, but he didn't want to slap her in the face with proof of it. The information would be safe locked in his desk. His deputies fiddled with surface stuff, but they both knew anything in the center drawer was for his eyes only. The spare key, hidden in a niche of the wall, was only for emergencies.

Rory came out just as David was pushing away from the desk and hooking his keys back on his belt. "Hey, boss, I thought you left for the weekend! No trouble, I hope."

David shook his head. "No." He met his deputy's curious gaze. "My daughter is with Ace and his family, so I sneaked away for an evening with my wife. Maybe I'll take her to Roxie's for a special supper or something."

Rory chuckled and nodded. "I get you. Having a kid around all the time —" He shrugged. "My people are big on family. Nothing is more important to us than our children. But, hey, every once in a while a man needs a little room."

A picture rose in David's mind of the lonely cot he'd occupied for a month, in the same room with his wife but not with her. He needed more than a little space, damn it. The heartbreak was he'd done nothing to earn it. He'd ignored Brianna when she tried to tell him the truth. He'd made light of her story, which must have half killed her to tell. When she'd laid him out with a slap, which he now realized had been well deserved, he'd told her to put her fist into it next time so she might give him a bit of a jolt. He'd screwed up in every imaginable way, mocking her, calling her a liar.

He could only pray God would have mercy on him. Stupidity had to count for something up there. Surely a man couldn't be condemned to hell on earth for being a pigheaded son of a bitch.

For her solitary chocolate-dunking party, Brianna had chosen to make David's wonderful coffee with a dash of salt instead of her usual tea. She sat at the round oak kitchen table, determinedly thrusting a piece of chocolate into the hot brew, sucking away the melted part, and then trying with everything she had to savor the taste. Only it wasn't the same without Daphne. She missed the little slurping sounds her daughter made and her muted groans of pleasure. Nothing, she realized, was the same without the child. And she missed David. His laughter warmed the rooms. His music lifted her spirits. The deep, velvety sound of his voice always soothed her. She dreaded going to bed this evening because he wouldn't be there, only a few feet away on the cot, to fill the night with his presence.

She'd fought not to love the man. She'd been betrayed a hundred times by the males of her species, and in as many ways. The kindly bosses who had turned into lecherous monsters. The bar patrons who'd gone from flirtatious to forceful, using their fists when strength of arm alone failed to over-power her. The bar owner, a wonderful old man, had come to her rescue each time, us-ing a whiskey jug as a club. To this day, Brianna remembered that gray-haired gentleman in her prayers, and she probably always would. He had saved her from meet-ing with the same fate Moira had, and he'd given her extra money to buy goat's milk for the baby.

As Brianna dunked the chocolate again, she pressed a hand over her breasts. During Daphne's infancy, they had ached and become swollen, as if her body was reacting to the baby's needs and desperately trying to produce nourishment. Nothing had come forth, of course, and Brianna would always feel that her own flesh had betrayed her. She and Moira had been so close, identical physically, connected emotionally. There had been an inexplicable mental link be-tween them. If Moira experienced pain, or if she felt afraid or sick, Brianna always knew, and vice versa. Even the afternoon of the rape, Brianna had sensed Moira's ter-ror. With a cry, she'd raced from the kitchen, sped through the hallways, and finally spilled out into the garden. Her sister, who had been assigned the task of trimming the roses and collecting bouquets, had been nowhere in sight.

But Brianna had known where Moira was. She'd gathered up her skirts and run for the conservatory. Now, all these years later, when she recalled that moment, the sound of her own screams echoed inside her mind. She'd found Moira sprawled on the floor, her body battered, her torn clothing soaked with blood.

The nuns, heralded by Brianna's terrified cries, had come quickly. Moira had been carried into the orphanage kitchen. Brianna couldn't remember if she'd helped to carry her sister or if she'd followed behind the nuns. One of the cots from the pantry had been dragged out so they could lay Moira's limp body on it. Brianna couldn't recall the rest, at least not clearly. All she saw in her mind's eye was a blur of crimson, bruises, and her sweet sister's face.

What had come later, after Moira had been saved, would haunt her for the rest of her life. For in the end, Moira had recovered initially only to die a horrible death later, her life's blood seeping slowly from her body.

Brianna dropped the hunk of chocolate onto the saucer and nearly gagged on the taste. Moira's favorite thing had been dunking chocolate. Brianna had tried to pass along the tradition to her daughter. Her whole life revolved around that child, and now Daphne no longer needed her.

Sobs built in Brianna's chest. The tears in her eyes made everything swim. She tried to steer her thoughts to the practical. She should fix something for supper. She should stitch seed pearls onto her gown. Instead she sat there and cried.

After leaving the marshal's office, David stood on the boardwalk in the deepening twilight, grabbing for a sense of calm that eluded him. He'd never been good with words, and he'd need to be tonight. He loved that woman and wanted to spend the rest of his life with her, but now that he knew the truth, he couldn't in good conscience force her to remain in the marriage. What if she wanted to leave No Name? He couldn't stop her. Hell, even if he'd had that kind of power over her, he wouldn't use it. When you loved a woman, really *loved* her, you wanted her to be happy. Making Brianna stay with a man she didn't love would be cruel.

With a weary sigh, he walked to the dress shop, used his own key to let himself in, and then moved up the stairs. A thin line of light shone at the bottom of the door, telling him that Brianna was inside, undoubtedly sewing seed pearls on her gown. She used every waking moment to accomplish something.

As he walked into the room, David expected to see her in the rocker with the lantern at her elbow. Instead she sat at the table with her face cupped in her hands. She jerked when she sensed his presence and straightened. Her eyes were puffy from crying, her pale cheeks still wet with tears.

"David," she said shakily. "What are you doing here? I didn't expect you back." Her eyes went dark with sudden fright. "Is it Daphne? Has she been hurt?"

"No, Shamrock, Daphne's fine." David hung his hat on the wall hook and joined her at the table, taking a seat across from her. "I have to talk to you, and I figured it would be better if Daphne wasn't around to overhear."

"Oh." She glanced over her shoulder. "I made fresh coffee a bit ago, just the way you like it."

David watched as she fussed at the stove, taking down a dainty cup and saucer, grabbing a towel to lift the pot and pour. As she moved back to the table, careful not to spill the hot brew, she asked, "Would you like a piece of chocolate to go with it?"

"No, thanks. Coffee suits me fine." As David added two chunks of sugar to his cup and gave a brisk stir, Brianna resumed her seat. He searched his mind, trying to think how to best start this conversation. Glancing up at her, he said, "You've been crying."

She wiped at her cheeks with shaky fingers. "Yes, well, a bunch of foolishness, that. I didn't think anyone would catch me at it."

David leaned back on his chair. "I don't often see my feisty Shamrock cry. I'm sorry Daphne hurt your feelings this afternoon. She's young. She just doesn't think."

Brianna turned her cup, gazing solemnly into the dark liquid. "It's a good thing that she wants to be with you. I'll adjust to it over time and try to be more encouraging. I was — well, I've done some soul searching, and I was thinking of only myself. The best thing for Daphne is to have strong bonds with her father and his family."

"That would be true if I were actually her father."

Her slender hand jerked on the cup and slopped coffee. Her green eyes flashed to his. All the color drained from her face. Even her lips, usually a shimmery pink, went as white as the cabinet doors behind her. "You — you *know*."

"I should have known all along. You told

me the truth that day by the stream, but I didn't want to hear it." David hauled in a tight breath. "It took the Pinkerton Agency and a background check to convince me you weren't lying. I can't begin to tell you how very sorry I am, Brianna, not only because I refused to believe you, but about your sister and everything you've been through. In my own defense, even now that I know Daphne isn't my daughter, I look at her and find it hard to believe. The family resemblance is amazing."

Brianna felt as if she'd been slugged in the solar plexus. The inevitable had finally happened. David knew everything. The ache of regret in his eyes brought more tears to her own, but she quickly blinked them away so he wouldn't see. "So," she said, struggling to keep her voice steady, "this is it, then." She pushed up from her chair. "Don't look so worried, David. I have no intention of making it difficult for you. We've never consummated the marriage, and both of us know the ceremony in Glory Ridge was a sham and most likely illegal."

She went to the sink with her dishes. The cup rattled on the saucer, a telltale sign of how badly she was trembling. Still, it was easier to get everything said when she wasn't looking at him. That dear face, every line of which had been engraved on her heart. Those eyes, always so compelling, now filled with regret. "Getting an annulment will be as simple as one, two, three," she said brightly. "It will be especially easy if we apply for the dissolution together." She turned off the water and clutched the edge of the sink. "I have only one favor to ask of you, David."

"What's that?" His voice sounded oddly thick and gravelly.

"Will you go with me to take care of the annulment in Denver? After it's done, I'll remain there with Daphne until the process is finalized just in case any wrinkles crop up. That way, Daphne will be far removed from No Name when word gets out, and none of the children here will tease her."

Not allowing herself to look at him, Brianna turned toward her bedroom. She knew one glance into his deep blue eyes would be her undoing. She couldn't allow herself to cling to a man who'd never really been her husband, or to a relationship that had been built on pretense. From the first, she had done everything possible to protect David, to make sure he wouldn't be legally shackled to her after he found out the truth. She refused to tie him to her now with tears and blubbering.

The trick was to be matter-of-fact and businesslike, allowing no trace of feeling to enter her voice. She didn't want him to suffer even a twinge of guilt or to have any second thoughts. He'd always dealt with her fairly and honestly, and she would grant him the same courtesy, no matter how much it hurt.

David stared after Brianna as she went into their bedroom. Tonight she wore the brown silk, one of his favorites on her, and she was so damned beautiful she made his heart hurt. He heard the swish of her skirts, the light pad of her footsteps as she moved about. A golden glow illuminated the other room, telling him she'd lighted the lamp. He caught the faint hiss of the wick as she turned it up. Nausea rolled through him. He could have sworn a full-size baseball was lodged at the base of his throat. Unless he could think of some way to stop her, she was going to leave him.

When he could stand it no longer, he rose and followed her. She had pillowcases on the bed and clothing piled at the foot. "Shamrock, what the hell are you doing?"

Keeping her face averted so he couldn't read her expression, she replied, "I'm getting ready to leave, David. The sooner, the better, don't you think? It will be easier for Daphne if we make the break quick and clean."

"But what about the dress shop? We have a contract. You're supposed to buy it from me. What the hell am I going to do with this place if you leave?"

David winced as soon as he spoke. To hell with the dress shop. Why had he even mentioned that when his legs had gone watery at the thought of losing her?

"I'm sorry to leave you in a mess." Her body rigid with tension, she began folding garments and stuffing them into a bag. "But there's no way around it. Even you must see that my staying here is impossible now. It would be even worse for Daphne, a nightmare. The children would taunt her constantly. Maybe some other woman in town would like to buy the shop — or possibly rent it. I know you paid cash, a sizable sum, and would have made some profit on the interest I insisted on paying." She glanced around at the wallpaper and frilly curtain at the window. "It was such a great opportunity that you offered me, a dream come true, but there is no way I can make it work now."

David didn't give a tinker's damn about

the money, but he couldn't think what to say. The only word that rushed past his lips was a strangled, "Don't."

Brianna sent him a bewildered look.

"Don't," he said again. "The Pinkerton report hasn't changed my feelings one whit. So far as I'm concerned, nothing is different. Daphne is still my daughter, and you are still my wife."

She searched his gaze for a moment, her green eyes glistening with unshed tears. "I know how much you've come to love Daphne, David, but your feelings for the child aren't enough for us to make a marriage work."

David stepped closer, determined to push out the words he needed to say. If she rejected him, his pride would take a beating, and so would his heart, but it was a chance he had to take. "From the start, my whole focus was about doing what was right," he said. "I freely admit that. But somewhere along the way, I not only fell in love with Daphne; I also lost my heart to you. I'm in love with you, Brianna. Can't you see that? This isn't about honor and obligation anymore. If you leave me, I don't know what I'll do. I *love* you. Not because it's convenient, not because it's best for Daphne. I'm head over heels in love with *you,* you and only you."

Brianna heard the passion in his voice and turned to stare at him. The pain she saw in his blue eyes nearly took her to her knees. She pressed her palms against her waist. "You mean that. I mean, you really, *really* mean it."

"Well, of course I mean it. I wouldn't say it otherwise. I don't know exactly when it happened, Shamrock." He raked a hand through his hair and released a quivery breath. "I wish I could say pretty words, something romantic about that first instant when I realized. But you sort of came on like influenza, a symptom here, and another symptom there, until I realized I was a goner."

"Influenza?" It was so like David to say something that caught her off guard. Choked with emotion, she gave a startled laugh that escaped through her nose. She fished in her skirt pocket for her handkerchief and dabbed at her upper lip. "Well, *that* was romantic." She blew her nose and wiped again. "Pray God you caught none of the spray."

David's gaze clung to hers. "Like I care? For once, Shamrock, can you forget about being a lady and just — oh, hell, I don't know — just be *you*. Because I have to tell you, it's not the proper lady I'm in love with. I'm in love with my Shamrock, who has a fiery temper, a mean right hook, and a tongue as sharp as a razor. I'm crazy in love with *you*, Brianna O'Keefe. No more lies, no more pretending. I want to spend the rest of my life with you."

"But what about Hazel Wright?"

He rolled his eyes. "I was never in love with Hazel. When I considered marrying her, I knew deep down that I was settling for second best. Thank God that bundle of letters came to save my stupid ass, because I would have been miserable shackled to her. She's got a nasty streak, in case you haven't noticed."

"Are you certain?" Brianna's chest felt as if it might burst. "I don't want to ruin all your plans and steer you completely off course. You have a right to the future that calls to you, a right to marry the woman of your choice."

"*You* call to me, and if you really want to honor my choice, stop questioning me and come here."

Brianna wasn't sure who moved first, but the next instant she was in his arms. "Oh, God, David, I love you, too. I tried so hard not to. I never dreamed you might return my feelings."

"How could I not? And I'm damned glad to hear you've got feelings for me because I wasn't sure if you did. And if you didn't — well, I don't know what I'd do."

He trailed light kisses over her forehead, tightened his arms around her, buried his face in her hair, and began to sway, holding her fast against him. His heat, his strength, the hardness of him against her — everything about the embrace felt absolutely right.

"All this time, I've wished for this, hoped for it, but, oh, David, I never thought it might happen. I knew you'd learn the truth eventually, so I held everything back. I didn't want you to feel trapped in a loveless marriage."

David laughed, the huffs of his breath stirring her hair. His warm, velvety lips moved to her ear, the gentle nips of his teeth making her knees go weak. "I don't feel trapped, Shamrock. I'll never feel trapped. I think I'm the luckiest man alive."

# CHAPTER TWENTY-ONE

Brianna surrendered, going pliable in his arms. When his mouth trailed to her throat, she let her head fall back to accommodate his lips, and the light touch of them against her skin made her nipples harden and ache. She wasn't sure how to do this, and despite the intoxicating pleasure that pulsed through her body with every pull of his warm mouth, a little voice way at the back of her mind called out faint alerts. She could tell that David had immense experience with women by the way his hands left her waist and moved firmly up her back to expertly start undoing her buttons. When the dress was unfastened, he nudged at her shoulder with his chin to push the silk down her arm.

In the lantern light, his hair drifted near her face like a mist of burnished gold. He smelled of fresh air, sunlight, leather, cologne, horses, and man. She clutched at his shoulders, her fingers finding only iron-hard muscle through the pliant leather of his duster. When she kissed his jaw, her lips encountered firm, masculine skin and the prickle of evening whiskers. He was all masculine, certain of himself, a practiced seducer, and by contrast, she felt as if she were afloat on a lily pad in a storm, with waves crashing over her from all sides.

"David?" she whispered. This was happening so fast she couldn't think. "I've never been with a man. I — um — it's not that I wish for you to stop or anything. But can we — you know — go a bit slower?"

"Shit."

The word erupted from him like a low, feral growl and made Brianna smile. Only David would utter that vile expletive while trying to seduce a lady.

His body snapped taut, and he moved slightly away. "Are you afraid, sweetheart? Because if you are, we don't have to do this right now. We can talk."

"About what?"

"About this. I mean — well, I doubt the nuns ever told you much about the birds and the bees, and even if they tried, what the hell do they know?"

Brianna buried her nose against his shirt and giggled. "Oh, David, I love you so." He was the only man on earth who could make her laugh at a moment like this.

"Say that again," he told her.

"I love you. And I'm not afraid." The minute Brianna said it, she knew it was true. She'd feared many men, but she would never feel afraid of David. "And, um, talking about it sounds rather unpleasant. I'd prefer that you just show me."

He tightened his arms around her again. "That I can do. But talking about it wouldn't be unpleasant, Shamrock. If you aren't sure how this goes, I don't —"

"I have a general idea. I lived at Ricker's place for six years. I saw farm animals mate."

He stiffened again. "What kind of farm animals?"

"Pigs, chickens, goats, cattle, horses, and one time even dogs."

"Well, hell." She felt his shoulders slump, and the next thing she knew, he'd swept her up into his arms and was carrying her toward the bed. "We've definitely got to talk. Pigs? Jesus Herbert Christ. They squeal, carry on, and create a God-awful spectacle. Watching that would be enough to make anybody afraid of having sex."

Brianna squealed herself when they landed full-length across the mattress, David somehow twisting as they fell to come out on top with his forearms braced to keep his weight off her.

"People don't do it like pigs, or horses, or cows, or dogs," he told her.

"They don't?"

"No, damn it, they don't." His blue eyes swam in her vision. "No wonder you're nervous."

"I'm not nervous."

He reared back to search her gaze. His firm mouth tipped in a grin. "Have I ever mentioned that you're a lousy liar?"

Brianna touched her fingertips to his jaw. "Okay, I'm a tiny bit nervous, but only because I'm not sure what to expect and I don't want to disappoint you."

"Shamrock, you could never disappoint me." He rolled to one side and gathered her into his arms. "Never in a million years."

Brianna rested her head on his shoulder. Her hand lay at the center of his chest, and she could feel the steady thrum of his heart against her palm. When he spoke, she felt the vibration. "We need to back up a bit and start over. And before we discuss the birds and the bees, I'd like to go back in time to that night by the fire when I asked who the bastard was who made you so wary of men. You gave me a blanket answer, saying it was nearly every man you'd ever met, or something like that."

Brianna sighed and closed her eyes. She'd never spoken to anyone about those days right after Moira's death, but somehow, with David, the words unlocked within her, and talking about it was easier. She told him about Daphne's infancy and how she had developed colic.

"She cried incessantly, and the owner of the tenement building kicked me out. I tried to find another room, but everyone took one look at my screaming baby and turned me away."

David ran his hand into her hair. She loved the feeling of his hard, warm fingers against her scalp. "Ah, Shamrock, it must have been sheer hell. Why didn't you just go back to the orphanage? I'm sure the sisters would have welcomed both of you with open arms."

"Of course they would have." Brianna sighed. "The nuns loved Moira and me. I know they would have adored Daphne, too. But I promised Moira that I'd raise her baby as my own, and I feared that I would lose control over Daphne if I went back to the orphanage. I would have had to work somewhere else in order to earn enough money to cover her needs, and most jobs didn't pay very much, so I would have needed two positions to support her. She would have seen me rarely. And she was so beautiful, David. You just can't imagine how perfect she was. What if a couple had seen her and wanted to adopt her? I was terrified of that possibility because I wasn't really her mother — the good sisters knew that, and I had no legal rights, plus I had little by way of money to recommend me as her guardian. Even the sisters, as much as they loved me, would have felt that their first responsibility was to the child. If a well-heeled couple had wanted Daphne, they might have decided that Daphne would be better off with them than with me."

David's arms tightened around her. "I didn't think of that at all. Dumb question. Naturally you were afraid to go back there, even though it was your only safe haven. Damn, Shamrock, you must have been scared half out of your mind."

"It was a frightening time. I knew Daphne would die if I didn't find shelter for her, and sometimes when I felt utterly hopeless, I almost broke my promise to Moira and went back to the orphanage. It was winter in Boston, and she was so tiny. I remember walking the streets, trying to think what to do. I needed a job, but I had no one to look after my baby if I found one, and I couldn't leave her alone." She fiddled with one of his shirt buttons. "Do you believe that God reaches down sometimes in answer to our prayers?"

"I do. Sometimes I don't get the answer I want, but then later, it turns out to be the best thing that ever could have happened." He pressed his lips to her forehead. "That day as I rode toward Glory Ridge, I prayed that Daphne wouldn't be my child and I'd be free to head home the next morning, no strings attached. Then, the instant I saw her, I *knew* she was mine. Or at least I thought she was. There was no way I could ride away and leave her, and you were part of the package. *That* ended up being the most wonderful gift God has ever given me — meeting you, coming to love you. I'm more glad than I can say that he knew better than I did what was good for me."

Tears filled Brianna's eyes even as she smiled. "I prayed for a miracle that day. The rent was due the following Monday morning, and I was a dollar short. Making so little per hour, I knew I couldn't come up with it, so I prayed for a miracle. Not a big miracle, only a little one, and instead God sent me *you.*"

David snorted with laughter. The sound

was contagious, and soon they lay wrapped in each other's arms, laughing like fools. When the hilarity subsided, Brianna sighed and wiped her eyes. "I thought God had lost his mind, I truly did, but now, looking back on it, I know he answered my prayer with a wondrous miracle named David Paxton."

"Ah, sweetheart. That makes two of us. Having you in my life is a miracle for me, too." He lay quiet for a moment, toying with her hair. "Back to Boston when you were wandering the streets and praying for help. What kind of answer did God send you?"

"A job as a barmaid."

*"What?"*

"I saw a sign on the door, and I was so desperate that I went in. The owner was a kindly, hunch-shouldered old fellow. A room came with the position. It was just off the main pub area and quite small, but it was warm and dry. Even more wonderful, the man loved babies and knew quite a lot more about them than I did. He was the father of seven and had twenty-three grandchildren. He said Daphne had colic because of the cow's milk. He handed me money and told me where I could get goat's milk. He also told me to stop off at the apothecary shop for some spirit of peppermint, which helps settle a baby's stomach. I was afraid to leave Daphne with him, but he refused to let me take her back out into the freezing rain. I was terrified he might harm her, but he gave me no choice, so I left her with him. When I got back, he was waiting on tables with my baby sound asleep on his shoulder.

"Daphne seldom slept. I couldn't believe my eyes. Come to find out, he'd dipped his finger in whiskey and let her suckle it off. He didn't give her a lot, only enough to ease her tummy pain, and she slept as if there was no tomorrow. When she woke up, I gave her warm water laced with drops of peppermint before I fed her the goat's milk. She never cried with colic again."

Brianna felt David's mouth curve in a smile against her hair. "So you had a happy answer from God." He waited a beat. "But I've got a bad feeling not all of it was good. Am I right?"

Brianna told him of the nights when she'd been attacked by bar patrons, and how the owner had clubbed them off to save her from being raped. Then she went on to tell him about looking in the classifieds for another position.

"When I saw Ricker's job post, I thought it would be perfect. I could work and have Daphne with me in a home environment.

He wanted an all-around housekeeper and tutor for his sons. I had helped teach at the orphanage as I grew older, but I didn't know much about cooking. I had, however, worked doing meal preparation in the orphanage kitchen, and I figured I could learn about farm animals. He wanted a young widow, with or without a child. By then, I knew how vulnerable a single young woman was, so I decided to dream up an errant husband who might resurface at any time. Across the street from the bar, there was a hardware shop called David Saxton's. I felt funny about using a real name for my fake husband, so I changed the last name to Paxton. Ricker lived in Colorado, so I thought he might like it if I had once lived in Colorado."

"So you dreamed up a place called Taffeta Falls?"

Brianna could laugh about that now. "Actually, until I met a very rude, relentless desperado named David Paxton, no one ever asked me where my pretend husband's ranch had been located." She sighed. "With my trumped-up qualifications, I got the position with Ricker. He sent traveling funds for me and Daphne. I took some of my money to buy a wedding band at a pawn shop, and off I went to Glory Ridge, with my story well memorized."

"And then all didn't go well."

She smiled at the memory. "I burned the food I tried to cook. I was terrified of the cow. The chickens pecked my hands bloody. I'm certain Charles would have fired me if he hadn't been worried about tossing a young woman and baby out on the streets in the dead of winter. He's a horrible man who used to whip his boys until they bled. But he worried about appearances and what people in town would think if he threw me out. I worked hard to learn how to do everything, and he worked equally hard at getting me to warm his bed. He would corner me when I least expected it, and one time I almost didn't get away. After that, I always carried a knife in my skirt pocket, buried deep in a potato so I wouldn't cut myself accidentally, and the next time he came after me, I put the blade to his throat."

"Sweet Christ."

Brianna smiled slightly. "I sharpened that knife every night after supper. He knew he'd be a dead man if he ever tried to touch me again. I also kept a chair wedged under my bedroom doorknob at night. We got along well enough after that, but he never turned loose of the idea of getting rid of me. I was a sore disappointment because I spurned his advances. He made me write letters once a week to my husband, David Paxton, who mined for gold in Denver. He dictated what I was to say, and I could only pray there was no one in Denver with the same name."

David chuckled. "There wasn't, but he did live thirty miles south of there."

"Yes, well, for a good many years, he never surfaced. After I became a good cook and farm helper, Charles resigned himself to keeping me on and went to town once a week to take care of his manly needs. During that time, he only occasionally insisted that I write to my husband, begging him to come for me and our daughter. Then, suddenly, he went to town more often and started making me write once a week again. He'd met a woman he wanted to marry."

"And when he got hitched, he finally booted you and Daphne out."

"Yes. That was frightening. I'd saved a bit over the years at Ricker's, so I was able to rent an attic room in the boardinghouse and purchase all the little things Daphne and I needed to call it home. She was old enough by then to be left alone. I hated doing that — leaving her, I mean — but necessity dictated. I did odd jobs, got hired to clean the restaurant at night, and landed a position with Abigail sewing." Brianna curled closer to David's warmth. "Adam Parks, the restaurateur, was supposedly a happily married man, but he had a wandering eye. He often returned to the restaurant late at night to bedevil me. One night, I clouted him on the head with a frying pan."

David said nothing for so long that Brianna wondered if he'd fallen asleep. "So tell me, Shamrock, how come you stifle your true nature, turn up your nose at nonsense, and always try so hard to be a perfect lady?"

"I promised." Brianna's throat went tight and scratchy. "When Moira was dying, I swore to raise Daphne for her. From the time we were little, Moira was a perfect lady, and I always fell short. When she drew her last breath and I took Daphne from her arms, I knew I needed to become like my twin in order to raise her daughter properly."

Again, David was quiet for a long while. Then he said, "So you stifle Brianna and try to be Moira."

"Brianna made stupid mistakes. She was rebellious and selfish. In the end, she was responsible for her sister's death. I was glad to tell her good-bye. All she brought was pain and suffering."

"Why do you think Moira entrusted you with her baby, Shamrock?"

"Because we were twins, and Moira knew

I'd love Daphne as much as she would."

"Did you ever stop to think maybe it was because you were all the things Moira wished she could be?"

Brianna lay still, thinking back. "She used to say we were incomplete without each other, that she was the calm, sensible one, and I was the adventurous, brave one. Together we created a perfect balance and could do anything."

"So when Moira died, you decided to be like her, and in the doing, you abandoned the perfect balance."

Brianna had never thought of it that way. David cuddled her close. "There's nothing wrong with trying to copy Moira's ladylike behavior, but if you toss away all of Brianna, you're a lopsided person. You need to show Daphne how to be a lady, but you also need to show her that having fun and laughing and being silly aren't wrong. Otherwise, you're raising her to be half of what she should be."

Brianna felt a moment of panic. "I don't know how to be Brianna anymore, David. She was wild, irresponsible, selfish, and thoughtless. I'm not sure I even want to be that person again."

"Ah, but without her, the Moira you're pretending to be is a wet blanket."

"A what?"

He nuzzled her ear. "A wet blanket, what you toss on a flame to put it out. Life is no fun without a little fire, Shamrock, and as a kid growing up with Moira, you were the fire. You owe it to Daphne to let her come to know both you and her mother. Otherwise, she'll never become the wonderful woman she should be. Does that make any sense?"

To Brianna, it made a horrible kind of sense. "She's rejecting Moira and becoming me," she whispered. "I see it in her all the time — headstrong, rebellious, always questioning the why of everything."

"The only reason she rebels is because you've forgotten how to have fun." He pressed his face against her hair, as if to soften the blow of those words. "In the morning, I'm going to teach you how to let loose again, to let the real Shamrock come through, but for tonight, I have another kind of lesson in mind." His voice had gone husky. "You ready to learn?"

"What are you going to teach me?" she asked.

"How to make love, sweetheart. No taking, no force, just sweet, fabulous sharing. You ready to go there with me?"

There was no other man on earth she

633

wanted to be her guide. "Yes, I'm ready. Still a little nervous, but, yes, I am ready."

He shifted, let go of her and sprang off the bed, exhibiting that incredible strength and agility she admired. Holding out a big hand to her, he said, "Of your own free will, come to me."

Brianna struggled to a sitting position, held out her hand, and with that fabulous anchor of steely weight, he lifted her to her feet, the forward momentum carrying her into his arms. She instantly felt at home against him. His heat surrounded her. His strength buoyed her. She knew in that moment that she'd never feel afraid of a man again, because David would be there to protect her.

"I love you so much, David," she murmured. "You sneaked up on me, kind of like influenza, a symptom here and a symptom there, until I realized I was a goner."

He laughed and then curled himself around her. "You, my high-minded lady, are the best case of flu I've ever had."

Brianna felt exactly the same. If he was a disease, she wanted him to infect every cell of her body. She felt her gown slip to the floor. Then David's hands went to work on her stays. When she started to say something, he covered her mouth with his, and she sank into the wet satin heat, startled at first by the invasion of his tongue, and then lost in the sensations he aroused within her. Somehow her corset fell away. Next her underskirts and bloomers departed, forming puddles on the floor with her other garments. He had finally divested her of everything but her chemise.

Nervous but not really frightened, Brianna caught his dark face between her hands, marveling at how pale her skin was next to his in the lantern light. Locking gazes with him — and, oh, my, she'd never seen his eyes in the heat of passion, darkening to a gunmetal blue that danced with sparks — she whispered, "Please do remember I've never done this."

He nibbled at the corner of her mouth, suckled at the V of her collarbone. "Neither have I, never with anyone I loved, anyhow. Just trust me, Shamrock. Can you do that? Forget everything and just come with me."

Her lungs grabbing for air, Brianna clung to him as if she'd been swept off the lily pad and was going under for the third time. "Just say you won't hurt me."

His mouth, warm and moist, found her bare shoulder. "I can't promise that, darlin', not with this being your first time. But I can promise that I'll make it as painless as I can."

Visions of Moira after the rape flashed through Brianna's mind, but then David's gentle hands were there, and the images dimmed, and when she searched his face, his chiseled countenance and those compelling eyes became her only reality.

"Just turn loose, Shamrock," he whispered, "and be with me."

He swept her up into his arms and laid her on the bed again. She felt exposed. Her chemise had drifted up, but when she started to cover herself, he touched a fingertip to her wrist. "No, don't do that. If you're feeling shy, I'll dim the lamp."

He lowered the wick, and then he started to strip. Off went the duster, then his shirt. Brianna couldn't jerk her gaze away from his chest — rippling mounds where she had breasts, striated muscle across his abdomen where she was soft and pliant. With quick flicks of his wrists, he took off his gun belt and draped it over the footboards. Next he took off his belt. Then he sat on the edge of the mattress to kick off his boots. Even in the dimmer light, she could see the play of strength across his back, large tendons and muscle bunching in his shoulder area, the massiveness tapering to a slender waist.

When he stood to kick off his pants, Brianna closed her eyes, afraid she might panic if she saw his erect manhood. But then he lowered himself onto the bed beside her, and his arms were around her, and she felt the throbbing hardness of him against her thigh, as silken on the surface as polished satin, but rodlike under the softness. She wondered fleetingly how something that big could possibly fit inside her. But then David made her forget that and everything else. He was *there,* all around her, his mouth, his voice, his strength, and his solid heat.

He tugged loose the front ribbons of her chemise, baring her breasts, and when he caught her aching nipple between his lips, she thought she might die of pleasure. Electrical zings shot through her body, pooling like blue fire low in her core. She could barely breathe. She made fists in his hair, inviting him to sample her other breast. Through half-opened eyes, she tried to take him in visually, the bronze gleam of his arms and shoulders, the mat of gold hair across his chest, but mostly all she could focus on was the feel of him.

"I love you," he whispered, his voice gone hoarse with desire.

And then his hand found that private

place between her thighs. Brianna gasped and her spine snapped taut. David used his weight to ride her back down to the mattress and touched her there, on that most sensitive area, until her nerve endings bunched, urgency built within her, and her breath came in jagged bursts as she raised her hips toward his hand, wanting more and more.

He gave it to her. *Tumbling off the lily pad into the waves.* She floated up, dived right, soared left, and the electrical ribbons of pleasure turned white-hot as the storm surrounded her. She didn't want to surface. Instead she arched, clinging to his shoulders. He buried his face in the lee of her neck. She felt out of control, distantly alarmed. Never in her life had she experienced anything like this.

"Go with me," he whispered near her ear. "Shamrock, turn loose. Trust me. Just go with me."

She remembered how he'd made such beautiful music on the prairie with his fiddle, his big hands expertly wielding the bow and pressing the strings, filling the night with magic. She stopped fighting and offered herself up to him. He didn't disappoint. Each touch of his fingertips, each stroke of his hands, each pull of his mouth made her pulse race faster, a fever pitch of need building within her. As if he knew, he increased the pressure and pace. Her body jerked and trembled. He took her higher and higher until she came apart with indescribable pleasure. She felt like a ray of light that exploded into hundreds of brilliant shards that began to trickle in fading bursts back to earth to land safely in David's arms.

He trailed kisses across her face and whispered to her. And then she saw him, magnificent in the dim glow of the lantern light, rising above her. For just an instant, she clamped her thighs together, fearing what was to come, memories of Moira invading her passion-drugged senses again. But then she found David's eyes, glassy and nearly black with desire, and all the fear left her. This was *her* David, the man who'd stood against three roughriders to protect her and her daughter, willing to sacrifice his life for them. How could she feel afraid of him, even for a second?

He poised himself over her, his knotted fists buried in the down mattress, his muscular body arched over hers, his eyes blazing as he met her gaze. Every inch of him quivered with restraint. "If you're afraid, I'll stop," he said raggedly. "This first time, I don't want you to feel frightened."

Brianna realized then that he truly would stop, and love for this marvelous, incredible man flooded through her, turning her bones to hot syrup. She realized he might pull away, and she grasped his hips, wanting to experience it all. Locking eyes with him, she lifted herself up. Moira's ghost turned loose of her, and for the first time in years, Brianna allowed her true, adventurous self to take over. "I'm not afraid. You asked me to come with you. Don't back out now."

He gave a harsh, broken laugh, and then he nudged his manhood against her opening. Brianna let her thighs part, trusting him as she'd never trusted anyone. He pushed in a little way and then stopped, his blue eyes fixed on hers, his body trembling with a need he refused to satisfy.

"You okay, Shamrock? I don't want to hurt you, and I know I will."

Brianna thrust up with her hips, hard and fast, taking the choice away from him. *Pain.* She sucked in air, stiffened, rode it out, and then sighed softly as the first onslaught became a dull ache.

Clutching his thick, hard upper arms, she whispered raggedly, "Come with me, David. Don't turn lily-livered on me now. Come with me."

He groaned, a shuddering sound, and

slammed forward with his hips. "No, Shamrock, you come with *me*."

Brianna couldn't imagine anything more wonderful than what he'd already made her feel with his hand, but David Paxton was a man full of surprises. He surged deep, withdrew, and plunged again, igniting her in places she hadn't realized she possessed. The initial pain was forgotten. Pleasure swept her under, a trembling, quivering delight that ended with a shattering orgasm. The wondrousness of it stole her breath and made her pulse pound like black fists in her temples. She clenched her arms and legs around him. *Yes.* This was love. This was why some women tittered and whispered. *This* was heaven on earth.

When it was over, David held her in his arms, pressing kisses to her brow. "Dear God, how I love you. Talk about miracles. I'll be thankful for the rest of my life that I got that bag of letters."

"And I'll always be thankful that God sent me a catastrophe."

He chuckled and gathered her close. They slept. Later Brianna awakened to his mouth at her breast, and she came instantly awake to ride the waves of pleasure with him again. *David.* She made fists in his hair and clung to him, loving him as she'd never loved anyone.

The third time they made love — or was it the fourth? — David whispered, "Where is my Shamrock, who once loved adventure, was fascinated by the outside world, and broke the rules?"

To Brianna, David was her *entire* world. She reared up on her elbows to peer at him through the golden gloom of the partially lighted bedroom. "Have I disappointed you?"

He kissed her deeply, impaling her with such sweet feelings that she forgot to worry. "Hell, no, you haven't disappointed me, but so far, I've taken command, and somehow I have this idea in my head that Brianna O'Keefe is a little rebel. She's in there somewhere. Tell her to come out and introduce herself to me."

For an instant, Brianna's chest clutched with dread. Letting go was so dangerous. When you behaved with abandon, the people dearest to you could die. She lay beside David, feeling frozen, searching within herself for that girl who'd once tossed caution to the wind. She was no longer there.

"Life killed her, David. I'll never get her back."

"Bullshit. She jumped out and decked me that day beside the stream. She came out again when I handed her my rifle, knowing she might have to learn how to use it without help and that she might have to ride a horse like the wind to save her daughter." He grasped her chin. "Damn it, Shamrock. You are *not* Moira. You're *you,* and trust me when I say that you are one of God's precious gifts to this world. When we're outside the bedroom, be a prim lady if you like, but behind closed doors, forget all that nonsense and just *be.*"

Brianna wasn't sure she could do that, but with coaxing and drugging kisses from David, she found that young girl within herself — the rebel who'd hated being controlled — and she broke every rule of ladylike decorum, touching him everywhere, tasting him everywhere, and reveling in the groans of pleasure that erupted from him when she closed her mouth around his shaft.

The sheets went flying; propriety went with them. The next thing she knew, she was flattened against the wall, with David's strong arms clenched under her thighs to hold her high. She cried out as his hot, silken mouth covered the center of her. His tongue caressed, flicked, and drew on her until she whimpered and disintegrated, clinging to his strong shoulders as he took her with him to paradise.

Brianna came slowly awake to sunlight glaring against her eyelids. When she lifted her lashes, she cupped her hands over her face to block out the brightness. Then, with a rush of horror, it struck her that she hadn't lowered the blind last night. She and David had made love for all the world to see. She lunged from the bed, grabbed the pull, and jerked it down to the sill with such force that she broke the rolling mechanism. The blind hung in folds, covering the window but lost forever to usefulness.

David sat up in bed. "What the hell?"

Brianna fluttered her hands, realized she was stark naked, and dove for a sheet that lay crumpled on the floor. Once she'd covered herself, she cried, "We made love with the lamp on and the blind up. Oh, my God, oh, my God."

David had no problem with nudity. He swung off the bed, and with two long strides, swept her into his arms. "Do you think people stay up all night to watch the Paxtons have sex? It's a back window. If it faced Main we might worry. As for anyone who might have sneaked out there to watch, to hell with them. They need something better to do with their time."

He reached out an arm and jerked the shade from the brackets, baring the window glass. Then he strode with her across the room, lifted her against the wall, and made love to her again. When she was a quivering puddle of pulsating nerve endings, he carried her back to bed and once again treated her to a journey with him to soaring heights and a dizzying plunge back to earth. Brianna came to her senses with both arms locked around his neck and her mouth open over his shoulder. She loved the taste of him — salt and man. She gloried in his strength, his power, his desire for her.

"You, sir, are impossible."

He laughed and nibbled at her temple. "And you, my high-minded lady, are irresistible. Hopefully, we haven't given our local hat maker a heart attack."

"She's a milliner," Brianna corrected, but the purr of fulfillment in her voice muted its bite. "Will you never learn how to speak properly?"

"Probably not, but I'll enjoy having you gripe at me about it for the remainder of my days."

David had kept his promise to teach Brianna how to make love, and after breakfast, as they were tidying the kitchen, he taught her how to turn loose and have fun. Wearing only her shabby nightdress, which she'd brought with her from the orphanage, Brianna dried the last dish as David pulled the plug in the sink. She put the plate on the shelf, turned to fold the towel, and put it on the counter. Just then David wet his fingers in the last of the water circling down the drain and flicked her in the face. She blinked, and he flicked her again.

"What," she said primly, "do you think you're doing?"

He cupped his hand in the remaining liquid and tossed it at her. She cried out at the splash, which got her on the chest. "Water fight! Where are you, Shamrock? You going to take that without firing back?"

Then he ran. Brianna grabbed hold of her drenched nightdress, thinking he'd lost his mind. But then the unholy urge to get even consumed her. She rifled through the cupboards for a big glass, filled it with ice cold water from the faucet, and went to find her attacker. She came upon him hiding behind the armoire in their bedroom. She looked him directly in the eye, smiled, and tossed sixteen ounces of cold water right in his face.

It was his turn to gasp and sputter. But he

quickly recovered. "Aha!"

He grabbed her glass and dashed for the kitchen. Brianna realized he meant to fill it and get even. She glanced frantically around, considered hiding under the bed, discarded that idea as too obvious, and instead climbed into the armoire. No easy fit. She had to fold herself double. Her gowns and his clothing hung around her face, and one of his spare boots poked her in the rump.

She heard him prowling around the apartment, looking for her in the broom closet, the living room, and Daphne's bedroom. Laughter bubbled up her throat. Sure enough, she caught the thump of his bony knees hitting their bedroom floor and knew he was looking under the bed.

"Shamrock," he called in an evil, lecherous voice. "Where *are* you? Come to Papa."

Brianna held her breath and ducked her head between her knees. He wouldn't *dare* douse her when she was in the armoire. The water would totally ruin her silk gowns. Not even David would be that rash.

Her nerves stretched tight, singing with alarm, when the armoire door creaked open. Before she could lift her head, a strong hand seized her by the arm. The next thing she knew, David was plucking her from her hiding place as if she weighed nothing. He pressed her against the wall. Looking up into his laughing blue eyes, she knew she was in for it. With a wicked grin, he held up the water glass, grabbed hold of the prim collar of her nightdress, and poured cold water down the entire front of her. She shouted at the shock. He ran back toward the kitchen. She needed another water glass. This was insane, totally absurd. Dumb, dumb, *dumb.* But she was already wet, so she ran after him.

When she reached the kitchen, she grabbed a glass and lunged for the sink. Before she had ammunition, he blasted her again, this time drenching her face and hair. Sputtering, she fought to gain control of the kitchen spigot. He managed to fill his weapon before she could fill hers. He got her again before she could fire back. And then he fled.

Brianna scooped her wet hair from her face, plucked her sopping nightdress from her breasts, and dripped a trail across the floor as she went searching for him. She found him in the water closet. He held up his hands.

"I'm unarmed. You wouldn't shoot a defenseless man, would you?"

Brianna let fly, nailing him right in the

face again. He choked and laughed, catching her around the waist as she turned to flee. Their glasses thumped to the floor. They ended up in the aluminum tub, which wasn't large enough to accommodate both of them. Somehow David made love to her there anyway. And afterward, when she lay limp, happy, and utterly exhausted, he left the tub, collected his vessel, filled it, and slowly dribbled the contents over her already soaked nightdress.

"Grab the bull by the horn, Shamrock, and you're liable to get gored."

"Oh, really?"

Brianna stood up and slowly, ever so slowly, drew her dripping nightdress off over her head. David almost lost his grip on the glass, his gaze traveling over her naked body. Brianna took advantage, threw her gown over his head, and tried her best to knot it around his neck.

They ended up on the bed again, going after each other as if they'd spent forty days in the desert. Afterward, as Brianna surfaced to awareness, she punched him in the ribs with her elbow.

"You *will* help me wash and hang the sheets on the line. Correct? And you'll also help me mop up all this water."

"For a price," he informed her. "You have

to do that again."

"Do what again?"

"Slowly strip off that stupid nightdress for me. My God, my heart almost stopped."

Brianna felt a grin coming on. She tried to stifle it, but it was no use. "I'll agree to those terms. But if you have a water glass in your hands, prepare to be drowned."

Later, they sat at the kitchen table, watching passersby on the street below. David sipped coffee; Brianna enjoyed tea. She felt oddly limp, and yet she also felt happier than she had in years. A water fight. She couldn't quite believe that she'd engaged in such foolishness. And if not for the fabulous intimacy between her and David that had followed, she would have wished Daphne could have been there.

David was right, she realized sadly. She'd worked so hard to be like Moira that somewhere along the way she'd lost touch with herself. Tumbling back through the years to childhood, Brianna could remember the first time Moira had told her, very simplistically, that without each other, they weren't complete. "You are me, and I am you," she'd whispered. "Without each other, we aren't right." Brianna had understood. Separated, they'd drifted all one way. Together they'd found balance.

Tears filled Brianna's eyes as she sipped her tea. David noticed. He searched her gaze. His mouth thinned to a grim line. "What is it, Shamrock? Talk to me."

She set down her cup and stared at the window glass. There were streaks. She needed to polish them away. "I was just thinking. You're right, you know. Moira and I — oh, David, you would have loved her so much. She was all that is good in me. Truly, she was an incredibly precious soul. And I was all that was bad in her. We were only about four when she reasoned that out and understood we needed to blend, that neither of us could ever be okay without the other."

"Shamrock, you weren't all that was bad in Moira. You gave her the freedom to be fanciful, and she gave you the structure to follow rules." He reached across the table to fold his hand around hers. Brianna reveled in the warmth of his grip. "You are *not* bad, and Moira was *not* an angel." He paused to stare out the window. "I don't understand the bond between twins. I met some twins once, and they were as close as skin is to an onion. They seemed to think together, bouncing ideas back and forth without saying a word. I was selling them cattle, and I never went up against better bargainers.

They sort of leaned into each other somehow, in a way me and my brothers don't. As close as I am to Ace, Joseph, and Esa, and as hooked onto them as I am, what I saw in those twins was different. It was almost as if one of them couldn't breathe without the other one drawing in air, too."

Pain lanced through Brianna's chest, for David had finally put her feelings about Moira into words. She gulped to steady her voice. "She was the other half of me. Without her — when she died — well, I can't describe how it felt. It wasn't like losing an arm or a leg. It was —" Brianna stopped, searching for words, but there were none to describe her relationship with her identical twin. "One time she got pneumonia. I wasn't sick, but she was burning up with fever. The sisters were gathered around her, building frames over her head and making a tent over her face with towels dipped in boiling water. I suddenly couldn't breathe." She looked at him, long and hard, knowing what she'd just told him was crazy. "I couldn't *breathe*. Moira grabbed for breath, and I grabbed for breath. Her chest rattled, and *my* chest rattled. I could feel her slipping away, and I felt myself slipping away with her." She folded her hands over the top of her cup, needing to feel the heat seep into her bones. "She nearly died, and I almost died with her. The nuns finally realized that we were somehow connected in a way they couldn't understand, in a way I still, to this day, don't understand, so they treated me as if I had pneumonia, too. And together, Moira and I got well."

David's eyes went suspiciously bright. His throat worked. "I am so sorry you lost her. I would have loved to know her."

Brianna inclined her head. "You would have adored her, maybe even more than you do me. She was so special, David." She forced her gaze to his. "Moira truly was an angel who walked the earth for a time. She was as close to perfect as anyone could be."

"Look at me," he said huskily. When Brianna lifted her lashes, he grasped her wrist. "I am sure I would have adored Moira, but I could never love anyone more than I love you. I'm too flawed to live with an angel. If she was as sweet and dear as you say, then fine, but Shamrock, you are sweet and dear, too. I like the spice and vinegar in you, and I'd never settle for anything less."

"You almost did. You almost settled for Hazel."

David threw back his head and laughed. His hair drifted over his shoulders, the strands only a shade darker than Daphne's. His eyes were like hers, too. "Thank God I didn't settle," he said, giving Brianna's hand a squeeze. "As for Moira, she's gone, up there in heaven somewhere looking down, and we have the job of raising her daughter. My big concern right now is what we tell Daphne. I think she needs to know the truth at some point, Shamrock. It isn't right to let a child grow to adulthood believing a lie."

Brianna bowed her head again. "I agree. If Moira had died differently, I would have told Daphne the truth from her cradle. But rape is a terrible thing, David. People often blame the victim instead of the perpetrator. I have always intended to tell Daphne the truth, but when I do, I need to know she's old enough to understand what really happened. Her mama did nothing wrong. It was *me.* I committed the wrong."

"You flirted with a young man," David corrected. "That was not wrong. You were young, innocent, and oblivious to his nature. If Moira hadn't gone into the garden that day, pretending to be you, it might have been *you,* Shamrock. Being a young girl, making eyes at a young man, and dancing away from him aren't sins. They're natural. A girl needs to learn how to be a woman. It wasn't your fault that the farmer's son was a bastard who beat your sister half to death, choked her, and raped her so roughly that he tore her up inside." He leaned over the table, demanding without words that Brianna look into his eyes. "What happened wasn't your fault. It wasn't Moira's fault. It was *his* fault, and I've got a good mind to pay the cruel-hearted son of a bitch a visit."

Brianna could barely see David through her tears. In the last twelve hours, he had brought her pain, joy, ecstasy, and now pain again. "I am finished with all the anger and the yearning for revenge. Now I just want to do what's right for Daphne. She needs to know about Moira. But when? When will she be old enough to grasp what happened? I'm thinking she should be about twelve."

David shook his head. "No way. She needs to be a lot older. We can go on as we have, Shamrock. Now we can be a *real* family. There's no need to fill Daphne's head with things that ugly, not until she's experienced an overzealous boy's advances and come to understand what happened to her mother." He grimaced. His eyes fell closed. When he looked at Brianna again, a glint of determination shone there. "No way is my little girl going to know about anything that horrible. Not yet. We'll know when it's time to tell her, when she can understand. Do you agree?"

Brianna had felt that way since she'd first taken the baby from Moira's stiffening arms. Daphne needed to grow up believing in goodness, not evil. "I definitely do. We'll know when she's ready, and then we'll tell her together."

David offered her his hand. "Shake on it?"

Brianna shook on it.

David convinced Brianna to leave the shop closed that morning and paid the off-duty Billy Joe to ride to Ace's ranch with a message that he had business to take care of in town that would prevent him from attending Little Joe's party and coming for Daphne until Sunday afternoon.

"She'll have fun," he assured Brianna. "Today they're having the party and a cookie bake. Little Joe is still too young to care if I'm there. Tonight they'll probably have a big family supper. She's got Sam, her cousins, and the kittens to play with, and my mother will undoubtedly keep her occupied the rest of the time."

Brianna smiled. "And what is the pressing business you have to take care of here in town?" she asked.

"Making love to my wife all day and all night."

"Is that a threat?"

He drew her up from the kitchen chair and into his arms. "It's a promise."

David Paxton was a man of his word. He did indeed make love to Brianna all that day and throughout the night. During brief rest periods, they ate, sipped wine he got from the Golden Slipper a few doors away, and then lay in each other's arms. Brianna felt as if they were the only two people on earth. In his embrace, she absorbed his warmth, sleeping, awakening, smiling when she felt his hard, hairy arms tighten around her. *David, her desperado.*

God truly had sent her a miracle.

# CHAPTER TWENTY-TWO

On Sunday, David rented a buggy, and he and Brianna drove out to Ace's ranch to collect Daphne. The whole family was there. When David parked in front of the house, Brianna saw Esa on the porch with Daphne, reading to her from his Bible. Little Ace was in the swing, pumping so hard with his feet that the back of the seat almost thumped the siding. Caitlin and Rachel spilled out through the door and down the steps, trying to hug Brianna before David could swing her from the conveyance and get her steady on her feet.

"It's good to see you again so soon!" Caitlin cried. Rachel beamed a smile and hooked her arm through Brianna's. "We missed both of you at the party yesterday. Come inside. We have some surprises for you."

The surprises were two lovely house-dresses, one pink and one yellow, which Caitlin and Rachel had made for her. Before

Brianna knew it, she was in the front bedroom standing on a stool, surrounded by female relatives who checked the gowns for proper fit and length.

"I don't know what to say," Brianna told them, and she truly didn't. "They fit almost perfectly, and oh, they are so pretty!"

Dory laughed. "You should have heard them, fretting aloud about having the audacity to make dresses for a fashion designer!"

"Why?" Brianna cried. "You do fabulous work! If you want a job at my shop, you've got it."

Rachel stood back. "I have to admit, you do look gorgeous in both colors, and now you can save your silk gowns for the shop. These are far more practical for out at David's ranch."

Brianna felt as if her insides were made of melting butter. For the first time, she was certain of the future. She *would* be at David's ranch often, and in these women, she'd found a mother and sisters. Both Rachel and Caitlin went straight to work doing minor alterations on the housedresses while Dory and Brianna adjourned to the kitchen to prepare a huge evening meal.

After a boisterous supper that featured tasty dishes, laughter, and a great deal of teasing, David brought out his fiddle. It was so wonderful to watch Ace gently guide his red-haired wife into a dance. Joseph handed Little Joe to Dory and swept Rachel into his arms next. Soon Esa took over playing the string instrument so David could waltz with Brianna. Dory blushed like a schoolgirl when Joseph plucked Little Joe from her lap, handed him to Ace, and bowed over her hand, asking her to take a spin with him. Even little Dory Sue bobbed around the room, looking adorable in a green frock.

When the evening grew late, David collected his family and assisted them into the buggy. Brianna held her two new dresses on her lap. Daphne was squeezed in between them. Sam lay under her feet. It was a glorious early-summer night, the breeze almost balmy and sweet with the scents of wildflowers and prairie grass. Daphne promptly fell asleep. Sam began to snore. Brianna gazed at the sky, trying to follow the point of David's finger as he showed her the North Star and explained how to navigate.

In that moment, only one direction mattered to Brianna, and that was forward. The future beckoned to her, filled with promise. In all her life, she could not recall ever having been so happy and content.

Over the next few days, Brianna and David

lived the blissful existence of newlyweds, sneaking to make love each night after Daphne fell asleep. Brianna was so happy that she felt frightened. What if something happened to spoil it all? David pooh-poohed the notion.

"I've waited all my life to meet the woman of my dreams," he told her, "and nothing and no one will *ever* take you away from me."

Daphne blossomed in the warmth that now filled the apartment. One evening after supper, she whispered to David, "I'm so glad you decided to spend more time brushing your teeth, Papa. Mama likes you a lot better now. It's so much more fun when she laughs and acts silly with us."

Midweek, Brianna accompanied David and the child to the ranch for two overnight stays to join in family activities. Each morning, it was a mad rush for Brianna to get back into town to open her shop. She seriously began to contemplate changing her business hours so she could be with her husband and daughter in a real home environment every single evening. She enjoyed traipsing around behind Daphne, who spent every spare second with her new pony, Blinky, or with the kittens. Sam was the child's constant companion, and Brianna came to adore the silly dog in a way she wouldn't have believed possible in the recent past.

David encouraged Brianna to embrace life with him. "I think you should change the shop hours," he said. "Open later in the morning. It's not as if you need the income. Designing gowns should be fun, not endless hard work. And why can't you hire a seamstress to help? There are plenty of ladies in No Name who could use an income."

Brianna was excited by the suggestion. "If I hire someone, I can assure you of one thing. I'll be a much better boss than Abigail ever was."

David hugged her close. "Yes, you certainly will be. Come live with me at the ranch. My deputies are well trained. We've driven away almost all the rowdies. It isn't really necessary for me to stay in town half the week. In fact, I see no reason why I can't make my nights there the exception instead of the rule as long as I'm in town to pull the day shift Monday through Friday."

Looping her arms around his neck, Brianna leaned back in the circle of his strong embrace. "That, sir, is an offer I simply can't refuse. It'll take me a bit of time to hire and train someone, but I shall get right to it."

Ever conscious of Daphne, David stole a quick kiss. "Put a rush on it. I soundproofed the walls of my house, and we can put our daughter in the room farthest away from ours. I'll teach you how to make beautiful music with mattress springs."

That was a lesson Brianna anticipated with bone-melting delight.

The next Friday night, Brianna made her grand entrance at the social, wearing her gorgeous burgundy gown, which sported a scalloped neckline beaded with seed pearls, outrageous puffed sleeves that narrowed at the elbow to skim her forearms, and an overskirt with scalloped edges and a flowing bustle that swept the floor behind her in a cascade of shimmering silk. Clinging to David's arm, she was immediately surrounded by ladies who admired her dress.

"I'm out of here," David whispered. "I'll be by the punch bowl."

Daphne raced away to find Ace, Caitlin, and Grandma Dory. Brianna was left to field eager questions and assure potential customers that she would happily consult with them if they came by the shop on Monday to make appointments. It was a victorious moment for Brianna. Her dream of becoming a respected designer was coming true, and she owed it all to David.

David felt as if he might burst with pride as he watched his wife hold court. She was breathtakingly beautiful in the burgundy gown. Over the last week, she'd fretted that the red in her dark hair might clash with the dress, but David could attest to the fact that it didn't. She shimmered like a bright flame, making the women around her look like drab hens. He felt certain that every lady at the social would be begging for Brianna's dressmaking services before the night was over, and he already had a plan in mind for advertising in Denver to net his wife a wealthier group of customers.

David ladled himself a cup of punch and scanned the hall to find Daphne. He spotted her waltzing with Little Ace at the edge of the crowded dance floor. Sam circled the children as if he were dancing, too. *Damn.* In nine or ten years, Daphne would be a handful of trouble with those perfect features and huge blue eyes and that glorious golden hair. The boys would be following her around like besotted puppies. David smiled as he watched her try to guide her cousin. Little Ace was all feet and as clumsy as a five-legged goat. Brad and Bess Thompson stood near David's family, Bess looking lovely in a pink gown, Brad bursting with pride when people came over to admire his infant son, Tobias, only a couple of weeks old.

"You stupid, pathetic imbecile!"

David jerked and nearly slopped punch down the front of his birthday shirt, his only concession to formal wear. He looked down to find Hazel Wright, up on her tiptoes, trying to get nose to nose with him.

"What put a bee in your bonnet?" he asked.

Wrong question. Hazel sneered. "I *know*," she said. "I know *everything*."

She held a cup of punch in her hand and was shaking so badly that David feared for her pretty yellow dress. "Doing right by a woman over a child that isn't even *yours?* You, David Paxton, are a fool, a stupid, gullible *fool*."

"What the hell are you talking about?"

"The Pinkerton report — that's what I'm talking about." Hazel's voice had risen to a shrill pitch. "I've read the entire, outrageous thing."

David's stomach felt as if it had plunged to his ankles. *Oh, dear God.* Hazel had found the spare drawer key and snooped in his desk. Rage snapped through his body like jolts of electricity. But before he could speak or control his reaction, he glimpsed a flash of burgundy at the corner of his eye and jerked around. Hazel turned with him.

Brianna stood there. The noise level in the hall was so high that David doubted she had overheard anything Hazel had just said, but it was obvious to anyone looking that the schoolteacher was on a rant. Brianna's face had gone pale, and the luster of happiness in her green eyes had vanished.

Hazel narrowed her gaze. "Ah, so here is the conniving little *harlot* and fiancé stealer! How delightful."

Brianna flinched at the words. "I have no idea what you're talking abou—"

Hazel stepped toward her. For David, everything slowed down. He saw Hazel lift her cup, saw her shoulders tense, and knew what she meant to do, but he felt like a bug trying to slog through cold honey. Before he could step in to protect his wife, Hazel tossed her punch in Brianna's face. Brianna jerked, squeezed her eyes closed, and stood there with her shoulders braced. The crimson punch beaded on her dark lashes, trickled down her cheeks, and cascaded in streams onto her bodice, possibly ruining the fabulous dress she'd worked so many hours to create.

"How *dare* you try to pass off your sister's

bastard child as David's?" Hazel shouted. "Were you stupid enough to think he'd never learn the truth? And now just look at the mess you've caused, you conscienceless little *bitch.* David loved *me.* We were planning to marry. Now he's chained to a liar and schemer who isn't worthy to kiss his feet!"

David couldn't quite credit his ears. Hazel was the schemer. She'd gotten into his desk on the sly and read a report meant for his eyes only. No one was allowed in that center drawer, not even his deputies, and Hazel had visited him at his office enough to know that. His brain felt frozen. He set aside his punch. His fists knotted at his sides. What the hell could he do? He'd never struck a woman in his life, and he wouldn't allow himself to knock Hazel Wright on her pompous ass. But, boy howdy, it was tempting.

He sent Brianna an encouraging look, trying to let her know she would have his complete support if she decided to let Hazel have it, but she kept her eyes squeezed closed. *Come on, Shamrock, let that Irish temper kick into play.* If Brianna decided to empty the entire punch bowl over the other woman's head, David stood ready to help her lift the damned thing. If ever a female had deserved a public set-down, it had to be Hazel Wright.

But, no, Brianna, always so controlled and conscious of propriety, merely opened her eyes, lifted her chin, and swept past Hazel with regal disdain.

"Oh, that's rich!" Hazel shrieked. "Try to run from the ugly truth! It won't work, I tell you. Before the night is over, everyone in this town will know what a lying, conniving whore you really are!"

David started to go after his wife, but then he remembered that, unlike Brianna, he hadn't been raised by nuns. He rounded on Hazel. "When did you sneak into my office?" he demanded. "And what gave you the harebrained notion that you had any business snooping through my paperwork?"

Shaking with anger, Hazel glared up at him through shimmering tears. "You have no call to take me to task. You're a cheating skunk! You broke my heart and made me look like a fool before the whole town. For weeks, everyone has been staring at me. I can't go into a shop without people whispering behind my back. I had *every* right to know before today why you left me in the lurch, and before this night is over, every person in this town will learn the truth. You didn't forsake me because you had a wife and patched things up with her. You were hoodwinked by a pretty, immoral opportunist who shackled you into marriage by leading you to believe you were the father of a child that isn't even hers!"

"Well, I sure as hell thank my lucky stars I never married *you*," he retorted. "Under that sugary act, you're as venomous as a snake." All Hazel cared about was saving face, and she didn't give a rip how many lives she destroyed in the process. "You even hit my dog! People like you disgust me."

"I disgust *you?*" Hazel said in a hoarse whisper. "You're nothing but a two-bit marshal in a dusty little town. That badge doesn't make you anybody. At least I have an education."

From the corner of his eye, David caught another flash of burgundy, and the next instant, Brianna stepped into view with an apple pie balanced on the upturned palm of her hand. Scarcely able to believe his eyes, David watched his wife pause in front of Hazel and silence her by slapping the pie dead center in her face. Hazel gasped. Apples clung to her shocked countenance, a chunk of crust dangled from the bottom lip of her yawning mouth, and blobs of gooey fruit decorated the bodice of her yellow dress.

Brianna smiled, set down the pastry plate, daintily dusted her palms, and said, "Perhaps in the future you will think twice before you cast slurs upon another lady's reputation."

Then, head once again held high, Brianna made another regal exit, her magnificent gown looking spotless from the back.

Hazel sputtered and squealed, wiping apple from her cheeks. David realized that a dozen people nearby had seen Hazel get the pie in her face, and their laughter was spreading around the room. It took all his self-control to gulp back a guffaw himself. Hazel had gotten precisely what she deserved, and David was so proud of Brianna. His Shamrock had finally come out of hiding.

There had been so much noise in the hall with the music, conversation, and the thumping footsteps of dancers that he felt sure only a few individuals had overhead Hazel's diatribe. Dripping chunks of pie, Hazel would flee for home to at least wash up and change clothes before she repeated the story to anyone else. He searched the crowd for Daphne, saw her still dancing with Little Ace, and spun on his heel to go after his wife. His family would look after his daughter. Right then, Brianna needed him most.

Typical of June near the Rockies, the night air embraced David with chilly arms, but he barely felt the bite. With three chinks of his spurs, he loped across the street and gained the opposite boardwalk. He was at the dress-shop door in thirty seconds. Recalling Hazel's insults, he smiled bitterly, thinking it didn't take long for a two-bit marshal to cover ground in a dusty little town. If she thought so little of the community that paid her teaching wages, why the hell had she moved there in the first place?

David let himself in and locked the door behind him. Taking the stairs four at a time, he reached the landing, opened the apartment door, and immediately spied Brianna, sitting rigidly at the kitchen table facing him. Pale and expressionless, she didn't look up. She sat as still as an alabaster statue. As David drew closer, he could see the tracks of tears on her cheeks, which had left white trails in the crimson punch that had dried on her skin.

"Oh, David," she whispered, her glassy gaze fixed on the tablecloth. "You're still in love with her, aren't you? That's the only reason I can think of for you to tell her the truth about Daphne's father."

David felt as if the floor had disappeared

from under his feet. *"No, God no."* He stepped closer. "You've got it wrong, Shamrock. I never told her anything."

"Really?" She finally looked up at him. There was a world of heartbreak in her eyes. "She knows every dirty detail — about Moira, about me. How could you do that, David? If you wanted to be rid of me and Daphne, you needn't have gone to such lengths. I offered to leave, to go with you to Denver and get an annulment. It was you who talked me out of it."

David sank onto the chair across from her. "I put the report from the Pinkerton Agency in the center drawer of my desk for safekeeping. *Nobody* is allowed to get in that drawer. It's where I keep things that are for my eyes only. My deputies know that, and unfortunately Hazel visited me there enough times to know that, too. I guess she found where I keep the spare key and sneaked in there tonight to go through my papers. I don't know what possessed her. Maybe she hoped to find some of the letters we supposedly wrote to each other."

David held her gaze. "Just know I didn't authorize her to get in my desk and that I never said a word to her about Daphne's parentage. She's a sneaky, sick-in-the-head, heartless little bitch." He planted his forearms on the table and leaned slightly forward. "You've got to believe me. I never told her anything. Have I ever lied to you?"

Brianna's mouth trembled. "No," she whispered. "Never so far as I know."

"Then please believe me now. She's all het up about me breaking it off with her. She feels like everybody in town is staring at her and whispering behind her back. Everything she did tonight was intended to discredit you and save her pride. I'm —" David broke off. "I'm so sorry she humiliated you." He leaned even closer. "But as bad as it was, I have to say I've never been so proud of anybody in my whole life. The way you smacked her in the face with that pie! I almost clapped my hands and threw my hat in the air."

Some color returned to Brianna's cheeks and she smiled slightly. "I did let her have it good, didn't I?"

"You certainly did." David couldn't squelch a grin. "I only wish you'd punched her lights out while you were at it."

Brianna sank back on the chair and covered her face with her hands. "I knew this would happen. I told you, remember? I was so happy, and I feared something would spoil everything. All I can think about now is how Daphne will be hurt." She dropped her hands. "If she hears a word of this, it'll break her heart."

In that moment, David knew exactly why he had come to love this woman so very much. No matter that Brianna had just been humiliated in public and called names. Her biggest worry was for her daughter.

David stepped around the table and drew her up into his arms. *"Nothing,"* he whispered, "is going to hurt Daphne. I'll run back over and get her posthaste. In the meantime, my family will circle the wagons to protect her. This will blow over. You'll see. If I have to, I'll say Hazel is lying about the whole thing. She's jealous. Anyone with brains can see that. I'll just spread the word that she sneaked through my files and is making up stories to get back at me. I won't suffer a moment of conscience if I do that. She came by the information underhandedly. And if she looks absurd, so be it. My first loyalty is to you and our daughter, not Hazel Wright. She's the one who tossed down the glove. Now she can suffer the consequences. I never loved Hazel. I've told you that, and I meant it from the bottom of my heart. I felt no magic with her. I never felt as if I'd die without her. I've felt that way about one woman and only one woman, and I'm holding her in my arms."

"Oh, David. Do you really think you can smooth this over?"

"I know I can. Hell hath no fury like a woman scorned. People will believe me. As far as I'm concerned, her teaching career in No Name is finished, and I'll be glad to see her gone."

Brianna had just relaxed in David's arms when a pounding came at the downstairs door of the shop. She and David raced to answer the summons and found Ace and Joseph on the boardwalk. Brianna knew the instant she saw their faces, even blurred by darkness, that something was horribly wrong.

"It's Daphne," Ace said gruffly. "She's gone."

*"What?"* Brianna cried.

She tried to bolt outside, but David held her back.

Joseph swept off his hat and slapped it against his leg. To David, he said, "After you left, Hazel continued her rant, wiping apple from her face and screaming crazy accusations to anyone who'd listen. Before anyone in the family could react, Daphne must have heard her carrying on. Ma saw her run from the building."

"Oh, no," Brianna whispered. "Oh, God, no."

"We all went looking for her immediately," Ace added. "Ma, Caitlin, Rachel, everybody. We've searched high and low. There's no sign of her."

Joseph broke in. "We left Ma, Rachel, and Caitlin to stand guard at the hall to watch the kids and be there in case Daphne comes back. It's time for us to execute a full-blown search." He searched David's gaze. "It's true, isn't it? What she's saying."

"It's true," David confessed. "I'm sorry I fed you the public version. It seemed best."

Brianna couldn't breathe. She clutched the front of David's shirt. *My baby.* In that moment, she detested Hazel Wright as she'd never detested anyone. How could the woman do something so cruel to an innocent child?

"Should we go over to the hall and ask for volunteers?" Ace asked.

David took control of the situation. "No, I want to keep this in the family if at all possible. The fewer people who know, the better off Daphne will be when we find her." He sighed and thought for a moment. "Okay, we need to do this smart, not run every which way, covering the same ground twice." Esa bounced up onto the boardwalk.

David acknowledged him with a nod. "Let's divide the town into four sections. With only one street, it won't be that hard to branch out and cover every inch of the town. Ace, you go south. Joseph, you take the north end. Esa can take the east section. Brianna and I will take the west side of Main because it's where Daphne spends most of her time, either at my office or here at the shop. She's more likely to come out of hiding if she hears her mother's voice. If anyone finds her, fire three shots in the air. If not, let's meet back here in two hours."

Brianna's knees were quivering. She watched David's brothers leap into the street, each heading his own way. She turned a frightened gaze on her husband. "Oh, God, David. What if we don't find her?"

He pressed a quick kiss to her forehead. "Don't be silly. It's a small town. Of course we'll find her. Grab your shawl."

Minutes later, they entered the marshal's office. David pulled his key ring from his belt to open the center drawer of his desk. "I want to make sure Hazel doesn't have that report in her possession," he told Brianna. "If she starts waving that under people's noses, we'll be sunk." He huffed with relief when he saw the Pinkerton report lying on top of the other documents, right where Hazel had left it. "Thank God," he said, stuffing the thick envelope inside his shirt and then relocking the drawer. "Now it will be my word against hers. She'll have no proof to validate a single thing she says."

"David," Brianna whispered.

His gaze followed hers to a yellow scrap of paper lying on the desk blotter. It was a note, written in Daphne's childlike cursive.

*I hate you both!*

Brianna held the piece of paper over her heart and sobbed. "Poor Daphne. She knows now, David. She knows all of it. How must she be feeling, and what foolish things might she do when she's this upset?"

David vowed that he would make Hazel Wright regret her actions this evening, but dealing with her had to wait. Right now, he needed to find his daughter.

Two hours later, David stood with his brothers again in front of the marshal's office. Nobody had found a trace of Daphne anywhere. Ace suggested that they repeat the search with lanterns. "She must have found a clever hidey-hole," he said, "and isn't answering when we call her name. We've got to look harder, leaving no stone unturned."

David could feel the tremors that shook Brianna's body and knew she was fighting down rising panic. He squeezed her close, trying to help her stay calm. As Ace suggested, they repeated the search with lights, checking every possible place a child might hide. Being so thorough took even longer, and another three hours had passed by the time they met in the street again.

"Where the hell could she be?" David said. "In a town this size, how can a child possibly vanish?"

David knew he had to keep it together. His wife needed him to be strong for her. But it wasn't easy. Daphne had now been missing for more than five hours. Ace cursed under his breath. Joseph spat. Esa hung his head, making David suspect he was praying.

"I've got a thought," Ace said. "Maybe she hid in one of the boxcars. A train left for Denver about five hours ago. The time frame is right. If she ran straight toward the tracks after she left the hall, she might have climbed in one of the cars and stayed inside when the train started to move."

"Denver?" Brianna's voice came out in a tremulous wail.

David almost lost his composure then. Denver had become a fairly large city.

Daphne could easily lose her way there. Dear God. If she wandered into a bad area, there was no telling what might happen to her.

He must have expressed his thoughts aloud, because Joseph spoke up. "Her shadow is also missing."

"Sam, you mean?" David glanced around. He'd been so worried about Daphne that he hadn't spared a thought for his dog.

"Yep, Sam," Joseph replied. "I'm guessing he's with her, wherever that may be. I haven't seen hide or hair of him. Normally he's right at her heels, David."

"You're right," David agreed.

Esa spoke up. "If Sam is with her, nobody will harm a hair on her head without going through him first."

It comforted David to know that Sam might be with the child. Then, as he thought about it, he knew there was no maybe to it. If the animal had been left behind here in No Name, he'd be with David. And he wasn't.

The train wasn't scheduled to return from Denver for four hours. Ace offered to send out another engine. "To avoid a collision on the tracks, I can telephone Denver to make sure the first train doesn't head back this way until the engineer is given the go-ahead."

"Do it," David bit out.

"Be at the depot in a half hour," Ace said. "The train will be ready to roll by then."

David took Brianna into his office to warm her up with a cup of coffee. Rory had returned from the social, and he'd be keeping an eye on things until Billy Joe relieved him early in the morning. The pot of brew on the stove was fresh. David had just filled a cup and handed it to his wife when the telephone rang. Everybody jumped. They seldom got calls at the office because so few places outside the greater Denver area yet had service.

His blood ran cold as he stepped over to grab the receiver from the hook. "Hello."

An operator with a nasal voice asked, "Is this Marshal David Paxton?"

"It is."

The woman said, "Please hold, Marshal. I'm patching you through to the Denver sheriff."

An instant later, a deep male voice came over the line. "Hello, Paxton. This is Sheriff Hansen. I need to powwow with you for a few."

David frowned and glanced at his watch. "I'm sorry, Sheriff, but you've caught me at a bad time."

"Well, you might better hear me out. About an hour ago, I was called downtown because a dog went berserk."

David's heart caught. "What kind of dog?"

"Yellow and white, fluffy like a collie. He looks a lot like the dog that was with you when you visited my office a couple of months back."

"Sam," David whispered, closing his eyes briefly. He felt Brianna clutching his arm. "Sounds like Sam's in Denver and attacked somebody," he told her.

The sheriff heard what David said. "You got that right. Some drunk down by the tracks went to pat a little girl on the head and damn near lost his hand for his trouble. He's got a record for accosting women on the streets, so I think he had it coming. The child refuses to give me her name, and I can't get close enough to collect her without shooting the dog."

"Oh, God, don't shoot him," David said. "The girl is my daughter. He's only protecting her. He loves her like no tomorrow."

"I figured that," the sheriff replied. "I've got two deputies standing guard over her, but they're keeping a safe distance away. It's a rough section of town. You need to get your ass up here."

"Thank you for your trouble, sir. I'll get there as fast as I can."

The sheriff gave David directions to where the child was located. When the phone conversation ended, David repeated what had been said to Brianna. "I can't believe Sam bit someone. He's growled a warning to me sometimes when a stranger comes around, but other than that, the worst he's ever done is bare his teeth."

"Thank God he did more than that tonight. That man might have harmed Daphne," Brianna said, her face as white as milk. "Please, David, we must hurry. Even with Sam there, she may be in danger."

David grabbed her arm and led her from the office.

Never had a trip lasted so long. Brianna kept turning to David, telling him that something had to be wrong. The train wasn't fueled correctly and was going too slow, or the engineer was lollygagging, not realizing the urgency.

Each time she complained, David glanced at his pocket watch. "We're moving along at a fast clip. It just seems slow because we're so anxious to get there. We'll be with Daphne soon."

Soon wasn't soon enough for Brianna.

After getting off the train, David led her along grimy, trash-littered streets with unerring accuracy until they finally came to the right place. It was a bad section of town, with windows boarded up and bars over all the doorways to prevent burglary. Bits of debris blew willy-nilly in the brisk night wind. Straining her eyes, Brianna finally saw Daphne. She was huddled against a building, her thin arms locked around her raised knees, her head hanging. Across the way, horrible, predatory men staggered along the walkways with whiskey jugs dangling from their hands. On Daphne's side of the street, two armed deputies stood apart at a distance under light posts to divert all foot traffic so no one would get close to the child.

Brianna's first instinct was to run to her daughter. David held her back. "Let me go first. She's not near a light, and a canine's eyesight isn't that good. In this wind, Sam may not be able to catch our scent right away. If he's going to bite somebody, I'd rather it be me."

When David tried to approach the child, Sam lunged forward, teeth bared, acting as if he might rip out David's throat.

"Well, now," David said softly. "I'd say you're all het up."

To Brianna's amazement, David sat down

cross-legged right in the middle of the walkway. She stood well back, afraid of Sam for the first time. He had a crazed look in his eyes, and froth dripped from his jowls.

David held out his hand. "Sam, old man, it's me. Sniff the air, buddy. Get my scent, you myopic mutt."

Sam crouched, his body bunching to leap, but he also whined, the tone questioning. Brianna's gaze was fixed on her daughter. Daphne looked so dejected. If the child heard David's voice, she gave no sign of it. She sat with the small of her spine pressed against a building, her head resting on her knees. Brianna wanted so badly to run to her, but she held fast, waiting for David to calm the dog down first.

"Well, now, Sam," David said, "ain't this a hell of a note? I raised you from a puppy. Get your head out of your ass. I know it's been a terrible night. But, hello, it's me. Stop acting like an idiot."

David thrust out his hand, and Sam dropped to his belly with a whine. Then he scooted closer, and then closer. Just as David was almost able to touch him, the dog scrambled back to Daphne, circled her, and barked joyously, wagging his nubbin of a tale until his whole rump quivered.

David pushed to his feet and moved

forward. "Good job, Sam. It'll be fine cuts of beef for you for at least a month. Aren't you something? I think I'll hang a deputy badge on your chest. What a dog you are! The very best! You fought for her, didn't you, and by God, you drew blood. You are amazing."

Man and dog met in a collision of strong arms and fluffy fur. Sam was so agile that he was able to leap up and tag David's jaw with glad kisses. David caught the squirming animal to his chest, released quickly, and then intercepted another joyous jump. Sam was clearly relieved to have reinforcements. Brianna, still standing back, felt tears slipping down her cheeks, and she knew she would adore that silly dog until he died.

But what held her gaze was her daughter. Daphne didn't react to the glad reunion taking place in front of her. She looked like a child who had dissolved and become nothing but skin, clothing, and a flow of hair draping over her clenched arms.

Brianna knew — sensed, as she had once upon a time with Moira — all of the child's feelings. Daphne was flesh of her flesh, blood of her blood, and heart of her heart. Sam, who now recognized Brianna, allowed her safe passage to her daughter. She sat down, drawing the folds of her burgundy gown close to her bent knees, not caring if her skirts were ruined.

Brianna tried to speak. Tears blinded her. Moira's face floated in her mind. She had so many things she wanted to say, important things that Daphne needed to hear, but she'd lied to the child for so long that the truth was difficult, if not impossible, to express. All that she could say was, "Daphne, I love you."

The child cringed away from her. "I *hate* you! Go away! I never want to see you again."

It nearly broke Brianna's heart to hear Daphne say that, but when she searched deep, she couldn't really blame the child. This was her fault, all her fault. Along with all the stale bread and cheese, she'd fed Moira's daughter lies. From the time Daphne had been old enough to understand the word *papa,* Brianna had spun grand stories, telling the child about her non-existent father who was looking for gold but loved her so much. Empty dreams, falsehoods. Daphne no longer had anything solid to believe in.

David finished praising Sam and came to sit at Daphne's other side. The dog promptly lay in front of the child, as close to her toes as he could get. Brianna could think of nothing she might say to soothe the child's pain. Regret stabbed her like a knife, and she wanted to weep, but she couldn't allow herself that luxury. She needed to be calm right now and think. The problem was, her heart was breaking.

David sighed and crossed his legs at the ankle. The men beneath the nearby light posts tipped their hats to him and walked away. David waved good-bye to them. Then he settled back. Brianna wanted him to say something, but he remained silent, apparently waiting Daphne out. The child refused to look up. When the wind lifted her hair, Brianna saw that her small face was puffy from crying.

"Go away!" Daphne finally screamed. "Just go away! Both of you! I hate you! I don't want you here! You're not my parents!" She sent Brianna a fiery look. "You aren't my mama. You're only my aunt!" To David she cried, "I don't have any of your blood. You said you were my papa, but you're not! You're both liars."

Still David offered no response. At his silence, Daphne rushed on. "I don't have a real mama and papa, only fake ones! I'm going to run far, far away, and neither of you will ever, *ever* see me again."

Brianna just sat there, feeling as if her

heart were shattering into a thousand pieces.

"Well, now," David finally said, "you've got one thing in your life that's not fake, Daphne, a dog that loves you so much he'd die for you."

Brianna wiped tears from her cheeks and sent David an exasperated look. This wasn't about the dog.

David ignored her visual warning. "Good old Sam," he said, ruffling the dog's fur. "He's loyal to a fault."

Daphne stifled a sob and rubbed her eyes. "He's my only real friend. When I got hungry, he brought me a bone he found behind a restaurant. I couldn't eat it, and it made Sam sad. Then that awful man came, and Sam bit him. He's my friend for always."

"Yep," David agreed. "He sure does love you, doesn't he?" He went silent for a moment. "That's kind of strange because, unless I missed something, you don't have any of Sam's blood. But he loves you anyway."

Daphne buried her face against her bent knees.

David let her cry for several seconds. Then, in a soft, velvety voice, he said, "Love has nothing to do with sharing blood, Daphne. It's a magical thing that happens in the heart." When Daphne refused to look up, David went on. "A long time ago, two baby girls who looked exactly alike were left on an orphanage doorstep in Boston. One girl's name was Brianna, and the other little girl's name was Moira."

"I don't want to hear a stupid story!" Daphne yelled, her small body shaking. "Just go away and leave me alone!"

David ignored her. "Those two girls were what people call identical twins. There's something very special between identical twins. Lots of times, it's as if they are one person in two separate bodies. Brianna and Moira were like that. They sensed each other's feelings, they were absolutely devoted to each other, and they shared everything. Sometimes they even pretended to be each other to fool the nuns at the orphanage. Then one sad day after they grew up, Moira died, and as she took her last breath, she asked her sister Brianna to raise her baby girl as her very own. That was an easy thing for Brianna to do because, way deep down, Moira had always been a part of her, and she'd always been a part of Moira. Does that make any sense?"

Brianna felt Daphne lean closer to her. She was almost afraid to breathe for fear of breaking the spell David was weaving. *Keep talking. Don't stop. You're getting through to her.*

"Anyhow," David went on, "Brianna loved Moira so much that she did exactly as her sister asked and raised Moira's little girl as her very own. When she reported the baby's birth, she listed herself as the mother, and from that moment forward, she *was* the baby's mother. She was loyal to Moira for always, just like Sam is to you.

"It wasn't always easy for Brianna to be a good mother." David stopped to stare up at the strip of sky that showed between the buildings. "But I don't have to tell you that, Daphne, because you're the baby girl she raised. Nobody knows better than you how hard Brianna worked to keep her sister's baby safe. And nobody knows better than you how much she loved you, through thick and thin, sometimes going without food herself so you could eat."

"Stop!" Daphne demanded in a thin, quivery voice.

David sighed. "I can't stop. This is one story you have to hear, pumpkin. It's the most important tale I'll ever tell you, barring none. No matter how bad things got, Brianna never broke her promise to Moira. She just kept on, trying her hardest to be a good mama, always putting you first, until somewhere along the way, she started to feel that you really were her little girl, at least in every way that counted. Do you remember all those times?"

"Yes," Daphne admitted.

"Do you remember writing letters to your papa, asking him to come for you? A man named David Paxton?"

"Yes," Daphne pushed out again.

"Well, one day all those letters, a huge canvas bag of them, were delivered to me in No Name. After I read them, I had no choice but to journey to Glory Ridge to see if that little girl, Daphne, might be my daughter. Remember how we met on the street when both of us bent over to pick up the same penny?"

"We almost bumped heads."

David chuckled and nodded. "Yep, and then I got a good look at you. It took the wind out of my sails, I can tell you that, because you were the spitting image of my mother, and you even had what I thought was the Paxton birthmark on the side of your neck, a mark almost exactly like mine. From that instant forward, I believed with all my heart that I was your daddy." He continued with a modified version of all that had taken place between him and Brianna ever since. "I didn't learn I wasn't your papa until just a few days ago."

Daphne had definitely pressed closer to Brianna during the story. Now she lifted her blond head to peer through the shadows at David, apparently captivated by what he was saying.

"It came as a huge shock to me," he went on. "And the news came way too late because I already loved you and your mama way too much to give you up."

"She *isn't* my mama, only my aunt." Daphne hid her face against Brianna's sleeve and said in a muffled voice, "I want a *real* mama and papa, not pretend ones."

"Ah," David replied softly. "So is Sam your *real* friend, or is he only your pretend friend?"

Daphne straightened to shoot him an indignant glare. "Sam is my *real* friend."

"But how can that be?" David retorted. "You have none of Sam's blood, and he has none of yours, but the friendship between you is real?"

Daphne nodded emphatically.

"So," David mused aloud, "why can't it be the same with people and love? Brianna isn't truly your mama, but she loves you as if she were. I'm not really your papa, but I love you as if I were. Why can't the three of us decide that love is more special than blood and go on from here? I'll be your papa, and your aunt Brianna will be your mama, and you'll be our little girl, for always."

"Because we can't!" Daphne cried.

David nudged back his hat to hold her gaze. "I think we can. All we have to do is believe in it hard enough." He touched the front of her frock. "Do you still have our lucky penny, or were you so mad at me that you threw it away?"

Daphne planted a hand over her waist. "I still have it."

David smiled. "Remember when I told you we should only make wishes on it for truly important things? I think our being a real family is one of the most important things in the world. Maybe if we wish for it to be true on our lucky penny, God will reach down and help us to make it happen. What do you think?"

Daphne tugged on the chain to pull the penny from under her frock. In the dim glow from the lampposts, the coin shimmered on her palm.

"See there? It's winking at us," David told the child. "I think there's still enough magic in it to make one great big wish come true. And then we'll just go home and pretend we never heard that ugly lady with the wart on her nose saying all those awful things. What do you say?"

Daphne sniffed and smiled faintly. "Miss Wright doesn't have warts."

"I'm certain I saw warts," David insisted. "You willing to place a wager on it? I'll put up a golden eagle and an ice cream at Roxie's that Miss Wright has a huge, ugly wart right on the end of her honker."

"I'd win," Daphne said. "There's no wart on the end of Miss Wright's nose."

David tousled the child's hair. "You can never collect on the bet if you won't come home with me and your mama to take another look at her."

Daphne stared down at the coin on her palm. Then she flicked imploring glances at both David and Brianna. "If we all three wished really, *really* hard on the lucky penny, do you think we could be a real family?"

Brianna locked gazes with David. She remembered that day when she'd railed at him about the penny and how he'd popped back, saying she was right, that people should turn to God, not objects, for help. But then he'd added that it never hurt to have special reinforcements.

Perhaps for Daphne, a little magic was needed tonight.

Fighting to find her voice, Brianna said, "I think all three of us should wish on the penny so we can be a *real* family."

David seconded the motion. Daphne stared at the coin for a long while and then clenched her fist around it. David and Brianna enfolded her small hand in theirs, and together, there on that grimy, dimly lighted walkway in a dangerous part of town, the three of them wished aloud that God would make them a family.

Sam seemed to understand. He whined and licked Daphne's face as if encouraging her to go home.

Daphne's eyes filled with tears again. "I don't feel any different. I don't think it worked. I want a *real* mama and papa, a *real* family."

It was all Brianna could do not to burst into tears when she saw the longing in Daphne's eyes. It was like going back in time. So often Moira had looked pleadingly at her and said the same thing. From Brianna's earliest memory, her sister had always yearned aloud for a real mama and papa. It was a wish Brianna had been powerless to grant to her sister, and now it was a wish she couldn't grant her niece.

"Well," David said in an authoritative voice, "that's only because we haven't made our wish official. What we need to do is see a judge and have him draw up a bona fide contract that all three of us must sign. I will promise to be your *real* papa, forever and always. Your aunt Brianna will promise to be your *real* mama, forever and always. And you will have to promise that you will be our *real* daughter forever and always. After we all sign the document, the judge will stamp it with his official seal, and then it will always be so."

Daphne's little face glowed with hope. "Can the contract also say that my mama will always be my papa's *real* wife, and that my papa will always be my mama's *real* husband? No more pretending?"

David flashed Brianna a twinkling look and nodded. Brianna knew that the circuit judge who came to No Name was a good friend of David's. He apparently felt certain the man would stamp anything they put before him if he realized how important it was to one beautiful little girl with a dimple in her cheek.

"Deal," David said, pushing to his feet.

As he helped Brianna to stand, she echoed him with, "Deal."

Daphne scrambled up between them. "Deal!" she cried excitedly.

■ ■ ■ ■

As the three of them walked to the train depot, hand in hand, with Daphne in the middle and the dog trailing faithfully at her heels, the little girl looked up at David. "Can Sam be in our contract, too, Papa?"

David was momentarily flummoxed. He wasn't sure how the judge would feel about that. But then he decided that anything could be included in a document that meant nothing legally. It would be an agreement conceived in a child's heart, and the judge would understand.

"Sure he can," he assured Daphne.

Daphne skipped along between him and Brianna, suddenly happy as only children can be after an earth-shattering event. A few minutes later, as David helped everyone board the train, he smiled, thinking that he now had the one thing he'd wanted all his adult life, true and everlasting love with the woman of his dreams, a beautiful daughter, and a fabulous dog.

In short, he finally had a *real* family.

# EPILOGUE

It was funny how things could turn out, Brianna thought as she walked with David and their daughter to see the circuit judge, who came to town every two months and had taken up temporary chambers at the town hall to conduct court business. It had been only six weeks since that momentous night on a dark Denver street. Now David and Brianna were about to make Daphne's dream come true.

Under his duster, David wore pressed jeans and the blue shirt Brianna had made him for his birthday, but outwardly, he still had a roughrider air about him. How odd that she now found that so attractive when it had once scared her nearly to death. Ah, well, the man was so handsome he almost took her breath away, and she seriously doubted that would ever change. There was just something about David Paxton that charmed her, and she suspected that she would be madly in love with him until the day she died.

Daphne walked between them. They each held one of her hands. Sam, ever faithful, trailed at the girl's heels. It was a sunny summer afternoon. The sky was powder blue without a cloud in sight, and in her new silk day dress, Brianna felt hot and vaguely nauseated. Doc Halloway, No Name's aging physician, assured Brianna that morning sickness was to be expected during the early weeks of pregnancy. Normally Brianna felt better by noon, but then she'd taken to staying indoors after the sun reached its zenith. Becoming overheated didn't sit well with her these days.

David sent her a questioning look. He'd become overprotective since she'd told him she was with child. Brianna smiled. "I'm fine, David. Just feeling a bit wilted. Stop fussing."

Instead of paying her any mind, he slowed the pace. He worried constantly that Brianna might start to bleed if she did too much, just as Moira had. That wasn't going to happen. Aside from a queasy stomach each morning, Brianna felt strong, right with the world, and perfectly fine.

Excited about signing a contract that would make them a *real* family, Daphne stepped out ahead of them, trying to hurry them along until her arms were angled out behind her. "Don't lollygag," she scolded. "We'll be late!"

Brianna had talked with David, and they'd decided not to tell Daphne that she would soon have a baby brother or sister until their contract to be a core family was signed and stamped. They both wanted the child to know she was as much theirs as any child that might come along in the future, and Brianna and David hoped to have a passel.

They reached the end of the boardwalk and stepped off onto packed dirt gone powdery in the heat. Up ahead, Hazel Wright's house stood empty, awaiting the newly hired teacher who would arrive in late August. After writing a lengthy letter of apology to both David and Brianna, Hazel had left town to take a higher-paying job in Denver, which she'd snagged only because Brianna, as the wife of No Name's marshal, had insisted that the woman be given a glowing letter of recommendation from the city council and school board. Loving David as Brianna did, she knew how badly she might have behaved if the shoe had been on the other foot. David Paxton was a man that no woman could easily give up.

Happily, Hazel's rant had carried little

weight with the townspeople. Why, anybody with eyes could see that Daphne Paxton was the spitting image of her papa and his ma. Gossip had it that if a jilted woman was going to spin lies, she'd best be sure they were believable. Daphne wasn't David's daughter? Pshaw! That little girl was Dory Paxton all over again.

Brianna was relieved to step into the community hall, where she was shielded from the sun. She waved a hand in front of her face. David swept off his hat and hung it on a hook.

Daphne dashed to the judge's desk, Sam circling around her legs. "We're here to sign an official contract to make us a real family."

Judge Claymore was elderly, with silver gray hair, kindly blue eyes, and a wry smile. He patted a stack of papers on his makeshift desk, a table normally used for buffets. "Your father gave me all the particulars ahead of time, so it's all drawn up and ready."

David curled an arm around Brianna's waist and led her forward. When they reached the table, he released his hold on her to shake the judge's hand. "Your Honor, good to see you. I hope this heat isn't getting to you."

"Not badly. One thing about Colorado is that you can always count on cool breezes in the evening." He stood, as any gentleman would, robed or not, to meet Brianna and shake her hand. Then he resumed his seat to proceed with business.

As promised, Daphne, along with her parents, was to sign a contract that would legalize her *real* family. The judge had good-naturedly prepared a document that would never be recorded, which stated in impressive-sounding language that her mama would always be her mama, and her papa would always be her papa, and she would always be their daughter. Even Sam got to sign. David pressed the dog's right front paw onto the ink pad and then the paper.

"Now you're my *real* mama and papa!" Daphne cried. She jumped around, flapping the skirts of the new pink dress Brianna had fashioned for her. "Forever and always!"

David's family members began to file into the hall. They had come to witness the nuptials between David and Brianna and the signing of adoption papers to make Daphne legally a Paxton. No one else had been invited because the secret of Daphne's true parentage had to be carefully guarded. The judge had deemed David and Brianna's first marriage to be slightly out of order, and with the adoption of Daphne and the coming of another child, he wanted the union to be unquestionably legal. Brianna had never agreed to the first marriage, and there had been only one witness. David was a fairly wealthy man. The judge wanted to be certain that Brianna's claim to David's estate, in the event of his untimely demise, could never be contested.

Brianna wasn't thinking about death when she and David said their vows. She looked into his eyes — those incredibly beautiful and compelling blue eyes, which were so very like Daphne's — and thought about that night, which seemed so long ago now, when she'd confessed to him that she had no sense of direction. He'd vowed then to teach her how to find her way.

And he had. Only the lessons had nothing to do with north, south, west, or east.

She'd once envied him his uncanny ability to know exactly which way to go, but now she had developed her own inner compass. As she stood in the midst of his family, which had become hers as well, and said, "I do," she knew that her compass needle would always direct her only one way, straight into David Paxton's arms.

The moment David and Brianna's union

as husband and wife was signed, stamped, and ready to be recorded, the judge turned his attention to the adoption papers. His expression was solemn as he leafed through the Pinkerton report. "According to this investigation, Stanley Romanik denied all charges and refused to acknowledge any biological connection." He stopped short and glanced at Daphne, clearly choosing his words carefully so the child wouldn't understand the import of what he said. "I see no legal obstacles to this adoption. There is no one to contest it."

Dory, standing off to Brianna's right, got a curious look on her face. She stepped closer to the desk. "Come again, Your Honor? Did you say Romanik, Stanley Romanik?"

The judge glanced up. "That's right."

Dory pressed her hands to her waist. "That report doesn't, by any chance, give the Christian name of Stanley Romanik's father, does it?"

Claymore pushed his glasses up his nose and leafed through the paperwork. After several seconds, his scowl lessened. "Esa Romanik. His wife's name is Hester."

For an instant, Dory looked as if she might faint. Her son Esa stepped to her side to loop an arm around her shoulders. "Ma, are you all right?"

Dory leaned against him, nodding as she focused a tear-filled gaze on Daphne. "Right as rain. Esa Romanick is my brother-in-law. Hester is my sister. I haven't seen them in years. They journeyed from Boston to visit me once in San Francisco when Stanley was about five. He was spoiled rotten, a holy terror, and I —" Dory broke off and swallowed, her attention still fixed on Daphne. "I guess my sister and her husband never saw the error of their ways with him. Stanley's behavior apparently never improved."

Brianna felt lightheaded. Moira's rapist, Stanley Romanik, was Dory Paxton's nephew? And David, the love of her life, was related to him? Closely related, first cousins, by her calculation. She wasn't certain how she felt about that.

"I remember that visit," Ace said. "Aunt Hester let that little brat get away with murder. So did Uncle Esa. The kid could do anything, and he was never punished."

"Are you certain the name isn't merely a coincidence?" Brianna asked.

David inserted, "I saw the name Romanik, but I never made the connection. Ma's maiden name is Jesperson, and —" He broke off and shook his head. "I haven't seen Aunt Hester and Uncle Esa since I was

706

young, and then only once. I don't recall if I was ever told their last name."

Dory met Brianna's gaze. "It isn't a common surname. I named one of my sons after Esa Romanik because I admired him so. There can't possibly be two men with that name in Boston married to a woman named Hester. Stanley is my sister's son."

Brianna fanned her face. Everyone in the room, with the exception of the judge and her sisters-in-law, was related to a man who'd been instrumental in killing her identical twin. How was a bride — especially a pregnant one — supposed to take that in without feeling as if she needed to sit down and ask for a glass of water?

"I know what you must be thinking," Dory said softly. "I'd be thinking it myself, Brianna. But I assure you this isn't a case of bad blood. My sister, Hester, is one of the most wonderful, loving individuals you'll ever meet. And Esa is as well. They were just deplorable parents. God forgive me for saying it, but it's a blessing that Hester could have no more children. They didn't get a chance to ruin another one."

Joseph spoke up. "I remember Stanley. The little shit stuffed Eden's cat in the hot oven. Ace rescued him, and we doctored his paws for days."

Dory straightened away from her youngest son. "Your cousin was, without question, a cruel, out-of-control child, and he obviously grew up the same." She looked straight at Brianna. "But he is no reflection on *me* or the children *I* raised. My sons are good men, and my daughter is beyond compare."

Brianna recovered her composure and searched the faces of David's brothers. They were honorable men, wonderful men. How could she ask for better brothers-in-law? Then her wandering gaze found David's. She felt as if she could drown in the depths of his blue eyes. They pulled and drew her in. The next instant, his strong arms locked around her, and Brianna knew she was precisely where she belonged — deeply loved and forever linked to him, heart to heart, flesh to flesh.

Daphne tugged on her skirt. "Mama, does this mean you and Papa can't adopt me?"

Brianna drew away from David and crouched to cup her daughter's face in her hands. There were some things Daphne didn't need to understand until she was much older. "No, absolutely not! We will proceed as planned. It only means that the adoption is merely a formality, dear heart. You're truly a Paxton by blood."

"I am?" Daphne beamed a huge grin. "That's wonderful, right?"

Brianna smiled up at Dory. "It's the most wonderful thing ever! You truly *do* have your grandma Dory's dimple."

Daphne scampered away to grab Dory's hands. "Grandma, did you hear that? I've truly got your dimple!"

Dory hugged the child close. "Yes, you certainly do! And my birthmark as well."

With a great deal of happy chatter pealing out around them, David and Brianna signed the paperwork to make Daphne legally their daughter. The judge stamped the documents with a loud bang as if to make sure the sound rang clear to heaven. Then he stood, looking regal in his black robe, and thrust out his hand to Daphne.

"Miss Paxton, I am pleased to make your acquaintance."

Daphne, ever outgoing, stepped forward to shake his hand. "And I am pleased to meet you, Your Honor."

With the formalities finished, the family was free to leave. A celebration was planned at Ace and Caitlin's. Brianna knew it would be an unforgettable evening, with delicious food, music and dance, and love abounding. And later, she would lie in David's arms while their daughter slept, secure in the knowledge that she belonged with him, and only with him.

As they exited the building, Brianna thought once again that it really was funny how things could turn out. Against all odds, Daphne was actually related to David. From the start, he'd kept saying, "I know a Paxton when I see one." And he'd been absolutely right. Either that penny truly was lucky, or God had reached down and shuffled the chess pieces on the board, lining them up so the outcome would be perfect, giving Daphne what Brianna and Moira had never had.

A *real* family.

The employees of Thorndike Press hope you have enjoyed this Large Print book. All our Thorndike, Wheeler, and Kennebec Large Print titles are designed for easy reading, and all our books are made to last. Other Thorndike Press Large Print books are available at your library, through selected bookstores, or directly from us.

For information about titles, please call:
  (800) 223-1244

or visit our Web site at:
  http://gale.cengage.com/thorndike

To share your comments, please write:
  Publisher
  Thorndike Press
  10 Water St., Suite 310
  Waterville, ME 04901